Also by Heidi Lang and Kati Bartkowski
A Dash of Dragon
A Hint of Hydra

A Pinch of Phoenix

Heidi Lang & Kati Bartkowski

ALADDIN

New York   London   Toronto   Sydney   New Delhi

ALADDIN
An imprint of Simon & Schuster Children's Publishing Division
1230 Avenue of the Americas, New York, New York 10020
First Aladdin hardcover edition July 2019
Text copyright © 2019 by Heidi Lang and Kati Bartkowski
Jacket illustration copyright © 2019 by Angela Li
All rights reserved, including the right of reproduction in whole or in part in any form.
ALADDIN and related logo are registered trademarks of Simon & Schuster, Inc.
For information about special discounts for bulk purchases, please contact Simon & Schuster Special Sales at 1-866-06-1949 or business@simonandschuster.com.
The Simon & Schuster Speakers Bureau can bring authors to your live event. For more information or to book an event contact the Simon & Schuster Speakers Bureau at 1-866-248-3049 or visit our website at www.simonspeakers.com.
Series designed by Nina Simoneaux
The text of this book was set in Adobe Caslon Pro.
Manufactured in the United States of America
2 4 6 8 10 9 7 5 3 1
Library of Congress Cataloging-in-Publication Data
Names: Lang, Heidi, author. | Bartkowski, Kati, author.
Title: A pinch of phoenix / Heidi Lang, Kati Bartkowski.
Description: First Aladdin hardcover edition. | New York : Aladdin, 2019. |
Series: The mystic cooking chronicles | Summary: "With elves waging war on scientists, it's up to Master Chef Lailu Loganberry to save both her restaurant and her city"—Provided by publisher.
Identifiers: LCCN 2018060873 (print) | LCCN 20190003 (eBook) |
ISBN 9781534437111 (eBook) | ISBN 9781534437098 (hc)
Subjects: | CYAC: Cooking—Fiction. | Animals, Mythical—Fiction. |
Elves—Fiction. | Robots—Fiction. | Fantasy. | BISAC: JUVENILE FICTION / Humorous Stories. | JUVENILE FICTION / Animals / Mythical. | JUVENILE FICTION / Fantasy & Magic.
Classification: LCC PZ7.1.L3436 (eBook) | LCC PZ7.1.L3436 Pin 2019 (print) |
DDC [Fic]—dc23
LC record available at https://lccn.loc.gov/2018060873

For Sean and Nick. Thank you for never doubting us, for supporting us on this wild writing journey, and for all the cake.

A PINCH OF PHOENIX

1

SURPRISE VISITOR

*L*ailu scrubbed a thick coating of her own homemade finish into the mark burned onto her cherrywood floor. The scent of beeswax and wine filled the air, drowning out the sweet aroma of her cockatrice cooking in the kitchen. But no matter how nice it smelled, or how hard she scrubbed, the burn remained. Taunting her. Reminding her of Wren's threat and her exploding spi-trons.

"*One . . . two . . . three . . .* die!" Lailu shuddered, remembering the way that creepy metal spider had chanted at her before exploding, leaving behind metal parts and the black streak now scarring her floor. Wren's little present, which apparently was here to stay.

"It's no use," Lailu sighed, sitting back on her heels. "It's not going away."

"Well, I think it looks much better," Hannah said. Hannah had been living with Lailu and helping out at Mystic Cooking for several months, but she had been Lailu's best friend for far longer. They had grown up together in the same snowy little village in the mountains before chasing their separate dreams to Twin Rivers, Lailu to attend Chef Academy and Hannah to enroll in Twin Rivers's Finest, a school for hair and fashion.

Unfortunately, school hadn't worked out too well for Hannah, who couldn't resist the temptation of all those glittery hair combs and had gotten caught "re-homing" one. Luckily, their sneakiest friend, Ryon, had noticed her light-fingered talents and had recently taken her on as an apprentice spy. Lailu still wasn't sure what that entailed, and she preferred to keep it that way. Spying was trouble, but she was very glad Hannah had stayed.

"I doubt any of your hungry customers will notice a little scar on the floor," Hannah continued. She took a sip of tea, then set her mug down on her table. "Not when they're enjoying your tasty cooking."

"Master Slipshod will notice." Lailu's former mentor had left Mystic Cooking to return to his old job: cooking for the king. However, he'd promised to drop in from time to time, and she didn't want him to see how she'd already let the place get damaged, not after he'd just turned it over to her.

Hannah shrugged. "It's not really his business anymore, is it?"

"I guess not." Lailu tossed her scrub brush into a wooden bucket, then subtly stretched her hands, her fingers stiff and achy beneath their thick bandaging.

"Still bothering you?" Hannah's forehead creased.

"It's not so bad," Lailu lied. She'd thrown one of Wren's spi-trons at Starling in self-defense. When it exploded, the blast had killed Starling and burned Lailu's hands. The constant pain felt like a reminder, both of the battle she'd fought and the war to come. Lailu knew Wren's attack last night was only the beginning, and she hoped her poor restaurant could handle whatever came next.

Lailu stood and stretched her back just as the bell over the front door rang.

A tall, well-dressed man entered the room. A man with the cold green eyes of a killer.

Lord Elister the Bloody.

Lailu's chest tightened. "L-Lord Elister," she greeted him. "Welcome to Mystic Cooking—"

"No need for pleasantries," he said. "I'm not here to eat."

Lailu gulped. She knew she was *not* his favorite person right now. Not after her hand in the death of Starling Volan, the talented scientist who had been working for him. True, Starling had been trying to kill Lailu and her friends at the time, but did that fact matter to someone like the king's executioner?

Elister looked the restaurant up and down, his gaze lingering on the burn mark.

"Search it," he said. Four guards swarmed inside, one of them stationing himself at the door while the other three made straight for the curtain that separated Lailu's dining room from the rest of the restaurant.

"Hey, stay out of my . . ." Lailu stopped. This all felt eerily familiar. On her opening day, her restaurant had been invaded by both the elves and a shady loan shark. She hadn't been able to stop them, either. She let her outstretched arm fall limply to her side and took a deep breath as the sounds of crashing and things falling came from her kitchen. Those guards weren't just searching her restaurant; it sounded like they were tearing it apart brick by brick.

She glanced at Elister. His face was as expressionless as one of Starling's automatons.

Until Lailu's mother came storming through the door, her fury swirling around her like one of her brightly colored skirts. "Eli!" she snapped. "What is the meaning of this?"

Lord Elister took a step back, then caught himself. He straightened. "Lianna," he said, almost pleasantly. "Since we appear to be dispensing with titles and formalities, I'll get straight to the point. Mystic Cooking is a business with ties to the elves. As you well know, due to the pandemonium they caused on the final day of Masks and their 'involvement' in Starling's murder, the elves have been banished from my city." He glanced at Lailu when he said "involvement," and she shuddered.

It was true that the elves had created fear and mayhem during the final day of the Week of Masks. Their magic had turned many of the citizens of Twin Rivers into the monsters they were masked as, but they had nothing to do with Starling's death. Elister knew that, Lianna knew that, and Hannah . . . Hannah had also been there when Starling died. The only ones who didn't know the real cause of Starling Volan's death were the guards. So . . . who exactly was this show for?

"Therefore . . . ," Elister drawled.

"Therefore what?" Lianna narrowed her eyes. "You're *not* shutting us down. We don't belong to the elves, we just owe them money."

Lailu noticed how her mother said "we," and her heart filled with warmth. Even if that warmth was surrounded by cold terror. Elister wouldn't really shut her restaurant down, would he? *Could* he?

Of course he could. He basically ran this city. Technically he was acting as joint regent with the queen until the king came of age, but everyone knew he was the real power behind the throne.

"I'm not shutting you down. I'm just ensuring that no elves are being harbored here."

"Why would we harbor any elves?" Hannah asked.

"Or anyone of elven descent," Elister added pointedly.

Hannah looked away, her cheeks reddening. Ryon was half elf. It was supposed to be a secret, but Starling had found out, so clearly Elister knew as well.

"There's no one here but us," Lianna said, her face giving nothing away. "As I'm sure you know. This really isn't necessary."

"Perhaps it would be less necessary if there were someone I truly trusted nearby. Someone who still worked for me, for instance . . ."

"Oh, stop with the weighty pauses," Lianna snapped. "You might intimidate everyone else, but you forget, I've known you a long time. And my work is here now."

Elister studied her, taking in the apron tied over her skirts, the flour smudged on the side of her neck. "I see that. I suppose that is . . . understandable," he said in a tone that suggested it was anything but. "Just as I'm sure *you'll* understand that part of *my* work is to search every business that has a connection to the elves, just in case." His lips curled back in a cold, hard smile. "For your own safety, of course."

"Of course," Lianna said blandly.

"And we'll continue to enforce our ban by any means necessary," Elister continued.

"Hey, there's a trapdoor in here!" one of the guards in the kitchen called, followed by the sound of more crashing and then, a moment later, the tinkle of glass shattering from below.

Hannah gasped. "Your wine cellar!"

Lailu clenched her sore hands into fists.

"If you use this display of force with all the businesses, you won't be making any friends on this side of town," Lianna warned. Pretty much every business near Mystic Cooking had some connection to the elves, who lived in the Velvet Forest just outside of this part of the city and regularly loaned money to the citizens in the poorer districts.

"My job is to make the city *safe,* not to make friends."

"Then maybe you should be more worried about this." Lianna pulled a newspaper out from one of her skirt's voluminous pockets and shoved it under Elister's nose.

All Lailu could see was the back advertisement about LaSilvian's special roast.

Elister snatched the paper from her hands. "I told them not to put that on the front page."

"My lord." One of the guards poked her head out from behind the curtain. "You'd better come see this. We've found . . . well. Something."

Elister rolled up the paper and tucked it under his arm. He looked at Lailu over Lianna's auburn head. "Is there anything you want to tell me?"

Lailu felt the color drain from her face like water from a colander. *Was* there something to tell him? Ryon did have a tendency to lurk around here. For all she knew, he was close by now. She really, really hoped he wasn't, but if he was . . .

Lailu shook her head.

"Very well. Come."

Lianna started forward.

"Not you," Elister snapped at her. "Or you." He pointed at Hannah. "Just Lailu."

As Lailu followed Elister, she caught Hannah's dark, worried eyes and wondered if it would be the last she saw of her.

THE GENERATOR AND THE SPY

Lailu's hand trembled as she brushed past her curtain into the kitchen. Her huge steam-powered stove, designed by the murderous—and now dead—Starling Volan, took up about a third of the floor space, and cupboards, pots, pans, and other cooking essentials took up another third, making the space in the kitchen pretty cramped. Normally Lailu found it cozy, but with Elister's imposing presence and the guard hovering over her wine cellar's trapdoor, it had become as claustrophobic as a hydra den. And as messy.

She had to step over several pots and pans, all heaped on the floor next to shattered dishes, and someone had left the stove door open. Lailu snuck a quick peek at her cooking cockatrice, glad that at least no one had destroyed that.

She turned her back on everyone and blinked away her tears.

All of the damage in here was fixable. Even though she knew she'd never get it all back in place before the dinner rush began, she could deal with it when Elister and his minions left. Still. It felt like a betrayal.

Elister had saved her life in this very restaurant. He'd helped her when she was dealing with the backstabbing loan shark, Mr. Boss, *and* he'd complimented her cooking. She thought he at least respected her as a chef. But this treatment of her restaurant? It was unforgivable. It was as bad as Mr. Boss, and she'd never thought Elister would stoop that low.

"What is it, Seala?" Elister asked the guard.

"I don't know. But it's large, glowing vaguely bluish, and humming."

Lailu turned away from her broken dishes. "The power generator," she realized. *Wren's* power generator.

Wren, Starling Volan's daughter, had convinced Lailu to let her "modernize" Mystic Cooking with hot and cold running water and lights that would turn on and off with the flick of a switch, all thanks to the generator installed in Lailu's cellar. Now that Wren wanted to kill her, coupled with the fact that Wren's inventions had a tendency to be a little . . . unstable, that generator suddenly seemed like a terrible idea. Lailu could practically feel its malice throbbing all the way through the floor, and she wrapped her arms around herself.

She had to get rid of it.

"Shall we?" Elister said, jerking his chin at the open trapdoor.

The guard fingered the cuffs of her dark-red uniform, which seemed a little large for her. Maybe she'd grow into it; with her wide brown eyes and wispy hair escaping the tight professional braids, she looked barely older than Hannah. She eyed that dark square leading below and then turned to Lailu. "Chef!" She pointed. "You first."

Lailu scowled. "That's *Master Chef* Loganberry."

"Exactly so," Elister said. "Go first yourself, Seala. Unless you're afraid to?" He glanced at Lailu. "Seala here is rather young and inexperienced, you see."

The guard's face tightened. She shot Lailu a murderous glare, as if Lailu had somehow set her up, before disappearing below, followed by Elister. Lailu sighed and reluctantly went down after them. The stairway was narrow and dark, but enough bluish light from the generator filled the room for them to see where they were going.

When Wren had first installed the generator a week ago, it hadn't given off more than a gentle glow. But over the past two days that glow had gotten brighter and brighter. It reminded her eerily of Wren's spi-trons and how their lights brightened right before they exploded. Just like the one that had killed Starling.

Lailu shook her head, pushing away the memory of two surprised green eyes caught in a glow of fire. Then she noticed her wine cellar. "What did you *do*?" She was shaking she was so angry. "You smashed half my bottles!"

The other two guards stood among the shards. "Don't worry. We spared the LaSilvian," one of them said. "Only a few of the Debonaire broke."

"You carry LaSilvian now?" Elister said, raising his eyebrows. "Interesting."

Interesting? All those smears of wine soaking into her cellar's packed-dirt floor like blood and *that* was his comment? "Is *this* protecting your city?" she demanded. "Or do you not consider *this* to be part of *your* city?"

"Don't worry, Master Loganberry. We will see that all damages are paid for." Elister turned his back on her, studying the generator. "Did Wren make this?"

The generator took up all of the wall space next to Lailu's icebox. Pipes stuck out of the top, sending out occasional bursts of steam, the whole machine humming continuously. When Wren had offered to install it, Lailu had pictured Mystic Cooking becoming the very image of a modern and revolutionary restaurant. Now, staring at it, the thing filled her with dread. Dread, and sadness.

Wren had been her friend back then.

"Yes, Wren made it," Lailu said stiffly.

Elister nodded. "I recognize the design. One of her mother's original creations. Such a pity."

"Sir?" Seala called. "There's something underneath it. It's . . . moving." She dropped her hand to the hilt of her sword, crouching to see better.

Click, click, click.

Cold terror shivered up Lailu's spine. That noise sounded exactly like the clicking of one of Wren's explosive spi-trons. But there was no way. . . .

Lailu moved closer, scanning the shadows beneath the hulking generator. Was that a glowing blue light? It moved, darting to the left, and Seala gasped.

One of the other guards moved in closer. "It's under the icebox," he said.

It moved again, farther back. *Click, click, click.* And then it vanished.

"Maybe it—ahh!" Seala fell back as something black and metallic shot out from beneath the generator, its long spindly legs extended toward her.

Lailu grabbed one of her intact wine bottles and smashed it on top of the metal creation, slamming it into the ground in a shower of wine.

Click! Click! Its legs trembled and jerked as the gears in its back crunched around the shards of glass, its single eye glowing the same eerie blue as the power generator. Aside from the clockwork gears and the many-jointed legs, it looked almost like a giant beetle, about the size of a frying pan.

"An elven spy." Seala pushed herself to her feet. "Should we arrest the chef?"

"Hey, I just saved you," Lailu said.

"From a trap *you* set." Seala's eyes narrowed to ugly slits.

"What?" Lailu looked down at the broken wine bottle in her hand. "I sacrificed one of my best wines for—"

"Stop," Elister commanded. "Both of you. Obviously this is science, not magic." He sighed. "Much less predictable. Unfortunately."

"But, sir," Seala began.

"We're leaving. Grab the beetle."

"Wait!" Lailu flung her arm out to stop them. "Last time Wren sent one of those . . . it exploded."

"Intriguing." Elister glanced at the guard, who had backed away from the spi-tron. Scowling, he grabbed the clockwork creature himself.

Lailu threw up her arms.

Nothing happened.

Elister wrapped his new pet in the folded newspaper he'd taken from Lianna and headed up the stairs, trailed by his guards. Seala paused at the bottom of the steps, blocking Lailu. "Just so you know, I didn't need your help."

"Are you sure about that?" Lailu asked.

"*I* didn't need to go to a fancy academy to learn a thing or two. Don't think I don't know exactly what you were doing."

Fancy academy? Lailu scratched her head. "Um, what was I doing?"

"Don't play innocent. You were trying to make me look bad in front of Lord Elister." Seala's scowl grew uglier, darker. "It won't work." She stomped up the stairs and slammed the trapdoor closed, leaving Lailu in the semi-darkness.

Lailu sighed. She had enough enemies already.

She spared one last glance for the generator, pulsing behind her. It did *not* seem safe, and the fact that a spi-tron had managed to hide beneath it made her feel about as secure as a lopsided cake. She'd prefer it openly attack her like last time, rather than scuttling around in the dark, doing the gods only knew what.

Lailu shivered and made her way up the stairs. One way or another, she'd have to get rid of that generator, or she was afraid she'd end up going the same way as Starling.

EMPTY HOUSE

ailu almost managed to forget that morning's encounter with Elister as she lost herself in the joy of cooking. The previous week, Master Slipshod had made her a special marinade for her cockatrice, and now the air was filled with the scent of expertly seasoned, freshly baked meat. Ah, it was going to be a delicious feast!

"Lailu?" Hannah stuck her head around the curtain, her long black hair pulled up into an intricate bun and secured with a fancy silver hair comb. "We have a problem."

Lailu followed Hannah into the dining room and immediately saw what she meant. Most days her restaurant was nearly full at this time, but today for some reason there were only three groups of customers, and none of them looked very happy.

Then Lailu heard voices outside.

"If you're really not an elf, then take off your hat."

Lailu rushed to the door. Two guards in dark-red uniforms were blocking the entrance to Mystic Cooking. One of them flipped the hat off the head of a middle-aged man in an expensive three-piece suit.

"Look at that," the other guard said. "He's not an elf after all."

"My mistake." Both guards laughed.

The man picked up his fallen top hat, dusted it off, and put it back on his head. "Do you have any idea who I am?" he sneered.

"You can't be anyone too important if you're eating at this dump," one of the guards said.

"Hey!" Lailu snapped.

The guard turned and smirked at her, and Lailu realized it was Seala.

"We'll need to check your wife, too," Seala added. "Make sure you're not trying to escort an elf inside."

"I can't even believe this," the woman said. "Elf? Me?" She shook her head. "Let's go, darling. We don't have to put up with this . . . this treatment." She glanced at Lailu and sniffed.

"It's not my—" Lailu began, but the couple had already stormed off. "Fault," she whispered, her heart sinking to her boots. How many customers had these horrible guards chased away tonight? "Why are you here?" Lailu demanded.

"Lord Elister's orders," Seala said. "He wants guards stationed here around the clock."

"We're to keep out the elves by any means necessary," her partner added, "for as long as is necessary." He held out a piece of parchment with Elister's signature and seal stamped at the bottom.

Lailu shook her head. How many more customers would they scare off tomorrow and the next day? She had opened up Mystic Cooking so *everyone* could dine like a king even if it was just for a day. But without a steady stream of customers, she didn't know what would happen to her restaurant.

Lailu clenched and unclenched her aching hands, but she could feel the customers inside watching her. They still needed to be fed. She only hoped that more would be willing to come through. Lailu stomped back to her kitchen to work, her eyes watering. Here she'd thought it would be the scientists or possibly the elves at war with her, not the rulers of the city itself.

"It wasn't all bad," Hannah said, breezing into the kitchen hours later and flopping down on the one chair.

Lailu grunted.

"I mean, at least *some* customers showed up."

"Not enough." Lailu scowled.

"Maybe more will make it through tomorrow. But in the meantime, don't you have a date with Greg tonight?" Hannah wiggled her eyebrows.

"Hunt!"

"Same thing, for you. What are you going to wear?"

"Hunting clothes, obviously."

"Better be warm hunting clothes!" Lianna called from the dining room.

"I swear her hearing is getting better and better," Hannah whispered. "Well, what *are* you hunting?"

"Greg said it was a surprise."

"He sure does love his surprises. Any hints?"

"Apparently we're going somewhere 'darker than night.'"

"Oooh! How mysterious!" Hannah clapped. "And romantic."

"It is *not*." Lailu remembered again the feeling of Greg's hand holding hers as they watched the fairy lights. . . . Her face burned, and she turned away before Hannah could notice.

"Someplace darker than night . . . ," Hannah mused.

"A cave." Lianna ducked into the kitchen carrying a tray full of dirty dishes. "I'll get these washed for you," she told Lailu.

"I can do it."

"What good is having your mom around if she can't even help take care of you?"

Lailu remembered how her mother had told Elister that her work was here now. Lianna had been one of Elister's spies for a long time; they'd had a bit of a falling out after Starling's death—Lianna didn't think Elister handled it well—but Lailu had always assumed her mother would flit off again on another one of his missions. But maybe those days were gone for good, and she was here to stay.

"I'm glad you're around," Lailu blurted.

Lianna smiled. "Me too, honey. Now, go grab some sleep. You look like you're about to fall over." She bustled around the kitchen, filling a tray with two bowls and heaping a generous portion of cockatrice into each.

"That looks like you're making more dishes dirty," Lailu said.

"Oh, this? I'm taking food out to the guards."

"You're *what*?" Lailu gaped. "Why? Why would you do that?"

"Because when you're hunting, it helps to use good bait." Her mom grinned. "Right?"

"We're hunting the guards?" Lailu said. "I know you're mad at Elister, but that seems a little extreme."

Her mother laughed. "It's just an expression. Hannah understands."

Lailu glanced at her friend, who nodded.

"Is this like all those other times you made me give away free food?" Lailu asked. Hannah had spent their opening week promising people free appetizers and full-course meals, despite Lailu's objections.

"Sort of like that," Hannah said. "If the guards like you, they'll maybe be nicer."

Lailu thought of Seala's furious expression. "Good luck with that," she said sourly. "Wake me when Greg gets here." She stomped up the stairs and into her room above the restaurant. Her head had barely hit the pillow before someone was shaking her awake.

"Honey, Greg is here." Lianna placed a lantern on Lailu's nightstand.

"So soon?" Lailu mumbled, squinting against the sudden light.

"You've been asleep for two hours. I'll tell Greg you'll be right down."

Lailu sat up and yawned, her jaw cracking. She stumbled out of bed, got dressed, and then rummaged through her hunting chest. She selected two of her larger chef's knives, both keen-edged and almost as long as her forearm, with slender handles. They fit into specialty sheaths that she strapped to her legs; a knife belt would be no good if she was crawling around in tunnels. After a moment's debate she slipped a pair of weighted steak knives into her boots too, just in case, then grabbed her rope, her grappling hook, and a coat and headed downstairs and out into the cold, where Greg was waiting for her.

Normally, Greg's unruly curls were jammed under a fluffy white chef's hat, but in the last week the weather had gotten so cold that he had traded his white puff for a warmer knit cap. His wool coat and trousers were as dark as hers, and he had his hunting gear slung in a bag on his back. Lailu was relieved to see several torch heads poking out, but no climbing harness.

This was the first time she'd seen him since the night of the Fairy Lights, the night they'd held hands, and for a second she felt almost shy. Until she realized he was chatting with the new guard posted at her door.

"I still can't believe it," the guard was saying. "You're *the* Gregorian LaSilvian! Youngest master chef in over two centuries!"

Lailu bristled at that comment. "Ahem!"

The guard ignored her. "I was there on your opening day! I proposed to my wife there, and she said yes." He dug around in his pocket, then pulled out a very wrinkled newspaper.

"Is that the article about my opening day?" Greg asked. "And you just had it in your pocket . . . ?"

"Oh, I carry it with me everywhere. Just in case. Can you sign it?"

Greg glanced warily at Lailu. She scowled.

"I don't have a quill," Greg said.

"I do!" The guard pulled one out of his other pocket and thrust it at Greg.

"Seriously?" Lailu sighed as Greg took the quill and paper. "We don't have time for this."

"To Jonah," the guard instructed, looking over Greg's shoulder.

Greg signed and passed the paper and quill over, and then finally he and Lailu headed out into the night.

Lailu shook her head.

"What?" Greg jammed his hands in his pockets. "Lailu, he had a quill. And the article. That he carried around. Just in case he ran into me. How could I say no to that?"

"Like you didn't love every second of it," Lailu muttered. "Do you know how many customers that guard has chased off?"

"I wanted to ask you about that. What's going on?"

Lailu told him about Elister and his plan to keep the elves out "by any means necessary." When she finished, Greg was silent, the only sound their feet crunching on the cobblestones as they approached the last of the poor houses. These were the ones with broken glass, or no glass at all, and missing shingles. The ones separating the city from the elves' forest. There was no outer wall here, nothing to protect the people who lived here, the families who had spilled outside the original outskirts of Twin Rivers decades ago.

Lailu's steps slowed as she reached the end of the road. It stopped a few feet from the nearest house, the cobblestones ending abruptly as if whoever had built it planned to come back and expand it someday. Past the end of the road, there was a cleared ring of about five feet with nothing but grass and a few shrubs, and then the first slender trees of the Velvet Forest began.

Clouds obscured the moon and most of the stars, but Lailu could still make out the white sign wedged firmly into the ground a foot in front of the nearest tree.

"That's new," Greg whispered.

Both of them headed toward it, walking so close their shoulders brushed.

Lailu's eyes traced the words carved forcefully into the pale wood:

elves be warned,

you are officially banished from these premises.
the punishment for trespassing is death.

signed,
lord elister
protector of twin rivers

Just past that tree stood a second sign, this one facing out toward the city. It read:

humans be warned,

you are officially banished from these premises.
the punishment for trespassing is death.

There was no signature on this second sign. None was needed.

4

Darker Than Night

Lailu kept glancing back as she and Greg left the signs behind and stepped into the Velvet Forest. She could feel the trees looming over her, the grass swallowing her foot-steps like it was trying to erase her presence.

"Why do you keep doing that?" Greg asked.

"Doing what?" Lailu glanced behind her.

"That." Greg looked back. "See? Now you've got me doing it!"

"They said the punishment for trespassing here is death." Lailu shivered. The trees seemed to be more alive than usual, the rustling and whispering of their branches reminding her uncomfortably of the soft hum of the generator lurking beneath Mystic Cooking. She would have turned around and left after seeing that sign, except they really needed the cooking materials.

"We're not really trespassing." Greg hunched his shoulders.

"The cave entrance is only a few feet into the forest, so I don't think that will count."

"So it *is* a cave hunt." Her mother had been right.

"Of course it's a cave hunt. What else could it have been?"

"Well, if it was so obvious, why didn't you just say 'we're hunting in a cave'?" Lailu said irritably. "Why all the 'darker than night' nonsense?"

"Maybe it was a test." Greg gave her a sideways look. "Trying to keep your brain sharp, now that you're not in school."

"My brain is always sharp."

"Oh yeah? Did *you* figure out the clue? Or did Hannah?"

"Actually, it was my mother."

Greg smirked.

"Whatever." Lailu scowled. "I would have figured it out too."

"Oh, yeah. Sure."

"I would have!"

"I'm not disagreeing."

"Yes, you are! You're making that face and using that tone, and, and . . . Just tell me what we're hunting already."

"Fine. We're hunting a raegnar."

She froze, her breath catching. "A raegnar? *Here?*" Giant bear-like creatures, raegnars didn't have any eyes, relying instead on an impossibly good sense of smell and an ability to read even the slightest of vibrations in a cave floor or wall.

"Slipshod said it attacked two people on the edge of town a few days ago. According to the papers, Elister has been too busy to send a contingent of heroes after it."

"The papers said that?"

"Yep, this morning, right on the front page and everything."

Lailu thought of the paper Elister had snatched out of her mom's hands. "I don't think Elister wanted people to know about the attacks," she said. At Greg's questioning look, she explained Elister's furious reaction in her restaurant.

"Yeah, my uncle was pretty surprised to see it in the papers too," he admitted.

"But . . . why? It seems like important news."

Greg shrugged, but he was making a weird expression. Like he wanted to say something and didn't want to say it, all at the same time.

"Spit it out," Lailu said.

Greg sighed. "Fine. I think Elister believes people are scared enough right now without worrying about random raegnar attacks. *Especially* the people on the outskirts."

"You mean the ones he's been hassling with all those guards?"

"You mean *protecting* with all those guards?"

"I meant what I said."

Greg frowned. "He's trying to keep order, Lailu. That's all."

"He's trying to prove some sort of point."

"Oh yeah? And what's that?"

"That he can go in and do whatever he wants, and none of us can stop him." She thought of the way his guards had rifled through all her stuff and broken her wine bottles. Bottles Elister had then replaced, which meant it was just for show the whole time. "He's trying to make us feel powerless," she realized. That was probably the real reason he didn't want everyone to know about the raegnar attacks; those attacks showed he didn't have control over everything. "And I think he does want us to be scared," she added.

"And why would he want that?"

"Because powerless, scared people are easy to control."

Greg shook his head. "I think this forest is getting to you."

"That's not it, Greg," Lailu said.

Greg pressed his lips together, his expression skeptical, and Lailu sighed and let it go. There was no way he'd understand anyhow. He'd grown up on Gilded Island. Things were a lot different there.

In silence, they picked their way through a large clearing, stopping next to a pile of rocks that had been stacked as a marker. Behind them lurked a giant hole in the ground that Lailu knew opened into a cave big enough to swallow her entire restaurant.

Lailu and Greg had been inside it once before when Master Sanford, Lailu's favorite teacher at Chef Academy, took her class out here on a field trip to study proper cave-hunting techniques.

"This cave isn't the problem," Master Sanford had said as they dropped into the dark beside him. "Lots of space to move around, and some of the beasties that live here make a mighty fine roast. But just be sure you don't get lured too far in." His single blue eye had caught the light from his torch, gleaming as he fixed it on each and every one of them.

"Why not?" Lailu had asked.

"Because this cave narrows into a tunnel that extends for miles beneath the ground, branching off like the veins in your arms. If you turn down the wrong branch . . ." He'd plunged their torch into the dirt at his feet, the flames sputtering and going out. Sudden darkness had pressed in on all sides, so dark Lailu couldn't tell if her eyes were open or closed. So dark she could imagine all the things that lived in it moving closer . . . things that didn't need to see to hunt.

"You think this is dark?" Master Sanford had laughed, the sound echoing off the rocks and bouncing around them. "This is a walk through a sunlit meadow compared to those tunnels. So don't you go wandering off now, you hear? You all stay close."

Lailu had stayed close. So had everyone else.

She blinked, letting the memory fade away.

The Velvet Forest around them kept silent watch over the field and the nighttime. "How far in are we going?" she whispered.

Greg smirked.

"And if you call me 'chicken,' I'll truss you up and throw you in by yourself," she added.

Greg's smirk wilted. "You are no fun." He pulled out one of his torches but didn't light it yet. "And we won't be going in far. It should be in this first outer cave."

The longer she stared at the opening to the raegnar's lair, the colder she felt. It seemed to suck in the light of the moon and give back none of it. "So, what's the plan?" She glanced sideways at Greg. "You do have a plan, right?"

"Last time I left the planning up to you, you made me into bait for a charging hydra. Of *course* I have a plan."

Lailu smiled, remembering their last hunt together when they took down a large seven-headed hydra. "That's the fastest I've ever seen you run."

"You know, there are only two times I see you smile: when you're cooking and when you're thinking about me suffering," Greg grumbled.

"You forgot one." Lailu's smile widened. "When I'm hunting."

Greg laughed. "Speaking of, look what we have to work with." He opened his bag. "We have torches." He pulled them out. "Rope, a net—pre-made, I might add."

Lailu took the net from him, letting its silky strands slide through her fingers. "Is this Aracillian silk?" Aracillias were super rare, and their silk very expensive. But the rope made from it was the lightest and strongest that any chef could ever ask for.

Greg nodded. "Just arrived from Mystalon traders three days ago."

"I kind of hate you right now."

"Don't hate me yet," Greg said. "Just wait until you see this last surprise." He reached in his bag and pulled out a large chunk of mottled grayish-green meat. It had been wrapped in something clear, but that hardly disguised its foul stench. "Bait." He dropped it on the ground between them.

Lailu nudged it with her foot. "Is that what I think it is?"

"Yep. I got that orc meat specially for you. Like old times, eh?" They had used orc meat on the famous dragon hunt some months back. "All we're missing is Hannah."

Lailu eyed that deep, dark hole in the ground. "Probably better she's not here," she said. She tightened her pigtails. "What's the plan, then?"

"We climb down there. We stalk the raegnar. And then we kill it."

"You want us to stalk it? Through the dark?" Lailu thought of Master Sanford's little demonstration again and imagined miles and miles of tunnels so deep even the dream of sunlight never entered. "I have a better idea."

"Oh yeah?"

"Pass me a torch."

Greg scraped a torch against a sparking pad sewn into the side of his bag, and it crackled with flame. "Pretty neat, right?"

"Is that from one of the scientists?" Lailu couldn't help the accusation that crept into her voice.

Greg's shoulders stiffened. "Not . . . exactly," he hedged. He handed her the lit torch. "It's . . . well, you know how some of them are branching out now, doing their own thing?"

"They are? I thought that wasn't allowed."

"Starling didn't allow it, but without her around . . ." Greg shrugged. "Anyhow, one of them made me this. He seems nice enough. Pretty harmless."

"I doubt that."

"Yeah, you're probably right. But this, at least, is a useful tool."

Lailu couldn't deny that. Still. "Let's just hunt this thing and get home, okay?" She dropped her torch down the hole, showcasing the gouge marks of the raegnar's large claws before landing at the bottom.

"So much for subtlety," Greg said.

"I'm not really big on subtle." Lailu took an iron peg from Greg and pounded it into the ground a few feet away. "Rope," she called. He tossed her an end, and she quickly looped it around the peg, then tugged on it. Nice and tight. When she turned around, Greg was already disappearing into the ground.

"What are you doing?" Lailu asked.

"Hunting," Greg said, shimmying further down the rope. "OBV."

"OBV?"

"Obviously."

Lailu scowled. "Well, *obviously* you're doing it wrong. No wonder you always got lower marks in hunting class."

"Not always." He grinned, and Lailu just knew he was thinking of the time he made her into bait and got all the fyrian chicken eggs himself.

"Watch it, you." She pointed her knife at him. "I'm not opposed to cutting your rope."

"Great. That will just get me down faster."

"Which would be a huge mistake."

"Why?"

Lailu shrugged. "*I* know how good the raegnar's sense of hearing is. Any tiny vibration, any little sound . . . like the sound of a torch hitting the ground . . ."

Lailu felt the ground shudder beneath her feet, and Greg's face paled.

"Help," he whispered. "Pull me up, fast."

Lailu hauled up the rope as Greg climbed. He'd just cleared the lip of the hole when they heard snuffling from below.

Greg slid forward, stretching out on his stomach, and Lailu lay down next to him, moving as quietly as possible.

The raegnar was nudging the torch with its massive nose. It looked almost like a vole the size of a bear, with scaly dry skin instead of fur. Its sloped face was all nose, but Lailu knew it could open its jaw wide and inside would be plenty of teeth. It padded silently on all fours, its claws retracted like a cat's. It lifted its long pointed snout in their direction, nostrils flaring.

The torch in the cave sputtered and went out.

"That can't be good," Greg whispered.

5

LAILU'S TURN

*L*ailu and Greg both held their breath, peering down into the inky darkness of the hole, waiting.

Eventually a soft scraping noise echoed up from below, the sound of the raegnar retreating farther back into its lair once again. They were lucky it had fed recently, or it would have clawed its way up and out to investigate, and their perch on the edge of the cave would have been about as safe as one of Wren's inventions.

Lailu slid back and stood, taking a few steps away from that opening. Just in case.

Greg followed her. "Did you see the size of that thing? Man, I'm glad we aren't stalking it through the tunnels. What a terrible plan that was."

"At least you can admit it. You're just lucky *I* always have a plan."

Greg chuckled. "I know. It's why I keep you around."

Lailu wondered if it was too late to shove him back down into the raegnar's lair. "Rig up the net above the hole," she said, "and then throw the meat on it. When he comes for the meat, we'll drop down with the net and take him out."

"That's it?"

"Simple is always best."

"That sounds *too* simple."

"Your brain is too simple," she muttered.

"What was that?"

"Nothing."

"Are you sure? 'Cause it sounded like a vicious and unnecessary insult to me."

"Oh, so you *did* hear me." Lailu grinned and found Greg grinning back. She used to hate the way he'd tease her, but lately she'd started appreciating how she could tease back, how it didn't feel like fighting anymore. It felt almost like a dance. He tossed her one end of the net, and they moved away from each other, pulling it between them like a fitted sheet across the hole. Despite the cold, sweat trickled down Lailu's spine. Raegnars were not beasts to take lightly, but she knew this was a well-made net and Greg wasn't so bad for backup. They could do this.

"Ready?" Lailu called out softly. The ground trembled beneath her boots. The raegnar was stirring again, unable to resist all the noise they were making so close to its home.

"Ready," Greg whispered.

Lailu kept one hand firmly gripping the edge of the net and groped around next to her with the other. Her hand brushed against the edge of the orc meat. She picked it up, her fingers sinking slightly into its decaying flesh, the sickly sweet scent of it filling her nostrils. She wrinkled her nose and tried breathing as shallowly as possible. Trust Greg to find the grossest possible bait. At least *her* orc meat had been half-frozen.

She tossed the meat onto the center of the net, the ropes bowing under the weight. Greg kept his end held tight, and she adjusted her own grip, waiting. Any moment now.

It happened in an instant. One second there was nothing but a slight vibration in the ground beneath her feet, and the next, jaws like a land shark's rose from the hole, snapping around the ropes holding up the orc meat.

"Now!" Lailu jumped down, still clinging to her side of the net, and tried not to think about how the battle would turn out if Greg didn't do the same. She had to trust him.

The raegnar bellowed in rage as it tumbled backward, carried by Lailu's and Greg's weight on the net. Lailu felt like they were falling in slow motion, the air whizzing by, the ropes digging into her hands, the blackness swallowing everything. Then a sudden jerk as the beast hit the ground, taking the full impact of the fall, before her boots crunched on solid ground.

They were inside the cave. "Hold it!" Greg yelled, just as the net tore right out of Lailu's fingers.

"Butterknives," she swore. She couldn't see anything, but she felt movement above her and ducked instinctively as something swished over her head. A raegnar paw, claws extended. She could picture it perfectly.

She drew her knife, trying to picture the rest of the creature. Every mystical beast had a weak spot, and the raegnar's was just under his left rib cage.

"Torch!" Lailu yelled, ducking again and sliding to the side.

"I'm a little busy," Greg panted, but a second later there was a *whoosh*, and his spare torch flared to life. Lailu had an impression of size, of bared teeth and raised arms and claws curved and deadly. She lunged in, not stopping to think, and shoved her knife between the raegnar's ribs as it swung at her, so close its talon sliced off a lock of her hair before it staggered and collapsed.

Lailu rolled away, breathing hard. She flexed her fingers, her hands aching under their bandages. Not much she could do about them now.

"We did it," Greg said.

Lailu looked over. He stood on the other side of their fallen foe, his hands on his knees. He'd lost his hat, and his hair stuck out around his head in a wild tangle of curls.

"See?" Lailu grinned. "My *simple* plan worked just fine."

"If you say so." Greg poked the raegnar with his foot. "No wonder it prefers darkness. This sure is one ugly beast."

"If by 'ugly' you mean 'delicious,' then yes," Lailu said, although secretly she thought Greg had a point. The raegnar's huge form filled the better part of the cave, its tongue sticking out between teeth as long and jagged as steak knives. And now that they were closer, Lailu could see that it did actually have fur. In patches.

"You know, I think we're getting a little better at these joint hunts," Greg said.

"Maybe."

"Maybe? Come on. This was almost *too* easy." He grinned, his cheeks dimpling in the torchlight. "Even *you* have to admit we make a great team."

Lailu's chest filled with a burst of warmth, but she admitted nothing. The last thing she wanted was for Greg to think she agreed with him on anything.

6

TRAPPED

lmost . . . there," Lailu huffed as she and Greg hauled together on the rope. The raegnar scraped through the small hole and out onto the ground, and Lailu and Greg collapsed next to it, sweaty and exhausted. Overhead, the first faint streaks of light filled the sky, reminding Lailu of the soft pink of a lightly seared filet mignon. Maybe that was how she'd cook this raegnar.

"That was way harder than the actual hunt," Greg said.

"It really was." The raegnar had been too heavy to haul out of the cave using just the rope, so they'd had to rig up the net to help support it. But then it hadn't fit through the hole, so they'd had to dig at the walls to widen them and then try again. And again.

Every muscle in Lailu's body throbbed, but nothing compared to the ache of her hands, which felt like she was holding them in the oven. Still. This should provide enough meat for a week's worth of meals, which meant it was all worth it.

"Hands okay?" Greg asked.

Lailu shrugged, and then almost jumped when Greg took one of her hands in his, gently massaging it.

"I'm sorry," he said.

"For what?"

"For not having a better plan."

"I'm used to it. You never have a good plan."

He laughed. "Your honesty is so . . ."

"Refreshing?"

"I was going to say painful," Greg said. "But refreshing, too, I guess. At least I know where I stand with you."

"My, my, isn't this a cozy little scene," Ryon said.

Lailu was instantly very aware of her shoulder against Greg's, her hand in his. She sprang up, tugging her fingers free, her face blazing. "What are *you* doing here?"

Ryon seemed like a shadow come to life, his clothing in shades of green and brown, his long hair pulled back into a low messy ponytail that Lailu knew Hannah would hate. Her friend had a thing against ponytails. "I'm lurking in the forest," he said.

"Truth," Greg muttered.

Lailu thought of Lord Elister's guards searching her restaurant. "Probably for the best," she decided. "I think Elister knows about your heritage."

"I guessed he would," Ryon sighed. "I take it I'm not welcome in the city, then?"

"Not so much."

"Ah well."

"That's it?" Lailu asked. "It doesn't bother you?"

"It's what I expected. It's why I've been staying here with the elves."

"And that's been okay for you?" The last time Lailu had seen Ryon, he'd been upset with his elven brother Fahr for running the scheme that got the elves banished in the first place. Between that and the fact that Ryon didn't get along with Fahr's second-in-command, Lailu doubted his stay with the elves was very comfortable.

"It's been . . . well . . . not the best." His lips quirked in a crooked smile. "I'm not particularly welcome in the forest, either. But Fahr's keeping an eye out for me, keeping me busy."

"Doing what?" Greg asked suspiciously.

Ryon ignored him, crouching instead to inspect the raegnar. "Nice work. Although, technically, you're both poaching." His eyes glittered, his face suddenly much too elf-like for Lailu's comfort. "You're just lucky that *I* was the one who found you hunting here."

Lailu shivered. Suddenly the trees felt like they had moved in closer, becoming their own kind of cave, just as dangerous as the one they'd escaped. "Maybe we should get out of here?" she suggested.

"I'd suggest so, and quickly. I don't know what the elves will do if they find you here." Ryon stood and brushed his hands off on his coat, then went still, his head tilting to the side.

"What is it?" Lailu asked.

"Nothing . . ." He turned in a slow circle, searching the trees. "Or something?"

"Not really filling me with a lot of confidence," Greg said.

Ryon glanced at him. "Weren't you leaving? Or did you need help with that?" He waved a hand at the raegnar.

"We don't need your help," Greg said quickly.

Ryon's lips quirked in a tiny smile. "That's too bad; I was really looking forward to it."

"I just bet you were," Lailu muttered.

"You know me, the soul of helpfulness."

"Not the first description I would use." Shaking her head, Lailu grabbed the net still tangled around the raegnar. Greg mirrored her on the other side, and together they dragged the heavy carcass behind them, lugging it over roots and around trees as Ryon practically skipped through the forest just ahead.

"I can't believe you're friends with that guy," Greg said.

"And I can't believe you stopped him from helping. This would have been a lot easier with three people."

"Like he was really going to help. Look at him up there. He's prancing. Just to rub it in."

"Well, what did you expect? You *told* him not to help. Of course he's going to be obnoxious about it." A branch cracked overhead, another behind. Lailu hunched her shoulders, trying not to imagine things lurking in the forest around them. "Let's just hurry, okay?"

"You feel it too?" Greg glanced around.

"Like we're being watched?" Lailu said.

He nodded, and they picked up their pace, catching up to Ryon. Just ahead, Lailu could see where the trees thinned out, the dirt road barely visible between them. Almost there. Another five feet. She adjusted her grip, then froze.

Greg kept right on walking, tearing the net from Lailu's hands, but she barely noticed. She had just spotted what was waiting for them at the edge of the forest. Or rather, *who*.

"I thought I heard the pitter-patter of little human feet crashing through our territory." Eirad stepped from beneath the trees, the shadows dripping away from his pale face and golden braids like sauce from an overflowing pan.

Lailu shrank back. She'd always found Eirad to be the most terrifying of all the elves; while Fahr seemed to at least care a little about the humans around him and the rules they made, his second-in-command held no such pretense.

"Did you not see our sign?" he asked her.

She thought of their NO TRESPASSING sign and swallowed hard. She could lie, but Eirad would be able to tell; the elves always seemed to know if someone was lying to them. "Yes," she said shakily. "We did."

"Then you know what the penalty for ignoring it is." A statement.
Death.

Lailu and Greg exchanged a look, and then both of them dropped their hands to their knife hilts.

Ryon moved, putting himself between them and Eirad. "A moment, cousin," he said, smiling pleasantly, hands out. "I was the one who discovered these trespassers, so I get to carry out their punishment. Isn't that so?"

"That only applies to full elves," Eirad snarled.

"A status that Fahr has granted to me."

"A status that can always be revoked." Eirad crossed his arms. "Tread carefully here, *cousin*. Some of us already think your loyalties are . . . questionable."

Ryon dropped his pleasant mask. "I have proven my loyalties, again and again. Fahr is satisfied; that should be enough for the rest of you."

"Maybe Fahr isn't as satisfied as you think."

A sudden breeze tugged at Lailu's hair and twirled through the branches above her, turning the forest into a sea of dancing leaves. And then it wasn't just the breeze moving through the forest.

"Lailu," Greg hissed, grabbing her arm.

"I know."

Elves, four of them, slid out from between the trees and formed a loose ring with Lailu, Greg, and Ryon at their center.

"Ah, I see," Ryon said, turning and looking around at the other elves. "You were too scared to face off against me alone this time. I get it." He winked. Right in Eirad's face.

Lailu caught her breath. True, Ryon had held his own against Eirad during their last fight, his ability to neutralize magic helping him counter Eirad's attacks and giving him an edge. In fact, she could still see the faded bruise on Eirad's cheek. But still, winking in his face? It was worse than tap-dancing through the cave of a hungry raegnar.

Eirad's nostrils flared. "I will face you anytime," he spat.

"Is that so? Perhaps we should test it?"

Eirad took a slow, deep breath, and then he smiled. It was terrifying, especially when he turned that smile on Lailu and Greg. They inched close together. "Actually, cousin," Eirad said, "I *will* allow you to carry out the penalty in this case. So, what punishment will you give these foolish little chefs?"

The way he said it made it clear this question was a trap.

Which made Lailu and Greg the bait.

Ryon didn't seem worried. "As you know, I can only give the punishment that has been ordered. So, since the penalty for trespassing is death, I'll be forced to carry that out." He shrugged.

"Seriously?" Greg said.

"You also set a death penalty for poaching," Ryon continued, so matter-of-factly, it was like he was discussing the weather.

"I did," Eirad agreed.

"Which means I'll be forced to kill these poaching trespassers twice."

"How are you going to kill us twice?" Lailu demanded, heart thumping.

Ryon put a finger to his chin in exaggerated thought. "That's a great question, Lailu. It's not possible, is it? Which means this is . . . What would you call it, Eirad? A loophole?"

Eirad went still. Elves couldn't lie, and their promises were binding, but they were masters of twisting around words to find the best possible outcome. Best for them, at least. "That is not how I would interpret it," he said after a long moment.

"Ah, but you did agree that I get to carry out their punishment, which means it's my interpretation that matters."

"So, you would pick these humans over elves?" Eirad's eyes were icy blue slits in the darkness.

"No. I'd pick *this* human"—Ryon tugged on one of Lailu's pigtails—"over an arbitrary elven rule. But you can have the other human, if you'd like, and we'll call it even."

"Hey!" Greg said.

"He's joking," Lailu whispered, even though she wasn't sure he was.

"And this is your final choice?" Eirad asked.

"It was never really a choice."

Eirad nodded once. "Fahr *will* hear about this. You are choosing your human side after all. He will be most . . . disappointed."

"For the last time, I'm not—" Ryon stopped. The elves had already melted back into the shadows, vanishing into the early-morning fog. "Huh," he said into the quiet. "That went well."

Lailu wasn't sure if she wanted to laugh or cry. Maybe both. "I thought for sure we'd have to fight them."

"I did too," Ryon admitted. "I'm surprised he's letting us go this easily, so we might want to hurry, yes?"

"Yes," Lailu and Greg said, picking up the net and hauling their raegnar the remaining feet.

Wham!

Lailu staggered, dropping the raegnar. "What the—" She reached forward into the empty space between two of the trees on the edge of the forest, and her hand stopped. There was nothing there. It was as if her hand just couldn't physically move anymore. Like her muscles forgot how to work the moment she reached that space.

Lailu dropped her hand, her fingers tingling.

"Oh, Fahr must have put up a boundary," Ryon said. "He said he might be doing that soon. I forgot to mention it."

Greg stalked closer until he was only inches from Ryon. "Is there anything else you've conveniently forgotten to mention?" he growled.

"Oh stop. You're not nearly as intimidating as you think," Ryon said. "Besides, I noticed you're missing all your pretty little knives."

"Lailu still has hers."

"Yes, but Lailu is smart enough not to threaten me." Ryon grinned. "Especially since I can get through the barrier, and I can bring you with me." His grin widened. "If you ask nicely, that is."

Lailu sighed. Her head hurt, and her fingers still felt like they'd fallen asleep. "Ryon, would you please take us through?" Best to get this over with.

"Not you," Ryon said. "I want to hear it from him." He jerked his chin at Greg, who scowled and crossed his arms.

"Just do it." Lailu nudged Greg in the side.

"I don't want to."

"We don't have any other options."

Greg winced. "Fine," he grumbled. "Fine." He dropped his arms, took a deep breath, and said, "Ryon, would you please take us through the barrier?"

Ryon's eyes narrowed. "Not good enough."

"What? Why? I said please and everything!"

"Ah, but you didn't say it like you meant it. Besides"—Ryon examined his nails—"I thought you didn't need my help."

"What now?" Greg asked Lailu.

"Ask again. Nicer."

Greg shook his head, but he turned back to Ryon and pasted a huge, insincere smile across his face. "Ryon, could you, pretty please, with all due respect, take us through the barrier? We would be ever so grateful."

"Let me think about it."

"Ryon!" Lailu snapped.

Ryon laughed. "Oh, all right. Here, I'll need to be touching both of you." He looped his arm through one of Lailu's, then looked at Greg.

"Ryon," Lailu growled.

"Do we have to take him with us?" he asked.

"Yes!" Lailu snapped. "Unless you're suddenly going to help with the raegnar?"

Ryon sighed and looped his other arm through one of Greg's. "Keep ahold of that beast. Ready?" And without waiting for a response, he stepped forward, Lailu and Greg stumbling in his wake.

For a second Lailu felt like she'd plunged through ice-cold water, so cold it burned. And then, as quickly as it washed over her, it faded, leaving her skin tingling as if she'd just scrubbed it down with a wire-haired sponge.

Ryon let them both go.

"We're through?" Lailu asked.

"You're through. And now it's time for me to head back to Fahr. Hopefully I'm still welcome." Ryon frowned. "You know, maybe I won't go back quite yet."

"Why not?" Lailu asked. "Will Fahr really hold it against you that you helped us?"

"He might. Not because of *you* specifically. But as you may have noticed, I'm not Eirad's favorite person."

"I had noticed that," Lailu said dryly.

Ryon's lips quirked in a half smile. "Fahr has started slowly shutting me out, I think thanks to Eirad's influence. I don't know how he expects me to be useful to him when he won't tell me anything, but . . ." He shrugged. "I guess it will make it easier, though, to know which side I'm meant to be on."

"S-side?" Lailu swallowed. "Why do there have to be sides?"

"Because we're at war. There are always sides in a war. Our side, and their side."

He was of course referring to the war between the elves and the scientists. They had been at odds with each other ever since the scientists kidnapped elves so they could experiment on them. But seeing how Lailu killed the scientists' leader, the war seemed rather one-sided. Granted, Elister seemed to be taking up Starling's place quite menacingly. . . .

"And which side *are* you?" Greg asked.

Ryon's grin this time didn't look forced. "I'm always on the same side." He winked. "My own. I'll see you both around." With a cheery wave, he sauntered down the road away from them.

"Wait, Ryon! You're not safe in the city!"

"I'll keep a low profile," he called over his shoulder, before vanishing into the shadows up ahead.

Lailu frowned. That had seemed a little *too* cheery. Even for Ryon. "Do you think he'll be all right?" she asked.

"Who cares," Greg said, shoving a muddy curl out of his face.

"I care! He *is* my friend." That was something else to consider: if Greg wanted to be friends with her, he had better be more accepting of all her other friends, or else it just wasn't going to work.

Greg opened his mouth to say something, then closed it again. "Let's just get going," he said instead. "Elister needs to hear about the barrier." He scowled at the forest behind him.

Lailu and Greg each grabbed their side of the net and set off down the road, dragging the raegnar behind them.

7

Those Left to Burn

The dead raegnar took up a good portion of Lailu's kitchen. She and Greg worked side by side, separating meat from bone and pulling away the sinewy, inedible parts.

Lailu finished slicing away another chunk of meat and tossed the bone into a large pot for soup, then set her knife down.

"Hands hurting you?" Greg asked.

"No," she lied. Paulie Anna, Twin Rivers's resident witch, had given her a special salve to rub into the burns on her hands. It had helped a lot, but dragging that raegnar through the forest and doing all this chopping had made her fingers extra stiff and achy. Sometimes she worried this was her new normal and that they'd never completely heal. But she could still cook, so she didn't need Greg hovering over her. "I'm just checking something." She glanced down at her old textbook.

"I still can't believe you're using *Gingersnap's Theories*." Greg shook his head.

"Whatever, Greg. Don't think I haven't noticed you checking it too." She'd caught him not once, but three times looking at the book to make sure he was doing his part right.

"What are we going to hunt next?" Greg asked.

"We?" Lailu blinked, surprised. "You want to hunt together again?"

Greg looked away. "I mean, if *you* want to . . ."

Lailu hesitated. Truthfully, she *did* want to hunt with Greg. And that worried her. She was supposed to be running this business on her own, a full master chef in her own right, and here she was getting dependent on another chef.

"I don't much care either way." Greg sniffed. "Although since we can't go into the Velvet Forest anymore, I did think of another perfect hunting place to go next week. . . . But if you don't want in on the action, then fine. More for me and my customers."

Lailu narrowed her eyes. "Where?"

He grinned. "I'm not telling. You'd have to see it for yourself."

"That's not fair."

He shrugged.

"Can't you give me a hint?"

"It's not the Velvet Forest."

Lailu sighed. "You and your surprise hunts." She looked around the kitchen. Between this and the remaining cockatrice in her icebox, she should have enough supplies for meals for a week. But after that? "Fine," she said. "It had better be truly amazing."

"Oh, it will be." Greg chuckled.

"Why are you laughing?"

"Why are you always so suspicious?"

"I just don't want this hunt to end up biting me in the butt."

"Okay, first of all, those chickens used fire, not teeth, and—"

"I don't want to talk about the chickens!" Lailu snapped.

"Are you sure? Because you do seem to bring them up a lot." Greg's eyes twinkled. Lailu's hands ached too much to throttle him, so she just gave him her best death glare.

Lianna strolled into the kitchen, looking way too cheerful with her bright skirts swishing around her, the day's newspaper tucked under one arm, a bouquet of flowers under the other. "My, my, I have been on the receiving end of that look plenty too," she said. "I feel for you, Greg. I truly do."

"He deserves this look," Lailu grumbled. She glanced at the bouquet, with its riot of red, pink, and white petals. "Nice flowers. Where'd you find roses at this time of year?"

"Oh, I didn't find them, dear. They're a gift for Hannah." She sighed. "From Vahn."

"On second thought, maybe they're not so nice," Lailu muttered. She didn't want to think about her old crush, Vahn. She had *really* liked him, but he had been a jerk to her *and* to Hannah. She still couldn't believe he had two-timed her best friend with Paulie Anna. And now he thought a bunch of stupid flowers would smooth that all over? Ridiculous. It also showed how little he knew about Hannah; if he had sent her hair combs instead, he might have had a shot.

"I'm sure he spent a pretty penny on them, for all the good it'll do him." Lianna chuckled, setting the flowers on the counter. "Now, what terrible thing did Greg do?"

"I offered to hunt with her again," Greg said. "And nice to see you again, Mrs. Loganberry."

"Please, call me Lianna. And Lailu is lucky to have you as a friend."

"Lucky my butt."

"I thought we weren't talking about that anymore," Greg stage-whispered.

Lailu shot him another glare.

He clutched dramatically at his heart.

"Stop showing off for my mother and tell her where we're hunting."

Greg shook his head. "Nice try, though. It's a surprise," he told Lianna. "Now that we've been barricaded out of the Velvet Forest—"

Lianna dropped her newspaper. "What?"

As Greg told her about the elves' magic barrier, Lailu scooped up the paper. Flames curled across the picture on the front page. Lailu frowned and opened it, and the fire resolved itself into the silhouette of a rampaging phoenix. A small village peeked out from behind it, the houses charred, the crops burned. It looked a lot like Lailu's home village, except that Clear Lakes sat on the top of a mountain, whereas this village nestled in a valley. Otherwise, the two places could have been twins. Beneath the picture, the article stated that a phoenix had been terrorizing the village for the past three nights in a row.

Lailu frowned, her eyes trailing over to the bouquet on the counter. Why hadn't a hero like Vahn been sent to take care of the phoenix? He clearly wasn't busy enough.

"—not allowing anyone in their forest," Greg finished. "They have a sign up, too, that claims no one can enter."

"Elister needs to know about this," Lianna said.

"I was going to tell him after we finish—" Greg began.

"No. Right now." Lianna made shooing motions, and Greg reluctantly stood up. "I'd go myself, but Elister and I . . . aren't on the best of terms right now. I'll help Lailu bundle up your portion and have it sent to your restaurant."

Greg gathered his supplies. "See you next week for the hunt of your life," he told Lailu. He grinned, then hurried out before Lianna could shoo him along again.

"The hunt of my life?" Lailu shook her head. "Somehow that's not comforting."

Her mom didn't answer.

"Mom?"

Lianna blinked. "Sorry. Lost in thought."

"About?"

"What this all means. For the people caught in between." Lianna picked up a knife and started chopping, her fingers moving swiftly. "Whenever there's a power clash between rival rulers, it never works out well for the little people."

The little people. People like Lailu. Lailu glanced at the newspaper again, at the burned houses in that small, poor village, and shuddered.

8

INCOGNITO

Lailu bustled about the kitchen, adding water to her broth, then rummaging in the cupboard for more vegetables and extra seasoning. She was running way behind.

"Lailu," Hannah hissed, poking her head through the curtain.

"Gah!" Lailu spun, sprinkling the floor with salt.

"Oh, sorry. It's just . . . the guard is hassling your first customer." Hannah pursed her lips. "And wait until you see who it is." Her head disappeared before Lailu could ask any questions.

"Better be good," Lailu muttered. Salt was expensive. Sighing, she stepped over it and headed out into the dining room. She could already hear the voice of the guard outside. Seala's voice. Great.

Lailu opened the door. "Is there a problem?" she asked.

A short man stood awkwardly on the doorstep, his arms wrapped protectively around his stomach. He wore a large brimmed hat and a shabby brown vest that hung loosely over a baggy white shirt. Most of his face was obscured by a mustache as ridiculously oversized as his hat, but beneath it his face was gaunt, the skin sagging as if he'd lost a lot of weight recently.

Still, Lailu recognized him immediately. A scientist. Her heart beat faster.

"I told you, I'm not an elf," the scientist said. "I'm just . . . I'm allergic to the sun. Hence the hat."

"And I told you, I don't believe you," Seala said.

"Why are you alone out here?" Lailu asked. "Where's the second guard?"

Seala frowned. "Jonah followed your chef friend back to Gilded Island."

Lailu remembered the guard from the other night and the way he'd carried around that old newspaper just in case he got a chance to meet Greg. She shook her head.

"I know," Seala said. "It's sickening."

"Want to take a lunch break?" Hannah asked her.

Seala scowled. "I can't leave my post. Unlike some partners of mine, I actually care about doing a good job."

"Oh, we'd bring the food out to you, naturally," Hannah said. "Since we do appreciate you keeping our restaurant safe."

"You do?" Seala asked. "I thought you hated having me out here." She pointed at Lailu. "I know *that* one hates it, at least."

Lailu gaped. "'That one'?" Who did this guard think she was?

"She's always glaring at me," Seala continued. "And she totally set me up in front of Lord Elister."

"Well, I'm sure she feels terrible about that now." Hannah

looped her arm through Lailu's and tugged her back toward Mystic Cooking. "We'll bring you a tray in a few minutes!" She closed the front door and leaned against it.

"Did you hear her? Did you?" Lailu curled her hands into fists, then winced.

"I heard her. And you should probably put some more salve on your fingers."

"Can't." Lailu sighed. "I used it up." She clasped her hands together, feeling the bandages underneath her gloves.

"Really?" Hannah frowned. "I'll ask Paulie to bring some more when she gets a chance. You should have told your mom this morning; she could have swung by on her way back from the market."

Lailu shrugged. "It's really not a big deal. . . ." Her eyes narrowed. The scientist had managed to sneak in. He huddled in the corner behind one of the tables, very obviously eavesdropping on everything. "Hello, Neon," Lailu said.

He started, almost falling. "Neon?" he spluttered. "Me? No, no, you are mistaken. Very mistaken."

"Your mustache is crooked."

His hand flew to his face.

Lailu could hardly believe that this frightened, twitchy man was one of Starling's scientists, the man who had invented the camera, who had helped capture Ryon, who . . . looked like he was about to pass out.

She hurried forward and pulled out a chair for him.

"Thank you." He sank gratefully onto it, dabbing at his face with the edge of his sleeve. His mustache was now barely hanging on, one end dangling down by his cheek. He didn't seem to notice. "Great place you've got here. I'm, er, new in town." He tried on a smile. It was about as convincing as his mustache.

"New in town. Really."

"Oh yes. Definitely. Just got here. The name's Alber—er, I mean, Fred. Al . . . fred." More sweat broke out on his forehead, and he wiped it away again. At this rate he'd be wringing out his sleeve on her cherrywood floor. "We've never met," he added.

"That's too bad," Hannah said, coming up beside Lailu. "We owed Neon, formerly Albert, a free meal."

"That's right," Lailu said. "I forgot about that."

"Did you say free?" their mysterious guest said. He patted at his shabby jacket pocket, then dropped his hand quickly.

"I'd even be willing to throw in appetizers and desserts," Lailu added, "in exchange for a tiny bit of scientific advice."

"But only from Neon," Hannah said.

"Right," Lailu said. "I wouldn't trust anyone else. But the man who invented the camedo—"

"Camera," the stranger corrected automatically.

"Well, he was so brilliant, I'm sure he could help us easily." Lailu waited. It didn't take long.

"Fine, fine," he muttered. He glanced around the room, then leaned forward. "I *might* be the man formerly known as Neon."

"No!" Hannah gasped dramatically, both hands clutching at her chest.

"Oh yes, but I go by Albert again. I'm incognito."

"Incognito?" Hannah asked.

"It means in disguise."

"Does it really?" Hannah's lips curved in a tiny mocking smile. Lailu elbowed her.

Albert, formerly Neon, didn't seem to notice. "This"—he pointed at his face—"isn't a real mustache."

"You mean mustaches don't normally hang off your cheekbones?" Hannah blinked wide, innocent eyes at him as he felt around his face. "And stop elbowing me, Lailu. I'm just having a bit of fun."

"You're being mean."

"Maybe a little. Did you see those flowers? I mean, how pathetic does *he* think I am? Honestly!" Hannah scowled.

"What flowers?" Albert asked.

"Not you," Lailu sighed. "Look, Albert, we know you're in disguise."

Albert pulled the fake mustache off and removed his silly hat. "I'm not very good at it," he admitted.

"You?" Hannah said. "I never would have guessed." She glanced at Lailu. "Sorry. I'll stop."

"I *have* been through a lot, you know," Albert said.

"Like what?" Hannah's gaze sharpened instantly. "How has it been since Starling . . . ?" She stopped.

"Since Starling died?" Lailu finished for her. She made herself say the words, feeling the rush of guilt they always brought. It had been Lailu's fault; she'd flung one of Wren's faulty contraptions at Starling, and when it exploded, the scientist had not survived the blast. Of course, Starling had been about to kill Lailu, Hannah, and Ryon, so Lailu tried not to feel *too* bad about it. Still. It was impossible not to remember how much she'd once looked up to Starling Volan, who had told her she had the eyes of a true chef,

who designed the stove Lailu still cooked on. And it was hard to think of Wren, her former friend, growing up without any parents at all.

"It's been terrible," Albert said quietly. "Some of the other scientists tried to leave and set up their own businesses. At least two of those have gone missing. That I know of."

"Really?" Hannah and Lailu exchanged glances.

Albert fiddled with the edge of his faded brown vest. "I think it was probably the elves. They hate us, you know. And we get no protection from Elister at all, not unless we're willing to be a part of the Nucleus."

"What's that?" Lailu asked.

"It's . . . what's left of Starling's original organization. Wren has taken over.'" Albert's mouth twisted. "They are working on some sort of secret agenda for Lord Elister."

"Wren took over?" Hannah frowned. "Isn't she a little . . . young?"

"So are you," Albert pointed out. "And your friend here, who is a master chef." He inclined his head toward Lailu. "And despite her age, Wren has the most drive, and also the backing of Elister. But she's been a terrible leader."

"Worse than Starling?" Hannah asked.

"Oh, definitely. Starling was ambitious, but she was also trying to save us. Wren is just . . . angry. And she doesn't care about saving anyone." He shivered. "Not even herself."

Lailu and Hannah exchanged looks.

"With so many enemies, it's only a matter of time before us freelance scientists begin getting picked off, one"—he tapped his fingers—"by one."

The door to Mystic Cooking chimed open, and Albert crammed his hat back on, clutching it protectively around his face.

"I'll go seat them." Hannah swept away.

"That just makes you stick out more, you know," Lailu said.

"Does it?" Albert slowly lowered his arms and cast a furtive glance at the new customers. "You won't tell anyone I'm here, will you?"

"Of course not," Lailu said. "But I really could use your help."

"What kind of help?" he asked suspiciously.

"I need you to look at something for me." Lailu glanced over her shoulder. Hannah was seating a family of four on the other side of the restaurant. They looked hungry, and she hadn't finished cooking the lunch special. Still, this was important. "Something Wren invented."

Albert straightened. "Oh yes?"

"I don't trust it."

"I wouldn't either, if I were you." Albert gazed off into the distance. "About this free meal . . ."

"And appetizers. And dessert."

"And all I have to do is take a look?"

"That's it," Lailu said.

He sighed and heaved himself to his feet. "Fine, fine. Lead the way."

Lailu led him into her kitchen and through the trapdoor down to her cellar. Wren's invention loomed over them, a pulsing metallic monster that glowed and hissed malevolently, a beast with wheels and buttons and spouting steam. Lailu could feel its evil intent

beating against her skin and knew this creation had the power to destroy everything she'd worked so hard for.

She peered beneath it, looking for spi-trons, but this time there was nothing. It didn't make her feel any better.

"Hmm." Albert cocked his head to the side and rubbed his chin. He stepped closer, running one finger carefully down the glossy front. "Hmm," he said again.

"Can you help me remove it?" Lailu asked.

"Remove it? This death trap? Holy logic, no. No. Much too risky. In fact, this whole thing could blow at any moment. Trying to move it . . ." He shook his head. "I'm sorry, but this contraption must stay."

Death trap . . . Could blow at any moment . . . Lailu's teeth chattered, the cellar suddenly way too cold. "Is it safe? Leaving it here?"

"Well, it hasn't exploded yet, and that's a good sign, a very good sign." He took a step back, then another. "I think, as long as you don't mess with it and nothing hits it, it should be safe enough. But see that valve there?" He pointed to the largest pipe, the one that let off puffs of steam like gentle summer clouds. "That's the most sensitive part. Tap that pipe even just the barest smidge, and . . . *kaboom.*"

"No." Lailu felt sick.

"Or maybe not. Maybe nothing would happen. I'm sure it's perfectly safe. Yes, definitely. Perfectly safe."

Lailu didn't think he looked sure. Sure people didn't usually sweat that much or have faces quite that shade of green.

"Er, about that food you promised me?" he said.

"I can begin on it now." Lailu started up the stairs.

"Yes. Great. And . . . can you make it to go?"

"Perfectly safe my butt," Lailu muttered. But if he didn't feel comfortable removing it, what could she do?

Nothing, except serve her customers and hope for the best.

9

SECRETS

"Four dinner specials." Lailu set the tray down. "Enjoy!"

"More water!" someone called out.

"Hey, can we get seated over here?" a man said from the front of the restaurant.

"We're ready to order," a woman chimed in from another table.

Lailu pasted on her best professional smile. Where the spatula was Hannah?

"Choose whichever seat you—" Lailu began.

"I'll take care of it. Oh, and I got the other table's order. Two more specials." Lianna swept past Lailu in a flurry of brightly colored skirts. "This table, by the window?" she asked the customers, leading them away.

Lailu turned and saw her mother had already refilled the water glasses. Lailu knew her mother was as reliable as one of Carbon's harnesses, so she was trying not to get used to counting on her being around. Still, she couldn't help but feel that this time might be different. That this time her mom would stay until Lailu didn't need her help anymore. Why else would Lianna have turned down Elister's job requests?

Lailu pushed the curtain back, then froze. Hannah leaned against the kitchen counter, whispering with someone. A woman with long, wavy black hair.

". . . won't know what hit him," the woman was saying.

"Oh, I can't wait to see this." Hannah giggled, then looked up. "Oh! Hey, Lailu."

The woman turned, her purple eyes locking with Lailu's.

"Paulie?" Lailu said, surprised.

"See?" Hannah grinned. "Didn't even need to ask her to stop by."

"I read your mind." Paulie tapped the small glass jar of salve in front of her. At Lailu's expression, she laughed. "Joke. I don't read minds."

"If you say so." Lailu shivered. Paulie made her nervous. Maybe it was the way her face looked, both old and young at the same time, youthful, but mysterious and knowing. Must be the cheekbones, Lailu decided, running a hand absently across her own face. Hannah had sharp cheekbones too.

She looked between the two of them, sitting close together, whispering and giggling, and suddenly she felt very out of place, like a spoon sitting forlornly in a drawer full of knives. She did not have the kind of cheekbones a person would notice.

"You heard about the phoenix?" Paulie asked.

Lailu nodded, and Paulie's expression sharpened, pinning her in place. Maybe it wasn't just the cheekbones, but those eyes, too, like cut gemstones, unnaturally bright.

"It's the first time in more than fifty years that we've seen a phoenix this close," Paulie said eagerly.

Lailu frowned. "It's been attacking the local villages. Burning down houses."

"Oh, I know, and that's unfortunate"—Paulie waved a hand like she was shooing a fly—"but do you know how much magic is in one of their tail feathers alone? If I could just get my hands on one . . ."

"I need to check on my customers." Lailu left the kitchen. She wasn't sure why she was so angry. Maybe it was the "that's unfortunate" or the casual hand gesture, but it was obvious Paulie cared more about getting some kind of magic talisman than she did about people's lives.

Lailu was so distracted that she didn't notice the thing scuttling into the middle of the dining room floor until one of her guests screamed.

Message for Lailu. Message for Lailu.

One of Wren's spi-trons spun in a slow circle, its blue orb glowing. As soon as the light touched Lailu, it brightened to a blinding white.

One . . . two . . . three . . . die!

Lailu grabbed the nearest bowl off a table and slammed it down over the spi-tron, holding it in place.

Boom!

The bowl shattered, shards and food and pieces of metal limbs splattering Lailu and cascading across the floor.

Hannah rushed over to her, holding a very familiar frying pan loosely at her side. "Another one? This has *got* to stop."

"Aww, you brought Mr. Smacky."

"Just in case." Hannah swirled the pan around, then froze, and that was when Lailu noticed it too.

Silence. Thick and choking like week-old salamander stew.

"Butterknives," Lailu whispered. Everyone in the restaurant stared at her, their eyes wide, mouths open, and worst of all, food forgotten in front of them.

"Sorry about that, folks." Hannah smiled brightly, holding her arms out like she was conducting a play. "Lailu is good friends with the late Starling Volan's daughter—"

Lailu almost fell over, but at a sharp look from Hannah, she bit her tongue.

"And Wren has been sending her, uh, gifts," Hannah finished. "Sometimes, as with any new invention, they don't quite work right. And, well, you see the result."

"I thought it said 'die,'" said a woman at the closest table, her eyes as big and round as the plate in front of her.

"Heh. Yes. Well. Er," Lailu tried.

"A joke." Lailu's mother appeared suddenly, stepping in front of Lailu. "Kids, you know?" She laughed. No one else joined her. "Now . . . I think a round of desserts for you all."

"What kind of dessert?" someone asked.

"The kind that is on the house." Lianna winked.

"My favorite kind!" another customer said, the people around him laughing.

"On the house?" Lailu hissed as Hannah pulled her away. She

had already given Albert free food, and then Hannah gave food to that horrible guard, and now this?

"We needed to distract everyone with something," Hannah said reasonably. She pulled the curtain tight behind them. "Maybe we should get a real door," she mused, studying the dark blue fabric.

"Don't you try to distract me, too." Lailu scowled. "And why did you say Wren was my friend? Clearly that is *not* the case." A wave of sadness hit her harder than any spi-tron explosion. "Not anymore," she whispered, remembering the first time she'd met Wren. She'd been catering her very first meal ever, for Elister the Bloody, no less, and Wren had helped her. She'd been a friend at a time when Lailu was feeling very much alone.

Hannah turned her back on the curtain. "Sometimes you need to stretch the truth a little."

"Disagree." Lailu crossed her arms. "That just makes things complicated."

"Things are already complicated. All of those people out there think the scientists are heroes, remember? They think they saved us all from the magic of the elves. We can't go around telling everyone that actually Starling tried to kill us, and now her daughter has taken up where she left off, now can we?"

"We could . . ." Lailu stopped. "But then no one would eat here, would they?"

Hannah shook her head. "It would be worse, even, than being hassled by the guards."

Lailu played with one of her pigtails. If she were completely honest, she'd have no customers. But the people out there deserved to know the truth. Didn't they? But why? What good would it do them?

She thought of Starling's face again, of her own conflicted feelings over the woman's death. She didn't want to think about Starling ever, but the woman was like freshly chopped onions, the smell always just at the edge of her awareness no matter what other scents might mask it.

"Things used to be simpler," Lailu whispered.

Hannah watched her for a long, silent moment and then put an arm around her shoulders and hugged her. "I know," she said gently. "I know."

"Wren isn't *really* trying to kill me, either. She'll get over this. She's just . . . lashing out."

Hannah chewed her lip and didn't say anything at all.

Lailu decided it was time to change the subject. "Where's Paulie?" she asked.

"She slipped out the back when the screams started," Hannah said.

Lailu pulled away.

"Don't judge her too harshly. She's . . . well. The people of Twin Rivers have always treated her like an outsider. So she treats them the same way." Hannah shrugged. "She means well, though. Mostly." She tapped the jar of salve sitting on the counter.

"What were the two of you talking about?"

Hannah smirked. "Revenge."

"On?" Lailu asked.

"Oh, I think you can guess." And Hannah dropped a handful of crumpled petals on the counter, red, and pink, and white, the edges brown with decay.

10

A Hunt for Amateurs

Lailu adjusted her grip on her knife and took a deep breath, trying to concentrate. It was hard to do with the thick aroma of raegnar bourguignon filling her whole kitchen, reminding her that supplies were running low. Good thing she had another mystery hunt with Greg coming up.

"Do you see it?" Hannah whispered. Her long black hair was twisted into a tight bun on the top of her head and pinned in place with a dragonfly hairpin Lailu had never seen before. Hannah noticed Lailu looking and touched it briefly. "I didn't re-home this."

"I didn't think you had," Lailu lied.

"I made it, actually."

"Really?" Lailu looked closer, impressed by Hannah's craftsmanship.

"Paulie brought over some supplies." Hannah looked away.

"Oh?"

"We should keep looking for the spi-tron."

"Maybe she didn't send one today?"

Hannah's mouth tightened, her knuckles whitening around the handle of her frying pan. It had been her idea to search for Wren's spi-tron before they had another incident in front of Lailu's customers. Apparently the guards outside were good at hassling people who wanted to come inside and eat but not so good at stopping actual threats, and Lailu couldn't afford to lose any more customers.

The bell over the front door rang, and Lailu peered around the curtain as Lianna strolled inside, another newspaper tucked under her arm. "Bad news, honey." Lianna casually tossed her paper on a nearby table, and Lailu glimpsed the top article:

Another Scientist Missing?

So-called freelance scientists have started disappearing. Some believe they are merely leaving the city, while other sources, who wish to remain "incognito," insist this is either the work of the elves, or the newly formed Nucleus. Whoever or whatever is causing this, today marks the third such disappearance in the past week, and . . .

(story continued on page 4)

"Another scientist missing?" Lailu said.

"What?" Lianna glanced at the paper. "Oh, that. Yes, that *is* bad. But I meant bad news about your pixie paprika. Bairn over at the Spice Rack said there's been a shortage this year. I was able to order refills on most of your other spices, though." She pulled a list out of one of the many pockets sewn into her colorful skirt and dropped it on a table next to the paper. "Oh, and were you expecting Wren here for any reason?"

"Wren here? What?" Lailu rushed to the door, then hesitated.

Wren *had* been sending those creepy spi-trons, and while Lailu truly believed her old friend didn't *really* want her dead, rushing out to greet her probably wasn't the best idea. Lailu ducked and peered out her window instead.

"What's she doing?" Hannah whispered, crouching down next to her.

Wren leaned against a horseless carriage parked across the street, her hand moving furiously as she scribbled in a large, leather-bound journal. Oversize goggles with more switches and gears than a clock sat perched on her red hair, and a long white coat with many pockets made her seem smaller and younger than usual. She looked like a kid playing dress-up in her murderous-scientist-mom's lab coat.

She finished writing, set the journal down in the carriage, and strode over to Mystic Cooking. Seala lifted a hand in greeting, not even bothering to try to stop her.

"Those guards are so useless," Lailu grumbled.

Wren pulled something else out of her pocket, a small tube that stretched out in a long line with numbers and dashes on it. She placed it against the side of the restaurant, walking until it was fully extended, then studying the number.

"I think she's measuring Mystic Cooking," Hannah said.

Lailu felt sick. "Why?"

"Who knows? But whatever the reason, I'm sure it's not good for us."

Wren glanced at the window, her eyes meeting Lailu's before Lailu could duck again. For one brief, terrifying moment they stared at each other, and Lailu realized this was the first time she'd seen Wren since . . .

Since Wren had tried to save Lailu and her friends and instead had accidentally set in motion the events that had led to her mother's death.

Lailu could see all the emotions playing across Wren's thin face. Sorrow followed by rage and then a bleakness that reminded Lailu of her brother Lonnie's expression every time they'd woken up to find their own mother had left them again.

Wren scowled and shoved her goggles down over her face, then yanked one of those weird boxlike remote-control things out of her pocket. She pointed it at Mystic Cooking, and a beam of blue light shot from the end of it.

Lailu ducked, covering her head—

But nothing happened.

Lailu straightened slowly and peeked out. Wren was back at the carriage, jotting something else down in her journal. She finished and, without another glance, hopped into her automobile and drove off.

"Well. That was strange." Lianna sipped her tea behind them, as calm as if grudge-holding scientists measured her home all the time.

"Strange," Lailu agreed. She felt like she'd swallowed a live vibber, her stomach all twisted and anxious. And beneath that worry, a thick layer of guilt. For that one brief second, Wren had seemed so lonely. It made Lailu wish she *had* gone out to talk to her.

Several days passed. As far as Lailu could tell, the generator didn't do anything other than pulse ominously, but her dreams were still full of explosions and wide green eyes and metal creatures with too many limbs, despite the fact that no more spi-trons had scuttled into her restaurant. Part of her wondered if maybe Wren was done sending them, but that didn't explain why she had been measuring Mystic Cooking, or whatever it was she was doing. None of it made sense, and the less sense it made, the more scared Lailu felt.

Meanwhile, the elves didn't do anything either. "They're planning something," her mother kept insisting. "The longer they put it off, the bigger it's going to be when it happens."

After that, Lailu's dreams included Eirad's cruel smile and masks that turned into people before transforming into raegnars, mouths open to swallow the world.

"You're not sleeping well," her mother remarked one freezing-cold afternoon a week after the raegnar hunt.

"Me? I'm sleeping just fine."

"The shadows under your eyes tell a very different story."

"You have shadows too," Lailu protested. It was true; instead of sleeping, her mother had thrown herself into organizing the restaurant and restocking all of the supplies, as if she could prepare them for any kind of attack. Some nights when Lailu lay awake in her bed, she could hear her mother still up, banging around in the pantry.

Lianna waved this aside. "Help me take this tray out to Seala."

"Another tray?" Lailu groaned. "Mom, she's horrible."

"I can hear you, you know," Seala called.

Lailu's eyes widened, and she pulled back the curtain so she could see into the dining room.

Seala was sitting at a table near the front of the restaurant, drinking a pot of tea and eating a tray of appetizers. All on the house, of course.

Lailu scowled. "You're not even guarding anymore!"

"Let's be honest. This is just a job of appearances. Lord Elister wants to pretend he's doing something without actually doing anything at all." Seala took a long, loud sip of tea. "Besides, it's ridiculously cold outside."

Still scowling, Lailu drew the curtain closed again. "I'm not taking any soup out to her," she told her mom.

"Be nice, honey. You know she's the oldest of seven kids. Can you imagine?"

"I don't care." Lailu crossed her arms.

"She joined the guard to provide for all her siblings."

"Still don't care."

"Her dad was injured in the Industrial District, so he's had a hard time finding work. Lost his leg and one of his hands."

Lailu tried to stay angry, but in the end she sighed and took the tray.

Her mom flashed her a smile. "That's my girl."

"Here's your soup," Lailu said stiffly, putting the tray down in front of Seala. "And . . . sorry about your dad."

"What?" Seala blinked. "Why?"

"His injuries."

"What injuries?"

"You know, from his job in the Industrial District," Lailu said.

"He doesn't work there." Seala took a slurp of soup. Everything she ate or drank, she did so at top volume. It was extremely irritating. "He sells spices in the market. You've actually met him before."

"I . . . have?"

"His stall is called the Spice Rack."

"Oh!" Lailu *had* met the owner of the Spice Rack, many times. He gave her the best deal on spices and other seasonings.

Seala took another loud slurp of soup. "You gave him dragon cuisine a few months back, and he hasn't shut up about it since." Slurp. Slurp. "You should have heard him when I mentioned I'd be guarding your restaurant." Another slurp.

Lailu couldn't take it anymore. Each slurp was worse than a hundred forks scraping on a plate. "Well, tell him I said hello." She backed away, ducking past her curtain. She turned to yell at her mother for lying about Seala's family, but Lianna wasn't around. Hannah sat slumped in the chair instead.

"Is Ryon out there?" she asked hopefully.

"What? No. Just Seala." Lailu peered at her friend. "Why? Are you expecting him?"

"Not really. Just . . ." Hannah shrugged. Ryon hadn't come by since the night of the hunt. Lailu had told Hannah how he'd stuck up for her and Greg when Eirad and the other elves had surrounded them, and Hannah had guessed he'd be skulking about their restaurant soon. "Two days tops," she'd bet, but that had been a week ago, and nothing.

"Do you think he's okay?" Lailu asked.

"I'm sure he's fine. He's *always* fine." But Hannah looked worried, her fingers braiding and unbraiding her long hair. And as Lailu watched her friend's anxious fingers, she wondered, suddenly, how Hannah really felt about Ryon. She'd been sort-of-almost-dating Vahn until recently. Maybe Ryon was just a friend.

Maybe she had a crush on him.

Lailu bit her lip and decided not to ask. After all, she wasn't completely sure how she felt about Ryon either. He was confusing. Probably all the winking.

Hannah sighed. "I think I'm going to head to bed. You're meeting Greg tomorrow, right?"

Lailu nodded, thoughts of Ryon vanishing in a wash of excitement. Greg had been sending little notes hinting at a truly epic hunt. Something within the grounds of the city. She had no idea what that could be, but she couldn't wait to find out.

Together they'd hunted dragon and hydra and even that most dangerous of all beasts, fyrian chicken. If this hunt was the "hunt of her life," then it had to be something amazing.

"I still can't believe you brought me out here to hunt *this*." Lailu held up a slimy creature, its lifeless, bulbous eyes reflecting both Lailu and Greg on the river shore like a distorted mirror.

"Hey, you needed somewhere to hunt, and Elister needs this colony of skilly-wigs thinned out before we have more boat crashes."

"More?" Lailu stuffed the dead skilly-wig into a bucket, pushing all twenty-four tentacles around it.

"Yeah, there was a small accident during the Week of Masks."

"How come I didn't see anything about it in the paper?"

Greg shrugged. "It happened the same day those automatons went berserk."

Starling Volan had created creepy metal men, and during the big parade where they were being showcased to the public, they went completely out of control and attacked all the bystanders, even the king! Luckily, no one was killed. But still, the food that had been wasted was a real tragedy, a hydra finger food tragedy.

"There were no real injuries," Greg continued. "Just a sunken party boat and a little dock damage." He gestured to the nearest dock pillar a few yards away. A large chunk had been gouged away, almost like a confused medusa fish got hungry.

Their buckets sat next to the docks, overflowing with skilly-wigs and a few other tasty sea morsels, enough for a seafood feast. Lailu was pretty sure she'd never get the smell out of her hands. Or the feel of their slime, the way it coated her skin and oozed under her fingernails. She shuddered. Unfortunately, they still had at least one more load to go.

"I am never going to forgive you for this," she said.

"So you keep telling me." Greg grinned. "I'm used to it."

She sighed. "Let's get this over with before anyone sees us."

"What's the matter?" He picked up an empty bucket. "Scared?"

"Skilly-wigs are for amateurs," Lailu muttered.

They loaded up their rowboat, then pushed it out into the river and hopped in. The water felt like ice against Lailu's bare feet, like the mountain streams near her old village.

"This looks far enough," she said once they were in the middle of the river. They stopped paddling, sliding the oars up and safely back inside the boat. "Bait?" she asked. "Or did you use it all up?"

Greg chuckled. "No way. I've finally learned my lesson. I brought plenty." He picked up a bucket and emptied a large, squirmy ball into the river with a splash, then glanced sideways at Lailu. "No need to look at me like that."

"Like what?" she asked innocently.

"Like you're disappointed you couldn't use *me* as bait."

"Well, you did trick me into hunting skilly-wigs."

Greg threw back his head and laughed. "I did! I totally did."

"Don't be so proud. We're out here, in the middle of the river." She paused. "Sure would be a shame if you were to slip and fall in . . ."

"Lucky for me, I brought an extra change of clothing."

"Really?"

"Oh yeah. I knew I'd better be prepared. Especially once you realized I'd tricked you into hunting skilly-wigs."

Lailu laughed. She felt strangely content, sitting here in this rocking boat, wedged in across from Greg. Despite the fishy stench of too many skilly-wigs packed into too small an area. Despite the growing tensions between the elves and everyone else in Twin Rivers. Despite Slipshod leaving her and Hannah becoming a spy and everything changing, Greg was still here, still as irritatingly constant as ever.

Lailu leaned back against the wooden seat.

"Okay, now I'm really freaked out," Greg said.

"What?"

"You've been smiling for, like, more than a minute. That can't bode well for me."

"Maybe I'm just happy. Is that so hard to believe?" Lailu huffed.

"I like seeing you happy."

Lailu froze. Greg was wearing a strange expression, almost like a smile, but softer. It made her insides squirm like one of their skilly-wig buckets. "Um, thanks," she managed, looking away.

"Lailu." Greg's voice had gone suddenly husky, but she wouldn't, *couldn't* look at him. "We never, you know, talked. About the other day."

"Th-the other day?" she squeaked. Her hands were all clammy, and her stomach churned like the water beneath their boat. She really, really didn't want to hear whatever it was Greg was about to say. At the same time, she desperately wanted to hear it.

She had never felt so conflicted before in her life. It was exhausting.

"You know, during the fairy lights, when I—"

"Churning," Lailu realized suddenly.

"Held your—what?"

"The water." Waves sloshed around the edges of their boat and began trickling inside. Skilly-wigs wouldn't be able to do this. Lailu stood abruptly, accidentally smacking Greg in the face with her shoulder and sending him tumbling backward. "Oh! Sorr—gah!"

Something large and metallic flew at her. She ducked and

scooped up an oar. The thing spun in midair, buzzing angrily. Lailu had the impression of a giant horsefly as big as her head, with a long, jointed tail and four sets of vibrating wings, before it flew at her again, faster than before. Two long black pincers shot out of its body and tried to clamp onto her throat. She managed to throw up the oar just in time to block, but already it was spinning and coming after her again, the buzzing louder, more aggressive.

Thwack!

Greg swatted it with his oar. It flipped end over end, then tumbled into the river. "What . . . the spatula . . . was *that*?" he asked, wide-eyed.

"I have no idea." Lailu gripped her oar tighter and peered over the side of the boat. "And stop using my expressions," she added. "It's creepy."

"Not as creepy as whatever that thing was," Greg muttered, joining her at the side.

There was no sign of the thing. Slowly the water calmed around them, and the first few skilly-wigs oozed their way closer, attracted by the bait.

"Maybe it's dead?" Greg suggested.

"It was never alive." Lailu leaned farther out. She'd feel a lot better if she saw the thing's mangled body.

"Wren invention?"

"Must be." She thought of those pincers, how they'd been coming straight for her throat. Maybe . . . maybe Wren really, truly wanted to kill her after all. It wasn't just her lashing out. It wasn't a game. It was deadly serious.

Lailu couldn't decide if she was terrified, or just really, really sad. She hugged herself. "I guess—"

"Look out!"

Lailu never had a chance to turn around; she heard Greg's warning at the exact same time something hit her hard from behind, knocking her out of the boat and into the freezing river water.

11

DEATH BY SKILLY-WIG

Centacles. Tentacles everywhere.

The skilly-wigs had come in force for Greg's bait, and they were in a full-on feeding frenzy. They swarmed all around Lailu, their inky orb eyes focusing on her like a tasty steak.

Skilly-wigs were not especially dangerous, but this many crowded together made it impossible to know which way was up or down. Tentacles buffeted Lailu from all sides, tangling in her pigtails and wrapping around her hands and feet, but that wasn't the worst thing. They also managed to ooze across her eyes, up her nose, and in her mouth.

She gagged and thrashed while the edges of her vision burst with light and her lungs screamed for air.

O God of Cookery, don't let me die like this! she prayed. Greg would never let her live it down.

She could picture him at her funeral saying, "Poor Crabby

Cakes, death by skilly-wig. Such an amateur." She paddled harder, kicking at skilly-wig heads and flinging off tentacles, the image of his mocking face spurring her on until finally she burst through a web of tentacles, her head breaking the surface of the water.

She sucked in a great lungful of air. "Greg—"

Tentacles snagged her ankles and tugged her back under. She swallowed a mouthful of water before a hand grabbed her from above and hauled her back into the bottom of the boat.

Lailu coughed up disgusting river water until she could breathe again. Sweet, wonderful air. It tasted better than the finest cuisine, better even than her full-course dragon feast. And that was really saying something.

Greg cut away the clinging skilly-wigs from her hair and clothes, then handed her a towel.

"Thanks," she managed. She could still feel the echo of those tentacles, the slime trails over her face, and she furiously scrubbed herself down with the towel.

"Hey, maybe leave some skin behind, yeah?" Greg gently took the towel out of her hands and passed her a thick wool coat.

Lailu shrugged out of her own soaked coat and fumbled with the new one, her limbs shaking uncontrollably in the cold and her hands clumsy under their wet bandages.

"Besides," Greg said, "we both know your skin is thin enough as it is."

Lailu scowled and shoved him. "Watch it, Greg. I am not in the mood for your jokes."

"Exactly my point." He grinned. "Mr. Waspy is gone, by the way."

"Mr. Waspy?" Lailu's scowl deepened. "Do *not* call it that, first of all. Only helpful things get names like that. And second, it was more of a crab than a wasp. Did you see those pincers?"

"You didn't notice the stinger on its tail?"

"It had a stinger, too?" Lailu clutched Greg's coat closer. "A scorpio-tron," she decided.

"That's actually pretty good."

"I'm good at naming things."

"Hmm . . . debatable."

Lailu narrowed her eyes, but she decided not to get into it. No one seemed to appreciate her names. "Where is it?"

Greg shrugged. "After it knocked you into the river, it just took off. Probably cuddling up to Wren right now."

Lailu tried not to picture it curled up in Wren's lap, but she could just imagine Wren stroking its metallic head like some kind of twisted pet.

Thump!

The boat rocked. "Skilly-wig," Lailu said.

"You got a good look in the water. How many skilly-wigs are left?"

"A lot."

Thump! Thump! Thump!

"A super lot," Lailu revised. She sighed. "I guess we'd better get back to it." Icy wind cut across the surface of the river, and Lailu shivered. Yes, Greg's coat was quite warm—warmer than her coat even before it got wet, but the rest of her outfit still held half the river. Still, a chef did what she had to do. Even if she really, really didn't want to see another skilly-wig ever again.

"I think," Greg said slowly, "that maybe we have enough skilly-wigs for the moment."

Relief washed over Lailu as quickly as the river water had. Still. "Are you just suggesting that because of me?"

"Pretty much."

"Because I could handle another round."

"I'm sure you could," Greg said. But he didn't sound sure.

Lailu narrowed her eyes. "I c-could," she said as firmly as possible around her chattering teeth.

"What was that?" Greg cupped a hand around his ear and leaned forward. "I couldn't understand you over the shivering."

Lailu scowled. "We're f-finishing this hunt."

Greg laughed. "I'll let you play 'toughest chef' later, okay?"

"It's not a game." Lailu checked the nets. "But if it were," she added, "I'd be winning." And she tossed the first net over, and waited.

"Winning?" Greg tossed his own net over the other side. "We'll see about that."

An hour later, and they'd both caught as many skilly-wigs as they could stomach, so this time when Greg called an end, Lailu agreed. Her hands were so tired they'd gone past aching and were simply numb now.

"If you want to count them, go ahead," Greg said, looking at their overflowing buckets. "Otherwise, I'm gonna call this a tie."

Lailu shrugged. "I'm calling it a victory for me, but whatever." She looked out across the river. Skilly-wigs still oozed all over the place, their tentacles occasionally breaking the surface of the water and glistening like oil in the sunlight. "Elister will still probably have to send a hero out here to deal with the rest of them." She hated the idea of so much death, and so much good meat going to waste. Mystical beasts deserved better than that. Even skilly-wigs.

"Maybe that's why Vahn is lurking over there on the riverbank."

"Ha ha."

"No, seriously."

Lailu turned. "Vahn?"

He stood heroically posed next to the water, chest out, chin up, the wind tossing his long blond hair back like a cape.

It reminded Lailu of when she'd first met him. The snow had been blowing in so fast and so thick it was like a curtain, howling through the trees and piling up in large drifts. Their whole village had been alerted that a shiver of striped vibbers was on the move, at least ten of them, hunting through the blizzard. With their two-headed snake bodies and their slit tongues, striped vibbers seemed almost reptilian, but unlike other snakes, vibbers loved the cold.

"Lonnie!" Lailu had been calling her brother's name so much her throat felt as raw as grated cheese, but the storm just grabbed her voice and threw it back in her face. "Lonnie, where are you?" He'd been missing for hours, and Lailu knew with a certainty as cold and fierce as the storm around her that something must have happened to him. "Lonnie!" she shrieked.

She thought she could hear the scrape of scales slithering beneath the snow, and she spun, one hand over her eyes to block the stinging snow as she searched all that white.

A shadow emerged from the nearby woods, too big to be her

brother. Lailu stumbled back, her boots crunching through the snow's crust, sinking her up to her knees.

The figure moved closer, and beneath warm coats and a fur-lined hood she glimpsed a boy with hair as blond as the magic folk from the northern country of Mystalon and eyes bluer than the frozen falls. He was the most beautiful thing Lailu had ever seen, like winter personified. So beautiful that for a second she didn't notice Lonnie slung across his shoulders, his black locks covering his eyes.

"Lonnie!" Lailu had struggled out of the snowdrift.

"Don't worry. He's going to be fine," the boy said, so confidently that Lailu had believed him immediately.

"A-are you a spirit?"

He threw back his head and laughed. "No, silly village girl. I'm Vahn. I'm a hero. Well, practically."

"Practically a hero?" Lailu hadn't known what that meant.

"I'm apprenticed to Rhivanna," he'd explained, "and I will make sure both you and your brother get back to your homes safely." He'd smiled then, the most gallant smile, and Lailu felt thawed down to her ice-tipped toes. Rhivanna was Savoria's greatest hero; even way out in Clear Lakes they'd heard tales of her amazing feats. If Vahn was *her* apprentice, he must be able to do anything. Lailu had followed him back to the village, through the snow and the wind, and she hadn't been the least afraid. And after that, for the longest time she'd thought Vahn was the boy of her dreams.

But then slowly she'd started to realize that her mother had been right all those years ago when she'd told Lailu that one good deed did *not* make a good person. And Vahn, with his too-pretty face and perfect smile, had been a jerk to her most of her life. Which wasn't great, but Lailu knew she would have gotten over it. Except then he went and hurt her best friend too. So now Lailu wanted nothing more to do with him.

She blinked, letting those memories fade, but the cold of that long-ago day seemed to have soaked in like the wet clothes on her back. And seeing Vahn standing there on the rocks next to the river, so heroic, still made her remember how she'd once felt about him. Even if those feelings were totally gone now.

Vahn finally noticed her looking. He grinned, the sun flashing off all those gleaming white teeth. Then the stone beneath him broke, dumping him into the river.

"Vahn!" Lailu stood, ready to plunge in to help, then hesitated. That water really *was* cold. Luckily Vahn's head popped back up a second later and he hauled himself out of the water. His hair now stuck to his face and seaweed dangled from his clothes as he staggered up the bank and left without a backward glance.

"That was weird," Greg said.

Wham!

The boat rocked so hard that one of their buckets fell into the water.

"Umm, Greg, maybe you should paddle a little harder."

The skilly-wigs weren't trying to climb aboard yet, but if too many more of them came they might tip the boat.

"You know," Greg grunted, "this would be a lot faster with a little help. Why'd you have to let go of your oar?"

"You mean when I almost died back there?"

"Almost died? Against skilly-wigs?" Greg shook his head. "Speaking of *toughest chefs* . . ."

"Watch it," Lailu said.

"Or you'll what? Drip on me? You need my muscle to get us across this river."

Lailu snatched the oar from Greg and began rowing the boat herself. It really was hard work; her arms and shoulders burned by the time they bumped to shore, but she did it. She turned to Greg triumphantly, then noticed he was leaning back, his legs stretched out, hands behind his head. "You did that on purpose!" she accused.

"What? Teased you so you'd take over rowing?" Greg grinned. "How could I possibly have known you'd react like that?"

Lailu scowled.

"Hey, it's not my fault you're predictable." He reached forward and tugged on one of her pigtails. Lailu smacked his hand away.

Predictable. She thought of Hannah's mysterious, knowing smiles, Paulie's sharp cheekbones. Neither of them would be considered predictable. Lailu felt a sudden intense longing to be one of them. Which was just ridiculous. Being predictable was the same as being reliable, and that was a good thing. But boys didn't really like predictable, did they? Even her father, who viewed consistent hard work as the highest quality, had chosen to marry someone like her mother.

"You all right there?" Greg asked. "You look like you swallowed a raw skilly-wig."

Lailu shuddered. "That's a terrible mental image. Thanks a lot."

"Anytime. Anytime. Speaking of skilly-wigs, let's unload them and be done with this hunt."

"Hey, this whole thing was your idea."

"I know, and I accept full responsibility," Greg said solemnly. "Let's agree to never hunt them again."

"Agreed."

They shook hands, then unloaded everything in silence. Lailu could hardly wait to get home and take a shower. It wasn't that long ago that she'd been covered in hydra blood. The feeling of slowly hardening skilly-wig slime was a hundred times worse. Still, she couldn't help but notice how Greg kept looking around, like he was expecting someone. It made her even more anxious, and finally she couldn't take it anymore.

"Is something wrong?" she demanded.

"Wrong? What could possibly be wrong? We just had a successful and epic hunt." He grinned, securing the last of the skilly-wig buckets in his cart. "I'll take care of initial prep work on these, by the way."

"Oh, thank Chushi," Lailu breathed. If she never had to touch another slimy skilly-wig, it would still be too soon. Then she frowned, eyeing Greg suspiciously. Was he trying to be nice? Unlikely. He must be up to something.

"I'm not plotting anything. I promise." He held up both hands. "I'm just doing my part, accepting responsibility."

"It's about time, I suppose."

Greg coughed. "Yes. Well. Speaking of time . . . I promised someone you'd meet them after our hunt, and we're running late."

"Who?" Lailu asked.

"Me," Master Slipshod said, stepping out from beneath the bridge. "I have news for you, and I'm afraid it's not good."

"Not yet," she admitted.

"No?" Slipshod turned on Greg. "You don't call her by her title?"

Greg took a step back. "Hey, hey, she doesn't call me Master LaSilvian either."

"And I'm not going to," Lailu sniffed.

"Well, it's nice to know some things don't change," Slipshod said, tapping a newspaper into his hand.

"I'd better get these back before they start smelling." Greg indicated the buckets, then added, "Or smelling worse."

"Is that even possible?" Lailu said.

Greg grinned. "Cook with me tonight?" he asked her.

"Make that tomorrow." Slipshod unfolded the newspaper. In big bold letters, a headline read:

Elves Warn The People Of Twin Rivers: Stay On Your Own Side Today!

Lailu and Greg exchanged glances, then both leaned in to read the article.

Fahr, the leader of our city's disgraced elves, has sent a warning to this paper. While we have been urged *not* to report on it by some of our city's leaders, this reporter, who wishes to remain anonymous, felt it was too important not to print. Here is the message in full:

Good people of Twin Rivers. On this, the Eighth Day of the Harvest Week, we, the elves, are declaring our rights to ownership of *our* city. Those of you who live in

12

Bad News

"**M**aster Slipshod!" Lailu beamed. Her heart lifted the way it did at the sight of an especially well-prepared feast. Master Slipshod had taken Lailu on as his apprentice when no other master chef would. Seeing him now reminded her of that day, even if her old mentor looked a bit different than he used to. She still couldn't get over the neatly trimmed hair, so recently cut short, and today he wore a clean, pressed suit, complete with expertly tied cravat, like some kind of aristocrat. Even Hannah wouldn't have been able to find fault with his appearance.

"Master Loganberry." He inclined his head.

Lailu froze. She was used to him calling her Pigtails. Having her mentor call her by her title made her feel like she was wearing someone else's apron.

He grinned. "Not used to it yet, are you?"

the shadow of the Velvet Forest, do not venture far from your homes. Turn away from your jobs in the market, away from your masters on Gilded Island. If you do not, you will have made your choice. Choose wisely; you do not want to be on the wrong side.

Signed,

Fahr

"But what does that mean?" Lailu asked.

"I have no idea," Slipshod admitted. "Except that I think you should stay close to Mystic Cooking tonight. Just in case."

"Your masters on Gilded Island?" Greg frowned. "It's like he's deliberately trying to create hostilities."

"You mean highlight hostilities," Slipshod said. "They're already present."

Greg's frown deepened, and he glanced at Lailu, then away. "I bet Elister is furious."

"This is the angriest I've ever seen him." Slipshod flipped through the paper and showed them an article on the next page.

The Wrong Response?

Lord Elister, Protector of Twin Rivers, has declared that any worker who remains home on this, the Eighth Day of the Harvest Week, regardless of reason, is to be no longer employed here in Twin Rivers. Fear of elven retribution has already created tensions throughout the city, and this latest response has only made them worse. "We have a right to stay home with our families in times of danger," said Nadine Rooney, local seamstress. "We shouldn't lose our jobs because we took a warning seriously."

"The elves don't lie, unlike certain rulers of our city," said another local worker. When asked if we could quote him, he turned white and ran away.

Others had questions regarding the specifics of this newest decree. "Does this apply to those who *live* on Gilded Island but *work* in the shadow of the forest?" asked Jonah Gumple, who currently guards a lesser-known restaurant location on the outskirts of town. In Gumple's own words, "The food is good, but it's no LaSilvian's."

The article continued, but Lailu had seen enough. "Lesser-known?" she demanded, furious. *"No LaSilvian's?"*

"Is that really the most important takeaway?" Greg asked.

"Yes!" Lailu fumed. She worked so hard, *so hard*, and Greg still got all the credit in the papers.

"Maybe this would be a good time to get your . . . skilly-wigs . . . home," Master Slipshod suggested, his lips curling around the word of that most embarrassing of mystic beasts.

Greg sighed. "Cook tomorrow, then?"

Lailu shrugged.

Greg hesitated, then shook his head and left.

Lailu realized Master Slipshod was studying her. "What?" she demanded. "It's not fair, how they always print good things about Greg's restaurant and—"

"Yes, yes." Slipshod waved a hand, cutting her off. "But the more important point is, Elister didn't want either of those articles printed, and they were printed anyhow. Which means . . . what, Pigtails?"

"You mean Master Pigtails?" Lailu sniffed.

"Don't you get snippy with me. I'm here against Lord Elister's express orders, you know."

Lailu's irritation oozed off her faster than skilly-wig slime. "Against orders?" She glanced around. They were in the shadow of the bridge, so anyone walking down the road wouldn't see them unless they were looking closely. Still, they weren't exactly hidden. She thought of all the extra guards she'd seen patrolling the streets on her way out to meet Greg and was suddenly nervous for her old mentor.

"It's why I'm dressed like this." Slipshod indicated his fancy suit. "And not in my chef's hat. Blending in."

"Then I guess we should hurry. What *was* the point of that horribly biased article?"

"Aside from the content? The fact that the elves are now beginning to escalate tensions? That Elister is trying to control the response and failing to read the people?"

"Yes, yes, aside from all that," Lailu said. "Lesser-known," she added disgustedly, half under her breath.

Slipshod grinned. "Ah, Pigtails. I missed you. Now, the *other* point is that when Starling was alive—don't flinch, now. When she was alive, she kept all the scientists firmly under her control, and since *she* was under Elister's control, he maintained his grip on all the new technology in the city. But without her, he's lost that. Wren is trying to fill her mother's shoes, but I think . . . I think the strain of so much responsibility on top of her age and lack of experience is beginning to take its toll. She's desperately trying to tighten her fist around everyone and everything, but it's all sliding out between the cracks in her fingers."

"That was . . . very eloquent," Lailu said, impressed.

"Well, I *am* cooking for the king now." Slipshod puffed out his chest. "Speaking of . . . I need your help." He glanced around. No one was near them, but he dropped his voice anyhow. Lailu had to lean in to hear him over the sound of the river. "I am sworn to secrecy in the king's affairs, and naturally, as his head chef, I take that very seriously. But . . ."

"But?" Lailu prompted.

Slipshod sighed, his fingers tightening around the newspaper. "Fahr has been in to see him. In secret."

"He's *what*?"

"Shh, Pigtails."

"He's what?" Lailu repeated, this time in a whisper.

"It's a well-known secret that the king is sick with the same thing that killed his father."

"The Mystalon Curse," Lailu said. The late King Salivar had been betrothed to the heir of Mystalon—a country to the south with a higher concentration of magic and magic users even than Lailu's own country of Savoria—but he had decided to break off the engagement and marry her sister instead. Rumors swirled that when the heir became ruler, she crafted her magical revenge in the form of a curse that caused extreme weakness and eventual death. A curse that would carry down through the generations until a cure was found.

Officially Matriarch Aurelia denied the existence of any such curse, and Mystalon and Savoria remained allies. And here in Savoria, Lord Elister stopped any rumors of a curse as efficiently—and often permanently—as he could. But still. People talked. Especially since the young king was now fifteen and still not taking on much of the ruling of the country, leaving it mostly in the hands of Elister and his mother.

"Supposedly, Elister had Starling working on a cure," Slipshod continued.

"Supposedly?" Lailu asked.

"The king is no longer so sure where Elister's loyalties truly lie."

"He can't think Elister wants him to die though. Can he?"

Slipshod shrugged. "Hard to know. Regardless, Starling is dead—stop flinching, we all know it wasn't your fault—and the king doesn't believe the remaining scientists will be able to find a solution, so he's been entertaining other . . . possibilities."

"Like Fahr and the elves," Lailu said.

"Exactly so."

"And Elister doesn't know?"

Slipshod shuddered. "I certainly hope not." He looked out across the river. "But I can't be sure of what he does and does not know. And I can't be sure of how he will or will not respond when he *does* find out."

"But I still don't understand. Why doesn't the king trust Elister anymore?"

"The king believes that if he remains cursed, it would be the excuse Elister needs to hold on to power indefinitely."

"No," Lailu said. "Elister wouldn't . . ." She remembered how he'd come into her restaurant, smashing it up like he was a low-level loan shark. Maybe she wasn't the best judge of what he was capable of.

"The king has brought up his concerns to his mother, but the queen is very loyal to Elister and refuses to believe him. Without her support, King Savon can't do anything to stop Elister, and all I can do is sit back and hope for the best. But you, Lailu, you have more flexibility."

"Me?" Lailu took a step back. "I'm a terrible spy, if that's what you're getting at."

"Don't think of it as spying. Think of it as simply . . . keeping an eye on things."

"And you'd want me to tell you what I see, right?" Lailu asked.

"Yes, that would be helpful."

"And you'll . . . what? Tell the king?"

"If it's important."

"So, in other words, you want me to spy," Lailu said flatly.

Slipshod ran a hand down his fresh-shaven chin. "Just . . . if Elister visits, or if you get wind of anything . . . suspicious . . . would you do your old mentor a favor and let me know?"

Lailu hesitated. She'd spied on Elister once before, and he'd caught her. And this sounded awfully similar to spying, no matter what Slipshod told her.

"Would it help if I told you the very fate of Savoria itself might be at stake?"

Lailu winced. "Not helpful, no." A cold breeze cut through her coat, reminding her that her clothing was only half-dry. Shivering, she studied her mentor. Master Slipshod had taken a chance on her when no one else would, and he'd helped her start Mystic Cooking. "Fine," she muttered. "I'm not spying, but I'll keep an eye out, if he shows up."

"Good, good. And I'll drop by when I can to visit and catch up. When things settle down a little."

"*If* they settle down," Lailu whispered, thinking of those articles Slipshod had shown her. With the elves escalating their war, Wren sending scarier inventions to kill her, and Elister trying to yank power away from the king, things might never settle down again.

At least Lailu had her restaurant, even if the world outside it was as chaotic as a river full of hungry skilly-wigs.

13

ALBERT'S DEMANDS

*L*ailu raced down the road toward Mystic Cooking. The front door was ajar, and there were no guards out front. She slowed down, frowning. Maybe Elister had called them back for the day?

When she nudged the door open, the dining room was empty. "Hello? Mom?" she called.

The voices of Hannah and Lianna floated from the kitchen before Lianna poked her head out from behind the curtain.

"Hey, honey. How was your *mystery* hunt with Greg?" Then she caught a whiff of Lailu and crinkled her nose. "What *is* that smell?"

Lailu looked down at her slime-slicked trousers and Greg's ruined wool coat. Sure the river water had dried . . . mostly . . . but it had done nothing to rid her clothing of the stench of skilly-wigs.

"It's, uh . . . skilly-wig." She stared down at her boots, her ear tips heating up like oil on a frying pan.

"Skilly-wigs?" Hannah called out from the kitchen. "Seriously?"

"I don't want to talk about it," Lailu said, and she could hear Hannah's answering laughter.

"Good," Lianna said. "I don't think you should talk about it, or anything else, until you wash up and change. Phew!"

"But I have to tell you—"

Lianna shooed her away, and Lailu trudged off to get clean.

What felt like hours later, Lailu found herself in the kitchen, where Hannah and Lianna were busy washing and cutting vegetables. Tired and wet for the second time that day, Lailu flopped on the kitchen chair and dried her dripping pigtails off on a small white towel.

"That is so much better," Lianna said, sniffing at the air. "And don't even *think* about putting your coat back on until it's been properly washed. You'll just have to use my black wool coat instead."

"Actually, that coat is Greg's," Lailu admitted.

Hannah giggled. "Good thing he likes you."

Lailu opened her mouth, then closed it again, her face way too hot.

"What was it you wanted to tell me?" her mom asked, amusement stamped all over her face.

Lailu took a deep breath, opened her mouth, and everything Slipshod had told her came spilling out like soup from a cracked bowl. When Lailu mentioned Fahr visiting the king, Lianna stopped cutting up vegetables mid-carrot and began pacing. Unfortunately, the kitchen really wasn't big enough for a good pace. And when Lailu finished, Lianna finally stopped moving back and forth and instead stood completely still.

"Mrs. Loganberry?" Hannah had stopped chopping too, her dark eyes fixed on Lianna.

"There's no other way," Lianna said. "I'll need to go talk to Elister." She put her hands on Lailu's shoulders, her hazel eyes bright. "Lailu, honey, I know I promised not to vanish on you anymore. But I need to take care of this. I imagine it'll be an overnight trip. Possibly several nights, but definitely no more than a week. Okay?"

Lailu nodded reluctantly. "But you'll be back?"

"I promise."

"Are you sure you should tell Elister?" Hannah asked. "I think that's the exact opposite of what Slipshod wanted. Not that I trust his judgment all that much," she added. Hannah and Slipshod had never gotten on that well together, although by the end of their time sharing Mystic Cooking with Lailu, they'd come to some sort of friendly-ish truce.

"I'll . . . be careful about what, precisely, I tell Elister," Lianna said. "But he does need to know about Fahr. It's for the good of Savoria."

The good of Savoria. It seemed like people were throwing that around a lot lately. It made Lailu wonder just how fragile her country really was.

Her mom was packed and out the door again in a matter of minutes, pausing only to collect Greg's coat. "I'll get this cleaned and back to your friend," she promised. And then she was gone.

"She really is good at leaving," Hannah said, impressed. Then she realized. "Oh, sorry, Lailu! That was really insensitive."

"No, it's okay. I know what you mean." Lailu sighed. "It sounds like the king needs someone to spy *on* Elister, not *for* Elister, though, if you ask me."

"Isn't that your job?"

Lailu scowled. "I'm *not* spying. I'm merely . . . keeping an eye out."

"Hmm."

"Anyhow, I was thinking maybe Ryon could help with—"

"Doubt it," Hannah said tersely, cutting her off. "You know how he is when it comes to Fahr. We can't trust him."

Lailu frowned. "Are you mad that he hasn't shown up here?"

Hannah picked up her knife and resumed chopping. "I don't even care what he does." *Chop. Chop. Chop.* "It doesn't matter if he can't be bothered to stop by." *Chop. Chop.*

"I'm sure he's just busy, Hannah. You know, keeping a low profile."

"I went into the market today to pick up these vegetables, and I saw him there. Not keeping such a low profile after all." Hannah's eyebrows drew together in a furious line. "Nope, he was joking and laughing and doing his whole winking routine. And did he say one word to me?"

"Um . . . no?"

"No is right!" *CHOP!*

"Maybe you should set the knife down," Lailu suggested nervously.

"It's not like I've been worried about him all week or anything—"

"Hello?" someone called timidly from the dining room. "Anyone here?"

Frowning, Lailu pulled back the curtain. Albert stood hunched on the other side. He still wore the silly wide-brimmed hat from last week, but at least he'd lost the mustache. Unfortunately, he'd replaced it with a bushy black beard.

"It's me," he said, pulling on the beard to show them his face.

"Ah, Alfred!" Hannah said.

"It's Al*bert*," he snapped.

"Are you sure? I thought Albert had a mustache. . . ."

Lailu shot her a look.

"Sorry," Hannah said. "I guess I'm still irritated, and he's such an easy target."

"What are you doing here, Albert?" Lailu asked. "I thought you decided this place was a death trap."

"I never said that. At least, not in those specific words."

"Whatever." Lailu crossed her arms. She hated the way the generator loomed below them like some kind of vicious beast, and she couldn't do anything about it. "Unless you've changed your mind?" she added hopefully. "You think you *can* remove Wren's generator?"

Albert fidgeted. "I don't know if I can remove it, but I'd like to look at it again. See if I can make it more stable."

"More . . . stable?" Hannah said. "Just how *unstable* is it?"

"He did say 'death trap,'" Lailu reminded her.

"I did not!"

"Then we don't need to worry about it?" Hannah asked.

Albert strode to the nearest chair, flipped it on its side, and pulled some sort of circle contraption out of his pocket. He pressed a button and the circle buzzed, blades sliding out of the sides and spinning furiously. It reminded Lailu of the knives hidden inside the fingers of Starling's deadly automatons.

She and Hannah crept closer.

Albert thrust the spinning blade at a table leg, turning the wood to splinters in the blink of an eye.

"Hey!" Lailu leaped forward, but she was too late; Albert wielded his blade faster than she would have thought possible, turning a second leg to splinters and then setting the chair carefully down on its two remaining legs. It wobbled piteously. Lailu wanted to hug it. Her poor chair. She whirled on Albert. "What are you *doing*? Those chairs weren't cheap!" Actually, Lailu had no idea how much the chairs cost. Slipshod had bought them with money he borrowed from Mr. Boss.

"I'm making a point," Albert said.

"You're destroying private property," Hannah countered, her tone as sharp as Albert's spinning knife.

He gulped. "Yes. Well. That was unfortunate."

"*Unfortunate?*" Lailu exploded.

"Let's throw this guy out," Hannah said, rolling up her sleeves. "I'll get Mr. Smacky."

"Wait. Wait!" Albert cried. "I can see now how that was maybe not the best strategy. But this chair here represents the generator."

Lailu looked at it. He'd left legs that were diagonally across from each other, but it certainly didn't look safe to sit on.

Albert nudged it, and it fell over with a loud crash. "*Kaboom,*" he added.

"Not necessary," Lailu whispered, staring at her splintered chair. "I'm pretty sure we got the point."

"Then you understand that you need me to fix this problem for you."

"Need you?" Hannah scoffed. "Last time you looked at it you were less than useless. All you did was make us even more worried. Lailu's been muttering 'death trap' in her sleep ever since."

"I have not!" Lailu protested.

"You have. It's very concerning."

"For the last time, I never said . . ." Albert sighed. "Anyhow, you *should* be concerned. But like I said, I believe I could fix it for you." He paused dramatically. "For a price."

Hannah narrowed her eyes. "What kind of price?"

"In exchange for my help, you need to promise to provide anything I need."

"Uh . . . ," Lailu started.

Hannah put a hand on her shoulder. "Let me." She turned on Albert. "Anything you need, huh? That's very open-ended."

"It's, well, it's what I demand."

"You get one thing," Hannah said.

"Fine. That's all I want," Albert said.

"And"—Hannah held up a hand—"you have to tell us what it is first before we agree."

Albert frowned. "There's no trust in this world anymore."

"And nothing like free food for life, either," Lailu added. She knew how much Hannah liked to give away free food.

"It's nothing like that." Albert picked up the broken chair and set it gently on its remaining legs. "All I need from you is . . . protection."

Lailu's eyes widened. "From whom?"

"From everyone," he whispered. He looked so small, so deflated, with that sad fake beard. When she thought of the confident, arrogant man he'd been just months ago compared to this husk, her heart softened like butter left on the counter.

"Okay," she said.

"Wait, Lailu—" Hannah started.

"I accept your terms." Lailu held out her hand, and Albert shook it—

And the front door flew open. A swarm of buzzing, chirping spi-trons scuttled inside.

"I was afraid of this," Hannah sighed.

14

CITY OF THE ELVES

Lailu grabbed Albert's mutilated chair. One of its remaining legs broke off in her hand, and she ran and threw it as hard as she could at the first layer of spi-trons.

They skittered to a stop, the wave behind crashing over them in a jumble of metallic jointed limbs. Lailu counted at least two dozen of the things, maybe more. She threw the rest of the chair. Most of the spi-trons managed to scuttle back, avoiding the splintering wood, before surging forward again.

"Butterknives," Lailu swore, heart racing. She yanked the nearest table onto its side like a wall, her hand going to the ever-present knife at her hip.

"Yaa!" Hannah leaped forward with her own favorite weapon, a large cast-iron frying pan Lailu had cleverly named Mr. Smacky.

Hannah whacked the closest spi-tron down before Lailu hauled her behind the table.

"There's too many of them!" Lailu kicked one back over the other side of the table, then threw her knife and pinned two others to the floor, where they sizzled and sparked.

Hannah hit another spi-tron so hard, it flew over the table and crashed into the wall. But it didn't matter; there were plenty waiting to replace it, their feet clicking and scrabbling against the wood of the table. They'd started flowing around it too, and Lailu knew in seconds it would be too late. She kept thinking of Wren's scorpio-tron, of the pincers going right for her throat. And the spi-tron that had attacked Ryon during the Week of Masks, sinking needles into his skin and stealing his blood.

What would these be capable of, if they got close enough? What would they do to her?

What would they do to *Hannah*?

The best strategy would be to leave, to sprint through her kitchen and out her back door . . . but Lailu couldn't do that. She couldn't abandon Mystic Cooking. Never.

Glass shattered, and another horde of spi-trons poured through the windows.

Hannah swore, her words far sharper than "butterknives." She swung her frying pan around in a complicated arc, but the spi-trons were learning, hovering just out of her reach. "At least we know why Wren has been so quiet lately. And where are Albert and his stupid fancy blades now?" Hannah growled, swinging her pan again and missing.

Lailu stomped on a nearby chair, reducing it to jagged wooden splinters. She grabbed the largest of them by feel. The glowing blue orbs of the spi-trons brightened, all of them tracking Lailu's movements. Any second they would surge forward in an unstoppable wave, washing over everything in their path.

Hannah adjusted her grip on her frying pan and widened her stance.

The nearest spi-tron lifted two legs in the air like antennae. The one next to it did the same, and the next, and the next, all the way down the line. Charging position, Lailu realized. They were out of time.

The spi-tron moved in a flurry of clicking limbs, spreading across the floor like the tide. Lailu kicked the table, hard, and it slammed into the first dozen spi-trons, but the rest managed to scuttle out of the way. They came at Lailu and Hannah, moving in from all sides.

Lailu took out the closest spi-tron with a well-thrown splinter of wood, but missed the one behind it. Hannah got that one with her frying pan. Another darted forward, then stopped, trembling. A shiver ran through all of them, and the hairs on Lailu's arms stood up. The air thickened like porridge left out overnight, the pressure in the room mounting. It felt like a storm was about to hit, and when it did, it would smash right on top of them.

"O God of Cookery, what now?" she whispered.

Beside her Hannah whispered to her own god, something Lailu hadn't heard her do since they'd left their village behind so many years ago.

A spi-tron lifted slowly into the air, its legs scrabbling frantically, trying to hold on to the smooth wooden floor. The spi-trons on either side rose as well, until in seconds every single one hovered several inches above the ground, the air around them glowing a gentle forest green.

"Elves," Hannah gasped, her face whitening.

"Better the elves than the spi-trons," Lailu said.

"Not sure I agree with that."

A tall figure with hundreds of golden braids stepped through Mystic Cooking's battered doorway, his icy blue eyes sweeping over the room. Hannah tried hiding behind Lailu, which was not very effective given their height differences, but Eirad ignored her. His gaze focused on Lailu, and he bared his teeth in a feral smile. "Hello again, little chef."

"Eirad," Lailu managed.

"I'm testing a new trick. Watch this." He snapped his long spindly fingers, and the clockwork creatures started spinning in place. Slowly at first, then faster and faster until they became a blur, a metal cyclone in the middle of the restaurant.

Eirad's eyes narrowed, his lips pressing together. He raised his hands, and the pressure in the room increased, tables screeching as they slid across the floor, chairs crashing to the ground beside them. Lailu clutched at her fluffy white chef's hat as her pigtails danced and tangled around her face.

"What are you doing?" she yelled, her voice caught by the rising, howling wind. "Eirad! Eirad!"

He slapped his hands together, and everything stopped.

Lailu's ears popped, and she staggered against a wind that had abruptly vanished. And not just the wind; the spi-trons were gone, the entire spinning mass.

"Lailu." Hannah clutched at her arm, her fingers digging in hard enough to bruise.

Something . . . *else* . . . sat on the floor of Mystic Cooking. At first glance it looked like one of Starling's humanoid automatons, with the same blinking blue lights for eyes and a torso full of metal gears and wires. Except instead of two arms, there were six, and as many legs. And its eyes had the multifaceted look of an insect.

"A beetle." Hannah backed away, pulling Lailu with her. "It's a giant beetle."

It fell forward, planting its arms and legs on the ground, and Lailu saw the wings, curved and metallic and definitely beetle-like. They opened and closed with a soft, far too-familiar *whir . . . whir . . . click-click-click.*

The bottom third of the smooth metal faceplate cracked open and giant pincers popped out.

Lailu took a step back. This *thing* had been a swarm of spi-trons, and Eirad had somehow transformed it. During the Week of Masks she'd seen his powerful magic transform people into creatures, but she never would have guessed his magic could do the same thing to the scientists' very inventions.

Eirad laughed. "Don't worry, little chef. My new toy won't hurt you."

Clackety-clack. The beetle-tron's pincers moved back and forth, its eerie eyes focusing on Lailu.

"Are you sure about that?" she asked.

"Oh, yes. You, at least, are quite safe." Eirad finally looked at Hannah, and his smile widened.

Hannah whimpered.

"Your thieving friend is safe too," he added reluctantly. "For the moment. After all, she's part of *our* city now, and we elves protect our own."

"Your city?" Lailu asked.

He stretched out his hands. Green fire licked around each fingertip, then swirled into a solid line, which he pointed at the beetle-tron. The fire wrapped itself around the thing's neck like a collar.

It turned toward Eirad, pincers clacking furiously.

"Why, yes," Eirad said softly. "You *can* return home. Give your former creator my greetings."

It reared back once and then scuttled out the door so fast its legs were a blur, Eirad's laughter following it as it vanished into the night.

"What is it going to do to her?" Lailu asked, throat tight. Sure, Wren had almost killed her several times now, but still. That beetle-tron was bigger than she was.

Eirad shrugged. "It's hard to know."

Lailu clenched her fists, wincing as pain lanced up her arms. It felt like some of her scars had torn open.

"And now for the fun part," Eirad continued. "Come along, come along." He walked outside Mystic Cooking.

"Why do I get the sense that his idea of 'fun' is going to be no fun at all?" Lailu asked.

Hannah clutched her frying pan, for all the good it would do her now.

Lailu didn't let herself look around at the broken tables and chairs, the shattered windows. If she looked, then she'd have to think about it, would have to calculate how much money it would cost to fix, how much work to get it all ready for the next meal. . . .

"I'll help you," Hannah whispered. "Once we see what that pointy-eared villain is on about, we'll get Mystic Cooking back into fighting shape." She gave Lailu a small, strained smile. "I promise."

"Thanks, Hannah," Lailu said, feeling a little better.

Until she stepped out her front door.

The night air smelled of damp soil and decomposing leaves. Insects chirped and buzzed joyfully. And all around them, foliage tumbled over buildings and burst from streets as the Velvet Forest expanded into Twin Rivers, greedy branches extending to swallow the whole city.

"See, little chef?" Eirad grinned wickedly. "I told you it was *our* city."

FAHR'S ANNOUNCEMENT

The poor district no longer looked anything like the Twin Rivers Lailu was used to. Trees, giant vine-covered redwoods, filled much of the empty space in between buildings. And through buildings too; a large tree had thrust its way from the roof of the apartment complex across the street. Brightly colored fairies flew as thick as forest insects, competing with the afternoon sunlight raining down between branches to illuminate the torn-up cobblestones of the street.

And the people. Dozens of people, all rushing outside, and more joining every second. A woman nearby sobbed and clung to her husband, but most of them just looked confused as they studied the trees, the fairies, and their transfigured homes.

The world swam, and Lailu put a hand against Mystic Cooking's comforting bulk behind her. Here she'd thought the powerful magic she'd felt inside Mystic Cooking had just been Eirad's work. This . . . This had to be the work of the entire gang of elves.

"I suppose we're fortunate no trees decided to grow through our roof," Hannah said bitterly.

"Fortunate?" Eirad raised his eyebrows. "We would never harm Mystic Cooking. After all, you still owe us money. In fact . . ." He studied the shattered front windows, raised his hands and—

"Don't!" Lailu cried, but it was too late.

Green fire crackled all around them, and Lailu's nostrils filled with the scent of pine and the crisp undertones of a cold mountain stream burbling quietly over rocks, trickling into a moonlit forest, sweeping away leaves and flowing, flowing . . .

"What the spatula did you *do*?" Lailu demanded, finally noticing Mystic Cooking. The front of her restaurant practically sparkled, every brick as red and crisp as if it had just come fresh from the kiln, the windows gleaming and unshattered.

Eirad staggered, his face gray. He caught himself and straightened, as haughty as ever. "I decided to be helpful," he said irritably. "And now I remember why I don't usually bother with that sort of nonsense." He brushed his hands together as if wiping away the evidence.

"What about Seala?" Hannah asked, frowning as she looked around for the guard.

"She wasn't there when I showed up," Lailu said.

"That's very unlike her. Especially since her dad contributed extra spices for today's lunch special."

"Did he really?" Lailu asked, impressed. Movement caught her eye, and she turned toward a towering fir tree in time to see

Fahr stepping out from its shadow. For a moment she was struck by his ethereal beauty. Even dressed simply in a dark green tunic and brown trousers, his black hair wrapping around his shoulders and back like a cloak of night, he looked almost too lovely, like a painting.

And then she remembered that *he* was really the one to blame for the masquerade during the Week of Masks that had injured so many people and frightened hundreds more. And suddenly he didn't seem quite so beautiful anymore.

"Master Loganberry," Fahr said, inclining his head. His eyes slid over Hannah like oil on a heated pan as he turned to look out at the street.

It was now packed with people, the noise level rising as conversations grew more heated, punctuated by crying and yelling. A group of kids chased one another around one of the intruding trees, giggling, but everyone else seemed very upset. Lailu heard a few muttered comments about "the elves," and with their superior hearing, she was sure Fahr and Eirad heard much more.

It didn't seem to bother either of them. Eirad smirked, his arms crossed as he watched the people like they were putting on a play for his benefit. And Fahr's expression gave nothing away at all, a pretty mask devoid of feeling.

Lailu realized that was the biggest difference between Fahr and Ryon. Even though Ryon had mastered the expressionless look so well that it could be impossible to know what he was feeling, she could still tell he was feeling *something*. Something about his eyes, despite all that winking. Or maybe because of it.

"Good afternoon, gentle folk of Twin Rivers," Fahr announced, stepping forward and raising his hands. Green flame flickered around his fingers, and all noise cut off immediately. Even the kids stopped playing, frozen by the base of the tree.

"You may have noticed a few small improvements made to this part of Twin Rivers. Do not be alarmed."

"Yet," Eirad added, teeth glittering.

Fahr shot him a look. "We mean you no harm," he told the apprehensive crowd. "We are merely giving the rulers of this city a message: that this part no longer belongs to them. It belongs to us." He turned, his outstretched arms taking in the entire crowd. "It belongs to *all* of us."

Lailu and Hannah exchanged confused glances.

Eirad stepped forward. "Regrettably, however, we've had to make a few other changes as well. Just to be sure those in their gilded palaces get the message." He grinned wickedly. "I hope none of you have any business in town for a while."

The crowd stirred anxiously.

"Eirad," Fahr warned.

Eirad's smile dropped away. "Do not be alarmed," he repeated. It was even less convincing when he said it.

The crowd's anxiety rose.

Fahr shook his head. "Return to your homes, friends," he said. "I'm sure you'll have plenty of questions, questions which we shall answer later." He clapped his hands.

Silence reigned for a second, another, and then—

"Do not be alarmed?" a woman demanded.

"What do you mean, no business in town?" someone else asked.

"If they think they can just get away with this—"

"Lord Elister will never allow—"

"—wouldn't dare if Starling were still alive."

Lailu winced and turned her back on the street and the growing torrent of questions and angry comments. Eirad and Fahr were both gone. Of course they were.

Lailu shook her head. "Let's go inside," she told Hannah. "I want to see what else that pointy-eared cretin did to my restaurant."

"Pointy-eared cretin?" Ryon stepped out from under the shadow of a giant redwood. "Now, *that* is a good insult." He grinned. "You're getting better."

"Ryon!" Relief rushed through Lailu even though Hannah had said she'd seen him earlier that day. In the back of her mind she'd been imagining him arrested by Elister, experimented on by Wren, held captive by the scientists. . . . She still remembered how Wren's spi-tron had attacked Ryon in the street, stealing some of his magic-neutralizing blood. At that time they'd been close to Paulie's house and the witch had been able to help him. Maybe she'd helped him this time too.

Lailu looked at the tree, then at Ryon. It had been the same trick Fahr had used, that whole appearing-in-the-shadows thing. As far as she knew, Ryon didn't have any magic of his own, except for the ability to cancel others' magic. For the first time she wondered if that was really true. Maybe he hadn't needed *anyone's* help.

"Well, well, look who decided to show up." Hannah crossed her arms, her frying pan tucked prominently under one elbow. "Actually going to talk to me this time?"

Ryon rubbed the back of his neck sheepishly. "Hey, Hannah. Nice to see you again too."

"Don't you 'hey, Hannah' me. And is that a *ponytail*?" Her eyes narrowed.

"You don't like it?" he asked innocently.

"Watch it, Ryon," Lailu warned. "She's still got Mr. Smacky."

Ryon laughed uneasily. "Maybe we should move our discussion inside." He opened the door to Mystic Cooking for them.

Hannah shot him one more glare, and then she and Lailu walked inside.

And stopped.

Ryon whistled. "Nice job. Are those lights new?"

Lailu's jaw dropped, and she spun in a slow circle, taking it all in. Her candelabra illuminated the room with glittering fairy lights. Orange and green and purple, all cascading over the newly shined cherrywood floor, highlighting the tables and chairs, all whole and unbroken and clean.

And the floor . . . bright and polished like opening day, not a burn mark in sight.

"It *does* look nice," Hannah said. She pursed her lips, like she'd just bitten into something sour. "Unfortunately."

"Elves aren't all bad, eh?" Ryon said.

"You're the one who told me they keep a collection of limbs," Lailu said. "You know, the ones they've hacked off people who displeased them?" She glanced sideways at Hannah, who had been one of those people personally threatened with limb removal a few months back.

Ryon followed her gaze. "Only the ones who deserve it." He winked at Hannah.

She tapped her frying pan against her hand with an ominous

smack, and Ryon stopped winking in a hurry. "Why are you here?" she demanded.

"I thought you were angry because I *haven't* been here."

"I am. But mostly I'm suspicious because you're suddenly here. Now. After all of this." She waved her frying pan wildly toward the chaos outside.

"Er, maybe you could set the frying pan down?" He edged a few inches farther away.

"Mr. Smacky is staying right here until we get some answers. Right, Lailu?"

Lailu adjusted her collar. "Um, right." Hannah seemed like a different person with that frying pan in her hand. Lailu was beginning to wonder if naming it had been a mistake.

"If you must know," Ryon said, "I felt a surge of elven magic and wanted to make sure my favorite chef was all right."

"R-really?" Lailu asked. She tried not to be pleased, but she felt like a morning pastry fresh from the oven, warm and content.

"And what am I, chopped liver?" Hannah grumbled.

"Oh, I knew you'd be fine. You're too sneaky to be in any real danger."

"I'm sneaky? *I'm* sneaky?" Hannah's expression darkened. "You come slithering in here and accuse *me* of—"

"Shh," Ryon hissed suddenly.

Hannah's eyes widened, then narrowed dramatically. "Did you seriously just shush me? You know, you—" She stopped. "Is that . . . ? Is someone yelling?"

"You hear it too?" Ryon said. "Sounds like it's coming from . . . below us?"

"What?" Lailu frowned. "I don't hear anything. . . ." But then she did. Someone yelling for help. "Albert?" She spun slowly. It did sound like it was coming from under her feet.

"Oh, Chushi," Lailu whispered, realizing. "The cellar." She locked eyes with Hannah and knew they were both thinking of Wren's generator.

16

DEATH TRAP

lbert crouched beside the generator, clutching some weird contraption with lots of gears and metal spokes against the large pipe that ran down the middle as if his life depended on it. And maybe it did. Maybe *all* their lives did.

"What's wrong?" Lailu asked, frantically scanning the room for spi-trons. But the rest of the cellar was empty. Only her hulking icebox in the corner, the wine racks on the side, and her spare pantry items stacked neatly in back.

"This . . . death trap . . . is about to blow," Albert said through gritted teeth.

"Aha! So now you admit it's a death trap!" Hannah said.

"Of course it's a death trap," Albert snapped. "Now come here and help me before it takes us all with it!"

Lailu rushed forward, Hannah close behind.

"I'll, er, keep an eye on things up here," Ryon called from the top of the stairs.

"Typical," Hannah muttered.

"Hold this," Albert ordered, jerking his chin at the pipe.

"Hold it . . . how?" Lailu pressed on it, then jumped. It rattled and slithered beneath her hand like a whole nest of vibbers.

"Keep your hands on it!" Albert snapped.

Lailu tentatively put both hands against the pipe.

"Firmly," Albert added, and Lailu pressed harder. "If you allow it to move, even the tiniest bit, it could destroy all of us. This whole room for sure. Probably this whole restaurant."

"I'll be outside if you need me!" Ryon yelled.

"So, so typical." Hannah shook her head. "What can I do?"

"You turn that knob over there." Albert pointed at something on the other side of the generator. "Slowly. Clockwise." He traced a finger in the air to show her what he meant. "Once it starts clicking, stop immediately." He moved around them, fiddling with gears, adjusting wires, and muttering under his breath. Finally, he stepped back and nodded. "You can let go. It should be stable now."

"Should be?" Lailu gulped, but she took her hands off the pipe. She waited. Nothing happened.

"Oh, good." Albert sagged against the wall, clutching his heart. "I thought for sure that wouldn't work."

"You *what*?" Lailu demanded.

"But it did—it did—and that's what matters. Yes?" He grinned weakly, pulled a wrinkled handkerchief from his pocket, and dabbed at his sweaty forehead.

Lailu resisted the urge to throttle him, but it was a challenge. She turned her back on the generator. It hummed softly, the noise ominous and low, like the growl of a vicious manticore. It raised the hairs on the back of her neck and made her stomach flip-flop, but only if she paid attention to it. If she ignored it . . .

No, that wouldn't help. "How stable is this?" she asked Albert.

"And be completely honest," Hannah added.

Albert sighed and shoved his handkerchief back in his pocket. "To be completely honest, it's fairly stable. For now. But I can't say how long that will last. If nothing bothers it?" He shrugged. "It would probably be fine for years. Maybe forever. But this most recent attack . . ." He hesitated.

"What?" Lailu asked.

"Two spi-trons came straight down here. As if they were drawn to it."

"Or sent," Hannah said grimly.

"Or sent," Albert agreed. "I stopped them, of course."

"How?" Lailu asked.

"I shoved them into your icebox."

"Really?" Lailu said, impressed. "Quick thinking."

"I thought so too." Albert stood a little straighter, and for a second he resembled the man he'd been months ago, the proud inventor of the camera, the self-proclaimed "most brilliant" of the scientists. "I wanted to study them. Maybe discover a way to destroy them, hopefully before . . . well. Before they destroy us."

"Us?" Hannah asked, her tone too casual.

Albert rubbed his chin, loosening the few remaining pieces of beard. "I believe—and I think you will agree—that it would be in your best interest to have someone remain close by to keep an eye on your generator. Someone who knows what he is doing and can ensure it remains in stable condition. Someone—"

"Like you. Yes, we get it," Hannah said. "Get to the point, Alfred."

"Bert," Albert said.

"Get to the point, Bert." Hannah's lips curled in a tiny smile.

"That's not my . . ." He stopped, drew himself up. "You're making fun of me again."

"Only a little."

"Hannah," Lailu sighed. "Why?"

"I'm sorry. He just makes it so easy!"

"You know, I could take my expertise somewhere else. A lot of people would be happy to see me."

"And a lot of people would be happy to see you *dead*." Hannah's smile vanished. "Isn't that right?"

Lailu felt like she'd plunged into the Dancing River all over again, it was such a shock. Hannah seemed almost like a different person. A *dangerous* person. Lailu wasn't sure she liked this new version. "Hannah, don't—"

"Don't what? He's trouble. And we already have enough trouble of our own. We don't need to borrow more."

"But he needs help. And honestly, so do we. Besides, I already promised him my protection."

Albert looked back and forth between them, his lips pressed together, hands held balled up against his chest. He just looked so frightened and sad, and Lailu hated seeing that. Albert was a genius; she couldn't have invented something like that camera of his, and who knew what else he might be capable of? "You're look-ing for a place to stay, right?" Lailu asked him.

"I . . . Yes. Somewhere safe. Preferably hidden. And with a good supply of food."

Lailu glanced at Hannah, who shrugged. "It's your restaurant," she said. "Your call."

Lailu sighed. "Okay, Albert. Once my mom comes back, she'll need that room again, but in the meantime . . . you can stay here." If *my mom comes back*, Lailu thought grimly. With Lianna, it was always an "if."

"Really? I can stay?"

"For a little bit."

"Oh, thank you, thank you. You won't regret this." Albert clutched at Lailu's hands.

"Doubtful," Hannah muttered.

"I'll just, er, go and get my things, then, shall I?" Albert scurried away up the stairs. Lailu followed more slowly, feeling Hannah's disapproval radiating behind her with every step.

Ryon waited for them in the kitchen. "What," he said slowly, "did you do?"

"Nothing," Lailu said.

"You just offered a renegade scientist safe haven. That's not 'nothing.' That's a very big 'something.'"

"And maybe it's also a very big 'none of your business,'" Hannah said. "After all, you just drop in here when you feel like it and head out when it suits you." Her fingers tightened on the handle of her frying pan.

Lailu's eyebrows shot up, and even Ryon took a step back.

"Whoa there, Sticky Fingers," he said. "I'm not Vahn."

"No, you're not," Hannah conceded. "But you do have some of the same annoying tendencies. Plus you're a snoop."

"It's my job."

"It's *supposed* to be my job too."

"Then maybe you should spend more time snooping and less time sniping at me, eh?" Ryon winked.

Hannah frowned, then tilted her head like she was considering his words.

"But in all seriousness," Ryon continued, "if you have a deal going on with the scientists, things could get a little awkward around here. The elves definitely won't like it, but I'll see what I can do to smooth things over. In the meantime, try not to invite anyone else here who might get us all killed, okay?"

"*Us* all killed?" Hannah shoved her frying pan inches from Ryon's nose.

He glanced down at it. "You're getting too attached to that."

Hannah snorted. "Whatever. We all know *you'd* be just fine, Ryon. You'd probably just leave."

He winced. "I can see I'm not making any friends here today. I'll take that as my cue. You know, to do what I'm good at." He left, the door slamming behind him.

"Okay," Lailu said slowly into the silence. "Want to tell me what that was all about?"

Hannah turned her back on her and bustled about with the kettle. "I'll make us some tea."

"Hannah."

Hannah sighed. "I don't know. I just . . . I went through so much to save him, and he hasn't ever thanked me—us. I mean us." Her face colored slightly, and she turned back to the kettle. "He hasn't really taught me anything else either. Maybe I didn't do a good enough job spying on Starling and he's decided I'm not cut out to be a spy after all. If he'd just talk to me . . . But no, he's too busy skulking about and disappearing every few seconds to give me a straight answer."

Lailu chewed her lip. She'd never really talked to Hannah about her role in the whole Starling affair. Hannah had been the one to work her way in with Starling and then had blown her own cover in order to warn Ryon. When he'd refused to listen to her and gotten himself caught, Hannah had then bravely accompanied Lailu to Starling's secret lair in order to save him.

He'd visited Lailu afterward. She remembered the way he'd sat framed in her bedroom window. *It was a lucky day when I started working for Mr. Boss, because it brought me to you.*

Lailu's cheeks felt strangely warm, and she was suddenly glad Hannah wasn't looking at her. Had he visited Hannah, too? Or just her?

Hannah sloshed boiling water in a mug and thrust it at Lailu.

"Thanks," Lailu murmured.

"It just . . . It's hard when you worry about someone and they don't even notice, you know?" Hannah said. "They don't even care."

"I know," Lailu said quietly, her thoughts drifting from Ryon to all the times she spent worrying about her mother when she went missing. So many sleepless nights, only to find her mother sitting there in the morning, all cheerful and acting like she'd barely been gone at all.

Hannah took a sip from her mug, then made a face. "This is just hot water, isn't it?"

Lailu sniffed her mug. "Yep."

"Probably better if I put the tea in it too."

"Probably," Lailu agreed, setting her mug down on the counter.

"Hello?" someone called from the dining room.

"Maybe we'll have a lunch crowd after all," Lailu said, perking up.

"You know it's practically dinnertime now, though, right?" Hannah said.

"Is it really?" Lailu hurried out of the kitchen. And stopped. Vahn stood looking at the new light fixtures, his thick blond hair pulled back in a braid.

Her breath hitched, just for a second. Vahn always had that effect on her. Even now. Although she'd let her feelings for him vanish like flour in the wind, she could still remember how excited she used to be to see him, the way her stomach tightened and twisted when he smiled at her.

He turned and smiled at her, all white gleaming teeth and . . . and . . .

Lailu stepped closer, frowning. "Spinach," she said, pointing.

"What?" Vahn's smile faltered, and he ran a finger down his teeth, missing the spot.

"Nope, still there."

"Really?" He half turned away from her, swiping furiously at his mouth. "That's funny. I didn't eat spinach today."

Hannah heard Vahn's voice and burst out from the kitchen, Mr. Smacky swinging in her hand. "Lailu, do you want to throw

him out, or do you want me to? Please say you want me to do it."
She thumped her frying pan in her hand.

"Oh, ah, hello, Hannah." Vahn tried out his smile again, but at
Hannah's look, it wilted around the edges like the spinach still stuck
in his teeth. "Did you, ah, get my flowers?"

"Oh, I got them all right." *Thump, thump* went the frying pan.
Lailu began to wonder if Ryon was right. Maybe Hannah had
grown too attached to it. "And I threw them away."

"What? Why?"

"Because I didn't like them," Hannah sniffed.

Vahn opened and shut his mouth like a fish. "What about . . . ?
What about the chocolates I sent you?"

"I threw those out too. Sorry, Lailu," Hannah added. "I know
you hate to see food wasted."

"And . . . my note?"

"Oh yes. Your 'note.' Your little non-apology." *Thump, thump.*

"But I did say sorry."

"You said you were sorry my feelings were hurt. You didn't apologize for your own actions."

"While I can see how some might misconstrue my actions—"

"Ooh, fancy words," Hannah mocked. "I'm intimidated already."

"I did nothing wrong," Vahn continued. "We weren't officially
dating, remember? You said you—"

"I know what I said." Hannah twirled Mr. Smacky. "I also know
what *you* said. Something about waiting for me? Forever if need be?"

Vahn gulped.

"And I also know what you said to *Paulie.*"

"Can we not bring her into this?"

"Oh, so *now* you don't want her involved?"

Vahn held up his hands soothingly, one of them clutching a newspaper as if it could shield him from Hannah's wrath.

Lailu frowned at that paper. She could only see a little of the front page, where flames crackled in black-and-white and the start of a caption read LOCAL VILLAGE IN ASHES . . . She transferred her frown up to Vahn's face and found him looking right at her.

"I'm actually here to see *you*, Lailu," Vahn said.

"Me?" Lailu's heart fluttered. Not because of his words, but because he'd gotten her name right. He *never* got her name right unless he needed something from her. He was definitely up to something. Something big.

"I have a fantastic opportunity for you." He unfolded the newspaper so she could see the full page. A blazing phoenix swooped over a burning field beneath the headline:

Local Village In Ashes. How Long Until Phoenix Strikes Twin Rivers?

"How would you like to be the first chef ever to successfully hunt, and cook, a phoenix?" He tried the dazzling smile once more. This time minus the spinach.

17

VAHN'S TINY LITTLE PROBLEM

aster Chef Gingersnap theorized that if there could be some way of stopping the phoenix's explosive combustible powers, then it would cook up into the tastiest bird roast ever. Of course, no one could figure out how to achieve that, so cooking a phoenix remained pure theory. Plus, Master Slipshod thought Gingersnap and her theories were all a load of salt.

Lailu shook her head. She had too many worries on her plate right now. She didn't need to add the impossible to it too. "It can't be done," she told Vahn. "As soon as anyone so much as harms that bird, she's going to go up in flame, then rise once more from her ashes."

"Not necessarily," Vahn said. "What if you had this?" He reached into a pocket and pulled out a cloth pouch, placing it on the table before her.

Lailu barely believed her eyes. "Is that . . . ?"

"Mal-cantation powder," Vahn finished. "I grabbed some just for you."

Mal-cantation powder was something the scientists had brought with them from their home country. It was very rare and very powerful—it neutralized all magic, although it did wear off quickly. Lailu could see how it might be very useful in a phoenix hunt.

Hannah's eyes narrowed. "Where did you get it?"

"Oh, I have my sources, and my resources." He flashed Hannah his biggest smile yet. "And may I just say, you are looking particularly beautiful tonight. Anger really suits you."

"Oh, it does, does it?" Hannah's nostrils flared, her eyes glittered, and she looked about as beautiful as the business end of a knife. "That does it, Lailu. Let's throw him out!"

Lailu couldn't blame her friend; if Vahn hadn't saved her brother Lonnie all those years ago, she would be happy to toss him out right now. But . . .

She glanced again at that paper, at the flames crackling on the cover. The same flames she'd seen in the paper a week ago. That phoenix had to be stopped. And maybe she *could* be the first chef to hunt and cook one. . .

"What's in it for you?" Lailu crossed her arms.

"Me?" Vahn widened his big blue eyes. "Why, nothing. Nothing for *me*. I just want to see my friend's little sister make history."

Friend's little sister.

After Vahn and Rhivanna had destroyed the local vibber nest that almost killed Lonnie, they'd remained near Clear Lakes for almost a year. None of the villagers knew why precisely, although rumor had it Rhivanna's quest was to keep an eye on the nearby border with the Krigaen Empire. While there, Vahn had become good friends with Lailu's oldest brother, Laurent. Back then Lailu had followed Vahn around, hoping he'd notice her. But he'd always seen her as just some little kid. Even now, as a master chef in her own right, with her own restaurant, she was just her brother's kid sister. Not that she cared what Vahn thought of her anymore.

She didn't. "I've *already* made history. I'm the youngest master chef in three hundred years."

"Second youngest," Vahn said.

Lailu scowled. "Greg is older than I am." The newspaper always gave Greg credit for being the youngest, the first, the best.

"If you say so," Vahn said, clearly unconvinced. "But for someone who's already made history, you seem to be in need of a little direction. I mean, you were hunting what this morning? Skilly-wigs?"

Lailu's face flushed hotter than phoenix fire.

"Oh, Lailu, honey. Don't let him get to you." Hannah glared at Vahn. "*You* got assigned the phoenix hunt, didn't you? And you can't do it."

"I . . . You . . . That's just absurd!" Vahn spluttered. "Me? Unable to complete a quest? Ridiculous!"

"So, then Lord Elister *didn't* assign the phoenix hunt to you?" Hannah asked.

Vahn looked away and mumbled something.

"What was that?" Hannah asked, cupping a hand around her ear.

"I said I might be responsible for ensuring that it gets taken care of. But he never said I had to be the one to do it."

"Oh, look at you with your fancy words and your technicalities. How very . . . elf-like."

Vahn staggered back a step, and even Lailu gasped. Coming from Hannah, that was about the worst insult ever.

"Well," Vahn said stiffly. "I can see that you're still upset."

"I'm glad you noticed."

"Why *aren't* you hunting the phoenix yourself?" Lailu asked.

"Yes, why aren't you?" Hannah crowed.

"I, uh . . . no reason."

"Well, if you can't at least be honest with me about that, then you can go." Lailu pointed at the door. "I've had a very long day."

"Er, can't we discuss this a little more?"

"No. Goodbye, Vahn."

"I mean . . . just imagine the papers: Lailu Loganberry, the master chef who took down the phoenix. Your name would blaze hotter even than—"

"She said it's time to go, Vahn," Hannah snapped. "Which is way more polite than I would have been."

Vahn looked back and forth between the two of them, then sighed, his shoulders slumping. "Fine. Just think about it, Lailu. Think about it." He took a step toward her, then tripped and landed painfully on his face.

"Are you okay?" Lailu asked.

"Bootlace broke, huh?" Hannah said, innocently looking at her fingernails. "That's some bad luck."

Vahn stood, carefully not looking at any of them as he brushed himself off.

"Are you blushing?" Lailu peered closer. Vahn turned away from her. "You are!" She'd never seen him embarrassed. It was surprisingly satisfying, like biting into a pastry and discovering chocolate filling.

"I've just . . . had a run of bad luck is all." He glanced at Hannah, then away.

Lailu remembered how the rock he'd stood on that morning had broken, sending him tumbling into the river. And how Hannah and Paulie were giggling mysteriously together the other day, plotting some sort of secret revenge. The glimmer of a suspicion wriggled into her mind. "How much bad luck would you say you've had?" she asked. "Much more than usual? Almost . . . magically so?"

Vahn winced. "Er, possibly."

Hannah gave him a tiny close-lipped smile that was somehow even more menacing than all her frying pan maneuvers.

Vahn took a careful step back. "I think I might . . . possibly . . . have a small curse on me."

A curse. Lailu thought it made sense, considering he'd been two-timing a witch. "And is that why you aren't hunting the phoenix yourself?"

"Maybe . . ."

Lailu studied him, with his red face and his broken shoelace. It was hard to imagine him as the hero from her imagination, the boy who had seemed like winter itself on that stormy day so long ago. Then she looked down at the paper, still sitting open on one of her tables, the flames rising around that poor village. Snow and fire . . . "I'll do it," she decided.

"You will?" Vahn's jaw dropped.

"Lailu!" Hannah snapped.

"Someone has to take care of that phoenix before it hurts more people. And if that someone wants to test out a good dry rub?" Lailu shrugged. "Might as well."

"You are not going to regret this." Vahn rubbed his hands together.

"Debatable," Lailu sighed. She could feel Hannah's anger radiating out at her, almost like she was a blazing phoenix herself.

"Leave at first light?"

At first light? Lailu glanced around her restaurant. No one had shown up yet for dinner, but she still needed time to prep. "The day after tomorrow," Lailu decided.

"But—"

"She already agreed to help you," Hannah snapped, swinging Mr. Smacky around in a complicated loop that narrowly missed Vahn's nose. "Don't rush her."

Vahn inched back. "Er. Okay. Right. I guess I'll just . . . be on my way, then."

"You do that," Hannah said.

He walked with his old confidence toward the door and pushed on it. It didn't open.

"Aren't you leaving?" Hannah asked.

"I'm trying." Vahn shoved on the door harder. "Stupid curse," he muttered.

"Oh, the curse has nothing to do with this," Hannah said. "This is all you."

"How so?"

"It's a pull door," Lailu sighed.

Vahn blinked. "Oh." He pulled, and the door swung open easily. Hunching his shoulders, he stepped through, just as the door swung abruptly back and smacked him in the butt.

"Now, *that* was the curse," Hannah laughed.

Lailu frowned.

"What? It's funny. And don't tell me he doesn't deserve it." Hannah's eyes narrowed, daring Lailu to disagree.

Lailu thought Vahn probably did deserve a run of extremely bad luck, but somehow this still left a sour taste on the back of her tongue. Revenge was a dish she didn't particularly enjoy. And not only that, but how was she supposed to hunt something as powerful as a phoenix with him if he could barely even manage to get out her door?

She might have just made a huge mistake.

"Has anyone ever successfully hunted a phoenix before?" Hannah asked.

"Not sure," Lailu admitted. "There are stories . . . but it's hard to know how true they are."

"So Elister assigned Vahn a potentially impossible task." Hannah tapped her chin, thoughtful. "I wonder if he's *trying* to get Vahn to fail?"

Vahn had helped the elves a few months ago, so maybe Elister wanted him out of favor? If so, Lailu had *definitely* made a huge mistake. But she'd promised; she was stuck for it.

The door opened again and Vahn poked his head back in, looking sheepish. "Forgot my paper," he muttered.

"You know," Lailu said, "you could always go talk to the person who cursed you, apologize, and ask her to remove it."

"I can't do that!"

Lailu glared at him.

"I mean, I really can't. As soon as I stepped into this side of the city, a huge magical wall came up behind me."

"Wait, what?" Lailu blinked.

"Oh, didn't you know? We're all trapped over here on this side, and everyone from the market on over is trapped on their side. It's literally a city divided."

Lailu thought of Slipshod. Her mother. Greg.

"There's no way . . ." And then she remembered the barrier in Velvet Forest and the paper that morning, warning everyone to stay near their homes. "They wouldn't." But that was another lie.

She needed to see this wall. Now.

18

Separated

*L*ailu rushed outside. And stopped. "What the . . . ?" She turned in a slow circle, mouth open. A few hours ago it had looked as though the forest had spilled into the city. Now it looked as if the *city* had spilled into the forest, as if their human buildings, their houses and businesses, were the intruders.

A canopy of leaves tangled overhead, blotting out most of the late-afternoon light. Roots tore up cobblestones and branches wove through windows. Grass sprouted in wild patches, and the air hummed with the sound of insects.

Lailu ran down the dirt road, hopping over rotting trunks that looked like they'd been there for years, dodging giant, luminous mushrooms, and swatting away flies. She could hear someone crying through the shattered window of the brick building across the street, but she didn't stop. What could she possibly say? Fahr had already told everyone that this part of the city belonged to the elves now.

Lailu remembered how Mr. Boss had tried to own her, back when she and Slipshod had first opened Mystic Cooking. They'd owed him money, and he'd tried to use that to control them. She'd had to bargain with the elves to get out of Mr. Boss's trap . . . and they'd threatened to own her too.

She scowled. She hadn't fought a mountain dragon all those months ago to win her freedom just to lose it now thanks to some fancy elven party trick. One way or another she'd see this part of the city returned to its rightful owners: the people who lived here.

Wham!

Lailu stumbled back. The air in front of her shimmered with rainbow flashes and sparks. "No," she breathed, putting her hand up. Her fingers stopped in midair, tingling, just like the barrier she'd encountered in the Velvet Forest.

Vahn hadn't been lying. They were cut off from the people on the other side of the city.

Lailu shook out her hand and tried again to push through the barrier. It felt like pushing her hand into a slab of raw steak: a little give and then nothing. She couldn't get through.

Panic squeezed her heart in sharp, jagged claws, but she shook it off. Panic never helped in a hunt, and it wouldn't do her any good here, either.

She took a step back and studied the barrier. Even though it was invisible, the trees sprouting all along this side of the city made its outline obvious. Lailu followed it, occasionally reaching to the side to brush her fingers against it as she made her way over to the main road into town.

People wandered nearby, on both sides of the barrier, the crowd growing as she walked. One man had both hands pressed against it, sweat beading across his forehead despite the chill evening air. On the other side, a woman watched him with sad eyes, her hands clutching at her chest. All around her were the scared faces of other city folk.

Another woman caught Lailu's eye and waved frantically. "You there!" she called, her voice distorted slightly, as if she were yelling across a canyon and not from a distance of two feet away. "Can you give a message to my son? He's on the wrong side! I told him to stay home, but he—"

"My wife might be over there, I haven't seen her since—"

"—looking for my friends. We were supposed to meet in the market, but they didn't—"

Voices. Too many voices. Lailu looked from one frantic face to the next, but their words all swirled together, a recipe for confusion and fear. And on Lailu's side, it was even worse; people crying, hugging one another, running into the barrier and being flung back.

Lailu skimmed the growing crowd, searching for a familiar face, but all she saw was a wall of people growing thicker by the moment.

"Lailu!"

She spun. Hannah sprinted toward her, then bent over, panting, her hands on her knees. "I tried," she gasped, "to catch up sooner." She straightened. "Whew! I really should run more often."

"Really?" Lailu asked, surprised. Hannah hated running.

"Of course not. It's a miserable thing to do. I don't know why I said that. It's just . . ." She indicated the wall, the people, everything. "How could this happen?"

"I think the real question is, what'll happen next?" Lailu remembered all her mother's warnings. She'd known something like this was going to happen. "I wish my mom were back," Lailu said, the words slipping out, and for a second it was like she was six years old again. "She'd know what to do."

Hannah looked away. "We'll figure it out too, though." Then she frowned. "Do you see that?"

"What?"

Hannah jerked her chin at a spot a few feet away. A man crouched beside the barrier, a giant metal box next to him with a multitude of pipes thrusting through the top. It almost looked like a stove, only without a door to open or a stovetop to use. Green-tinted steam puffed out of the largest pipe in short, regular bursts.

Lailu looked past the box at the man next to it. He looked a lot like Albert, actually: short, with skinny arms and legs and a ball of a stomach in front. Only he had hair, and lots of it, all standing up in jagged white spikes on the top of his head. "Interesting hair," Lailu said.

Hannah shot her a look.

"What? Like that's not the first thing you always notice on a person."

"Well, yes, but Lailu, I think he's trying to break down the barrier."

"Do you think it'll work?" Lailu asked.

The scientist bent one of the smaller pipes until the end of it pointed at the barrier. He pushed it as close as he could, and then he flicked a switch on the box.

More green-tinted steam poured out of the top of the largest pipe, but other than that nothing happened. Frowning, he flicked another switch, then bent a second pipe and thrust it at the wall. Sparks shot out of it, then ricocheted back, zapping the box. It quivered, and even from this side of the barrier, Lailu could hear a high-pitched whine screaming from the gears inside it. People on that side of the barrier clapped their hands over their ears and backed away.

The box vibrated, and then stopped, all the glowing lights inside going dead, the pipes quieting.

"Probably not," Hannah decided.

The man kicked the box. It imploded in a burst of green light and smoke, and he leaped back, yelling, his face stained with soot.

"Definitely not," Hannah amended.

Lailu sighed. Then she noticed the group of people standing just behind him. One of them was tall and imposing, with silver-streaked hair and cold green eyes. Lord Elister. He wasn't saying anything, but his expression was angrier than Lailu had ever seen it. And that anger wasn't directed at the elven barrier but at the scientist beside it.

"I'd hate to be that guy right now," Hannah whispered.

"Me too." Lailu shuddered. Elister was speaking softly to the scientist now, too quiet for them to hear, but they could see his face growing pale beneath the soot. Lailu noticed a couple other scientists, all inching away from the furious tirade. Among them stood Wren, with her bright red hair, still wearing a leather apron and a pair of too-large goggles perched on her head.

Lailu took a step back, her heart racing furiously. She felt . . . guilty. Even though everyone told her, again and again, that it wasn't her fault that Starling died, that she'd been protecting herself and her friends, that Wren was just lashing out, looking for someone to blame. Still, Lailu could feel the guilt enveloping her like a swarm of skilly-wigs, choking and slimy and nearly impossible to wash off. And beneath that guilt, her fear. This Wren, with her hard gaze and her deadly inventions, was a different person from the friend Lailu had once known. This Wren was dangerous.

"I'm going to head back to Mystic Cooking to make sure Vahn left," Hannah said. "Meet you there?"

Lailu nodded, still watching Wren. She was talking to Elister now, his face going from extreme anger to polite attention as she spoke. He nodded, said something, and then Wren trotted over to the box. Lailu wandered closer, unable to help herself. From this distance, Wren's face seemed thinner, with deep purple shadows under her eyes, and her tangled red hair looked like it badly needed a wash.

Was anyone looking out for her? In her overlarge leather tunic, she looked even younger than her eleven or twelve years. And now she didn't have a mother—

Lailu forced herself to remember the flood of spi-trons, the scorpio-tron, the generator. All the ways Wren had made her life harder. As she pictured that scorpio-tron, she corrected herself: all the ways Wren had tried to make her life *shorter*. Still. "How are you doing, Wren?" she asked.

Wren looked up, green eyes widening, and for a second she looked like she might be happy to see Lailu. Then her expression hardened. "I don't owe you any answers. Murderer."

Lailu flinched. "Okay. I can see this isn't going to be a productive conversation."

Surprisingly, Wren smiled. It reminded Lailu eerily of the smile Hannah had given Vahn, and chills snaked up and down her spine. "I see you've chosen to join the elves."

"I haven't *chosen* anything." Lailu scowled. "I'm stuck on this side, the same as everyone else over here."

"Oh really? Then how do you explain this?" Wren pulled open the lid of the mysterious metal box. Lailu had to stand on tiptoes and crane her neck to see inside, but she caught a glimpse of a glittering automaton head in the shape of a beetle, with wires plugged beneath its metal plates and connected to gears and coils built into the corners of the box.

Lailu felt like her own insides had turned to metal. What kind of experiment were they doing with that? Would Eirad's magic still be trapped inside the metal? She didn't know enough about either the elven magic or the science behind the original spi-tron creations to know what this could mean. "That wasn't me," she managed.

"I recognize my own inventions, and I recognize elven magic when I see it." Wren shut the box with a resounding clang. "I spent days on those. They were supposed to destroy Mystic Cooking, take it apart brick by brick. And you with it."

"Is that really what you want, though?" Lailu asked, trying to keep her voice gentle even as her blood pounded in her ears.

"Yes," Wren said simply. "I plan to be as ruthless as necessary."

"You know, you can kill me, but it won't bring back your mother."

Wren flinched. "How dare you?"

"She was ruthless too," Lailu continued. "And it didn't work out well for her."

Wren's eyes narrowed. "I might not be able to get to *you* anymore while this barrier is still up. But I'll figure out how to remove it, and in the meantime, I have some things of yours over here on my side. And I can get to *them* just fine."

"Some . . . things?" Lailu asked, confused.

Wren scowled. "This is why I don't deal with hyperbole and vague statements. *People*, okay? I have some of your people over here. And I can hurt them. I can *kill* them."

Immediately Lailu thought of Slipshod, her mother. Greg . . .

"You wouldn't," Lailu whispered, but she kept remembering those pincers, aimed right at her throat.

"Ruthless as necessary," Wren repeated. She took a step back, then another, her eyes cold and much too grown-up.

"Wait, Wren—"

Someone jostled Lailu from behind.

"Sorry, little miss," a man said. "So sorry. I thought . . . I'm looking for my daughter. I thought you were her." His face crumpled like a used napkin. "She was supposed to meet me in the market."

"I'm sorry," Lailu told him. And she meant it. She really did. But she couldn't do anything to help him or the people staggering around behind him.

She turned back to the barrier, but Wren was already gone. Only that blackened box sat there, alone and forbidding, a reminder of Wren's threats.

19

On the House

*L*ailu felt hot and cold all over, dread pooling in her stomach and spreading through her limbs like the forest spilling into the streets around her. The man who had bumped her cried softly into his hands. Other people wandered behind him, sad and afraid. Down the road, two kids took turns hitting the barrier with sticks, while a woman watched them from the other side, her face drawn and pale.

Lailu turned away from the barrier and started back through the foresty streets. As she got closer to Mystic Cooking, she passed more and more people, all of them looking as lost as she felt. They must have taken the elves' warning to stay home today seriously, but despite that, many of them were still dressed in their typical worker smocks and bowler hats, as if they didn't know what else to do. She wondered what they'd do tomorrow. Would they continue to get dressed for jobs they could no longer get to?

An older gentleman, his eyes lined with his years and his hands gnarled and calloused from hard work, sat on a fallen tree and stared down at the ground. He looked up at Lailu as she passed. His mouth opened and then closed again silently, as if there were no words.

The dread in Lailu's stomach curdled and turned into something else. Something softer, lighter. This man, this hopeless man, reminded her of her hardworking dad. He always wore the same dazed expression when Lianna left, his eyes staring off into a distance that never seemed to get closer.

In the days and weeks and sometimes months that stretched without Lianna, he would disappear into his workroom, consumed by the one thing that never left him: his work. A shrine carving for one family, a wooden statue for another . . . It had gone on like that for years. Eventually, Lailu's oldest brother, Laurent, joined him as an apprentice, and then it was just Lailu and her other brother, Lonnie.

One lonely afternoon during one of their mother's longest absences yet, Lonnie had confided that it felt like both their parents were gone. He'd been so sad, Lailu felt like her heart was breaking just looking at the droop in his face, the slump in his shoulders. Food always cheered him up, so she'd decided to prepare an elaborate meal. Something special, better even than her mother's cooking. Her very own recipe.

The smells had reached her father's workshop, and he'd actually joined them in the house for dinner that evening. "You put a lot of work into this meal. It deserves my full attention," he'd told Lailu. She still remembered the way his eyes widened after his first bite, and the smile he gave her when his bowl was empty. For the first time since their mother left, his face relaxed. It was like her food had filled the empty places inside him. "A talent like yours will need a lot of nourishing for it to really grow," he'd said, before making her promise to cook dinner for the rest of the week.

Lailu looked around at all the scared people clustering nearby, the memory of her father's pride lingering like the aroma of that long-ago feast. She might not be able to bring the rest of Twin Rivers back to them, but she could give them a place to gather tomorrow and the comfort of good food to fill them with more than just fear.

Lailu walked over to the old man first, her footsteps lighter than steam.

The next morning Lailu stirred a large pot of raegnar soup, the smell flavoring the air with the gentle aroma of a hint of lebinola spice. She breathed it in, feeling better than she had in days. It was like she'd swallowed a rock the day Starling died, a rock that had slowly expanded and grown heavier and heavier, and now for the first time it was beginning to dissolve.

She smiled and even hummed a little as she scooped soup into a row of small ceramic bowls.

Hannah pushed open the door from the upstairs, yawning. "Did I oversleep?" She brushed a tangled black lock out of her face and pulled her robe tighter around herself.

"No, I'm just getting started early today," Lailu said.

"You know, we'll probably have a slow day, what with most of the city cut off from us." Hannah flopped down on the single chair in the kitchen. "I would have slept longer, but I dreamed I could hear the voices of a crowded restaurant coming up through the floorboards." She rubbed at her eyes. "Funny that. I'm still hearing it."

"Well, that's because we've got a fairly full restaurant." Lailu finished scooping soup into the last bowl and began arranging them all on a tray.

"How do we have a full restaurant already?"

"Oh, because last night I promised everyone appetizers on the house today." Lailu beamed, expecting Hannah to be proud of how much she had changed. For the first time, *she* was the one offering people free food instead of yelling at Hannah for doing so.

She was not disappointed. Hannah was so surprised she slid right off her chair. "You *what?*"

"I would've done more, but seeing how the skilly-wigs are still with Greg, I only have enough for appetizers until I get a chance to hunt again tonight."

Hannah picked herself up. "You can't just give away free food like that!"

Lailu's smile wilted. Clearly Hannah was *not* proud. "Why not?" she asked. "You do."

"It's different. I'm not trying to give *away* food. I'm trying to bring *in* customers."

Lailu sniffed. "Well, it seems the same to me."

"I was trying to get you more business, so you would make *more* money. Not give away all your hard work. It's very, very different."

Hannah put her hands on her hips. "Very different. I mean, these people . . . I'm assuming they're all the poor folk who live nearby?"

Lailu nodded.

"Most of them can't afford to be regular customers here. Don't you remember when I tried that neighborhood discount? It didn't help. They're not about to go bringing all their friends by either, because most of their friends can't afford it, too."

"But isn't that the point of a restaurant? So everyone can dine like royalty, at least for a meal?"

Hannah pursed her lips. "Well, yes, but these people are stuck here. If they wanted to dine like royalty, they would have had to come to you anyhow. You didn't need to give them food to get them to come. Do you see what I mean?"

Lailu looked down at the soup on the tray in front of her. "I don't care about that," she said quietly. "Right now it's not about the money."

"We're running a business! It's *always* about the money."

Lailu gently turned one of the soup bowls. The raegnar broth caught the light, its telltale rainbow sheen gleaming. "Not to me it isn't," she said. "To me, it's always about the cooking." She looked up, meeting Hannah's eyes. "Those people out there are scared. Most of them have friends or family on the other side of the barrier, and they don't know what's going to happen to them *or* us. *I* don't know what's going to happen either, but at least I can feed them and give them a safe place to gather."

"That's really not your job."

"Then whose job is it? Besides, I know what it feels like."

Hannah's hard expression shattered like the ice on their village lake in spring. "Oh, Lailu," she whispered. "I understand. And your mom will be fine."

"I know she will. She always is."

"We'll be fine too," Hannah added. "Just don't go bankrupting yourself again. Okay?"

Lailu scowled. "I haven't been bankrupt in weeks."

"And let's keep it that way." Hannah studied the trays full of soup and sighed. "I'd better get dressed so I can help."

"You're not dressed?"

"Lailu, honey, I'm wearing a bathrobe." Hannah grinned, then sashayed up the stairs, the hem of her nightgown poking out beneath her fluffy white robe.

"Hmm. Not sure how I missed that." Lailu shook her head, picked up her tray of soup, and carried it out to her frightened customers. While she had been talking to Hannah, another table had filled up. Lailu immediately recognized Albert's bald head and round tummy. She assumed the other men and the woman sitting with him were scientists too.

As Lailu passed out the soup, she noticed that Albert and his friends seemed to be in a furious discussion, with large arm gestures and dramatic facial expressions. One of them even slammed his fist on the table.

"Shh," Albert hissed.

Lailu frowned and drifted closer, but before she could find out what they were discussing, the bell over the front door chimed.

Lailu's whole restaurant fell silent. She turned. Fahr stood framed against the open door, his blue-gray eyes glittering, the midmorning sunlight highlighting his dark hair. He waited another beat and then strode inside, followed by Eirad and half a dozen other elves. Ryon slipped in behind them, quietly closing the door.

Trapped. Lailu felt a gnawing sense of horror as she looked between the elves and her customers. Including Albert and his little group of scientists. Eirad was currently circling their table like a hungry shark, malice shimmering in the air around him. The tall scientist with a monocle turned the color of soured cream, while Albert mopped at his bald head with a cloth napkin, probably regretting his lack of disguise.

Eirad caught Lailu's gaze over the heads of the scientists and smirked, his lips drawing up just enough to display the tips of his sharp white teeth. The gnawing sense in Lailu's stomach froze into sheer dread. She had promised Albert that she would protect him. . . .

She put a hand to the knife always at her hip.

Eirad lifted his eyebrows in silent challenge, ready. She'd never beat him. They both knew it.

Lailu swallowed, and—

And Ryon hooked his arm through hers. "Easy there, tiger," he whispered. "No one is here to fight."

"Oh, I don't know," Eirad said. "A fight would make this whole outing much more entertaining."

"Eirad," Fahr warned. "We talked about this."

Eirad sighed. "I know. It's not always about my entertainment." He looked back down at the table of quivering scientists. "Today, at least."

"Then what is it about? Today, at least?" Lailu added.

"This," Eirad said simply, jerking his chin at the room. Lailu noticed the other elves had spread out, each of them sitting at different tables around the room, and . . . talking? Yes, they were talking to the people. And people actually seemed a little less scared.

Lailu frowned.

"Let's go to your kitchen, where we can talk," Ryon told her.

Still frowning, Lailu led the way. She glanced back once more.

"Honest, they're going to be okay. Fahr has promised no harm will come to anyone in your restaurant. Today, at least."

"People keep using that modifier," Lailu said. "It's not as comforting as you all seem to think."

Ryon laughed and pulled the curtain closed behind them. He glanced around.

"Hannah's getting dressed, if you're looking for her," Lailu said.

He grinned. "I'm getting too obvious. I'll have to watch myself." He turned the chair around and plopped down on it backward, propping his chin in his hands on the back. "So, is she still mad at me?"

"Am I still the youngest master chef?"

"I thought Greg was."

Lailu scowled. "Yes, she's still mad! And now so am I!" She forced herself to take a deep, slow breath. She knew Ryon was just trying to annoy her. And doing an amazing job of it. "Now, what the cutlery is going on?"

20

WHAT THE CUTLERY IS GOING ON?

"What the cutlery?" Ryon laughed. "What happened to spatula?"

"Greg started using that expression," Lailu grumbled, crossing her arms. "I've had to get a little more creative."

"Considering you're the mastermind behind such gems as 'Mr. Frosty,' 'Mr. Icy,' and my personal favorite, 'Mr. Smacky,' I have to admit I'm impressed."

"Watch it, Ryon. You are not my favorite person right now."

"You're no one's favorite person around here," Hannah added, pushing open the door to the upstairs. She stepped through, letting it swing shut behind her. "And I heard you insulting my frying pan."

Ryon's eyes widened, and for a few seconds he just stared at Hannah. Lailu couldn't blame him; her friend looked *amazing*. Even more so than usual. She had twisted her long black hair up into two elaborate buns on the sides of her head, each bun secured by a thin silver cage with a long, glittering chopstick thrust through. It made her face appear more heart-shaped than normal, with just a few tendrils curling around her eyes and ears.

"What?" Hannah's cheeks colored slightly, and she ran a hand over the front of her outfit self-consciously. Not a dress, either, Lailu realized. It was more like the outfits Hannah had tailored for Starling: an emerald-green vest cinched in at the waist and then flaring out at her hips over snug black pants and a pair of knee-high gray leather boots. "Why are you staring at me like that?"

Ryon blinked, then smiled. "Just checking to see if you have your frying pan hidden behind you."

Hannah looked a little disappointed. "No, I've been told I should give Mr. Smacky a rest." She looked pointedly at Lailu. "But I'm just looking for any excuse to swing him again."

"I take your point." Ryon stood in one smooth motion. "So I'll get to mine. You asked what was going on. Well, the elves have realized that ultimately there's no way they can win this fight alone."

"Perhaps," Eirad said from the kitchen doorway.

Hannah flinched back.

"What are you doing in my kitchen?" Lailu demanded. If Eirad really wanted to harm her, he would have done it already when she was trapped in his forest, Ryon or no Ryon, so there was no point in being afraid of him. Still, she'd prefer a healthy distance between them. Like a mile. Or several.

"I thought this was where the real discussion was happening," Eirad said. "Not out there among the sheep."

"My kitchen isn't big enough for everyone," Lailu said.

"Then maybe those who aren't useful can see themselves out." Eirad looked hard at Hannah.

She swallowed but didn't budge.

"I don't know, Eirad. Everyone in this kitchen is extremely useful, with a specific purpose," Ryon said. "Except for you."

Eirad's cold blue eyes narrowed. "Speaking of useful, didn't Fahr assign you a job? Maybe you should be taking care of that, hmm? Wouldn't want to disappoint him again, would you?"

They glared at each other, the air between them hotter than any of Lailu's burners.

"This display of macho bravado is inspiring and all," Hannah said, "but Ryon was about to tell us what's going on. Maybe we could get back to that? I want to see if he'll give us a straight answer. For once."

Ryon winced.

Eirad gave Hannah an approving nod for the first time ever. "I, too, would like to see this."

"As I was saying before we were interrupted," Ryon said, "Fahr has realized it would be helpful to get the people in the nearby districts of the city on his side. We know the scientists are up to something, something big. And we need to be ready to counter them."

"Not just counter." Eirad held up one long-fingered hand and clenched it in a fist. *"Crush."*

"What a delightful demonstration," Ryon said dryly. "So helpful. So illuminating."

"How are you getting them on your side?" Lailu asked suspiciously. "They don't like the elves. They think Star—" Lailu stopped, Wren's face swimming in her memory, how happy she looked that last holiday night as she sat by her mother's side. It was the first and only time Lailu had ever seen Starling praise her daughter. Lailu clenched her fists. "They think the scientists saved them from you elves on the final Night of Masks," she finished.

"Oh, yes, but Fahr can be very persuasive," Eirad said. "Isn't that right, Ryon?"

Ryon looked away, his mouth a hard, thin line.

"Persuasive how?" Hannah asked, her eyes narrowing.

Lailu frowned and cocked her head to the side. It sounded like … cheering? She pushed past Eirad and out into the dining room.

The first thing she noticed was Albert huddled in the corner, looking scared. And past him, several men and women on chairs, their fists in the air. Gathered around them, everyone else had gotten to their feet and were cheering as well as Fahr stood on a table in front of them all, his pointed elvish chin thrust forward, long black hair rippling behind him, both his arms raised.

And a triumphant smile stretched across his delicate face.

Lailu realized the people were shouting, "Down with Elister! Down with the monarchy!"

"That's right!" Fahr said. "Those people don't care about you. They don't know you. But we live beside you. We work with you. You're in our city now, and we mean to spread that city. We mean to make the whole city *our* city."

And people cheered harder. Lailu couldn't believe it. Didn't they see this was all a trick? Yeah, maybe the aristocracy didn't care about these people, but neither did the elves. How could they forget that these elves had been taking years from their lives for generations, had been whittling away at their businesses all this time?

She remembered something Ryon had said, the night Starling died: *Sometimes you see in a person what you want to see in them and not what's really there.* Maybe these people were all so desperate for someone to save them that they were willing to pretend the elves were their allies rather than face the fact that they had none.

"So convenient, you know," Eirad whispered next to her. "You gathering all these people in one place for us."

Lailu turned slowly, horror-struck.

Eirad's grin was sharper than the pain of a thousand vibber bites. "We really must thank you for that."

21

POINTY-EARED CRETIN

Lailu sat on the edge of the old well behind Mystic Cooking. She wrapped her arms around her legs, buried her face in her knees, and cried. She didn't even try to fight the tears. Heaviness wrapped itself around her shoulders and dragged her down until she felt as low as the caves beneath Velvet Forest—and twice as dark.

"Lailu?" Hannah called.

Lailu didn't bother looking up.

"Oh, Lailu." Hannah sat down beside her and put an arm around her shoulders. "Don't cry, honey. It's going to be okay. Please, please stop crying."

But Lailu couldn't stop. Tears poured out of her until she thought she might choke on them. All those people. Scared. Lost. Alone.

Vulnerable.

"I did this," she sobbed. "I set them up."

"No, you didn't. You gave them a place to meet. You gave them food. *Free* food. You were trying to help them feel better, and that's a good thing." Hannah ran her fingers through Lailu's hair, which had come loose from her pigtails. "Those elves . . . they know how to take something good, something you love, and twist it."

Lailu sniffed, but she didn't say anything, and after a moment Hannah stopped stroking her hair. Silence built around them, but it was the kind of silence a watched pot made, like it was going to boil if you just gave it time and didn't look too closely.

"I never told you," Hannah said quietly, "but remember how I, uh, re-homed that hair comb a few months ago? The one that belonged to an elf?"

Lailu nodded. Considering that had led to her first dragon hunt, there was no way she'd ever forget it.

Hannah sighed deeply. "I think it was a test. It's like they knew . . . They *knew* I wouldn't be able to resist it. I mean, none of the elves ever came to Twin Rivers's Finest. Except that day, when that one elf showed up, wearing that comb. And requesting that I assist her."

"Really?"

Hannah nodded. "I think they wanted to see if I could do it. And then when I could . . . they used that as leverage against me."

"But . . . why?"

"That's the part I've never figured out." Hannah touched her own hair combs, the glittering nets Lailu had admired earlier. "Sometimes I wonder if Ryon . . ."

"You think he was involved? No. No way."

Hannah shrugged. "Probably not. But . . . maybe? I mean, what do we really know about him?"

"He's our friend."

"But is he? Is he really?" Hannah cocked her head to the side, her dark eyes intense. "Ask your mom about him sometime, okay? About the things she's heard. I know he seems so friendly, all winking and making his little jokes, but . . . I don't think that's who he is at all. I think it's just another mask." Hannah's face crumpled, and for a second it looked like she might cry too, but then she took a deep breath and her expression smoothed out.

And Lailu realized if anyone knew about masks, it would be Hannah, who wore them so effortlessly even Lailu hardly noticed they were there. Lailu wiped her sleeve across her eyes and under her running nose. She felt empty from crying, like a fruit with all its seeds scraped out.

"His loyalty is always going to be to Fahr first," Hannah continued. "We're *supposed* to be working together. We had a deal. But—"

"But then I started working for Fahr again." Ryon stepped out from the shadows around them.

Lailu almost fell off the well, but Hannah didn't look surprised at all.

"I was wondering when you'd come out" was all Hannah said. "How long have you been listening?"

"Long enough." He walked toward them. Lailu could never tell if this serious Ryon was the real Ryon, or if the winking version was real, or maybe Hannah was right and she'd never even seen the real Ryon.

He knelt in front of Hannah and took one of her hands in his. It was a strangely intimate gesture, and suddenly Lailu felt very uncomfortable, like she shouldn't be there. She poked at that feeling, like stabbing holes in a piecrust before baking. Was it jealousy, or just awkwardness? She'd liked Vahn, and he'd picked Hannah over her. And now there was Ryon, who had been Lailu's friend first . . . who said nice things to her and made her laugh and who, despite all that awful winking, was actually kind of, sort of . . . cute.

She was still trying to decide how she felt when Ryon suddenly took one of her hands too, his fingers warm around her frozen ones. "You are both very important to me. I can't promise I will never lie to you, because *that* would be a lie. But I *try* not to lie to you. Which is why, Hannah, my sticky-fingered assistant, I've been staying away. I owe Fahr. Until I've paid off that debt, I don't think it's right to bring you into it."

"Why do you owe him?" Hannah demanded.

"He's my brother," Ryon said simply.

"So?" Hannah said.

"So, blood is important."

Hannah studied him. "Especially yours," she said, and something about her tone was off, like a soup without enough salt. Like she had some sort of secret. "But sometimes family isn't who you're related to. Sometimes it's who you choose."

Ryon's smile was small and sad. He let go of both of their hands and stood. "Fahr protected me when I was born. The other elves wanted me destroyed, and he stood up for me. He's the only one who's ever been willing to accept me."

"Hey!" Lailu protested.

"Not counting you. Obviously." He winked. "But I need to help him now, in this one last thing. He needs leverage against Elister if the elves are going to survive. And, Hannah." He turned back to her. "I hope once this is done you'll still want to work with me."

Hannah chewed her lip and looked away.

"What is Fahr up to?" Lailu asked. "Can you tell us anything? Are those people . . . the ones I invited . . . will he hurt them?"

Ryon shook his head.

"But that's not entirely true either, is it?" Hannah said. "He might not hurt them directly, but a lot of them will be injured or even killed in this clash that's building."

"That's their choice, though," Ryon said. "That's not Fahr's fault."

"Yes, it is!" Lailu said. "He's getting them involved!" Her voice caught on the last word, turning it into a half sob.

"They were already involved. They're the pawns of the city. The poor are always the pawns." He ran a hand back through his dark hair, his movement sharp and agitated. "Besides, the people on the other side of the barrier aren't necessarily much better off."

Lailu remembered Wren's threat again. Slipshod, her mom, and Greg. Slipshod would be fine. He was surrounded by the king's guard. And her mom? Probably well hidden. But Greg was easy to find. Greg would be a very convenient target.

"I need to see Greg," Lailu realized.

"Why?" Hannah asked.

Lailu didn't want to admit she was worried about him. "I need to see if he'll be my backup in the phoenix hunt tomorrow."

"That hunt is such a bad idea," Ryon said.

"Why are you here?" Hannah pushed herself off the edge of the well. "You said you don't want me to work with you, you're not making Lailu feel any better, and you're not telling us anything helpful. Why do you keep lurking around us like some kind of ghoul?"

Ryon tilted his head, his gray eyes solemn. "Do you want me to leave?"

It was a question with weight buried inside, like a well-planned pot pie. He didn't just mean tonight. He meant forever. "No," Lailu said.

Hannah glanced down at her, surprised. Then she shrugged. "No," she agreed.

Lailu managed a weak smile. "You're our friend, Ryon. Even if you are also a pointy-eared cretin."

Hannah sighed. "What she said."

A smile unfurled across Ryon's face. Not his usual sneaky smirk, but something genuine and happy that tugged at his eyes and shimmered around his face for one fleeting moment. Maybe *this* was the real Ryon. But then it was gone, and he'd wrapped his usual swagger around himself once again. "I'm not *such* a cretin. Would a cretin offer to take you through the barrier?"

Lailu blinked. "You . . . can do that?"

"Only if you ask me real nice." He winked.

"Please?"

"I don't know. . . . Do we really have to visit Greg?" Ryon asked.

"Yes," Lailu said. "Besides, he owes me some skilly-wigs."

"Oh yeah. I heard about that last hunt." Ryon shook his head. "Embarrassing."

"Your face is embarrassing," Lailu muttered, even as her cheeks flushed. Did *everyone* know about the skilly-wigs? It was a good thing she'd decided to hunt the phoenix; her reputation needed the boost.

Hannah giggled. "You never change." Then her eyes narrowed. "You know, speaking of change, I have the perfect outfit for you to wear when you leave."

"Outfit?" Lailu frowned. "Do we really have to go through all this again?" Every time she had to go into the city, Hannah took that as an excuse to dress her up. And now that she'd thought about Wren's threat and what an easy target Greg would be, she wanted to get through the barrier and check on him as quickly as possible. She knew he could take care of himself, and he was probably fine. Probably. She'd just feel better if she saw that for herself.

"Actually," Ryon said slowly, "getting dressed up would be a good idea. Something that will help her blend in on the streets of Gilded Island." At their confused looks, he added, "There are a lot of guards patrolling the streets right now."

"Also, you need to take her to see Paulie first," Hannah said, already dragging Lailu toward Mystic Cooking.

"Why?" Lailu asked, following her friend inside.

"Because Paulie's curse was supposed to affect Vahn, not you. Right now he's a danger to himself, which doesn't bother me one bit. But if you're really set on doing this hunt with him, he'll also be a danger to you. Besides . . ." Hannah waited until the door shut behind them, leaving them alone in the kitchen. "I have something I need you to give to Paulie. Secretly."

22

THROUGH THE WALL

*D*o you think my mom is in trouble?" Lailu asked.

Hannah adjusted one of the metal nets in Lailu's hair and stepped back, pursing her lips as she studied her work.

"Hannah?" Lailu said.

"I'm thinking." Hannah tapped her lips with one finger, then nodded. "Yes."

"Yes, she is?"

"Yes, that looks amazing. I think this is your new look." Hannah beamed.

Lailu scowled. "Focus, Hannah! My mom has been gone almost two days now, and we don't know where she is. That's a lot more important than my hair."

"Maybe."

"Maybe? *Maybe?*" Lailu spluttered.

Hannah sighed. "We know she went to see Elister, and this is hardly the first time she's vanished. She can take care of herself." She pursed her lips. "But you're right. It would be good to know where she's gone."

"How?" Lailu asked suspiciously. Hannah wore a look like she was up to something. It was the same look she'd worn when she told Lailu about her habit of "re-homing" other people's hair combs.

Hannah shrugged. "Can you give this letter to Paulie?" She handed Lailu an envelope. It was sealed shut. "It's . . . probably best you don't read it."

"Okay." Lailu tucked it into her vest, trying not to feel hurt about Hannah and Paulie sharing secrets without her. Idly, she touched her hair. It looked just like Hannah's, with her pigtails wound up in buns and then trapped beneath silver nets. Instead of the chopsticks securing Hannah's hair, however, Lailu's had small jeweled clips, each in the shape of a phoenix.

"For luck." Hannah tapped one of the clips.

"Do you think Greg will help hunt it?"

Hannah rolled her eyes. "You're so dense sometimes, Lailu."

"What?"

"Of *course* Greg will help you. Especially with how cute you look in that hairstyle." She grinned.

"Knock-knock," Ryon said.

"You're not supposed to say 'knock-knock,'" Lailu said, relieved by the distraction. "You're just supposed to knock."

"What can I say? I'm a rebel." Ryon winked. "Ready to go? Love the hair, by the way. It suits you."

"Th-thanks." Lailu touched one of her buns again, her finger tracing the pattern of the delicate silver net. She glanced over at Hannah, who had gone still. "See you soon."

Hannah nodded, her mouth a thin line.

Scrape. Scrape.

"What's that?" Ryon asked.

"Oh, probably just Albert moving in," Lailu said casually, slipping on her mom's warm wool coat since hers still stunk of skillywig from her swim the other day.

Ryon sighed. "Terrible idea. Don't you remember how he helped kidnap me?"

Lailu shrugged. "That was a long time ago."

"It was a couple of *weeks* ago."

"Things were different then." She pushed past Ryon and headed out. She didn't want another lecture. They had no time for that.

Silence fell around them as they walked through the forest that had been city.

"You probably should have complimented Hannah on *her* hair," Lailu said suddenly, remembering Hannah's expression.

"Nah. She gets enough compliments."

Lailu couldn't argue with that. Still. Hannah's expression bothered her, and the fact that she hadn't said goodbye when they'd left. She hadn't said *anything*.

Lailu was still frowning when they reached the barrier. To

her surprise, Ryon didn't try to go through it. He just turned and walked alongside it.

"Um, aren't we going through?"

"Oh, we're not going *through* the barrier," Ryon said. "We're going *around* it."

"Around it? Like . . . the edge runs out?" Lailu had just assumed it enclosed them, like a bubble, instead of a more traditional wall.

"Not exactly," Ryon said.

"But—"

"I'm not going to tell you anything else. So unless you want me to start winking at you again, I'd suggest saving your questions."

"Fine. But—"

He winked.

"Argh! You're so irritating!"

Ryon chuckled.

Lailu clamped her mouth shut. She didn't have any good insults, and something told her Ryon would just laugh at any of her attempts. They walked on in silence, until her boots began to pinch and her legs told her that she had been doing far too much walking lately, which meant she needed to do more cooking. "How far do we have to walk?"

"Not too much farther." Ryon looked back at her and smiled. "We're practically there, in fact."

"Good," Lailu grumbled. And then she noticed Ryon's coat. A *nice* coat, one that would not look out of place on someone on Gilded Island. Why hadn't he worn it before? And why did it look so out of place now?

She stopped dead in the middle of the street. The poor and

the less savory walked past, eyeing her and Ryon, trying to judge if robbing them might be worth their time. And Lailu knew exactly where they were. And even worse, where they must be going. Because right around the corner was Mr. Boss's old lair: the Crow's Nest.

23

EVENING

"hy are you stopping?" Ryon asked.

"Why are we here?" Lailu demanded.

"You said you needed to talk to Greg for some reason, so like the good friend I am, I offered to take you."

"No, why are we *here*?"

"And where is that?" Ryon asked.

Lailu scowled. "Stop acting so innocent." She stalked forward until she could see the old three-story building looming around the corner. *"Here!"* She pointed at it, then stopped, stunned.

The Crow's Nest was a broken, wheezing version of its former ominous self. One of the walls had been partially blown away, leaving the blackened insides laid bare like the intestines of some slaughtered beast. Charred wood surrounded that jagged hole and snaked down the entire side of the building. No one went in or out of the building anymore, and someone had painted over the crow on the creaky hanging sign, covering the whole thing in thick red paint, like fresh blood. Lailu had never thought she'd feel sorry for this particular building, but it was strangely . . . sad.

"Didn't realize it had been so damaged, did you?" Ryon said quietly.

Lailu dropped her arm. "No." Starling's face swam through her memory, the wide green eyes reflecting back the flames that would destroy her. Lailu tried to shake the image, but it haunted her now more than ever.

This had been the place. Right there, in that upper level, where the building was torn open. Her friend had lost a mother, and Lailu had gained an enemy.

She hugged herself and turned away.

"Come along and I'll let you in on a secret." Ryon strolled closer to the ruins, and Lailu reluctantly tagged along behind him. "Whenever the elves vanquish a worthy foe, they get a little boost to their magic in that location. So, since this was once Mr. Boss's lair, and then later Starling's secret lab, they felt it would be poetic justice to turn the Crow's Nest into a doorway."

"Poetic justice," Lailu whispered. The words tasted bitter in her mouth, and she couldn't help remembering Fahr at the front of her restaurant, getting all the people on her side of the city riled up. All so he could use that anger, direct it the same way the spout on a kettle directed water.

Ryon ignored the front door and instead walked into the narrow alley tucked behind the broken side of the building. The paint on the wood here had all peeled away, the exposed beams dark with charcoal.

"Is this like the doorway Eirad took me through the first day of the Week of Masks?"

"Exactly like."

Lailu remembered Eirad's warnings about that particular doorway, hidden in the Western Travel District where the elves had destroyed Twin Rivers's resident goblin population. According to the elf, the magic around the doorway was unstable enough that it could take the skin off a person as easily as Lailu could peel an orange. She eyed the darkened wood in front of her. "Is it *safe?*"

"Have I ever taken you somewhere that wasn't safe before?"

She glared at him.

"Wait, wait, don't answer that." Ryon laughed.

"I wasn't going to. I know we don't have all night."

"Look at you!" Ryon crowed. "Another good insult! I'm so proud. And to answer your question, of course it's safe."

"Are you sure?"

"Well, as long as you go through with me. If you try using it on your own, the consequences could be . . . disastrous." He smiled, and Lailu half expected a wink, but then he froze.

"What is it?" Lailu whispered. She looked around. The shadows seemed somehow darker than they had a moment ago. Colder, too.

Ryon circled slowly, eyes squinting into each dark corner. Then he shrugged. "Nothing. I just thought I heard clicking."

Lailu's eyebrows shot up. But then, it wouldn't be completely shocking to find one of Wren's contraptions here in the spot of her mother's death. She inched closer to Ryon.

"Whatever it is, it can't follow us through the doorway." He grabbed her arm and pulled her toward him, wrapping his other arm around her in a tight embrace and then falling back against the wall.

Lailu barely had time to feel awkward about being crushed against Ryon's chest before she realized they were still falling, right through the elven doorway.

A cold, gooey substance enveloped her, like chilled tapioca pudding, squeezing against her eyelids, her ears, up her nostrils. The pressure pushed and pushed and then *pop!*—they were through to the other side.

Lailu staggered away from Ryon, gasping for breath.

"Huh. I wasn't entirely sure that would work," he said.

She whirled around and punched him in the shoulder.

"Kidding! Kidding!" he laughed.

"That . . . was . . . *horrible*! I never want to do that again!"

"Bad news on that," Ryon said. "Unless you'd prefer to stay here on this side of the city?"

Lailu shuddered and ran her hands down her shoulders, her skin crawling with remembered stickiness. It was almost as bad as skilly-wig slime. "You should have warned me." She gave Ryon one last scowl, then looked around.

The doorway had spit them out under a weeping willow in a beautiful, wide-open park. A giant fountain burbled across from her, the water cascading from a marble bust. Past the fountain stretched a wide cobblestoned path with carefully manicured trees on either side and the occasional well-placed bench.

"Is this Gilded Island?" she asked.

"Yes, as promised. Do I deliver, or what?" Ryon winked.

"Don't test me," Lailu muttered. She recognized the park now as Ruby Park, a place for the social elite to stroll around and show off their wealth. She could already see a couple of richly dressed girls gossiping on a marble bench, and past them she noticed guards posted at each entrance of the park, guards walking up and down the streets outside the gates, even one guard walking the edges, all wearing that familiar deep brownish-red uniform. The color of dried blood.

Elister's color.

"Elister moves quickly," Ryon said, noticing her gaze. "As soon as the barrier went up, he mobilized. Of course, after what happened to the guards posted on *your* side of the city, you can't really blame him."

"The guards on my side?" Lailu thought of Seala, who'd been missing since just before the last spi-tron attack. "What happened to them?"

"Let's just say they won't be guarding anything for a long, long time," Ryon said grimly.

The lights around the park clicked on like magic, just as the shadows started to grow longer. Lailu flinched away from those glowing orbs, so much like the ones in the Industrial District. Only this light didn't waver and buzz. The scientists were getting better.

She realized Ryon was already striding down the wide path, leaving her behind.

"Wait, what do you mean about the guards?" Lailu asked, jogging to catch up to him.

He pulled a pair of white silk gloves from his pocket and slid them on over his hands, then adjusted his coat, flipping the collar up to frame his face. "We'll talk about it later," he said.

"Will we really?" Lailu asked, doubtful.

"It's possible." He passed a wealthy couple, the woman in puffy skirts and sleeves with a dramatically cinched waist, while the man wore a coat very similar to the one Ryon had on. Ryon nodded once at them and received a nod in exchange. Equal to equal.

Lailu looked down at her own clothing, glad that Hannah had insisted on dressing her up. Still, she felt like that couple could tell she didn't belong here by the way they both seemed to look down their noses at her. Or maybe she was just being sensitive.

She caught up to Ryon just as he adjusted his top hat.

Lailu blinked. "Where did you get a hat?" That thing would not fit in his coat, would it?

"That would be a secret." He winked. Of course he winked. "Oh, and please call me Rhone while we're here."

"Wait, what?"

"The name Ryon is getting a little too known for my liking."

They strolled out of the park under an archway that would someday hold roses, but not this bitter-cold season. It made Lailu miss home. Around her village the winter roses were the prettiest of all.

As they continued down the wide, tree-lined path, Lailu was very aware of the way the gossiping girls stopped talking and stared at Ryon, and even more aware of the way he inclined his head and smiled at them. He swept out of the park and past the guard posted at the gate, acting as if the guard didn't exist. Lailu tried to do the same thing, even though she felt like she was being scrutinized all over again.

Lailu's frown deepened as they left the park behind. The change in Ryon as he strutted down the street bugged her. It made her think of her recent conversation with Hannah about Ryon's many masks. If she hadn't known about the wrinkled shirt and the half-buttoned vest under his coat, she would say that Ryon looked the Gilded Island part perfectly. Like he'd grown up in one of the fancy houses on one of these fancy streets. And maybe he had. She really had no idea.

She didn't know Ryon at all.

He slowed his pace until she was walking beside him, stealing little sideways glances in his direction.

"You know," he said finally, breaking the gnawing silence. "If you keep looking at me like that, you might make your little chef friend jealous."

Lailu's face flushed, but she refused to be drawn into that. "You really don't like him," she said instead.

"Not particularly."

Lailu thought this over. *Everyone* liked Greg. It was one of the least likable things about him. "Why not?"

"I think you summed it up quite nicely when you called him a jerk." They turned off the main road just past the Gilded Island Bridge and onto a side street. Still wide, the cobblestones were smooth and glossy beneath those ever-present lights.

Lailu crossed her arms. "Plate calling the frying pan flat."

"What?" Ryon laughed. "I've never heard that one before. And actually, I don't really care one way or the other for Greg. I just think you deserve better. And here we are, Paulie Anna's."

For the first time in her life, Lailu was relieved to see the witch's doorway up ahead. She needed an exit from this conversation.

"I'll wait out here," Ryon said.

"You don't want to see Paulie? I thought she was your friend."

"Oh yes, but she'll ask awkward questions that I'm not in the mood to answer." He made a shooing motion. Lailu swallowed, then walked up the steps and knocked on the door. She glanced behind her once, but Ryon had already done his melt-into-the-shadows trick and was gone.

The door opened.

"Lailu!" Paulie's purple eyes lit up, and she drew Lailu inside, kissing her on both cheeks like they were the best of friends. "How nice to see you! How are your hands?"

"Oh! Um, better." Truthfully, her hands ached all the time, her fingers were stiffer than day-old bread, and she worried they'd never heal all the way. But Paulie's salve had helped a lot, and there was no reason to make her feel bad it hadn't done more. "I'm actually here about something else."

"Oh?" Paulie leaned back against her crowded countertop. Her shop looked the way Lailu remembered it from before the automaton attack, with shelves full of dried herbs and jars of salves stacked neatly, the air filled with the scent of lavender and cinnamon and something Lailu couldn't quite identify. Something spicy that smelled like it would be the perfect complement to a savory curry.

Lailu blinked, remembering her mission. "Would you take the curse off Vahn?" Immediately she knew she'd made a terrible, terrible mistake.

Paulie's eyes had gone as flat and cold as the lake in Lailu's village. "No," she said. "Never."

Lailu took a small step back. "It's not that I don't think he deserves it—"

"That selfish, conceited, arrogant . . ." Paulie took a deep breath, her nostrils flaring. "He deserves far worse than that silly little curse, but I don't dabble in black magic. Only the occasional shade of gray." She turned her back on Lailu and started shelving vials of powders, periodically checking a label.

"Please," Lailu begged. "He can't perform his hero duties with your curse on him."

"It's really not my problem."

"But he needs to hunt a phoenix."

"Still not my problem."

"It's been attacking a nearby village. Yesterday's paper said it burned down half of Wolfpine, and you know that's not that far from here."

Paulie pulled out a stopper and gave the jar a tentative sniff. "Needs more wormroot," she muttered, putting the jar on her kitchen counter and then finally facing Lailu. "Look, I like you, Lailu. I really do. But we both know Vahn can always go and inform Elister of his little problem"—she smirked—"and Lord Elister will put someone else on the case."

"He can't do that! Have you met Lord Elister? He'd *murder* Vahn." Elister was a man who viewed people as useful tools. What would he do with a hero who couldn't handle his missions?

Paulie regarded her coolly. "Regardless, Vahn can break his own curse. That is, if he's a *true* hero."

"What do you mean?"

"Well, every curse has a way for the cursed to break it. They just need to figure out how." Paulie picked up a box of pickled griffin feet. "In Vahn's case, he needs to get his head out of his butt and learn his lesson. In my opinion, the more painful the lesson, the better." She shoved the box onto the shelf with a little more force than necessary.

Lailu chewed her lip. She couldn't exactly blame Paulie; Vahn really did have his head up his butt. Not that Lailu would ever say that out loud. "Okay," she said instead, her shoulders slumping. "Well, thanks for your time."

"You're still planning on helping him, aren't you?"

"Yeah," Lailu said. "I have to."

"Why? He wasn't particularly nice to you either, as I recall."

Lailu shrugged. "Family debt."

Paulie paused, her hand stilling on her rows of jars. "I understand about family debt."

"Then . . . you'll help?"

Paulie sighed and leaned back against her shelves. "Breaking a curse is . . . complicated. It would take time and effort, and frankly I've wasted enough of both on that big oaf. But"—she smiled—"I might be convinced to try."

"Really?" Lailu gushed. "That would be—"

"If," Paulie continued, holding up a hand, "you brought me back a phoenix tail feather."

Lailu hesitated. That meant she'd still have to help Vahn hunt, and he'd still be cursed while *on* the hunt. But . . . she could tell it was the best deal she'd get. "I'll see what I can do," she said.

"Cute hair, by the way."

That reminded Lailu of Hannah's note, and she pulled it from her vest and passed it to Paulie. "Hannah sent that."

Paulie broke the seal and read quickly, her eyebrows shooting up. "Did Ryon take you through the barrier, perchance?"

"Yes." Lailu considered. "Well, more or less."

"Interesting." She folded the letter and tapped it against her mouth, deliberating. "I have something for you," she said abruptly. "And for Hannah. Wait here." Paulie disappeared into the back of her small shop. A few minutes ticked by. Outside, Lailu could hear the street filling with more people as the evening rolled closer. What was happening at Mystic Cooking? Were the elves still there? Were there people gathering, even though Lailu wasn't there to cook for them?

"Here." Paulie reappeared with two small boxes cupped in her hand. She opened one and drew out a pair of dangling rubies. "May I?"

"Um, sure . . ." Lailu was too nervous to tell Paulie not to do whatever it was, and she froze as the other woman clipped the rubies to the phoenix pins in her hair. "Thank you."

"Give this set to Hannah, okay?"

Lailu took the other box and slipped it inside her inner vest pocket, then turned to leave.

"Oh, and Lailu?"

Lailu turned.

"Tomorrow there will be a freezing rain, right about midmorning. That would probably be the best time to hunt the phoenix."

Lailu nodded.

"Good luck."

"Thanks," Lailu said. She knew she'd need it.

She left Paulie's shop, her mood plummeting with each step. How was this hunt going to work? Vahn wouldn't be much use, and Lailu honestly had no idea how to hunt a phoenix. Oh, she'd read *Gingersnap's Theories*, of course. But even those were a bit vague. Not that she'd ever admit that to Greg.

Greg.

She turned back toward Gilded Island and started walking. A few seconds later she became aware of Ryon walking next to her. "Smooth," she told him.

"I know, right? I'm getting sneakier. And even *I* didn't think that was possible."

He was so smug, Lailu didn't say anything else, and moments later they arrived at LaSilvian's Kitchen.

Greg's uncle had a lot of money, so it wasn't like he'd had to work hard to get this huge stone and wood-paneled building. It wasn't like it made him a better chef, either, just because he had those people willing to throw money at him. Still. She was always equal parts resentful and awed when she stood in front of that massive iron-lined door. What must it feel like to cook in there? To have the best cooking supplies, the newest inventions, and crowds of people eager to eat in your fancy restaurant?

The door opened, and a group of handsomely dressed men stepped out, the sound of voices floating out behind them. Greg's place seemed packed already, even though his dinner hours had just barely begun.

"Evening," one of the group said, tipping his hat to Ryon.

"And so it is," Ryon muttered, watching them leave. He shook his head. "I've never understood that. It's not like he's wishing me a pleasant evening, or any kind of evening at all. Just stating the time of day, as if I can't see it for myself."

"Would you prefer he wish you a terrible evening?"

"Maybe." Ryon pulled his top hat down lower until it completely shadowed his eyes and most of his face. "I guess I'd prefer he wished something at all, instead of these empty phrases."

"Most people who wish you a pleasant evening are only reciting an empty phrase too," Lailu pointed out. "It's just a longer empty phrase. They don't really care what kind of evening you have."

Ryon smiled. "That is absolutely true. Especially in this place."

And Lailu found herself smiling too. Because she'd discovered a truth about Ryon, one even his masks couldn't hide. He definitely did *not* come from Gilded Island. He didn't belong here any more than she did, or he wouldn't even notice the hollowness hidden beneath the glitter surrounding them.

"Well, this is where I leave you," he said.

"Wait, you're not coming in with me? Again?"

"To visit Greg?" Ryon snorted. "I'll pass. Besides, I have a few errands to run."

"What kind of errands?"

"The kind you probably don't want to know about." He winked, and Lailu wondered what job he was doing for his brother. "But I'll be back in an hour to collect you and take you through the doorway." He took her hand, his silk glove cool beneath her fingers. "Don't let that smug chef in there give you a hard time, okay?" And he brushed his lips over her knuckles, like she was some kind of aristocratic lady herself.

Lailu's body was ice, her cheeks fire, as Ryon released her and walked away.

Much as she hated to admit it, she liked the way his coat looked, how the fabric rippled with his movement.

She pressed the backs of her hands against her hot face, then squared her shoulders and stepped inside LaSilvian's Kitchen.

24

GREG'S DECISION

Dante LaSilvian, Greg's aristocratic uncle and co-owner of LaSilvian's Kitchen, had never liked Lailu. She could tell by the way he stopped walking to turn and scowl at her that nothing had changed, despite Hannah's fancy outfit. And it wasn't just a scowl; Lailu herself was quite fond of scowls in general. It was the way his lips curled at the edges, how his long nostrils flared, like he'd just bitten into a flaky golden pie and discovered a raw skilly-wig in the middle.

Lailu knew she should be used to that kind of look. The gods knew she'd received it plenty of times while at the Chef Academy. That look coupled with whispered comments about her secondhand uniforms, snide remarks about "scholarship students," and how the Academy would just let anyone in these days. The first time it happened, she'd been so shocked she'd just stood there, quivering like a fork stabbed into a hunk of meat while tears streamed down her face.

Master Sanford, her favorite teacher at the Academy, had found her frozen in place an hour later, still crying. "Student Loganberry," he'd barked. "You stop those tears this instant."

And she'd tried, but they'd just kept coming, no matter how quickly she'd wiped them away.

He'd scratched at his beard, regarding her with his one good eye. "Let me guess: you had to deal with cutting remarks and whispers back at your village, didn't you?"

She'd nodded, remembering all the times the other kids back home had made fun of her for her hunting and cooking obsessions and her mother's long absences.

"And you thought the whispers would stop once you arrived here, didn't you? That here you'd be around people who understood?"

She'd nodded again.

And he'd thrown back his head and laughed, loud and booming, the same way he did everything. She'd been so surprised her tears had stopped instantly. "I'm going to let you in on a secret," he said, still chuckling. "They almost never understand. They don't *want* to. It's much easier to see what you expect to see. Digging beneath those initial impressions takes work, and people are lazy. You'll find that's the truth no matter where you go, tiny village to big city."

"What should I do, then?" Lailu had whispered. "They hate me. They think I should leave."

"Do *you* want to leave?"

"No!"

"What do *you* want? And don't think about your answer," he snapped. "I want the truth, not some pretty package."

"I want to be the greatest master chef in all of Savoria." The words had slipped from Lailu before she could swallow them down, and she'd waited for Master Sanford's booming laugh again.

Instead, he'd nodded once, like that was a perfectly reasonable goal. Like he'd expected nothing less. "Then remember one thing, Student Loganberry: you sharpen a knife by scraping it against a dull surface." He'd stepped in closer, his grizzled face filling her field of vision. "And don't let me catch you crying over this again. Lazy people don't deserve your tears."

After that day Lailu always managed to keep her chin up and her tears hidden. Sometimes she'd retreat to her tiny closet of a room and cry until her eyes burned and her mouth was dry. But she never let the others know their comments got to her. Never let them see the hurt.

And she wasn't about to start now. She met Dante scowl for scowl, her head held high.

"What are you doing here?" he sniffed. "I thought you and your ilk were trapped outside the city."

Lailu blinked. "You mean trapped on the *other side* of the city."

Dante frowned. "You know what I meant."

"You know," Lailu said quietly, "I do. I know *exactly* what you meant." She thought of what Fahr had said back at Mystic Cooking, about these people in their gilded homes. About how none of them cared about the poorer districts, those Twin Rivers citizens who clung to the outskirts.

The elves didn't care about them either, except as useful tools. But at least it meant they *had* a use for them. Was it better to be used, or forgotten?

Before she could decide, Greg walked out of the kitchen, laden with an overflowing tray. He glanced over, his eyes meeting hers across the crowded restaurant, and stopped, a slow, disbelieving smile unfurling over his whole face. Lailu grinned back, relief flooding through her. He was fine. She hadn't realized how worried she was until this moment, how much Wren's threat had soaked into the back of her mind, like bread dipped in soup.

He dropped his full tray on the nearest table and sprinted over.

"Greg, is this really professional behav—" Dante started.

Greg ignored his uncle completely, grabbed Lailu in a hug, and spun her around in a circle before setting her back down again.

She laughed, giddy. "Nice to see you, too, Greg."

His grin was uncontainable, bursting from his eyes and radiating outward. "I never thought I'd hear you say that."

"Don't get used to it. This will probably be the only time I ever use those words in that order."

"Nice hair, by the way."

"You like it?" Lailu touched one of her buns, her finger sliding along the silver netting. "Hannah's creation." She bumped one of the dangling gems. "And Paulie's."

"It's very cute."

"Ah-hem," Dante said.

Lailu and Greg both turned to look at him.

"I hardly think this lack of decorum suits you," he told Greg, his tone icy. "Or my establishment."

"You mean *our* establishment?" Greg's smile vanished.

Dante stiffened, his eyes flicking to the side. Lailu followed his gaze, noticing first an ugly burn mark in the hardwood floors. A very familiar sort of burn mark. The kind an exploding spi-tron might make. She forced herself to look up past the burn to the wall above it, where a certificate hung, proclaiming him "Master Chef LaSilvian" and granting him joint-ownership status of LaSilvian's Kitchen.

Dante swiveled back to face his nephew. "As your *partner*, I'd suggest, respectfully, that you take your . . . business"—he jerked his chin at Lailu—"into the back."

Greg pressed his lips together and nodded sharply, once. "Would you be so kind as to serve my customers, Uncle, while Master Chef Loganberry and I continue our discussion in the kitchen?"

"Nothing would give me greater pleasure," Dante said, even as his eyes told a different story. Lailu could feel those eyes stabbing her in the back as she followed Greg through the crowded restaurant.

"I think nothing would give him greater pleasure than carving me up as one of your specials," she muttered once they were safely inside the kitchen.

Greg ran a hand back through his thick, curly hair. "Sorry about that. He's been having a rough day."

"Plus he hates me."

"Plus he hates you," Greg agreed. His stove rattled, one of the burners turning on, then off, then on again, the metal glowing a bright cherry red. Greg sighed. "I'm having a rough day too, actually." He stalked to the stove, twisted a few dials, then smacked the side for good measure.

Lailu winced. Greg had an amazing stove, even better than her own, if she were honest. It filled the whole side of his kitchen, giant pipes thrusting through the back wall, eight burners on top, and an oven big enough for Lailu to sit inside comfortably. "Be nice," she cautioned as Greg whacked it again.

"This *is* nice," he grumbled. "This thing has been randomly turning off and on all day." He fiddled with it for a few more seconds until the burner finally turned off and stayed off. "Anyhow. I'm almost ready to buy out my uncle's share of the restaurant. Once I do that, he'll go back to his vineyards and leave me in peace."

"Really? You're planning on buying out your uncle's interests?" Lailu had always assumed Greg liked the legitimacy his uncle brought to this restaurant. After all, Dante was well respected among the nobility. His name attached to this restaurant had been a large part of its immediate success.

"I've found that often my uncle's interests don't align with my own," Greg said, eyes on her. "Besides, now that you own Mystic Cooking by yourself, I need to catch up. Can't let you get ahead, even by an inch."

"I've noticed that about you," Lailu muttered. "So, what's up with the burn mark out there?"

"One of Wren's little spi-trons paid me a visit. Scared the pudding out of Uncle Dante." Greg smirked. "But I took it out pretty quickly."

Lailu fiddled with the ends of her shirt. So, Wren *had* attacked Greg.

"You look worried," Greg said. "Didn't think I could handle myself in a fight without you?"

"Do you really want me to answer that?"

"No, probably not." Greg laughed. "So, how did you make it over here? Did Elister's pet scientists get the barrier down already?"

Lailu shook her head and told him about Ryon's escort.

Greg frowned. "A really nice coat, huh?" he said when she was done.

"Is that seriously your takeaway? The elves have another secret entrance into the middle of the city!"

"Which is terrible but not surprising. We knew they had to have another way in and out. Now, back to this coat. How nice would you say it was?"

"Would you stop with the coat?"

"It's just, you never mention clothing. If you were Hannah, I wouldn't even have noticed."

"I'm sorry I said anything about the coat," Lailu grumbled. "Can we drop it? I actually have a favor to ask of you."

"Oh?" Greg's eyes lit up. "You know I love doing favors for you. It means you owe me."

"I know." Lailu sighed. She looked around the kitchen. Skillywigs in various stages of cookery cluttered every surface. Skillywigs. She shook her head. They'd really sunk low. "I'm actually probably doing *you* a favor, inviting you in on this action. I've lined up a new hunt for us." And she told him about Vahn's request to hunt the phoenix.

She thought Greg would be excited, but by the end he was frowning, not looking at her. "Let me get this straight," he said. "You want me to help Vahn hunt a phoenix?"

"To help *me* hunt a phoenix," Lailu corrected.

"But *for* Vahn, right?"

She hesitated. This might be like Ryon's coat all over again, one of those details she shouldn't have shared. "Um, it would help him, yes," she began carefully, "but it would also help us. Glory and fame. Actual decent mystic cuisine."

Greg shook his head.

"What do you mean by that?" Lailu asked.

"Usually when someone shakes their head, they mean *no*."

Lailu scowled. "I know what it usually means. But in *this* case, what does it mean?"

Greg matched her scowl for scowl. "It means no, I will not help Vahn hunt a phoenix."

Lailu could hardly believe it. She'd just assumed Greg would be a part of this hunt, that he'd want to help her. It felt like she'd followed a new recipe perfectly only to discover its list of ingredients was all wrong. "You won't help," she said flatly, when she could find the words again. "May I ask why?"

"Because it's impossible to hunt and cook a phoenix."

"Master Gingersnap says—"

"I don't care what Master Gingersnap says! It's impossible, okay? And besides, Vahn brought this trouble on himself. If you want to go running any time he bats his big blue eyes and asks for help, then fine. Whatever. But I refuse to be a part of it." He crossed his arms.

Lailu gaped at him. "You . . . you . . ." She took a deep, slow breath. "You might not remember, but Vahn saved my brother's life once. Even though I don't like how he treated Hannah, and I agree he brought this curse on himself, I still owe him. He asked me for help. I'm going to help." She narrowed her eyes. "With or without you."

"Then it will have to be without me," Greg said. Behind him, his stove flared up again, all eight burners turning on. He didn't even flinch.

"Fine." Lailu crossed her arms, mirroring his pose.

"Fine."

Knock, knock. Knock.

"What?" Greg snarled, not taking his eyes off Lailu.

The kitchen door opened. Dante stepped in, looking happier than Lailu had ever seen him before in her life. "The city guards are here for your *guest*," he said.

Three armed guards brushed past him, crowding the kitchen. "Lailu Loganberry?" one of them asked.

Lailu nodded.

"You're to come with us. Immediately."

"Why?" Greg dropped his arms.

The head guard, a woman with a narrow face and short dark hair, looked him over briefly, then sniffed. "It really doesn't concern you, Master LaSilvian."

"Am I being arrested?" Lailu asked, her mouth dry.

"Yes," said one of the other guards, a tall, balding man with a nose the color and shape of a tomato.

"For what?" Greg demanded.

The guards exchanged looks. "For being short?" Tomato-nose suggested.

"What?" Lailu spluttered. "Being short is not a crime." Her lack of height used to bother her, but ever since she'd opened Mystic Cooking and achieved master chef status, it just didn't seem to matter anymore. Still, she could tell Greg found this hilarious and knew she'd be hearing about it again. Probably often. She scowled.

"Okay, fine, you're not being arrested," the head guard admitted. "But your accompaniment is mandatory."

"That doesn't make sense," Greg said. "If she's not being arrested, you can't make her go with you."

"Told you we should've arrested her," Tomato-nose muttered.

"What's that smell?" another guard asked, his nostrils flaring. "Smells like . . . burning. And . . ."

"Gas," Lailu realized, glancing at the stove. All eight of the burners were now so hot, they'd gone past red and straight into white, with blue flames licking up. And beneath the stove itself . . .

A flash of blue, the scuttle of little metal feet. A spi-tron.

Lailu reacted instantly, grabbing the closest weapon to hand—the head guard's long metal baton—and lunging forward. Behind her, she heard the guard yelling and the sounds of crashing, but Lailu was already sliding forward on her stomach. She thrust the baton under the stove, stabbing it into the spi-tron and crushing the metal thing against the wall.

"What was that?" Greg asked, wide-eyed.

"Another spi-tron," Lailu said grimly. "You might want to

check the rest of the room. I think it was trying to make your stove explode." She pushed herself to her feet and looked at the shocked faces around her, then handed the head guard her baton.

"O-kay," the guard said slowly. "I'm not sure what just happened, but you're definitely under arrest now."

"Wait, what?" Lailu blinked. "I just saved everyone!"

"You stole my baton."

"I gave it right back!"

"Doesn't matter." The guard smiled, triumphant. "Stealing a weapon is a criminal offense."

25

ELISTER'S GAME

"This was hardly necessary." Lord Elister's face gave nothing away, those green eyes as cool as ever, but his tone was disapproving enough that all three of the guards flinched back.

"But, sir, she was up to something in that restaurant," the head guard said, her narrow face turning red under Elister's critical gaze. "And you did tell us to bring her to you."

"Bring her, yes. Not arrest her." Elister sighed.

"Er, sorry, sir. Our apologies, sir."

"Oh, go away, would you?" Elister waved his hands. "You're dismissed. Go . . . patrol."

"Yes, sir. Of course." The guards bowed and practically ran into one another on their rush out the door.

Elister ran a hand over his face. He was sitting behind a small table, and across from him sat a very familiar redheaded girl. Even though Lailu could see only her back, she knew it was Wren, and her fury burned hotter than Greg's malfunctioning stove. Wren could have killed Greg! And he had *nothing* to do with her mother's death.

"And what were you up to in that restaurant?" Elister asked.

Lailu scowled. "Maybe you should ask Wren what *she* was up to. She almost destroyed Greg's restaurant! *And* Greg," she added. She realized some of her anger was reserved for Greg, too. She'd gone through all this trouble to get to him, and he wouldn't even help her.

"Wren?" Elister said pointedly.

Wren's shoulders hunched up around her ears. "I . . . wanted to send Greg a message."

"And what kind of message?" Elister asked, his tone coaxing but stern, like a mother asking her toddler what was in her mouth. "Did you send one of your creations to threaten him?"

Wren nodded.

"Wren Volan, that is very disappointing. We've talked about this, haven't we?"

She nodded again.

"And what did we say?"

"There's a time and a place for attacks," she whispered.

"And Gilded Island is never the place," Elister finished. He looked up at Lailu. "There, all settled. Wren won't do that again. Right, Wren?"

"Right."

Elister smiled at Wren. It was the same kind of smile he'd once given Walton, the automaton Starling and her scientists created and the best butler Elister had ever had. A fond smile with actual warmth in it.

Lailu's jaw dropped.

"Now," Elister told Wren, "as I was saying, in this game, controlling the king is the key to winning. But the king itself is a weak piece." He moved something on the table. Lailu craned her neck, noticing the black-and-white board, and the pieces, and recognized it as a game of chess. Her father used to carve the boards and pieces, and they always sold out whenever a trade caravan passed through their village. For all she knew, this was one of his.

"The queen, however," Elister continued, "can move all over the board. Take the queen out, and the rest is easy."

Lailu pressed her lips together. She knew some people believed that the queen was the most valuable piece, but her father had always taught her not to underestimate the other pieces.

"Do you disagree, Miss Loganberry?" Elister asked abruptly.

Wren turned to look her full in the face, her eyes dark with fury. *Murderer*, she mouthed.

Lailu glared right back, her usual guilt gone in the face of Wren's most recent attack. Still angry, she met Elister's amused stare. "My father taught me that the other pieces on the board have more rigid movements, but if you place them in the right place at the right time, they can win you the game while your opponent is distracted, watching that queen."

Elister steepled his fingers in front of his chin, considering her. It reminded Lailu of the way she studied her pantry when she was deciding what to use in her next special. "Your father is a wise man." He turned back to Wren. "This is another good lesson for you. A piece that moves in only one direction *can* be just as deadly as a queen, if placed in the right spot, at the right time." He moved a rook.

"Can't I take that piece now, though?" Wren asked, studying the board.

"Oh, yes."

"So . . . you sacrificed it?"

"Absolutely. But you see how that sets you up for my next move? That's the third important lesson." He looked up, catching Lailu's eyes. "Know which pieces are expendable, which can be sacrificed to bring you closer to your goal."

Lailu went cold at his words. It didn't sound like he was talking about the game at all. She straightened, the ropes around her wrists scraping her skin.

Elister frowned. "Did they seriously tie your wrists? Oh, for the love of . . ." He stood and strode around the table, sliding one of his infamous curved blades out from its secret sheath in the back of his shirt, and sliced through the ropes around Lailu's wrists in one swift, terrifying motion.

Lailu shook out her hands until blood flowed back into her fingers.

"I see they left your knives on you, though. Not very thorough. I'd prefer they not have tried to arrest you at all, but it's even worse that they failed to *properly* arrest you." His frown deepened, and Lailu flinched back. "Don't make that face, Miss Loganberry. My displeasure is not aimed at you."

Lailu hadn't realized she was making any kind of face, although her heart hammered much too fast, and now that blood was flowing into her hands again, they were all sweaty and gross. The last time she'd seen Elister, he'd been overseeing the abuse of her restaurant, and coupled with Wren's presence, she felt about as safe here as an unattended plate of fresh-baked cookies. The sooner she could get out of this office and back to the safety of Mystic Cooking, the better.

"I should clarify," Elister said. "My displeasure is not aimed at you . . . as long as you tell me what I need to know."

Lailu gulped. "And what is that?" Then she realized. "You want to know how I'm over on this side of the barrier." Should she tell him? Would that be a betrayal of Ryon? Of the elves? What would they do to her if they found out she told their enemy about their secret doorway? What would they do to Ryon?

"You're making that face again. Relax. I don't understand why everyone is always so tense around me. I'm not an unreasonable man."

"O-of course not," Lailu managed. "But you do have a tendency to, uh, kill people."

"Only the ones who get in my way." He smiled.

Lailu wanted to point out that this was exactly why people were tense around him. But even she wasn't that brave.

"I already know about the secret doorway into Gilded Island, by the way," Elister continued. "I'm assuming that's how you got to this side?"

Lailu blinked. "Er, yes."

"Don't look so surprised. I have eyes and ears all over the city."

"Then what did you need to know?"

Elister leaned back against his desk, his face unreadable. "Correction: I have eyes and ears all over *this* part of the city. Including within the palace itself." His face twitched, and Lailu wondered if her mother was the one spying on the king for him. Would she do that? Would she really be more loyal to Elister than to the king himself?

Lailu tried to keep all of these thoughts off her face, imagining her features as dough being gently rolled flat.

Elister frowned.

"I'm making that face again, aren't I?" Lailu said.

"Honestly, I don't know *what* kind of face you're making. But I'll get to the point. Now that I'm cut off from the outskirts, I have no way of knowing what Fahr is up to. What is he planning? Surely this split through the city is only a temporary measure, a lead-in to some other, more permanent outcome."

Lailu thought of Fahr in her restaurant, talking to all the people, turning them against Elister and the rest of the Gilded Island aristocracy. What would Elister do to those people if he thought they might rebel against him? She swallowed. "I'm . . . not sure, sir. Fahr doesn't share his plans with me. None of the elves do." It was mostly true. Maybe Hannah was right; sometimes you really did need to stretch the truth a little.

"And you haven't noticed anything? Any hints at what he might want? Aside from the destruction of the scientists, which I cannot allow."

Lailu shook her head.

"Very well, then. We'll have to do this the hard way, Miss Loganberry."

"Master Loganberry," she corrected, her voice quavering. If he was going to attack her, she wanted to die with her title intact.

Elister's frown slid right off his face. "I was wondering if you would correct me. Excellent. I see I am putting my trust in the right hands after all."

Wren made a disgusted face, but she didn't say a word as Elister pulled an envelope from his inner vest pocket and passed it to Lailu, the paper thick and glossy beneath her fingers. "That is for Fahr. It's an offer for peace between our two camps. If he will tell me what it is he wants, perhaps we can come to some mutually beneficial arrangement. I'm hoping you, Master Loganberry, will help broker that peace."

"Me? How?" Suspicion pooled in Lailu's stomach like an under-cooked skilly-wig. "You don't need me to spy on them, do you?"

Elister laughed. "If I needed a spy, I would not be coming to you."

Lailu tried not to feel insulted.

"No, in this case, your inability to spy will be its own advantage. I believe the elves trust you as much as they trust any human. Your honesty will be what convinces Fahr that I mean what I say."

"And do you?" Lailu asked.

Elister regarded her. "I cannot afford to have the city divided at this time. Not with the Krigaen ambassador due within the next few months. One way or another, I must have peace, and I must have it soon. Do you believe me?"

Lailu nodded.

"Then help me get Fahr to negotiate."

"I'll do what I can," Lailu whispered, the envelope heavy in her hand, filled with the weight of that promise.

"Excellent. I leave it in your capable hands, then. And now"—

he turned to Wren—"would you be so good as to escort Lailu outside?"

"I can find my way—" Lailu began.

"I would hate for you to get lost," Elister said firmly, and Lailu wondered if there was something around here that he didn't want her to see.

"Is my mother around?" she asked quickly.

"I . . . haven't seen her," Elister said, but he said it in that careful way the elves had of talking. Like he wasn't lying, but he wasn't saying the whole truth.

Lailu frowned. "Isn't she spying for you?"

Elister tilted his head. "You know I could never honestly answer that. All I can tell you is that she's not here now, and I don't know when she'll return from . . . wherever it is that she is."

Lailu opened her mouth to ask another question.

"That was a dismissal," he said sharply.

"Come on," Wren said, tugging Lailu toward the door.

"Oh, and, Wren?" Elister called. "Escort her through the city, if you would. I'd prefer she not be accidentally arrested again."

Wren nodded and closed the door. "He's extra cranky right now because of the king," she told Lailu.

"Oh yeah? What's the king doing?"

"He seems to think *he* should run the kingdom, when everyone knows Elister is the best option."

"Everyone knows that, huh?" Lailu said.

"Everyone important," Wren said. She stopped, her eyes narrowing. "Why am I talking to you?"

Lailu figured Wren was pretty lonely, all shut up here with

only Elister and the other scientists for company. "Maybe you just wanted someone to talk to?"

Wren put her hands on her hips. "We're *not* friends."

"Oh, trust me, I know that. Especially now that you tried to kill Greg."

"Kill?" Wren blinked. "No . . . I'm saving that for you. I told you, I was sending him a message."

"Blowing up his stove?"

Wren frowned. "It was supposed to dismantle his stove. Not blow it up."

"Well, that's not what it was doing."

"They've been a little rebellious lately," Wren muttered. "All of my inventions. I think it's the magic—" She clapped a hand over her mouth.

"The magic?"

Wren slowly lowered her hand. "We're not talking anymore."

Lailu glanced up and down the hall. Elister's mansion always gave her the creeps. Maybe it was the too-high ceilings, even here, in the hallway, or how extremely well lit it all was. "Fine. We don't need to talk."

They started down the long hall in complete, icy silence. Lailu was very aware of the space between them, the sound of Wren breathing. Twice Lailu started to say something, but both times the words died before they could escape her mouth. What could she really say? Whatever friendship they'd had was more broken than Lailu's old shrine to Chushi.

26

Disastrous Consequences

*L*ailu stepped out into open air and breathed a sigh of relief. Then Wren stepped out next to her, and her heart sank. Apparently Wren really *was* going to escort her through the city. Lailu waited for Wren to do something, but she just walked, her face scrunched around the edges like one of Greg's fancy pie-crusts.

Wordlessly, they continued side by side down the paved path away from Elister's house and past the horseless carriages parked nearby. Lailu glanced at them, remembering the time Wren had given her a terrifying ride home in one back when they were friends. On that ride Wren had confessed Lailu was actually her *only* friend.

"Mama doesn't usually approve of my fraternizing with children," Wren had said. "But she likes you well enough. I'm allowed to be friends with you." It had seemed so lonely, imagining Wren wanting to play with other kids and having a mother who wouldn't let her, who kept her isolated. And now that she and Lailu were enemies, Wren wouldn't have any friends at all.

Lailu bit her lip, fighting off a wave of sadness. Wren had brought this on herself. Besides, Wren had not only attacked her, but now Greg, too. Still, as angry as she was about all that, she couldn't bring herself to hate Wren. After all, Wren *had* saved her from her own mother. Starling would have killed Lailu—and Hannah and Ryon—if Wren hadn't tried to stop her.

Maybe that was the whole problem right there. If Wren hadn't done anything, Lailu would be dead but Starling would still be alive. Lailu mulled that over, softening it in her mind as she walked. She'd never thanked Wren, mostly because she'd gotten caught in that explosion, and when she woke up, Wren had already been trying to attack her. And how *did* you thank someone for helping you when it meant the death of their mother?

Lailu glanced at Wren, walking stony-faced next to her. She should say something. She should at least try. But the words dried up in her mouth faster than overcooked fyrian chicken, and before she could think of what to say, they'd arrived at Ruby Park. "I guess this is goodbye," Lailu said.

"I'm supposed to follow you all the way to the doorway so I can report back to Lord Elister where it is."

"I thought he already knew."

"Not the precise location. I mean, he'd find it eventually. But I'm speeding up the process. Staying useful to him, so he'll let me live here longer."

Lailu frowned. "Would he really kick you out if you weren't useful?"

"I don't know."

Lailu remembered the way Elister had smiled so warmly. "I think he likes you, Wren," she said.

Wren missed a step, stumbling, then caught herself. "Really?" she managed.

"Really. He almost acted like you were, I don't know, a favorite niece or something."

Wren seemed to consider this as they walked through the park, stopping next to the giant weeping willow at the opposite end. Then she shook her head. "Elister's just like that with everyone."

Did Wren really think people were only nice to her if she was useful to them? But then, that was exactly how her mother had treated her. As long as Wren did what Starling told her to, she'd paid attention to her. Otherwise, Wren was discarded faster than week-old pastries.

Lailu glanced around. Ryon was nowhere in sight. It had definitely been more than an hour, though. Would he come back for her? No one else was around, either. Not even the guards from earlier. She frowned. "Where is everyone?"

"Elister instituted a curfew. Makes it easier to spot those who don't belong." Wren gave Lailu a pointed look.

"I'll be gone soon," Lailu said. "Trust me, I don't want to stay here any longer than I have to either."

"Then what are you waiting for?" Wren cocked her head to the side. "Ryon, right? You need him to go through the doorway safely, don't you?"

Lailu hesitated. Wren had a bad habit of attacking Ryon and taking his magic-neutralizing blood.

"I'm not going to do anything to him," Wren said. "I promised Elister I'd be on my best behavior, and there will be plenty of time after . . ."

"After what?" Lailu asked.

"You'll see." Wren smiled coldly.

Lailu sighed. "Wren, I know you hate me now, and I understand. You tried to help me, and it led to your mother's death, and—"

"Stop talking," Wren said.

"And I'm sorry that happened." Lailu forced herself to continue. "I'm sorry I never thanked you for helping me—"

"I said *stop talking*!" Wren put her hands over her ears, tears streaming down her face.

Lailu's eyes widened. "Wren?"

"I didn't mean . . . I didn't . . ." Wren gasped. She dropped her hands. "It's *your* fault. It has to be. Because if it isn't yours . . ." She turned on Lailu, her expression determined.

"It was an accident." Lailu took a step back. "But if there was anyone at fault, it was Starling herself."

"Don't you *dare* blame my mother," Wren snarled, shoving Lailu backward.

Lailu stumbled, her foot catching on one of the willow roots. Then she fell, right into the elven doorway.

It held beneath her for a second, and then the air itself seemed to melt away like cheese on a frying pan, bubbling under her weight before parting.

Lailu clawed at the air, but it was too late; she was falling through, and nothing could save her.

Wren's green eyes widened, her hand reaching forward. Then darkness swallowed everything, pressing in on all sides.

Lailu waited for pain, for the feeling of her skin peeling back like an orange, or worse, but all she got was the same icky sensation she'd had earlier. Like she was fighting her way through a wall of skilly-wigs.

Wham!

Lailu blinked up at the sliver of evening sky visible beneath the rotting slanted roof of a three-story establishment. The ground beneath her felt like hard cobblestone, and just beside her a puddle had formed around the mold-covered water pump that belonged to the Crow's Nest.

"I'm alive." Her fingers traced one of the cobblestones beneath her. Why was she alive? She sat up, moving slowly. Everything ached, but her skin was most definitely still intact. She breathed a silent prayer to Chushi and mentally promised she'd get a new shrine made as soon as this whole city-at-war thing was over.

Click, click, thud. Click, click, thud.

Lailu froze. Maybe Wren's creepy spi-tron had made it through the elves' doorway too.

Drag-thud. Click, click, click. Drag . . .

Lailu stood as silently as possible and turned in a slow circle, her hand dropping to her knife, but nothing was visible in the night in the dark, dark alley.

Drag, thud!

Goose bumps shivered up Lailu's spine. She might not be able to see it, but it was close—whatever it was—and *a lot* bigger than a spi-tron. Maybe Wren had invented something new. Something worse.

Lailu couldn't take it anymore. She turned and sprinted, leaving the old Crow's Nest behind as quickly as possible, and she didn't stop running until she reached the softly glowing sanctuary of Mystic Cooking.

Lailu's feet slowed, then stopped. Someone inside was awake. She shoved open the door, still breathing hard from her run.

Crash!

Hannah tumbled off a chair, then sprang to her feet with a mumbled, "I didn't take it!" She blinked at Lailu, then rubbed her eyes and looked around. "Oh."

"Guilty conscience?" Lailu asked. "Been re-homing anything lately?"

"Of course not. That was a different life." Hannah dusted off her robe, carefully not meeting Lailu's eyes. She stretched her neck, wincing, then sat back in her chair. "I must have dozed off there for a minute."

Hannah had clearly settled in for the long haul. On the table beside her, a teapot sat on a little heat cloth next to an empty teacup. Next to that lay a notebook with a rough sketch of the back of a woman's head, her hair in the nets Hannah had designed.

Lailu pulled out the chair across from Hannah and sat. "So, why are you still up?"

"I was worried about you, going off through some weird elven portal with Ryon like that."

"You were?"

"Of course I was! You're my only family here."

Lailu felt warm all over. "Aww, Hannah—"

"That, and Albert snores something awful." Hannah grimaced. "Listen, you can still hear him from down here."

Lailu cocked her head to the side, and sure enough she could hear the great mighty snores of Albert, formerly known as Neon.

"He's like some sort of wildebeest," Hannah continued. "Hard to believe one person could make so much noise."

"Yeah, almost sounds like three people. Maybe four."

"It's just temporary, though, right? We're agreed on that?"

"As soon as my mom gets back, he's out," Lailu promised. She frowned. *If* her mom came back, that was.

"So." Hannah's eyes twinkled in the low-level light. "How did it go with Greg?"

Lailu's frown deepened.

"Uh-oh. *That's* not a good face. I take it you guys got into another fight?"

"Not just that." Lailu sighed. "He said he won't help me. Then Wren set a trap for him, and I got arrested by Elister—"

"What?"

"And now Lord Elister wants me to set up a meeting between him and the elves. Then Wren tried to shove me through the elven doorway. Or maybe she didn't mean to do that—I don't really know. But I fell through and somehow miraculously survived." Lailu took a deep breath.

"Wow . . . ," Hannah said. She picked up her teacup, glanced inside, then frowned and set it back down again. "Empty," she lamented. "But it would've been cold anyway."

"Really? Wren just tried to kill me, and all you have to say is that your teacup is empty?"

"Eh, Wren's tried killing you several times already," Hannah said, waving this off. "Honestly, I'm more surprised that Greg told you he won't help you. That doesn't sound like him."

"Sounds *just* like him to me." Lailu swallowed hard. He had seemed so happy when she first got there. How did it all go sour like that?

"Let's start from the beginning. And I mean the beginning of your whole Greg encounter," Hannah added hastily. "All that other absurdity can wait." She twisted her long black hair into a bun, shoving her teaspoon into it to keep it in place.

Lailu cringed and whispered a silent prayer to the God of Cookery that he wouldn't strike her friend down for the obvious cutlery disrespect.

"So, spill," Hannah said.

Lailu spilled, about Paulie refusing to lift the curse, Ryon escorting her to Greg's door, Greg's snooty uncle, and then Greg's refusal to help because it would be helping Vahn, too.

"Really nice coat, you say," Hannah said, looking thoughtful. "How nice?"

Lailu sighed. "I really have to stop mentioning the coat."

"Did you mention it to Greg?"

"Maybe . . ."

Hannah shook her head.

"What?" Lailu said.

"Aww, honey, isn't it obvious? Greg's jealous."

"Of a coat? That's ridiculous."

"No, of . . ." Hannah stopped, scrutinizing Lailu's face. Her lips curved in a small smile. "Never mind." She fiddled with her charcoal pencil. "Are you still going to help Vahn with the phoenix hunt tomorrow?"

"Yes," Lailu said.

"You know he does *not* deserve your help."

Lailu shrugged. "I know that, but I still owe him."

Hannah reached across the table and laid her hand on Lailu's shoulder. "I know," she said. "I remember when he brought Lonnie home. It's why I liked him too. Well, that and his beautiful eyes," she admitted. "And that smile. I liked that, too." She lapsed into silence, then shrugged. "What can I say? I'm a sucker for pretty, sparkly things."

Lailu laughed.

"Speaking of pretty, sparkly things," Hannah said, "I saw your new gems. Paulie?"

Lailu touched the rubies pinned to the nets in her hair. "She gave me a pair for you, too."

Hannah's eyes lit up, and she thrust her hand out so fast her teapot wobbled. Lailu slid the small box from her vest and passed it over. "So shiny," Hannah murmured, looking inside the box. She bit her lip, then looked up at Lailu. "I know you told me not to keep secrets from you unless they were spy secrets."

"Yes?" Lailu asked carefully.

Hannah looked away. "Paulie kept . . . something . . . she got a while back. And she wanted to experiment with it. She asked me if I'd help her. I mean, I wasn't sure if I should, but she promised me some sparkly gems *and* she gave me the silver wire to use in my hair combs."

"I know how you are about hair combs."

"Pretty, sparkly things," Hannah repeated, shrugging. "Anyhow, that's where these gems came from."

"From . . . something that Paulie had?" Lailu asked, still not understanding.

"Yes, and they're the reason you were able to go through the barrier without Ryon."

"Really? Why?"

"She put something . . . special . . . inside them."

"I'm almost afraid to ask."

Hannah paused for a moment, grimacing guiltily. "Ryon's blood."

Lailu tried yanking the clips out of her hair.

Hannah laughed. "Here, let me." She walked over and gently unclipped them, then pulled off the nets so Lailu's hair tumbled around her shoulders in messy waves. "You know, that's a good look for you too."

"Focus, Hannah! I was wearing Ryon's *blood*?"

"Yes, but just a little of it. A few drops. Barely any blood at all."

Barely any blood at all. It was like Hannah had become a different person. Lailu shivered. "Does Ryon know about this?"

"Nope! And I don't intend to tell him either." Hannah winked. "He's not the only one around here who can keep a secret."

"Still mad at him, then?"

Hannah shrugged. "I'm not mad, really. Just . . . I feel like he doesn't think I know what I'm getting myself into, with this spying thing. But I do. And I know I dropped my cover with Starling, but I had to do that. I'm sure I can do this." She looked away. "I just need to show him."

Did Hannah like Ryon? Lailu had wondered that a few times, but she didn't have the courage to ask, and it was impossible for her to tell how Hannah felt. Was it just a need to prove herself as a spy? Or . . . something more?

Lailu studied Hannah's profile: her long, slender nose, those dramatic cheekbones and large dark eyes. Hannah was definitely the prettiest girl Lailu had ever seen. It was no wonder Vahn had been interested in her. And Ryon . . . Lailu didn't know how he felt about her friend either. He never said anything about Hannah's beauty, since he claimed Hannah got enough compliments, and that was probably true.

But he gave Lailu compliments. And he didn't like Greg. *I just think you deserve better.* How did Ryon feel about *her*?

Lailu hugged herself, her insides tangling in one confused knot, like skilly-wig tentacles. She didn't know how *she* felt either. This was why cooking was a thousand times better than anything else. If you gathered the right ingredients and followed the right recipe, you'd end up with exactly what you expected.

"Anyhow," Lailu said, "I think we should both get some sleep."

An especially loud snore shook the ceiling above them.

"*Try* to get some sleep," she amended.

27

PROBLEMS AND SOLUTIONS

Lailu woke slowly, a sunbeam gently caressing her face. It was hard to believe winter was just around the corner. She stretched and sat up. And then remembered: she was supposed to be hunting at first light!

Lailu leaped out of bed and frantically got dressed. How had she overslept? Why didn't anyone wake her? She looked across the room at Hannah's empty bed, then hurried past it and down the stairs.

"Oh, thank the gods you're up," Hannah said the moment Lailu opened the kitchen door. "I didn't want to wake you since you looked so tired yesterday, but we've got a problem."

"Is Vahn here?"

"What? Oh, no, he hasn't shown up yet. It's ... well." She pushed open the curtain to the dining room.

Lailu poked her head out. A dozen faces looked back at her.

"It's the chef!" one of them shouted.

Another banged her empty bowl on the table, and suddenly they were all doing that.

Bang! Bang! Bang!

And beneath that noise, they were chanting, "Hun-gry! Hun-gry!"

Lailu's jaw dropped.

"You all stop that right now," Hannah snapped. *"Now!"*

They stopped.

Hannah set her mouth grimly. "This is a business we're running here. Master Loganberry, out of the extreme kindness of her heart, gave you free food yesterday, but she didn't promise you anything today."

"But . . . we're hungry," a girl whined. She had to be about eight, with huge brown eyes and hair as curly as Wren's.

Lailu swallowed, mentally reviewing her cabinet space. She hadn't hunted anything since the skilly-wigs, and she'd been so distracted by that whole Greg-saying-no thing, not to mention the whole being-arrested thing, that she'd never packed up her portion of the slimy beasts. She didn't really have any food to make. Unless she kept it simple, used up the rice in her pantry and—

"Don't you dare," Hannah hissed.

"What?" Lailu said.

"I recognize that look. You're meal planning, aren't you?" Hannah glanced at all the people, then dragged Lailu through to the kitchen and yanked the curtain shut behind them. "Lailu, you can't just feed all these people! None of them can pay, and anyhow, we don't have any meals prepped."

"What kind of chef leaves people hungry?"

"A chef who is trying to run a successful business. And more to the point," Hannah sighed, "a chef who is rapidly running out of supplies."

"I still have all that rice in the cellar."

"Gone," Hannah said.

"All of it?"

"Most of it."

Lailu frowned. "Well, I froze a few carpe fish fillets, so I can—"

"Also gone."

"What?" Lailu shook her head. "That's impossible. But maybe . . . Maybe I used them up earlier." She would have remembered though; she had a very good memory for food. "Okay, how about that last hunk of mountain dragon? I froze about ten pounds for a rainy day." The nice thing about dragon was, as long as you prepared it correctly, it would keep for up to a year.

"You're not seriously considering feeding these people free dragon cuisine, are you?" Hannah crossed her arms.

"If that's all I have left, then yes."

"No."

Lailu was getting awfully tired of hearing that word. "It's *my* restaurant." She crossed her own arms.

"Fine. But you'll have to hunt a new dragon, then, because that meat is gone too."

Lailu gaped at her. "Are you sure?"

"I did a full inventory sweep when the first people trickled in here. Just in case I couldn't talk you out of feeding everyone."

"Okay, maybe my mom implemented a new storage system before she left. Or—"

The trapdoor to the cellar opened, and Albert poked his bald head out. His eyes widened, his cheeks bulging with . . . something.

"Or maybe someone is stealing your food," Hannah finished grimly.

Albert chewed, chewed, and swallowed. "Uh, just checking on the ol' generator," he said.

"Not as tasty as I remember, but I guess it's not fresh anymore." Someone else's voice carried up the stairs.

Albert went pale. "Shh," he hissed.

"What's the holdup?" another voice demanded.

"Who's down there with you?" Lailu asked.

"Um, no one. It's just me."

"Your lies are about as convincing as your disguises," Hannah said, her eyebrows drawing together. "And are you seriously eating *frozen dragon*?"

Lailu gaped. "What? You can't do that!" She'd leached all the poison out of the meat before freezing it, but still, eating it that way was a huge waste, a crime against good cuisine.

"It's only partly frozen," Albert mumbled, not looking at either of them. Then he stumbled to the side, and another head poked up. A head full of short, wiry gray hair sticking out in all directions beneath a bowler hat.

"Oh," the newcomer said, noticing Lailu and Hannah. "Hello there. I'm Zelda, formerly Zinc."

"And I'm Ignacious, formerly Magnesium." A third head, also covered in wiry gray hair, had poked up from the cellar. "We're siblings," he added, pointing at Zelda.

"Thank you for letting us stay here," Zelda said. "It's very kind of you. Even if your food is, er, rather stale."

"Wait, what?" Hannah said. "Stay here?"

"Stale? *My* food?" Lailu demanded.

"Just how many people are staying here with you, Albert?" Hannah asked.

"Stop pushing! Stop pushing!" Albert windmilled his arms, then slipped down the stairs with a series of thumps, followed by a muffled curse.

"Oops," Zelda said.

"No, that was me," a new voice said. A skinny man with a thin, ratlike face climbed his way past the siblings and into the kitchen. "Krypton," he proclaimed, grabbing Lailu's hand and enthusiastically pumping it up and down. "The others are reverting back to their old names, but I never liked mine, so I'm staying with Krypton."

"Tim is a perfectly fine name," Ignacious said.

"Quiet, Iggy," Tim/Krypton snapped. "Anyhow, we're all enjoying our accommodations very much. Quite lovely, you putting us all up like this, especially with Wren's most recent decree that she will, and I quote, 'personally tear apart anyone who harbors us the same way her mother used to rip the limbs off insects as a small child.' She's not lying about that either. I knew Starling as a child, and she used to take apart everything just to see if she could put it back together. Brutal girl."

"You didn't have to yank me down the stairs," Albert complained, joining the others in the kitchen.

"And how did you all get in?" Hannah demanded.

"Back door," Albert said sheepishly, pointing at the door that led out to Mystic Cooking's well. "You really should put a lock on that thing."

"Oh, we will. Immediately," Hannah assured him, eyes narrowing.

"So, you're all, er, staying here, then?" Lailu managed weakly.

"Albert said we could," Zelda said.

"Albert," Hannah growled. She turned to Lailu. "Where's my frying pan?"

"What the cutlery is going on here?" Ryon demanded.

Lailu looked past the scientists cluttering up her small kitchen. Ryon stood in the back door, his eyes wide, mouth a hard, thin slash.

"I'd really like it if you'd all stop stealing my lines," Lailu grumbled. And then she noticed the boy standing behind Ryon. "Greg?"

"Hey, Lailu." Greg smiled weakly. "I've reconsidered my answer."

For a second Lailu wasn't sure if she felt relieved or angry. Both, she decided. "So now you *want* to hunt a phoenix for Vahn?"

"I want to hunt a phoenix with *you*. Our own fame and glory and all that."

"I thought you said it was impossible."

He shrugged.

"That wasn't an answer," Lailu said.

"I'm still not sure it's possible, but I'm willing to try, okay?"

Lailu put her hands on her hips. "What makes you think I still want your help?"

"I thought you'd be happier to see me," Greg muttered.

"And *I* thought you'd always have my back. So I guess we were both wrong."

"Hey, I came here, didn't I?"

"Eventually," Lailu said.

"You know," Ryon began, and Lailu was suddenly very aware of all the people in her kitchen, all staring at her and Greg, "I hate to interrupt . . . Actually, who am I kidding? I enjoy interrupting very much." He grinned. No one returned it. "Tough crowd. Anyhow, Greg here took his time, but finally gathered up his limited courage—"

"Hey!" Greg protested.

"Only you were already gone," Ryon finished.

"Because Elister had me arrested," Lailu said. "Sort of. Which Greg knew."

"But after that. You left Elister's . . . and came here. Without me." Ryon's smile was gone, and Lailu realized what he was really asking: how had she gone through the doorway without him? She glanced at Hannah, then away.

"That's true," Krypton said. "You came through the barrier too."

"And who are you?" Ryon asked.

"Krypton, at your service." Krypton stuck his hand out. Ryon did not take it, so after a second the scientist just reached forward, grabbed Ryon's hand, and pumped it up and down like he was shaking a dead fish. "Pleasure, truly."

"Weren't you helping Starling drain the blood from elves?" Ryon tugged his hand free and stuffed it in his pocket.

"Er, well, yes," Krypton admitted.

"All of us were," Zelda added.

"But it was under duress," Albert said.

"You helped kidnap *me*." Ryon pointed at Albert.

"Me? No! Never!"

"I remember your face. You and your creepy metal people

cornered us at Paulie's place. Don't think I've forgot"—Ryon froze, his finger hovering in the air a few inches from Albert's nose—"ten," he finished, his arm drooping. "Paulie has some of my blood, doesn't she?" He turned to look at Lailu. "Paulie, who you visited first." His eyes narrowed, shifting from Lailu's face over to Hannah's.

Hannah lifted her chin and gazed back, giving nothing away. Lailu was impressed; she could feel her own face going pink and was sure their secret had been branded across her forehead. If he looked at her again, it would come spilling off her tongue like a mouthful of hot soup.

"What have you been up to, Hannah?" Ryon asked quietly.

Someone crashed through the curtain, tearing it right off the doorway and landing painfully in the middle of the kitchen. Ryon and Hannah didn't even flinch, just went on staring at each other, but everyone else jumped back.

Lailu looked at the figure struggling to get out of the curtain and knew there was only one person it could be. She sighed. "Hi, Vahn."

He finally managed to get his head and arms free, and lurched to his feet, his hair a giant tangle around his face. "Sorry I'm late. I ran into a few . . . complications." He raked his hair out of his eyes. "But I'm here now." He bundled up the curtain and thrust it at Albert. "Make yourself useful, would you?"

"Don't you order him around," Hannah snapped. "This man here is a brilliant scientist."

Albert stood up taller. "That's right."

"Then fixing the curtain should be no trouble for him." Vahn flashed his smile, then started forward, banging his shin on the edge of the counter and catching his toe on the kitchen's single chair before hobbling to a stop by the back door. "Ready to hunt?" he said, wincing.

"So . . . I'm guessing you'll still want my help after all," Greg said.

Lailu shrugged.

"That wasn't an answer," he pointed out.

"Well, it's the best you're going to get." Lailu tried to hang on to her anger, but she could hear people chanting "hun-gry" in her dining room, her kitchen was overflowing with renegade scientists, and she was about to embark on an impossible hunt with a cursed hero. To survive any of this, she needed Greg's help the way a good hydra feast needed lebinola spice. Her shoulders slumped. "Fine. I'm glad you're coming."

Greg smiled at her. "Me too. And not just because you'll owe me another favor."

"I will not!"

"Are we going?" Vahn asked. "Or arguing?"

"We can do both," Lailu decided, heading for the door.

"Uh, quick question," Greg said. "How are we going to leave? We're trapped on this side of the barrier."

"Ryon could—" Lailu stopped. Ryon and Hannah were huddled in the far corner of the kitchen having a very quiet, very heated conversation. Hannah's face had gone pale, all except for two bright spots on her cheeks, and her eyes glittered. Ryon's face had gone even more expressionless than usual as he gestured sharply.

"I think Ryon is busy," Greg whispered. He glanced at Lailu. "Do you know what they're arguing about?"

She nodded.

"It looks serious."

She nodded again. If Hannah had told him about the blood, it *would* be serious. How would Ryon take something like that? From the looks of it, not well. She bit her lip. Then she remembered something. "What did you mean by 'you came through the barrier *too*?'" she asked Krypton.

"Oh, didn't you know? We—"

"Shh," Iggy hissed. "We agreed to keep it a secret."

"Quiet, Iggy," Krypton snapped. "*I* never agreed. This charming young lady is putting us up in her restaurant and feeding us her stale leftovers—"

"Would you stop calling my food stale?" Lailu huffed.

"Least we could do is tell her about our newest discovery," he finished.

"And what is that?" Lailu asked.

The scientists all looked at Albert, who fiddled with the edge of his baggy vest. "I, um, figured out a way to break through the elves' barrier."

28

A Bad Idea

Albert led the way, hunched forward, a giant pack on his back. Krypton trotted along behind him. Iggy and Zelda had stuck around Mystic Cooking, promising to listen to Hannah and take care of the restaurant in Lailu's absence.

"I'll take care of all . . . this," Hannah had said, gesturing grimly at the chaos in Lailu's kitchen. "I'm going to make Albert's little freeloaders figure out a way to feed all the people out there, *after* they install a very big, very effective lock on the back door for us. You do what you have to do with the phoenix. And stay safe."

"I'll try," Lailu had promised.

"If all else fails, Vahn will make a great human shield," Hannah had added. She'd refused to talk about Ryon or their argument, only gave Lailu a quick hug and sent her on her way.

Lailu tried not to worry about it. Hannah and Ryon would work it out, one way or another. Instead, she focused on stepping over roots and dodging branches while Vahn tripped and stumbled through them next to her.

"Here we go," Albert said as they reached the barrier. The city around them had turned even wilder, with trees tangling overhead in a riot of greenery that looked like it had been there for generations. It was hard to believe that mere days ago this had been a normal street full of normal brick houses.

Lailu shivered and pulled her mom's thick coat tighter around herself. Paulie had said there'd be freezing rain later this morning. Since they were leaving so late, they'd probably be stuck hiking up through the mountains just as it hit. Not ideal.

Albert opened his pack and removed a spi-tron.

"Whoa!" Lailu leaped back. "What are you doing?"

"Don't worry, it's not dangerous." Albert rubbed his chin. "I think," he amended. Lailu, Greg, and Vahn all took another step back. Vahn tripped over yet another root and landed on his butt.

"This is going to be some hunt," Greg muttered.

"Quiet," Lailu hissed. "It'll be fine."

Albert set the spi-tron next to the barrier. It looked a little different, Lailu realized. Almost like someone had taken a spi-tron and combined it with a candelabra. One of *her* candelabras, to be exact. "Did you steal that from my restaurant?"

"I live there now, too!" Albert protested.

"Just for a short time." Lailu narrowed her eyes. "And growing rapidly shorter. Especially if this doesn't work."

Albert gulped and bent down, fiddling with the gears. A puff of green-tinted smoke burst out of the back in a little ring. "That's what Wren's scientist at the barrier did," Lailu said. "Only his didn't make it through."

"That's where Albert got the idea," Krypton piped up. "Only his is way better, because his will work."

"You sure about that?" Greg asked.

"It's how they all got through," Lailu reminded him.

"If they say so," he muttered.

"You don't believe us?" Krypton shook his head. "It breaks my heart to see such cynicism in one so young. Truly it does. But! There's no need to worry, because Albert here understands what he's working with."

Albert didn't say anything, just twisted another knob, pulled a thin cord from his pocket and attached it to one of the legs, and bent that up. Another puff of greenish smoke shot from it, but as far as Lailu could tell, nothing else happened. "Uh-huh," she said skeptically. "And what's he working with?"

"Isn't it obvious?" Krypton said. "It's a mating of science and magic."

"That terrifying blond elf gave me the idea," Albert panted, twisting another leg up. "Your description of the way he transformed the spi-trons . . ." He stopped and wiped the sweat from his forehead.

"Wren had the right idea, but she didn't quite know how to convert magic into energy in place of steam," Krypton added. "Poor little motherless thing."

Lailu flinched.

"Er, she's not such a poor little thing," Albert said, glancing back at Lailu. "She's quite capable all on her own."

"I suppose she is, after all." Krypton sighed. "Especially now that she has Elister backing her. Deadly combination. But I remember how she used to bully *you* way before that." He patted Albert on the arm. "It was pathetic. Truly a sad sight to behold. Bullied by a ten-year-old."

"Okay, first of all, she's almost twelve—"

"Oh yes, because *that* makes a huge difference." Krypton rolled his eyes.

"*And* she was the daughter of our leader." Albert had turned a ripe purple-red. "I *had* to listen to her. Anyhow." He coughed. "More importantly, I'm about to launch this spi-bert."

"Spi-bert?" Greg said. "Has Lailu been giving you naming lessons?"

Lailu smacked him.

"What?" He grinned.

"I don't name things like that." She scowled. "My names have dignity and grace."

Greg snorted.

"Pay attention!" Albert snapped. "This invention is molded by magic, which means it's no longer steam powered, but magic powered. That makes it powerful but also unpredictable. This is no laughing matter!"

Lailu and Greg inched back a little farther. "You probably want to move too," Lailu told Vahn. "With your luck . . ."

His eyes widened. "Good point." He staggered back a few feet, then crouched and put his arms over his head.

Albert gritted his teeth, twisted the remaining legs up, turned another lever, and stepped back. Another puff of green smoke shot into the air, then dissipated. "Hurry!" He waved his arm at the barrier. "It won't last long."

"It's . . . open?" Lailu stepped forward, putting her hand out. Nothing. Only empty air. "That was it?"

"That was it," Albert said.

"Well, now I just feel foolish," Vahn grumbled.

"You're about to feel even more foolish if you don't move your butt," Albert said, and Vahn, Lailu, and Greg hurried forward. Lailu and Greg made it through no problem, but Vahn crashed into something and stumbled back. "Duck, you idiot!" Albert said. Vahn ducked and lunged forward, and a few seconds later Lailu felt something crackling behind her. She put her hand back, her fingers tingling. The barrier was back up.

"Probably two feet wide by, hmm . . . How tall are you, boy?" Krypton pointed at Vahn.

"I'm six feet," Vahn said, rubbing his head.

"Just under six feet, then," Krypton said. "Terrible luck."

"I know." Vahn sighed.

"And the opening lasted . . ." He checked his pocket watch. "Seven seconds."

"That's it?" Lailu said.

"This is the problem with magic as a fuel source. Powerful, yes. The possibilities . . ." Krypton gazed up at the sky, his eyes wide and dreamy. "But it's very short-lived. We would need to find some sort of renewable magic as a resource. Still, one small step here, eh? And all thanks to this man." He clapped Albert on the shoulder.

Vahn had put his hands against the barrier, fingers spread. "I can't believe that worked." He looked at Albert. "You really *are* a brilliant scientist. Sorry about that whole curtain . . . thing. Can you break curses too?"

But Albert wasn't listening. He was gazing into the shadows gathered beneath the trees next to him, his face the grayish white of overcooked oatmeal. Lailu couldn't see what he saw, but she heard someone clapping, a slow, ominous sound, and then Eirad stepped out onto the road.

"Impressive." He bared his teeth in a wicked smile. "Much more impressive than I would have thought. I had you pegged as just another pawn."

Albert and Krypton shrank back from him, huddling together.

"Don't you hurt them!" Lailu pressed against the barrier, sparks flashing, her skin tingling all over.

Eirad lifted one eyebrow. She couldn't get through, couldn't do a thing to stop him, and they both knew it. "Perhaps you'd like to make a deal?" he asked her.

"No," Greg said.

"What kind of deal?" Lailu asked. She'd promised the scientists her protection, after all.

"Oh, I don't know . . . We could always do the standard. One year of your life for every scientist."

"The last years I won't even know I'll miss, right?" Lailu said grimly. Eirad had tried to make her a deal like this before, back when she owed Mr. Boss money. She hadn't taken him up on it then, but that time he was just offering her gold. And money was never worth it. But the lives of people she'd promised to protect? "I—" she began.

"You said you weren't going to hurt anyone in *your* city." Vahn stepped in front of Lailu. "That included these scientists. Therefore, you can't touch them. By your own word are you bound." Vahn said the last words almost like a chant, like something he had memorized a long time ago, and their effect on Eirad was instantaneous and shocking: the elf stood ramrod straight, blue eyes blazing, face pale and drawn.

"You dare remind me of our pledge?" Eirad's long fingers curled into fists at his sides.

Vahn shrugged. "You seemed to need the reminder."

Eirad regarded him for a long, tense moment. Blood thrummed in Lailu's ears, and it felt like she was staring down a long tunnel, everyone at the sides of her vision vanishing in a wash of dark as she waited to see what Eirad would do.

"Very well. I will not hurt these . . . people." Eirad shook his head. "So disappointing."

Lailu sagged against the barrier, then straightened. She didn't like the way the magic made her feel. "Wait, Eirad!" she called, suddenly remembering.

"What are you doing?" Greg hissed.

"Yes, little chef?" Eirad tilted his head. "Still want to make a deal?"

"Absolutely not." Lailu crossed her arms. "But Lord Elister asked me to pass along a message to you."

"Oh?"

"To all of you. Will you share it with Fahr?"

"That depends."

"On?" Lailu prompted.

"On whether or not I feel like it." Eirad grinned.

"Let's just go," Greg said. "We can find Fahr later. Or Ryon, I suppose." He grimaced.

"You might not want to speak with Ryon anymore." Eirad's grin twisted, becoming something small and sly and ugly.

"Why not?" Lailu asked.

Eirad didn't answer.

"Come on." Greg tugged on Lailu's arm.

Eirad sighed loudly. "Oh, very well. I promise to pass this message on to Fahr, for all the good it will do you. Now. Tell me."

"Elister would like to meet with you to discuss a possible peace treaty. He wants to know what it is you would like. Aside from the destruction of the scientists, which he cannot allow." She glanced at Albert and Krypton, who both stood there silently, like they were hoping to be forgotten. "He hopes you can negotiate with him."

"Is that so?" Eirad's face gave nothing away, but then, it never really did. "And does he mean it?"

"I think so," Lailu said truthfully. "He said he cannot afford to have the city divided right now." She patted her mother's coat. She'd been in such a state running home last night and then hurrying to get ready this morning that she'd never emptied her pockets. Her fingers found the edges of the slightly crinkled envelope, Elister's crimson seal gleaming on the front. "He gave me this for Fahr."

Eirad reached through the barrier, his hand slowing for a few seconds before popping out the other side. Lailu dropped the envelope into his hand and took a step back.

"I'll pass on the message, little chef. And if Fahr accepts, we will send word to Elister ourselves." The envelope disappeared down one of his long sleeves.

Lailu wondered how they planned to send him word. Would they just show up at his house? But then, according to Slipshod, Fahr had been meeting with the king. It made sense that they had other spies in that area.

Spies . . . like her mother.

Lailu wondered if her mother was spying on the king too. Was she safe? Lailu didn't want to think about it, but fear had already shivered down her spine, as cold as the waters of the Dancing River.

"In the meantime, I shall take good care of your little pets." Eirad put an arm around Albert and Krypton's shoulders. "Enjoy your hunt."

Albert's eyes widened, and he shrank away from Eirad.

"You promised," Lailu reminded Eirad.

"So I did."

She remembered how he'd explained "loopholes" to her and how elves always found ways around their promises. But there wasn't much else she could do right now.

"Let's go," Vahn said. "They'll be fine. They are brilliant scientists after all."

"I hope so," Lailu whispered.

"We'll come back this evening!" Krypton called as Eirad herded him and Albert back down the road. "Meet us here, and we'll let you back through!"

Lailu nodded and let Vahn and Greg pull her away, but she couldn't help feeling anxious, like she'd forgotten to turn the stove off. Leaving the scientists in Eirad's care was a bad idea. She just knew it.

29

Doomed!

Should have left him at home," Greg muttered for the hundredth time.

"Stop it," Lailu said, her patience wearing as thin as angel hair pasta. True, Vahn had already proven . . . challenging. But they were nearly to the mountains now, and it was too late to do anything about it. It had rained really hard for an hour and then stopped, but she could feel the threat of more rain hanging over their heads, and everything was mud and cold air and gray bleakness. Plus her hands ached like she'd been chopping vegetables for hours. She didn't need Greg's whining on top of all that.

She glanced back at Vahn, trudging silent and determined behind them. They were heading to Wolfpine Village, near the base of the mountains. As the last-known sighting of the phoenix, they'd all agreed it would be the best place to start their hunt. She and Greg had once hunted a mountain dragon with Hannah only a few miles from that very spot. Unlike that hunt, this time she had no plan at all. Vahn claimed he had a plan, but he also hadn't been willing to share any of the details, and Lailu wasn't about to hold her breath.

"You know he's just going to get in the way," Greg continued.

"Still," Lailu said, "he has to come. It's technically his quest."

"He'll probably get us all killed."

"I can hear you, you know," Vahn snapped.

Greg shot him a glare. "We weren't talking to you."

"You were talking *about* me. Which is impolite," Vahn muttered, looking down at his feet just in time to avoid stepping on a sharp stick. "Ha! See? I'm getting bett—ack!" He missed the sharp stick, but got his foot stuck up to the ankle in a hole hidden in the mud. He flailed, his arms windmilling, and managed to pull his foot free.

But not his boot.

Vahn's big toe stuck out of a hole in his mud-spattered sock. He looked down at it, then sighed. "Can one of you get my boot?"

"No," Greg said flatly.

"Please? If I try to get it, I'll probably just end up losing a glove in the mud too." His shoulders slumped.

Lailu felt a twinge of pity. She remembered all the times Vahn had called her Lala, or Lillie, or Lulu. And, of course, how he'd played Hannah, which had earned him this curse in the first place. But still. She crouched down by the hole, dug around, and yanked his boot out with a sucking, squelching *pop*.

"Thank you," Vahn said stiffly, putting it back on and lacing it tightly.

The lace snapped.

"Are you crying?" Greg asked, peering into his face.

"No. Heroes never cry." Vahn wiped at his eyes with the back of one gloved hand, smearing mud all across his face.

"Is someone still a hero if they can't handle their own quests?" Greg mused.

Vahn drew himself up. "I could handle this quest just fine on my own. I invited Lailu here as a favor. A favor to *her.*"

"Wait, what?" Lailu's sympathy thawed faster than Greg's orc meat.

"You were hunting skilly-wigs, of all things," Vahn said pityingly. "Obviously you needed a proper quest, someone to give you direction. Enter me." He grinned, tossing his head back confidently.

The clouds parted, dumping freezing rain down his back and soaking him in seconds.

"It's only raining on me, isn't it?" Vahn asked.

"Yep," Greg said cheerfully. "I sure do love this weather. Don't you love this weather, Lailu?"

"I do. I really, really do. I also love this nice warm raincoat."

"Me too," Greg said. "It would sure be awful not to have a raincoat right now, wouldn't it?"

"It sure would," Lailu said, and now she was grinning more broadly than Vahn ever had, her bad mood evaporating.

"I told you, I *had* a raincoat," Vahn snapped, his earlier bravado gone, "but it was stolen off my back." He shifted uncomfortably, his wet shirt sticking to him. "By squirrels," he added miserably.

Greg burst out laughing.

"Greg, be nice," Lailu said.

"But . . . squirrels!" Greg was crying now, tears streaming down his face.

"I don't know why you're laughing," Lailu said darkly. "We're about to face off against a phoenix, and one-third of our group just lost a battle to a bunch of squirrels."

"I know." Now Greg was in hysterics. "We're so doomed!"

"Hey, those squirrels were no joke," Vahn said defensively. "But I'll be fine against a phoenix. It's basically just a giant chicken."

Lailu froze, one foot squelching in the mud.

"Doomed," Greg repeated, laughing harder than ever. He was still laughing when they turned around the bend and came up against a wooden blockade stretching across the road.

The blockade had been hastily constructed, just two large trees that had been chopped down, stripped of branches, and then nailed together with boards to form a wall about four feet high. A rough fence stretched on either side of it with posts every few feet.

"Stop!" A man leaped out from behind the rough-hewn wall. He wore the tan-and-red uniform of a Savoria soldier, but it was wrinkled and covered in dirt, his hair and beard tangled. "The road is closed. And trust me, you do *not* want to go farther." Then he eyed Vahn and his soggy attire. "Are . . . are you a hero?"

Vahn tossed his wet mane over his shoulder and took a dramatic stance, one foot on the fence. "Why, yes, I—ahh!" A post on the fence gave out, dumping him on his face at the guard's muddy boots. He pushed himself up, spitting mud and water out. "I'm a hero," he finished.

The guard frowned. "Are you sure about that?"

"Yes!" Vahn snapped.

"Well, then. I guess you'd better come on in."

Just Temporary

I thought they said Wolfpine was only partially destroyed," Greg whispered, his eyes wide beneath his mop of hair as they walked past the barrier and down the dirt road. About two dozen tents were pitched up ahead, all close together, all made of rough canvas and wood. Villagers wandered in groups between them, most of them looking as dirty and disheveled as the guard, and all of them wearing that same lost expression Lailu had seen on the people of Twin Rivers after the elven barrier first went up. But at least most of the people in their city had homes to go back to. These people had almost nothing. Those tents couldn't be very warm, and when winter came in earnest . . .

Greg's hand gripped the hilt of the knife at his side, and he kept darting glances up at the sky.

Lailu couldn't blame him. She was doing the exact same thing.

"You of all people should know the papers exaggerate and twist things," she said.

"I've always found them to be quite honest." Greg managed a small, tight smile.

Lailu scowled. "Very funny."

"Still, though, this is terrible. All of these people forced to flee their homes . . ." Greg's expression grew serious. "Why didn't they send anyone out here to help before now?"

"Er," Vahn said. "Yes. Well." He coughed.

"Were you supposed to come out here sooner?" Lailu guessed.

"Not exactly. I mean, the city is literally divided right now, as you know. Lord Elister has more important things on his mind. And also . . ." He coughed again, mumbling something.

"What was that?" Greg cupped a hand to his ear. "I thought I heard you say you screwed up?"

"Me?" Vahn drew himself up, his chest out. "I am on track to become Savoria's greatest hero. *I* don't screw up." He looked around at the tents, the people standing in small, scared clumps around them, and he deflated. "But I had no idea it was this bad, or curse or no, I would have come."

"Yeah, right," Greg snorted.

"I believe you," Lailu said quietly. "I know you wouldn't have left these people to suffer." She could feel Greg's displeasure radiating like a stove burner turned up too high, and she purposely didn't look at him. But it was true. Vahn, for all his faults—and there were many—didn't leave people to suffer.

They stopped near the first row of tents. "Paulie said she'll consider lifting your curse," Lailu said abruptly.

Vahn whipped around. "Really? That's great news! Fantastic!" He grinned, and it was a surprisingly unpracticed expression, crooked and almost boyish. Lailu's heart twinged. For a second she remembered the first time she saw him, how handsome he looked with his hair billowing behind him. How *heroic*. And with that memory came a rush of all her old feelings, the same way eating a thick salamander stew always made her feel homesick.

You don't like him, she reminded herself. He was heroic, but he was also fake and definitely a jerk. Still, her face felt hotter than normal, and she kept her back to Greg, sure he'd notice. "She said she'll *consider* it," she continued, "but only if we bring her a tail feather from the phoenix."

"Why a tail feather?" Greg asked.

Lailu shrugged without turning around.

"Normally I take Master Chef Gingersnap's theories with a very large grain of salt," Greg said carefully, "but she *did* say the tail feather can be used to—"

"Who cares what it's used for?" Vahn said. "What matters is once we successfully hunt this bird, I'll not only complete my mission, but also get this inconvenient little spell lifted." He pushed his hair back from his face. "Consider it done. A hero always accomplishes his mission. This bird is as good as bagged."

"Are you coming?" the guard asked, turning back.

Lailu, Vahn, and Greg hurried to join him.

"We thought Lord Elister would send a hero sooner . . . a lot sooner." He led them past the first few tents lining the dirt road, his pace quick enough that Lailu had to practically jog to keep up. "We've been asking for help for weeks! That phoenix . . . Well, she's a blazing demon is what she is. Kept coming back no matter what we did. We tried water, magical charms. We even had a catapult at one point, but that's ashes now. Heck, the phoenix was here just the other night, circling right at sundown, like she's following us. But she's already taken everything . . ." His steps slowed. "Almost everything," he amended.

"*Almost* everything?" Lailu asked.

The guard kept walking and didn't answer.

Lailu and Greg exchanged nervous glances. "How long have you been out here?" Lailu asked next.

"Me personally?" He rubbed his chin. "Been stationed in the village now for . . . almost a year, I think?"

"Really?" Lailu said. "In Wolfpine?"

"Oh yes. It's not that close to the Krigaen border, but still. Sometimes they'll sneak scouts down through the mountains. Not enough heroes were available to make regular rounds, so Lord Elister decided to station some of the reserve troops out to live among the villagers." He shrugged. "It's not so bad. Or, it wasn't."

"What about this camp?" Greg asked. Vahn walked next to him, too busy concentrating on putting one foot ahead of the other without falling to say much himself.

"This camp has been here four . . . no, five days now. Took us two days to set it up after our village burned to the ground a week ago."

"A week?" Lailu had thought it had only been a few days. The paper really was way off base.

Those first two days were hard. I'm not gonna lie. Cold, so cold, and practically nothing to eat. Like I said, we thought for sure we'd have help soon, and some extra supplies did arrive a few days later. No heroes with it . . . But the important thing is that you're here now, eh?" He clapped Vahn on the shoulder.

Vahn's feet slipped, but he managed to stay on them.

"Why didn't you head into the city?" Greg asked.

The guard gave him a strange look. "We wanted to. Believe me, we wanted to. But when we sent a few scouts ahead, they were turned back. Apparently there isn't space for us there right now."

"Not space for you?" Greg said, confused. "Why wouldn't there be space?"

"Because of the barrier." Lailu sighed. Sometimes she forgot that Greg had been born an aristocrat. He'd never experienced this kind of thing. "Elister wouldn't be able to send these villagers over to the poor side of town, and the people of Gilded Island wouldn't want them cluttering up their streets."

"That's not true," Greg said.

"No, Greg, it's true. Trust me, it's true." Lailu could still remember the looks she'd gotten her first day at the Academy, wearing her secondhand uniform and carrying her battered books. How the other kids avoided her, or acted like she smelled weird, or made fun of her pigtails. They hadn't wanted her at their school. And as she looked around at the Wolfpine villagers, she knew the aristocrats of Gilded Island wouldn't want these people in their space either.

Greg frowned, but he didn't argue, and they walked the rest of the way in silence.

The guard stopped in front of the largest tent in the camp. Like all the other tents, the canvas material was a thick, muddy brown that blended in with the rocky foothills just behind it. "This here's our mess tent." He pulled open the flap. "I'll show you what supplies we've got, see if any of them are of use to you, Sir Hero." He ducked inside, followed closely by Vahn, who thankfully didn't manage to bring the whole thing crashing down . . . yet.

Greg held the flap open. "Coming?"

Lailu glanced back at the camp of displaced villagers. They had the same dark curls and tanned skin as Greg, rather than the straight black hair and lean frames of most of the people from her own village, but she still felt a strong kinship with them. They might not look the same as her, but they'd had similar lives, and she recognized their grim determination, like the villagers of Clear Lakes when they were weathering a particularly bad winter. Or how even though this camp was temporary, they'd set it up so much like a small village that Lailu could close her eyes and imagine the wooden homes of Wolfpine snuggled in its valley between the foothills. She just hoped they got to see those homes again soon.

"Lailu?" Greg tugged on one of her pigtails. "You okay?"

She sniffed, then nodded, ducking under his arm and into the mess tent.

Unlike its name, the mess tent was actually quite neat and organized, like a well-thought-out kitchen. Tables and shelves set in rows had everything the villagers would need for their stay: extra bedding, hunting equipment, tent-repair kits, medical supplies, and even weapons for defense, all laid out in orderly piles.

Vahn had already snagged himself a new coat and was placing a crossbow back on a top shelf when Lailu noticed him. She frowned. "Are you sure you want to—"

Crash!

The shelf collapsed, taking out the three shelves beneath it. Vahn tried to catch the items cascading down and managed to knock another shelf over before two people in official Savoria uniforms rushed over to help.

"Are you sure that man is a hero?" their guide asked, keeping his voice tactfully low.

Greg chuckled.

Lailu elbowed him. "Yes, we're sure. He's just had a run of bad luck lately." She winced as Vahn attempted to help with the shelves, only to have them fall again. "Really bad luck. But he'll pull it together during our hunt." *I hope*, she added silently.

The guard watched Vahn dubiously. "Best we're gonna get, I'm sure," he muttered. He glanced at Lailu and Greg. "I need to show you something." He led them to a sectioned-off part of the mess tent in back. It felt like entering their own little room. Tucked beneath a loose flap of canvas sat a small wooden chest. He slid it out and opened it, displaying a beautiful red-gold feather.

"Is that . . . from the phoenix?" Greg whispered. He glanced at Lailu, and she could see they were both thinking the same thing: the tail feather. This was what Vahn needed, sitting right here.

"We believe so," the guard said grimly. "I told you Lord Elister had us stationed here to keep an eye on the Krig, and that's true . . . but it's not the whole truth." He glanced around, then dropped his voice. "I'm only telling you this 'cause I'm not sure what else to do, you understand me?"

"Absolutely," Greg said, and Lailu nodded fervently.

"I'm not one to blab about secret missions. Not me, nope.

But . . . Lord Elister ordered us to search the surrounding mountains, to find anything unusual, any kind of magic artifacts. And on one of those patrols, me and two other soldiers found a nest. Or, what we believed to be a nest, full of soot and ash, and inside lay that there feather." He jerked his thumb at it. "As per our orders, we took it back to the village, and we've been arguing about whether or not to get rid of it ever since."

"Get rid of it?" Lailu said. "Why?"

"Weren't you listening earlier? That phoenix is searching for something! It kept returning to the village, night after night, until there wasn't enough village left to return to. And then last night, it came here, to this camp."

Lailu's heart beat faster. That went against everything Gingersnap had theorized. According to her, phoenixes were extremely rare, and never sighted in the same place twice. Like a fire, they burned hot and fierce and then moved on.

"If you think there's a chance it might be looking for the feather, why keep it at all?" Greg asked.

"Because . . . Lord Elister ordered us to keep it." The guard frowned down at the feather. "If it were up to me, I'd destroy the blasted thing right now. I'm hoping, in fact, that *you'll* take care of it for us. If you take it, no one can complain. If Elister himself sent you to help us, then surely you can make your own decision on this feather, and . . . he won't blame us."

"We could give it to Vahn," Lailu said.

The guard's eyes widened. "That man out there is Vahn? The hero who trained under the famed Rhivanna?"

Lailu nodded.

"I thought he was supposed to be good."

"Stories are often exaggerated," Greg said. He shot Lailu a look. "Or so I hear."

Lailu couldn't stop the small smile that crept up her face. "Jerk," she whispered.

"Grouch," Greg whispered back.

"Are you going to take the feather, or aren't you?" the guard said.

Greg picked it up, turning it over in his hands before passing it to Lailu.

The moment her fingers closed over it, Lailu felt the rest of the world drop away into the background, just like when she was cooking. Only her hands and the feather existed, as flames oozed from it, licking up and down her arm, gentle and tickling like a puppy's tongue.

The familiar pain in her hands throbbed once, twice, and then faded to nothing more than a tingling sensation.

She blinked. She was still standing there over the open chest, Greg saying her name next to her. A few seconds had passed, if that. "Are you okay?" he said, and it sounded like he'd asked that a few times.

"I . . . don't know." Lailu felt dazed, her hands still tingling. Carefully, she tucked the feather inside her vest. Whatever had happened, she knew she shouldn't leave it here to cause these people more damage. "I'm fine," she said, and she almost believed it.

"The nest you saw," Greg said, turning back to the guard. "Did you find any eggs in it?"

Lailu frowned, her attention sharpening. If the phoenix was a new or soon-to-be-mother, it was against the mystical chef code of ethics to hunt it; however, the phoenix had been attacking the people of Wolfpine, so it was also their obligation to help them. Which would take precedence in this situation?

"There were no eggs that we could see," the guard said. "And with a bird that size, I imagine their eggs would be hard to miss."

"But is a phoenix born from an egg, or from flame?" Lailu tapped her lip in thought. "In my old village we had some stories about the phoenix, and how when a new country was 'born' four phoenixes sprang into being, one for the north, one for the south, one for the east, and one for the west. I don't know if I ever truly believed that story, but as a young kid it was nice to think that maybe we were protected by these four guardians."

"Wait," Greg said. "You believe that the phoenix might be some kind of sacred guardian, and you still want to hunt it?"

"We had lots of stories like that. We even had some about dragons, and we hunted and ate one of those," Lailu pointed out. "Some of our children's stories are more about teaching us a life lesson than they are about giving us facts."

The guard cleared his throat. "I've heard similar tales in these parts. A lot of villages have legends like that. Do you think there is anything to them that could help us now?"

"Maybe," Lailu said. "There's one that's been digging at my memory, like a spoon on solid ice." She scratched her head. "Something about 'when down meets dust.'"

"What the spatula is that supposed to mean?" Greg asked.

Lailu frowned. "Would you stop using that expression?"

"Nope." He smirked, and then he tilted his head. "Do you hear something?"

"Yelling," Lailu said, hearing it now too.

Greg shrugged. "Probably Vahn."

"No, wait," Lailu said. "They're saying . . ." They looked at each other.

"Phoenix!" The screams grew louder, more desperate.

"O God of Cookery . . . ," Lailu prayed. Then the roof of their tent burst into flame.

DOWN AND DUST

The fire around them made the chill air evaporate like water on a frying pan. Already smoke snaked down in all directions, stifling the air as villagers and Savorian guards grabbed items from the shelves and raced from the burning tent. Lailu and Greg each grabbed an armful of supplies and hurried out with them; with winter around the corner, these people would need all the supplies they could get.

Lailu thrust her pile of blankets and dehydrated food at their guide. "Load your wagons and take these villagers as far from these mountains as possible," she ordered.

"But the tents—"

"Leave them. Just go, and quickly!" Flames roared all around them, people ran screaming. "If she's a nesting phoenix, she won't follow you, but if you stay—" A nearby tent went up in flame. "If you stay, you'll die."

"Understood," the guard said. "And if she's *not* a nesting phoenix?"

"Then we'll have to hope she really is looking for that feather," Lailu said grimly. "I'll keep it with me, and we'll distract her as long as we can."

Another tent burst into flame, the phoenix shrieking overhead. "Hurry!" Lailu said.

"But . . . where can we go?"

"Head to the city. If Lord Elister won't take you in, then make your way to Mystic Cooking and I'll find you all places to stay."

"Where?" Greg demanded. "You don't have room—"

"I'll figure something out," Lailu snapped. "If you can't get through the barrier, then wait there for me, and I'll help you."

The guard studied her face for the briefest second, like he was searching for something, and then he nodded. "I believe you will," he whispered. "Thank you." More fire crackled nearby, and the guard took off sprinting. Lailu and Greg ran in the other direction, dodging people and veering around flames.

"Plan?" Greg panted next to her.

Lailu scowled at him. "You've really got to stop doing that!"

"I know. It's a terrible habit. You're just so good at coming up with them, being the top student in our hunting class and everything. . . ."

"You can stop now." The sky had darkened considerably since they had entered the mess tent, bleeding away the vivid colors of the day. Shadows gathered, collecting in the folds of the mountains rising up on either side of them as Lailu searched the frantic crowd for long blond hair. "Where the apple peeler is Vahn?"

"Apple peeler?" Greg said.

"I'm trying it out."

Silence fell, nothing but the wind and the crackling of the nearby flames.

"It's not very good, is it?" Lailu said.

"No. No, it's not," Greg agreed.

"At least that means I don't have to worry about you stealing it—"

Screech!

Lailu clapped her hands over her ears and looked up.

The shape of the phoenix was outlined against the gray sky, wings spread wide, steam sizzling off its feathers where the icy rain hit it. And so brightly colored, crimson reds and golden yellows mingling until it resembled the heart of the sun. It was impossible to judge its size, even as it glided closer; flames licked around its feathers like fire on the wick of a candle, making it appear larger, but she guessed from head to tail that it was about the length of a grown man. Definitely bigger than Greg had been when he'd been transformed into a phoenix with elf magic the final night of the Week of Masks.

It spun in midair and dove toward the villagers, the fire flickering around its body leaving a streak across the evening sky. As it soared past, it turned in a sharp arc, coming back around for another loop.

Lailu crouched, scooping up a large stone, and then waited until it was near before throwing the stone as hard as she could with the deadly aim she'd honed in years of hunting classes.

Whack!

She got the beast square on the beak, knocking it off its course and sending it wobbling into the side of the mountain.

It shrieked in fury, scrabbling for purchase on the rocks before launching back into the air.

"Great job," Greg said. "Now you made it angry."

"At us, so we can lead it away."

The phoenix plunged toward them, its blazing eyes focused right on Lailu and Greg. "Dive!" Lailu shoved Greg one way as she rolled the other.

The phoenix smashed into the path as a ball of fire, right where they had been standing, then rose back into the sky again.

Someone hauled Lailu to her feet. She blinked against the sunspots dancing in her vision. "Vahn?"

"Got anything sharper than a rock?" he asked. She pulled her trusty chef's knife out of her hip sheath. "Better."

"Did that phoenix really just turn itself into a bird-shaped fireball?" Greg squeaked.

"It certainly looked like that," Vahn said.

"She's coming back." Lailu adjusted her grip on her knife. Greg pulled his own out, and Vahn drew his sword. A second later the phoenix was on them, its heat flattening them down like a panini. Lailu wasn't sure what happened next: a brief flurry of flames and feathers and the slashing of knives that couldn't seem to cut anything.

"Watch it!" Greg yelped as Vahn's sword missed him by inches.

Lailu felt the whoosh of air overhead as Vahn's next swing sliced just above her, and she fell back. Vahn spun again, his sword a blur as he parried the sharp thrust of the phoenix's beak and then sliced back at a wing.

The sword slipped from his hand, embedding itself into the rocks next to them.

The phoenix stopped and looked at the sword quivering in place, then looked at Vahn's empty hands.

Squawk, squawk, squawk.

"Is it . . . laughing?" Lailu whispered, horrified.

It launched itself up into the sky in another blast of hot air, sending Vahn sprawling backward. He slammed into Greg, both of them tumbling into Lailu.

"This . . . is not going well." Vahn wiped a sooty hand across his face.

"You think?" Greg climbed to his feet. "Should we run?" he asked Lailu.

"Run?" Vahn drew himself up. "A hero never runs from a quest."

"I wasn't talking to you. I was talking to the person here least likely to accidentally stab me to death."

"Thanks," Lailu said. "Your confidence in me is really inspiring." Up above, the phoenix tucked its wings against its body and dove straight for them again. "Yes, run!" The three of them took off.

"What's the plan?" Greg called.

"You need to ask? The plan is to kill the—"

"Shut it, Vahn!" Lailu yelled. "Plan is to get it farther away from the villagers. And then . . ." Lailu didn't know what the rest of the plan would be. Their weapons hadn't done much good, and she had no idea if the mal-cantation powder Vahn had given her earlier would make any difference.

The mess tent had collapsed in a smoldering pile of ashes, but a quick glance beyond showed Savorian officials leading villagers away with wagons laden with supplies. They had listened to Lailu and were heading away from the foothills.

Lailu, Greg, and Vahn led the phoenix farther into the mountains, weaving past the last of the tents and then darting down a path no bigger than a deer trail.

The path wound its way along the side of the mountain, up a small hill and then back down, through rock piles and small bent trees with reddish bark, their leaves gone already for the winter. The air here tasted like smoke and the promise of more rain, and Lailu prayed to Chushi as she sprinted that the skies would open up and drench the phoenix.

It dove at them, screeching, and they scattered, jumping through brambles that burst into flame and scrambling down small rocky trails.

"Trees," Greg called, pointing up ahead at a small copse clinging to the side of the mountain. "Trees burn."

"Good point." Lailu reversed course. They'd bought as much time for the villagers as they could. It was time to get back to the road. The air behind her sweltered, and sweat dripped into her eyes as the phoenix closed the distance. She'd have to take a chance, and soon.

Lailu pulled the pouch of mal-cantation powder out of her bag and put on a burst of speed. As soon as she hurtled back out into the main road, she spun, the bag in her hand. But before she could throw it, Vahn slid a crossbow from his back, his elbow knocking into her as he turned and took aim.

"Got you," he told the bird.

His crossbow jammed. Frowning, he lowered it, checking the bolt, and the whole weapon snapped. Vahn fell heavily backward, his crossbow bolt disappearing into the night.

"Vahn!" Lailu yelled.

The phoenix shrieked with victory, swooping right at the fallen hero.

Dimly, Lailu was aware of Greg racing toward them, knife raised, but most of her attention had tunneled down to the phoenix, its claws mere inches from Vahn's handsome face, beak open wide.

Lailu tossed a handful of powder right into the bird's mouth.

The phoenix shuddered violently, crashing into the road a few feet from Vahn.

Lailu leaped toward it, then stopped. Its feathers were melting, running like hot wax off its body until it resembled a giant plucked turkey, the skin grayish pink and saggy. It gave a piteous, mewling cry as it shrank. Now it was the size of a small child. A few seconds later and it was the size of a small dog and still shrinking.

Lailu, Greg, and Vahn looked at each other. "Should I . . . attack it?" Lailu asked. It didn't seem right.

Squawk! Squawk! The phoenix lifted its now-tiny beak and screamed defiantly into the sky. And then *poof!* It collapsed in on itself in a puff of ash.

Greg scratched his head. "Are you thinking what I'm thinking?"

"Yeah," Lailu sighed. "How are we supposed to cook that?"

Greg dropped his hand. "That's not what I'm thinking."

"I'm thinking all's well that ends well." Vahn rubbed his hands together. "Good work, team. Shall we venture back?"

"I . . . guess?" Lailu had never ended a hunt without taking something back to cook. It felt strange to leave now, like she'd forgotten to salt the soup.

"Hey, do you still have that feather?" Vahn asked.

"How did you know about the feather?" Greg asked.

"I turned to find you after those poorly put-together shelves collapsed, and I could hear you talking on the other side of the tent partition."

"So, you snoop, then run off when the phoenix attacks?" Greg glared at him.

"I went out to help the villagers escape," Vahn said. "Obviously." Then he turned back to Lailu. "So, do you have it?"

Lailu pulled the feather out and showed it to him.

"Can I have it?"

"I don't know if that's wise," Lailu started, but before she could stop him, he snatched it out of her hands.

"Hey!" Greg snapped.

"Relax, I'm just looking at it—ah!" A sudden gust of wind caught the feather and pulled it from Vahn's grip . . . and right onto the pile of ash that had been the phoenix.

The ash shimmered, turning the same radiant colors as the feather, then billowing in a giant cloud. It expanded rapidly, forming the outline of the phoenix.

"When down meets dust," Lailu breathed. "When feather meets ashes?"

"Uh-oh," Greg whispered. "Now what?"

"I don't know," Lailu said.

"I say we—"

"No one cares what you say, Vahn!" Greg said.

Vahn's eyes widened, and he backed up a step, then another. "Run," he squeaked. *"Run!"*

A shadow fell over Lailu, and she hesitated for just a second, glancing back.

The phoenix stood in the middle of the path, twice as large as when they first saw it and four times as angry. It flapped enormous wings, sending eddies of flame out as it slowly rose into the air.

SQUAWK!

Lailu ran. She ran as if a hydra, a dragon, and a cockatrice were all after her, because this phoenix felt as dangerous as all of those creatures combined and almost as frightening as a fyrian chicken. The charred remains of tents went past in a blur as she ran straight down the main road. Up ahead she could see the wooden barrier and prayed to the God of Cookery that it would provide them with enough protection. Vahn raced toward it in the lead, Greg right on his heels, and Lailu a few steps behind. Heat scorched her back, the shadow of the phoenix covering everything. It was practically on top of them.

Just before Vahn reached the wall, his sword belt snapped, and he stumbled, the sword tangling in his legs. One of his flailing hands caught Greg, and they both fell, right as Lailu sprinted past them.

She screeched to a halt and turned back.

"Go!" Greg yelled, his face illuminated in the fireball billowing toward him. Flames engulfed him and Vahn, and they vanished from view.

"No!" Lailu stumbled toward the flames, her eyes blurry, her nostrils full of the stench of burning hair. Two shapes hurtled out of the flames and crashed into her, all three of them toppling back through the gate and onto the road outside the camp's boundary.

Greg rolled until the flames were out as Vahn thrashed next to him.

Lailu leaped to her feet and poured the last of the mal-cantation powder into her hand. Just as the heat threatened to sear right through her, the beast close enough that she could see herself in its eyes, she threw all the powder at it.

This time she didn't get any in its beak, but it still had an effect; the phoenix made a strange gurgling noise, the flames around it abruptly going out as if it had been hit with a bucket of water, and it froze, hovering in the air only inches from Lailu. Her hand crept to the hilt of the knife at her side, but the fury in the creature's eyes stopped her, that black beady gaze intent on her face. As if it were memorizing her features.

Its eyes narrowed, the beak curving, and then it turned and sailed away, vanishing into the overcast sky.

Lailu's heart hammered loudly in her ears. That curved beak had looked almost like . . . a smile. But not the good kind. In fact, it reminded her a lot of Eirad's smiles, like a promise of danger to come.

She had no idea what to make of that, but right now she had bigger concerns. "Are you okay?" she asked Greg, checking him over. His raincoat had melted in places, and there was a nasty burn already bubbling across his left cheek.

"I'll be okay," he told her, catching her hands and squeezing them. "Oh, sorry. I forgot about your hands."

"They feel fine." Lailu flexed her fingers. Actually, they felt better than they'd ever felt before, as if all the stiffness had been burned right out of them. She remembered the strange way the phoenix feather had made her hands feel. The feather that Paulie wanted badly enough that she'd remove Vahn's curse in exchange for it. "You know—" Lailu began.

Vahn groaned.

Lailu glanced at him, then froze. "O God of Cookery," she breathed.

Vahn slowly opened his eyes, which were bloodshot and bleary, his face streaked with soot and speckled with a few small burns. His shirt was almost completely singed away, a series of larger burns zigzagging across his pale skin. But most shocking of all . . .

He put a hand to his head, frantically feeling the back of his scalp and neck. "My hair! My *hair!*"

His long golden locks had been burned away, leaving only clumps of char crackling against his soot-stained face.

32

NOT SO BAD

L ailu had never felt so defeated. They'd failed at a hunt. She'd *never* failed at a hunt before. Even that time Greg had set her up against a whole pack of bloodthirsty fyrian chickens, he'd still managed to get the eggs. And all the credit.

Now Lailu felt defeated and angry.

Greg glanced sidelong at her, then moved a few inches away. "You're thinking about the chickens again, aren't you?"

Lailu blinked. "You can tell that?"

"Oh yes. You always get a very . . . *specific* look on your face." Greg shuddered. "It's not pleasant."

"Well, neither was being roasted by those treacherous, feathered—"

"Hey, you know, it's been years. Maybe it's time to let that go, yeah?"

"Never," Lailu vowed.

Greg sighed.

From behind them Vahn mumbled something.

"What was that?" Greg asked him.

He mumbled a little louder.

"Did you understand that?" Greg asked Lailu.

"Sounded like 'my hair.'"

Vahn mumbled it again.

"Yes, definitely 'my hair,'" Lailu decided.

"I guess that's progress?" Greg said. Vahn hadn't spoken a word since they'd left Wolfpine behind an hour ago. Lailu had begun to wonder if he'd ever speak again.

"Your hair will grow back," she said. She glanced at the charred clumps. "Probably."

Vahn didn't look at her, just kept his eyes on the muddy road, his feet barely lifting as he trudged along. If she felt defeated this one time, Vahn looked as if he'd never win again.

Greg shrugged. "I think it's kind of an improvement," he whispered.

Lailu glared at him. "Be nice."

"I *am* being nice," Greg muttered. "Trust me, this *is* nice. Nicer than he deserves. Remember how often he called you Lala? Or Lillie? Or Leeloo? Or—"

"I remember, okay? It's just . . . Look at him. Have you ever seen such a sad sight in your life?"

Vahn stopped trudging. He lifted his chin, finally making eye contact. "For the last time, I *can* hear you," he snapped.

"It speaks!"

"Stop it, Greg," Lailu hissed. "Look, Vahn, it's going to be okay. When we get back, Hannah can give you a nice haircut and . . ." She thought of Hannah, holding sharp scissors so close to Vahn's face. "Someone *other* than Hannah can give you a nice haircut," she corrected, "trim away the burned parts, and you'll look just fine."

"You think I care how I *look*?" Vahn said.

"I think you care a lot about how you look," Lailu said.

"Definitely," Greg agreed.

Vahn shook his head. "That's not the problem. The problem is the feather. I *lost* the *feather*!" He ran a hand through his once-gorgeous locks. A few pieces broke and crumbled to ash. "The hair is . . . not ideal either. But without that feather I'll be stuck like this forever. How can I be a hero if I can't complete my quests?"

Lailu didn't have any answers for him. "Let's just get back. Maybe . . . Maybe Paulie will take pity on you."

Vahn snorted.

"Paulie also said that you can break the curse yourself if you learn your lesson."

"My lesson? And what lesson is that?" Vahn shook his head. "I did nothing wrong."

Lailu's jaw dropped. "You two-timed a witch. With my best friend." Suddenly she was no longer feeling quite as sympathetic.

"Technically Hannah and I weren't dating. Because she was under the impression that I wasn't nice enough to you, for whatever reason. And Paulie . . . well. We never had *the talk*."

"The talk?" Lailu said.

"You know. The talk." He peered at her. "Or, actually, you probably don't know."

Lailu scowled. She had no idea what "the talk" was, but he didn't need to say it so condescendingly.

"It's when you discuss whether or not you're actually dating," Vahn explained. "Until then you're still technically free. So technically I didn't do anything wrong."

"That's a lot of 'technicallys,'" Greg said.

"And I heard you telling Hannah you'd wait for her forever," Lailu added. "Isn't that talk?"

"It's not the same, okay?" Vahn hunched his shoulders. "I don't deserve this curse. It's not *my* fault women find me irresistible."

"Told you his silence was an improvement," Greg said.

Vahn frowned. "You couldn't possibly understand."

"You're right," Greg said. "I couldn't."

Lailu felt like the two of them were having some sort of silent conversation consisting entirely of intense eye contact. It made her uncomfortable. "Let's just get back, okay?" she said. "We're going to be hiking through the night as it is." The sun had already sunk below the horizon, and its light was fading fast. She could see the edges of the mountains fading to purple against the gray evening sky, and even though the rain had stopped, the chill in the air was growing, gusts tugging at Lailu's hair and freezing her nose. Plus she was worried about Albert and the other scientists, no matter what Eirad had promised. And part of her kept expecting the phoenix to reappear. All in all, it made her anxious to get home quickly.

Vahn's foot sank up to the ankle in one of the few remaining soft patches of road, and he lurched to a stop. He sighed, his shoulders slumping. "I know you both think I deserve this, and maybe I do deserve some sort of punishment. But . . . if I can't break this, if

I'm not a hero anymore . . . what am I?" He shook his head. "What am I?" He pulled his foot free, then continued trudging sadly down the road.

Without a word, Greg crouched and pulled Vahn's boot from the hole, carrying it by its laces. A few minutes later he stopped and grabbed Vahn's second boot from another hole as Vahn continued marching determinedly forward in bare feet. Lailu wondered if he even noticed.

Vahn was obnoxious and conceited and definitely deserved to be punished. But to not be a hero anymore? That would be like her losing her ability to cook.

"I know," Greg sighed. "We have to help him."

"You want to?" Lailu asked, surprised.

"Not really." He adjusted his grip on Vahn's heavy boots. "But I know you do." He shrugged. "So I'm in."

Lailu had the strangest urge to hug Greg, but she managed to stifle it. She'd never been the hugging type before, and she wasn't about to start now. "You know," she said instead, "you're not always so bad."

Greg stopped walking and put a hand to his heart. "Was that . . . actual praise? From the lips of Crabby Cakes herself?"

Lailu scowled. "I take it all back." She stomped away, but after a few steps her scowl crumbled like Vahn's charred hair. Obnoxious or not, she knew Greg had her back. And that made her feel like she could deal with anything.

Even whatever was waiting for her inside Mystic Cooking.

CELEBRATIONS

e made it," Vahn said as they entered the city. He'd had to talk to the guards stationed at the gate, but luckily they both knew him and let them all in easily. "I'm going to, uh, run some errands."

"At this hour?" Greg said.

"I'll see you both later." Vahn hesitated. "Thanks," he added, and then he turned and lurched into the night.

Lailu rubbed at her eyes with one numb hand. Every part of her was either aching with exhaustion or frozen, and she felt like they'd been walking forever. It had to be the middle of the night by now. Greg had a couple of fancy torches to light their way, but it still felt like she was hiking through a tunnel of night. Lailu always felt vulnerable in the dark, even with her keen sense of smell. Now, though, with the lights of the city around her, she felt even more exposed.

"He's probably going home to cry," Greg said.

Lailu frowned. It just seemed wrong to think of Vahn feeling sad, like a pasta dish without any sauce. "You can go home, too," she told Greg. "I can make it back from here."

He shook his head. "I'll walk you home."

"I can handle myself." Lailu tapped the knife at her hip meaningfully.

"Oh, absolutely. I'm worried about my own safety, really." He grinned, his teeth glinting against the shadows of his face, and even though he was obviously lying, Lailu decided not to fight it. She actually liked having his company as they wandered through the half-deserted streets. Not that she'd ever tell him that.

It seemed to take forever, but eventually they reached the place where the scientists had let them out of the elven barrier to go on their hunt. "Made it," Greg said wearily. "You think Albert is still wait—ah!"

A shadow unfolded itself from beneath a tree. "It's about time," Ryon said flatly. "I thought I'd be waiting out here for you all night."

"Where's Albert and the other scientists?" Lailu asked.

"They're busy entertaining the elves," Ryon said.

"That sounds ominous," Lailu muttered, nervous.

"Well, hurry up then, would you? Eirad left a sliver open for you right here." Ryon pointed at a spot in front of him. It looked exactly the same as all the other spots, but Lailu trusted him and went through it with no resistance. As soon as she and Greg were on the other side, Ryon began striding back to Mystic Cooking. He didn't say anything to either of them, didn't ask how their hunt went, nothing.

A few minutes passed like that, and then Lailu couldn't take it anymore. "Are you okay?" she asked.

"I'm wonderful. Splendid. Never better."

"Glad to hear it," Lailu said, matching Ryon dry tone for dry tone.

He glanced sideways at her, then sighed. "Did you know?"

"Know what?"

"About the gems Paulie gave you? About Hannah's plan?"

Lailu flinched. "No," she whispered.

"What plan?" Greg asked. "What gems?"

Ryon ignored Greg so completely, it was like he hadn't said a word. "That's what I thought," he told Lailu, his shoulders relaxing. "I was worried maybe you were in on it too. And if I can't trust you, who can I trust?"

"You can trust me."

"What are you talking about?" Greg tried again.

"I'll tell you later, Greg," Lailu said.

Greg frowned, then dropped back behind them, wrapping his hurt feelings around himself like a second coat. Lailu knew this was going to be another argument, but it would have to wait. *Greg* would have to wait.

"Hannah didn't mean—" Lailu began.

"She used me," Ryon said bitterly. "Just like everyone always does. She saw my talent, and she used it."

Lailu chewed the inside of her mouth. She wasn't good at this sort of thing. It felt like going hunting without any weapons, or light, or a plan. Like she was floundering in the dark against something she didn't understand. "She wasn't trying to use you," she managed, feeling her way along. "I kind of think she was trying to impress you."

Ryon frowned. "How so?"

"She wanted to show you she could do this whole spying thing on her own."

"By stealing my blood? By *exploiting* me?"

"Okay, maybe her methods weren't the best. But it's Hannah. Sometimes . . ." Lailu sighed, thinking of all the trouble her friend got into. "Sometimes she's a little impulsive. But she doesn't use people. If you trust me like you say you do, please trust what I say. Hannah isn't like that. And besides, Paulie promised her a hair comb." She shrugged, like that explained everything. And with Hannah, it probably did.

Ryon's frown grew deeper, shadows gathering beneath the downturned corners of his mouth and turning his face into a mask. "I'll think about it," he said. "Maybe . . . maybe you're right. And besides, I suppose we all do things sometimes that we need our friends to forgive us for." He glanced at Lailu, and for a second his mask slipped, and guilt colored his face. Lailu only had a moment to wonder what *that* was about before it was gone and he was turning back to Greg. "You can rejoin us now. The adults are done talking."

Greg scowled, but moved up to walk next to Lailu.

"Why do you do that?" Lailu asked Ryon.

He shrugged. "I guess sometimes I can't help myself." He managed a half smile. "Maybe I'm a little impulsive too. And speaking of impulsive . . . you might want to prepare yourself."

"For what?" Lailu asked.

"For the scene inside your restaurant." Ryon rubbed the back of his neck. "It's . . . Well . . . You'll have to see for yourself."

Lailu and Greg exchanged glances, then followed Ryon to the end of the road. They were still a few feet away from Mystic Cooking when the first wave of sound crashed over them: people's voices, laughter, cheers, and above it all, the clatter of dishes.

"What the fork and knives is going on?" Lailu said.

Greg gave her a sideways look. "If you promise to never say that again, I'll stop saying 'what the spatula.'"

"Promise?" Lailu asked.

Greg nodded, and they shook on it, then headed to the door.

"Hey, Lailu?" Ryon called.

She turned back.

Ryon remained standing a few feet down the road, his face almost completely in shadow. "I . . ." He hesitated. "I need to tell you something."

The door to Mystic Cooking opened, and Eirad poked his head out. "You're just in time. We're throwing a party in honor of your successful hunt!" He lifted a fist in the air, and everyone inside cheered.

"To the hunt! To the hunt!" a couple of people chanted.

"Come. Come." Eirad pulled Lailu and Greg inside.

"Wait—" Lailu glanced back at Ryon, but he was already gone. It left an uneasy feeling in her stomach, like she'd eaten too many raw ingredients. "That was weird."

"Not as weird as this," Greg said.

Lailu turned to face her restaurant, and her jaw dropped. This went way beyond weird. The room was full of elves and scientists.

She recognized Albert, Krypton, Zelda, and Iggy, all arm in arm and singing with a group of elves, one of them raising a large tankard in the air and bobbing it along to the beat. Dishes of food cluttered the nearby tables. Lailu could tell it was middle-of-the-road fare, nothing she'd ever serve here. On another table, a large paper with scribbles and drawings all over it was partially obscured by a cluster of empty glasses, and everyone was shouting and laughing like they'd been partying all night.

And maybe they had been.

"Lailu!" Krypton appeared at Lailu's side, grabbing her hand and pumping it up and down. "Excellent. So glad to see you! Did you bring the phoenix? Because we have a plan! A plan for your generator!"

"What?" Lailu managed to pull her hand away. "No, I didn't. What plan?"

"We'll transform it," Albert said, joining them. "With *magic.*" He waved his hands. "Picture it—"

"No! Absolutely not!" Lailu couldn't believe this. Albert had just said how unpredictable and powerful the combination of magic and science could be. And he wanted to *transform* the *generator*? What was he *thinking*?

"Another photo!" one of the elves called.

"Just a sec! Lailu, Greg, come join us." Albert pulled the two of them along, lined them up, and then whipped out his camera.

"What the fork and knives indeed," Greg said, his eyes as wide as Lailu's felt. "Are they all friends now?"

"Looks that way."

"We're celebrating!" Zelda yelled.

"We failed in our hunt," Lailu said.

"Doesn't matter! Still have a lot to celebrate." Zelda grinned, her wiry gray curls bouncing as she bobbed up and down. "There's going to be a peace negotiation!"

Lailu felt like her world was spinning too fast. "What? When? Where?" She looked around. She didn't see either Hannah or Ryon anywhere, but a second later Eirad materialized, and for once she was almost glad to see him. "What is going on?" she demanded.

"Elister accepted our initial demands for peace negotiations. Therefore, we'll be meeting for dinner tomorrow . . . actually, tonight." Eirad glanced meaningfully out the window, where the first hint of light brightened on the horizon. Morning was inching closer. "Fahr has promised to take down the barrier at first light as a show of good faith."

"Meeting . . . where?" Lailu asked, suspicion pooling in her stomach.

Eirad raised his eyebrows. "Oh, didn't you know? Elister requested we meet here, at Mystic Cooking. It was the only demand we were able to agree on immediately." He grinned. "I quite look forward to whatever meal you're able to cook up in that time."

34

GET COOKING!

*L*ailu kicked everyone out of Mystic Cooking immediately. "But I live here now!" Albert whined.

"Not today, you don't!" Lailu snarled, slamming the door in his face. He'd helped bring this on her, he and the rest of his scientist renegades, all buddying up with the elves. And now look! She was once again hosting a meeting between Elister and Fahr, between the scientists and the elves. Why did this keep happening to her?

"I'll bring back some supplies," Greg said.

"You mean skilly-wigs?" Lailu wrinkled her nose.

Greg sighed. "It's all we have. It'll have to do."

Lailu imagined feeding Lord Elister a plateful of skilly-wigs and shuddered. Still, there wasn't much else she could do. "You don't—" she started.

"Don't," Greg said flatly.

"Don't what?"

"Don't tell me that I don't have to come here and help you cook. You always say that, but you and I both know you need me."

Lailu opened her mouth, then shut it again. She *had* been about to tell him that, and she *did* need him. She hated when he was right. "Fine."

"You just need to say the words," he added.

"The words?"

He grinned. "You know the ones. Go on."

"Thank you?"

"Oh no. I'm not letting you off that easy. They're five simple little words."

Lailu scratched her head.

"Come on, you've said them before." His grin was so wide, it was a wonder the top of his head didn't pop right off.

Lailu sighed. She knew *exactly* what words he wanted. "I owe you a favor," she mumbled.

"Yes, you do!"

Lailu knew she was going to regret this. Last time she'd owed him a favor, she'd been forced to hunt a charging hydra and had ended up embroiled in a murder mystery. Who knew what he'd drag her into this time?

"But," Greg said slowly, "I might be willing to drop the favor. Just this once."

"Why?" Lailu asked.

"You don't need to sound so suspicious. Maybe it's just 'cause I'm such a nice guy?"

"Now I *know* you're up to something."

He laughed. "Then maybe I just want you to promise something else instead."

"What?"

"A talk. You and me, once this next feast"—he indicated the waiting restaurant—"is done."

"A . . . talk?" Lailu took a tiny step back in the direction of her kitchen. "What, uh . . . What kind of talk?"

"I think you know what kind of talk." He was still smiling, but it had gone funny around the edges, like ice left outside on a warm spring day, and his eyes seemed strangely bright and so intense Lailu couldn't look away from them.

She took another small step back toward safety, heart hammering, mouth dry. She remembered how in the boat Greg had wanted to talk about the night of the fairy lights, the night they'd held hands. Maybe that's what he wanted to say now. Maybe he wanted to hold her hand again. Maybe he wanted . . .

She wasn't sure what he wanted, but she was suddenly desperately afraid to find out. It was like going on a hunt without a plan. Lailu hated not having a plan.

"I . . ." She swallowed. "Maybe a favor is not so bad."

Greg's eyes widened, and then he shook his head. "I never thought you'd be such a coward."

"A coward?" She couldn't believe it. "Me?"

"Afraid of a few little words."

Lailu scowled. "I'm not."

"Oh yeah?" He took a sudden step, closing the gap she'd created, and caught one of her hands before she could so much as blink. "I like you, Lailu. I've liked you for years. And I . . . I'm not really sure how you feel about me, so this is terrifying. But I think . . . I think maybe you like me too? Or at least you don't actively dislike me anymore."

Lailu's mouth dropped open. He'd liked her for *years*? "I . . . I don't actively dislike you," she managed.

Greg's mouth twisted into a rueful smile. "Well . . . not quite what I was hoping for, but . . ." He shrugged, then let her go. "I guess I'll, um . . . I'll just see myself out." He turned and strode for the door.

Lailu's hand felt suddenly cold where he'd been holding it. "Wait, Greg?"

He stopped but didn't turn around.

"We can have that talk, if you want. Later. I just . . . I can't focus on anything else. Not right now."

"Okay," he whispered hoarsely, and then he was gone.

I like you . . . I've liked you for years.

Lailu looked around her restaurant, finally empty of people. Dishes cluttered the tables and some of the chairs were knocked over, and she knew she had so much work to do. So much. But she couldn't stop thinking of Greg's words, of his eyes when he said them. She couldn't stop thinking about Greg.

She hadn't handled that well. Not well at all.

Lailu put the backs of her hands against her hot face, took a deep breath, and forced herself to get to work.

An hour later and panic had driven every other distraction away. She didn't have enough supplies in her pantry to feed *any-*

body, let alone host a feast. She was going to have to hope Fahr had kept his word about dropping the barrier, because she needed to visit the market.

Lailu burst into Mystic Cooking, the straps of her bags digging painfully into her hands and shoulders. It was like a huge party out there, everyone celebrating in the street that the barrier had come down. Lailu wanted to warn them that it might not last; if the elves could put it up once, they could do it again. But she didn't have the heart to say all that, not when everyone seemed so happy, so instead she'd just put her head down and dodged people as she rushed back home.

She dropped her bags on the nearest table and stretched her back, glad that Bairn would be bringing over the rest of her market supplies later today. Then she instinctively flexed her fingers. They were tired from carrying the bags, but otherwise they felt good as new. No scars remained, no lingering stiffness.

It was too bad they'd lost that phoenix feather.

She shook her head. She couldn't think like that. Sure, it had healed her hands, and she was curious what else it could do, but that phoenix had been trouble. And anyhow, she would have had to give it to Paulie.

Paulie, who'd been experimenting with Ryon's blood . . .

Lailu didn't want to think about that, but she couldn't shake the image of Ryon's angry face out of her mind, how he'd claimed Hannah had just been using him. Her stomach twisted, imagining him saying those words to her friend.

Hannah never handled fights well. The one time she and Lailu had gotten in a fight, she'd run away and hidden at Greg's restaurant.

"Hannah?" she called hopefully.

Nothing.

The silence felt cold and stale, and Lailu hoped that her friend was okay, wherever she'd gone.

Ding!

Lailu whipped around, then froze at the sight of Greg in her doorway. His earlier words came rushing back, and suddenly she couldn't look at him, her face too hot, the room too small. He looked away too. "Um . . . I brought your skilly-wigs," he mumbled, pushing his cooling and containment cart inside.

"Oh. Uh, thanks," Lailu mumbled back. This was ridiculous. How were they going to cook together? And besides, he was the same old Greg as before.

I've liked you for years.

She resolved not to think about that.

"I also brought something else," Greg said. "Something better than skilly-wigs."

"What could possibly be better than skilly-wigs?" Lailu asked dryly.

"You'll see." Greg pulled open the door, then spread his arms dramatically.

Lailu's jaw dropped. "Master Slipshod?"

He still had a more put-together look than he ever had while working at Mystic Cooking, but instead of the fancy Gilded Island garb she'd seen him in last, he wore a casual blue shirt and wool trousers under an egg-white apron, crisp and ironed, peeking out beneath his warm wool coat. "It's good to be back, Pigtails . . . at least for the day." He pushed his own cooling and containment cart inside and closed the door, then pulled the wool hat off his head and replaced it with his fluffy white chef's hat. "Now, let's get started, eh?"

"But aren't you supposed to be cooking for the king?" Lailu felt like she'd entered some sort of dream, with Slipshod and Greg both in her kitchen, ready to save her butt from the frying pan.

"Well, as it happens, the king heard about your event today— no thanks to you, I might add—"

"I wanted to tell you," Lailu said quickly. "But I wasn't sure how to send you a message—"

Slipshod waved this off. "I know you've had a lot on your plate. But seeing how this negotiation may affect the safety of not just the city but all of Savoria, he decided that your need was more import- ant than his." Slipshod stood up taller, almost like he was some sort of official royal ambassador. "And even more importantly, I couldn't leave my favorite apprentice at a time like this."

"Favorite by process of elimination?" Lailu asked.

"Exactly."

Lailu and Slipshod shared a grin, and Lailu realized how much she missed cooking with her old mentor.

"So, what are we making?" Greg asked. "I've got plenty of skilly- wigs in here." He tapped his cart. "Mmm, mmm, mmm."

Lailu's shoulders sagged. "Skilly-wig soufflé?"

"And doesn't that sound like the best thing ever." Greg pumped his arms enthusiastically.

Lailu's eyes narrowed. "Why are you so happy about this? We're about to go down in history as the chefs who served skilly-wig at an important peace-treaty negotiation."

"Are we?" Greg waggled his eyebrows.

Lailu looked from him to Slipshod, both of them grinning. "What's going on?"

"We have other options," Slipshod said. "I brought another tasty beastie for us to cook up." He popped the lid of his cooling and containment cart. "We can't have the fate of Twin Rivers decided on a stomach full of skilly-wig."

Lailu peered inside, feeling the brisk air on her face. "Is that . . . ?"

"Yes," Slipshod said. "Caught it myself just yesterday. Fresh and ready for cooking."

Lailu grinned, the most delectable idea popping into her head. This feast would be fantastic after all!

35

Phoenix Tales

Since Lailu's kitchen wasn't *quite* big enough to host three master chefs cooking simultaneously, they set up most of their prep work in the dining room. With the blue curtain pulled back and all their supplies on the tables closest to the kitchen, they could move from one room to the other without much delay.

"Ever thought about getting a door?" Greg asked, carrying out an armful of spice bottles.

"No," Lailu said. She created a mound of flour on her table. "I like my curtain. It reminds me of home." She cracked an egg in the middle of the flour, like a little volcano, glad that someone else had had to suffer the wrath of the chickens. Next to her Slipshod was kneading dough. "How's the skilly-wig doing?" It turned out they didn't have quite enough food without cooking at least a little supplemental skilly-wig. Since Greg had been so obnoxious about it, Lailu had put him in charge of all skilly-wig food prep. With Slipshod backing her, Greg didn't have a hope of getting out of it, even though he kept trying.

"How's skilly-wig ever *really* doing?" Greg muttered.

Lailu shot him a look.

"I mean, it's doing great!" He plastered a huge cheesy grin on his face. "I just added the veggies, and I'm waiting for it all to boil once more. Everything should be ready by the time the noodles are done." He let his grin drop. "Still not sure why *I* have to be the one to cook them, though."

"I thought you loved skilly-wig," Slipshod spoke up. "I seem to recall LaSilvian's Kitchen serving skilly-wig and sea-orchids on their opening day. Remember, Pigtails? There was a whole article about it, criticizing our choice of kraken calamari."

Lailu gasped. "I'd . . . forgotten about that."

Greg laughed uneasily. "Hey, what's that I hear? The water's boiling?" And he retreated back into the kitchen.

The nice thing about cooking skilly-wigs was unlike other more challenging mystic beasts, skilly-wigs had no poison in their bloodstream. Some chefs even claimed they shouldn't be considered mystic beasts at all because their only real magical talent was their ability to regenerate their tentacles like hydra heads.

Unlike the sea-wyrm, which was what Slipshod had brought. Those had very impressive abilities, and therefore needed to be prepared much more carefully.

Sea-wyrms could grow to the size of a small ship but were able to disguise themselves as much smaller fish, their scales the color of molten gold. When an unsuspecting fisherman caught one in his net, the wyrm would reveal its *true* form. It was lucky for the nautical folk nearby that Slipshod had caught this beastie before disaster struck.

"What do *you* think about skilly-wigs?" Lailu asked Slipshod. "Should they be classified as mystic beasts?"

"Hardly."

"But Master Chef Gingersnap says—"

"Gingersnap? *Gingersnap?* Don't even get me started about her and her ridiculous theories." He shook his head. "She doesn't have enough recipes in her to fill a plate." He began making another mound of flour. "I've told you before, and I'll tell you again: take all of her theories with a huge pillar of salt."

Greg rejoined them, setting several pot holders on the table. "The water boiled, so I set it to simmer. Now, what did I miss? Are you talking about Gingersnap?"

"That's *Master* Gingersnap." Lailu narrowed her eyes at him. "And you just want to hear Slipshod criticize her."

"Ahh! It's like music to my ears."

Lailu elbowed him. Greg had never liked Master Gingersnap; she'd been one of the few teachers at the Academy who had given him average marks, refusing to fall prey to his charm and flattery. Lailu, on the other hand, got top marks in her class.

"You can't still be a fan of hers," Greg said. "I mean, she claimed we could successfully hunt and cook a phoenix, and we all saw how *that* turned out."

"True. But we also had a disadvantage. I doubt Master Gingersnap ever predicted we'd be hunting that beast with a cursed hero in tow."

"Wouldn't have mattered." Slipshod cleared his half of the table and set a large wooden cutting board in the center. "Hunting a phoenix is always, *always* a terrible idea. I could have warned you about that blasted bird had you asked."

"Why?" Lailu put her last dough ball next to Slipshod's. After the dough sat for a little while, it would be ready to be rolled out, stuffed with skilly-wigs, and twisted into tortellini.

"It just is."

Lailu peered at him.

"What?" Slipshod demanded. "Do I have flour on my face?"

"No . . . but I think you're hiding something. How do *you* know hunting a phoenix is such a bad idea?"

He sighed. "Because . . . I tried to hunt a phoenix before too."

Lailu and Greg gaped at him.

"Mind you, I was quite a bit younger and a lot less well-known." He chuckled.

"*Really?*" Lailu said.

"Let's go check on those skilly-wigs, and maybe—I repeat, *maybe*—I'll tell you about it." Slipshod rose from his chair.

"I'll finish up the tortellini if you want to start mixing up the wyrm glaze," Greg said. "I even brought out your favorite spice, lebinola. Just don't be too heavy-handed with it."

"Excuse me?"

But Greg had already escaped back to her kitchen.

"I'll show him heavy-handed," Lailu muttered, gathering the materials she would need for a sweet glaze.

Greg and Slipshod weren't in the kitchen for long before

Slipshod returned with half the massive sea-wyrm slung over his back—the other half he had left back in his icebox at the castle to prepare later for the king. The creature's torso far exceeded even Slipshod's girth, and its shiny scales glowed like the furnace of a blacksmith. Greg followed with a large pot of skilly-wigs, which he carefully placed on the pot holder.

"So, phoenix hunt?" Greg said.

Slipshod didn't answer, just settled himself in to work, wyrm held firmly down on the cutting board with one hand, while his other hand drew his sharpest knife. The scales flecked away, revealing rainbow skin underneath.

"Phoenix hunt?" Lailu prompted again.

"You're not going to let this go, are you?"

"Is that really a question?" Lailu asked.

Slipshod shook his head. "Fine. Get going with that glaze, Pigtails, and I'll tell you."

Lailu scrabbled for her bowl, lebinola, and special dragon sauce.

"Now, to tell the truth, after hearing your tale of woe, my story is quite tame. There were no curses, no burnt villages, and no special science that stopped the beast's magic involved. It was just me, my chef's knife, and a fiery bird of prey." He slid the sea-wyrm up to get to a new section of scales. "Back in those days, I had barely had my chef's hat on my head before I grew hungry to prove myself, and Gingersnaps's theories seemed like a good place to start. That's how old she is, by the way; she was a teacher even back in *my* day."

"Which means she must be very wise," Lailu said loyally.

Greg snorted.

"Anyhow, being young and foolish and eager for fame, I packed myself a hunting bag and left in search of a phoenix."

"Did you find one?" Lailu asked, then noticed that Greg had stopped working to listen. "Tortellini!"

Greg jumped, gave Lailu a sheepish smile, then got back to work rolling out the dough.

"As you know, phoenixes are extremely rare. Weeks bled into months. I chased rumors of sunbirds and fire creatures, ended up investigating every giant bird sighting myself, just in case. Which is how I found myself accidentally in a roc's nest . . . but that's a whole different story. But the phoenix . . . I never found it."

"You didn't?" Lailu asked, disappointed.

"Nope. But it found me."

"It found you?" Greg asked in disbelief.

"I had tracked it to a range of mountains just south of your village, Lailu. I had been seeing evidence of the beast for days . . . burnt trees, bits of animal bone and the like. Then I stumbled upon its empty nest, and there, lying on top of a pillow of ashes, was a single, long, golden-red feather."

Lailu leaned in to listen as she worked.

"I took the feather," said Slipshod, "and I carried it back to my campsite. Only then did I make a *horrible* discovery."

"What did you find?" Lailu whispered.

"A phoenix doesn't hatch from an egg. Oh, no. It's the tail feather that allows a phoenix to regenerate. So whenever a phoenix loses one of those feathers, it *always* tracks it, no matter who has it, wherever it goes."

Lailu's mouth fell open, and she looked at Greg. His face mirrored hers, and she knew he was also thinking back to the way the phoenix had seemed to search for something, how it kept returning to follow those villagers, night after night. The guard had been right; it was seeking its feather.

"But . . . birds grow new tail feathers all the time," Greg said. "Whenever one gets damaged, birds will molt and grow a new one. So why would a phoenix care that someone has its feather?"

Lailu remembered that tingling sensation she felt right after touching the phoenix feather. She glanced down at her hands, all pink and scar-free, as if she'd grown new skin. As if her hands had regenerated, like a phoenix. They didn't hurt anymore either; she hadn't felt so much as a throb since the phoenix hunt. "Maybe it doesn't want anyone to have its magic," she suggested.

"Maybe," Slipshod agreed. "Or maybe it's not *like* other birds. We really don't know. No one has been able to study a phoenix in depth, so mostly we're just going on rumors here. And some of those rumors are pretty wild."

"Lailu said people in her village believe the phoenix is some kind of guardian," Greg said.

"I told you, it was just a story," Lailu grumbled. "No one *really* believes that. Or at least, not completely."

"I've heard those rumors, and more," Slipshod said.

"Like what?" Greg asked.

"Oh, that the phoenix is a god, that it can grant wishes or protection, that it can give a person immortality. Things of that nature. And even if none of that is true, it certainly *is* powerful. One thing I've learned in my many years is that there is always, always a weakness. The greater power, the bigger weakness, if you know where to look. So it's possible that when a phoenix loses its tail feather, it will not grow a new one until it regenerates. A bird can fly without *one* tail feather, but much more than that . . ."

"So, what happened when you found the nest?" Lailu asked.

"Well, by that point I'd already decided not to hunt that beast. The chef code of ethics is very strict about such things, as you know, and that phoenix hadn't been bothering anyone. But I still wanted proof of my discovery. I *wanted* that feather." He scraped off the last of the scales, his knife moving slowly, deliberately.

"So, what happened?" Lailu asked.

"That blasted fiery beast stalked me through the mountains, nearly burned me to a crisp. Fortunately, I figured it out, so on the third night I gave it back its feather. After that it left me in peace, and I moved on to hunting dragons. Much safer." He set the skinning knife to the side and pulled out a giant cleaver. "I never attacked that phoenix, never truly angered it. Which is lucky, because I've heard if you anger a phoenix, it will use a tail feather to mark your territory as its own. And then it will hunt you down."

Whack!

He separated the head of the sea-wyrm from the body, his blade quivering where it stuck in the thick wood of the cutting board.

"And that is why hunting a phoenix is a terrible idea."

36

NEGOTIATIONS

"D o you think we should move the table?" Lailu asked, double-checking for the hundredth time that it was set and everything was ready. "It seems awfully close to the kitchen."

"Slipshod wanted it here," Greg reminded her.

"Where is he?" Lailu asked.

"I think he's still in the wine cellar. He should be out soon, though. How about Hannah? Is she coming?"

"I don't know when she'll be back. She just up and disappeared after her fight with Ryon." Lailu had no idea where Hannah would have gone, and even though she had enough on her plate right now without worrying about her friend, she couldn't help the unease that curdled in her stomach like old milk.

Greg's lips pressed together in a thin, disapproving line. "That guy." He shook his head. "I never understood what you saw in him."

"Really not the best time for this talk." Outside, the sun had begun its slow plummet to the horizon, and she knew Elister and Fahr would be arriving at any moment.

"On the contrary, I think this is a lovely time."

Lailu and Greg both spun around.

Ryon leaned against the doorway to the kitchen, arms crossed. He smirked at Greg. "Go on, tell me how you really feel."

"I should have known you'd be lurking around here," Greg muttered.

"I wasn't lurking. I was merely skulking about."

"What's the difference?" Lailu asked.

"One sounds cooler." Ryon winked.

"Why are you here?" Lailu asked. "And don't give us a silly answer, or another wink, or whatever. We don't have time for your usual nonsense."

"Yeah." Greg glared at him.

"Oh, stop," Ryon told him. "I can't take you seriously."

"I'll kick you out," Lailu warned.

"Fine. I'm here because I finally made my decision. Your annoying friend there"—Ryon jerked his chin at Greg—"once asked me whose side I was on. And now I know."

"I thought you were on your own side," Lailu said.

"Turns out that answer isn't super popular. I was forced to reconsider." He pushed away from the kitchen doorway. "So I chose your side, Lailu."

"M-my side? Which side is that?"

He shrugged. "Hopefully the right side, whatever that is."

"I thought you were on the side of the elves," Greg said, still frowning.

"I . . . may or may not have done something tonight that will make them very unhappy with me."

Curiosity burned through Lailu hotter than phoenix fire, but before she could ask, the bell above her front door chimed, and Elister stepped inside.

"Master Loganberry." He inclined his head, then noticed Ryon, his eyebrows drawing together. "I was under the impression this was a closed meeting?"

"What can I say? I'm a rebel." Ryon grinned.

"Ryon," Lailu hissed. You couldn't talk that way to Elister the Bloody! Her friend was going to get himself killed. "He's, um, with me." She ignored the sharp look Greg gave her.

Elister nodded once, then turned and called outside, "Wren? Are you coming?"

Wren hurried in, the door swinging shut behind her.

Lailu took a small step back before she could stop herself. Wren had pushed her into a magic doorway during their last encounter; who knew what she would do this time.

Wren glanced at Lailu and then away again quickly, almost guiltily. Her hair had been twisted into a messy bun, and she wore a long leather apron over a white coat, various gadgets and tools sticking out of its many pockets. She pulled one of those gadgets out now. It looked like a horseshoe, but in place of nails there were eight tiny glass orbs, each the size of Lailu's smallest fingernail, running in a line through the middle.

Wren snuck a quick peek back at the room, and then she slipped a small hammer from another pocket and whacked a nail, right there, into Lailu's front door.

Lailu's jaw dropped. "What the lemon zester do you think you're *doing*?"

"Well said," Greg whispered.

Wren hung her horseshoe gadget on the nail and took a step back, considering it.

"What *is* that?" Lailu tried again.

"I wouldn't worry about it," Elister said.

"But . . . that's my door!"

"And I'll pay to replace any damage once this is done." Elister's tone made it clear this matter was closed.

Lailu tried one last time. "But what does it do?"

"It's, um, for luck," Wren said, not meeting Lailu's eyes. She scurried toward Elister, slipping on the floor in her haste and bumping right into Lailu. Only Lailu's quick reflexes stopped them both from going down.

Wren clutched at Lailu's apron to catch her balance. "Sorry," she murmured. She met Lailu's eye again, and there was a strange heaviness to her expression. Almost like she really *was* sorry.

Greg inched closer, and Wren moved quickly away. "You okay?" he whispered.

"I'm fine," Lailu said. She smoothed down her apron, her hand freezing. There was something in her pocket. Something that hadn't been there a second ago. She had no reason to trust Wren or anything Wren might have given her, but that look in Wren's eyes was enough to weigh down her hand, to stop her from yanking it out into the light of Mystic Cooking.

"Ah, Fahr, old friend," Elister said, and Lailu dropped her hand.

Fahr moved inside so silently, it was as if he'd just wafted in like a plume of smoke. The silver shirt he wore belted over black pants added to that image.

"No Eirad?" Elister asked.

"Oh, he's coming," Fahr said. "He wanted to do a quick check around the perimeter first."

Wren visibly started, her lips pressing together so hard they were almost white.

"And why is that?" Elister asked. "Do you have reason not to trust me?"

"Of *course* we have reason not to trust you, *old friend*," Fahr said. "You had us banished."

"Only after you attacked my citizens."

"You mean King Savon's citizens," Fahr corrected. "Or have you forgotten who truly rules this country?"

"I think perhaps *you've* forgotten." Elister's fingers twitched, and Lailu wondered if he had his infamous crescent blades tucked in the back of his shirt. *Silly question*, she realized. He *always* had those blades on him. She was hardly an expert, but this didn't seem like a good start to a peace talk.

"Um, maybe we should all sit and I'll get you your appetizers?" she said.

"Excellent idea," Slipshod said, coming out from behind the

kitchen curtain and bowing to Elister. "Welcome back to Mystic Cooking, Lord Elister."

"Sullivan? I . . . did not realize you would be here." Elister's face gave nothing away, but Lailu got the impression he was not happy to see him.

"Just assisting my former apprentice." Slipshod adjusted his fluffy white hat, the picture of innocence.

"Finally," Lailu muttered. He'd certainly taken his sweet time in the wine cellar.

"Your spy didn't tell you he was coming?" Fahr raised his eyebrows. "Surprising. Unless your spy has gone mysteriously . . . silent."

Elister only glanced at Lailu for the briefest of seconds, but it felt like he'd plunged her deep beneath the icy river, like she was struggling to the surface through a wall of skilly-wigs all over again. Something had happened to his spy. *He has other spies*, Lailu told herself, but that look told her it was her mother. Something had happened to her mother.

Lailu bit her lip, her anxiety rising higher than a three-tiered cake.

Eirad strolled inside. "Good evening, good evening," he called cheerfully. "I see you've brought a scientist with you. Even though, as I recall, that was against the rules of the peace treaty."

"Technically she is a scientist-in-training," Elister said. "And we all know how you elves love your technicalities."

Eirad laughed. "Well, in this case we can be lenient. You see, we invited some of our *own* scientists." He whistled, and Albert poked his bald head in the front door. With an anxious look at Wren, he scurried inside, followed by Krypton. Lailu half expected Krypton to shake everyone's hands, but for once he kept his hands to himself.

Wren's face twitched. "Traitors," she hissed.

"What is this?" Elister demanded.

"You said no other elves were to be present," Fahr said. "You said nothing, however, about other scientists."

Elister's green eyes grew so cold it was a wonder he didn't turn to ice on the spot.

"Um, about those appetizers?" Lailu tried again.

"I suppose this will still work," Elister muttered. "Shall we?" He indicated the table.

"After you," Fahr said.

Lailu had put together three tables and covered them with her best tablecloth, a silk-woven fabric in a deep purple shot through with silver that Hannah had given her. Lailu had to admit it looked lovely with the newly improved candelabras glinting in their own reflected firelight, the sky outside clear and crisp so they had a perfect view of the sunset peeking out from between the various tree branches.

Elister sat at one end of the table, with Wren on his right. At the other end, Fahr took the main seat, with Eirad on his right and Ryon taking the spot on his left. The other scientists filled in the spaces between, although there was a brief struggle over who would be stuck sitting where. In the end Albert got stuck next to Wren.

Elister noticed Lailu hovering nearby. "Is there to be food served, or . . . ?"

"Right away, sir," Lailu said. She, Greg, and Slipshod all retreated a few feet to the kitchen, pulling the curtain closed behind them.

"I already prepared their food and wine." Slipshod pointed at the counter where a tray full of steaming bowls sat, ready to be carried out, with several bottles of LaSilvian wine resting beside it.

"Whoa, you *are* prepared," Greg said, impressed. This was like a whole different Master Slipshod. More than the shorter hair and the nicer, cleaner clothes, this made Lailu realize how much her old mentor had changed since she'd first started working with him. The man crouching beside her now was competent, his wits as sharp as the knife at his belt.

"Now," Slipshod said, still very quietly, "here's our plan: We serve the food quickly, and then leave quickly so they forget about us. And then . . . we listen. And be ready."

"Listen?" Lailu asked. And then she registered the murmur of voices out in the dining room. If they crouched by the curtain, they'd be able to hear everything pretty clearly. "That's why you wanted the table there," she realized.

"Precisely. Now, let's move."

"I, um, have to check something," Lailu said.

Slipshod shrugged and picked up the tray, leaving Greg to grab the wine bottles. As soon as they disappeared into the dining room, all conversation stopped immediately.

Lailu hurriedly dug inside her apron pocket and pulled out a thick sheet of paper, heavily folded. She unfolded it and scanned the words, all written in Wren's familiar script:

Lailu,

I don't think I want to kill you anymore. I felt awful after pushing you through that doorway, when I thought you might be dead. Mama told me revenge was the only way to feel better, but I think maybe she was wrong. So I'm warning you instead.

Elister has a backup plan if the peace negotiations don't go his way. I promised I'd help him, so I made something, something dangerous, and it won't listen to me, and I don't know how to stop it. And it's coming here. Elister thinks I can control it, but I can't.

You should leave. All of you.

-Wren

37

COUNTDOWN

Lailu slowly lowered the paper, her kitchen swimming around her. She didn't want to believe Wren's note, but she knew however murderous and manipulative her former friend might be, she was no liar. So, what kind of backup plan did Elister have? And what kind of dangerous thing had Wren created?

Lailu crumpled the note. Why couldn't Wren have given her more specifics? This warning was about as helpful as a pot with a hole in the bottom.

"We'll return with the main course shortly," Slipshod said, ducking into the kitchen, Greg right behind him. They pulled the curtain across and crouched by it.

Lailu stuffed her wrinkled note back into her apron and joined them. "I have to tell you—"

Slipshod put a finger to his lips, and she stopped. He pointed to the dining room, where the conversation had resumed.

"I still can't believe they're serving us skilly-wigs," Lailu heard Elister grumble, and all thoughts of warnings and traps faded in a wash of fury. If he'd told her she would be hosting this meeting, she would have prepared better.

"Although . . . for skilly-wigs, this is excellent," he added.

Lailu scowled, only a little appeased.

"Are we really here to discuss the food?" Eirad demanded. "Or are we here to discuss our terms for peace?"

"You brought down the barrier," Elister said. "As we had agreed would be your show of good faith to match my own, consenting to meet over here. First requirement met on both sides. What is your next requirement?"

"Next requirement," Fahr said, "is that we elves are tired of being kept on the outskirts of the city. We used to own this land, and we intend to reclaim it. Or at least, a part of it."

"Reclaim it . . . how?" Elister's tone was cool, giving nothing away.

"Nothing drastic, old friend," Fahr said, his tone slightly mocking. "The king is practically of age now. Which means he'll be ready to take over the running of this kingdom."

"Not until he has completed his apprenticeship with me," Elister said.

"Some people might think there's a conflict of interest there," Eirad cut in. "You being the one who decides when that apprenticeship is complete . . . and you being the one who gets to hold power *until* it's complete."

"Are you saying I am being unfair?"

"We're not accusing you of such a thing," Fahr said smoothly.

"Not within his hearing, at least," Slipshod muttered. He shifted position. "We'll bring out the next course in a few minutes," he added softly.

"I prefer to be blunter than Fahr," Eirad said. "Elister, we all know you would like to hold on to power."

"That's not true," Elister said. "I just want to make sure our kingdom stays on the right course."

"Same thing," Eirad said dismissively. "You want to keep power. The king wants to gain power. Eventually there's going to be a struggle, and if you don't act now to take care of that, our city, and the whole kingdom, will be divided and weakened enough for the Krigaen Empire to just sweep on in and gobble it up like one of these surprisingly tasty skilly-wig tortellinis." There was a loud *slurp!*

Lailu and Greg exchanged startled glances.

"Told you they could be tasty," Greg whispered.

"Currently, only the queen's favor and good graces are keeping you in charge," Eirad continued, voice slightly muffled. Lailu wondered if he was talking through a mouthful of food. "But that, too, will end eventually, especially as her son grows older."

"Therefore, we have a proposition for you," Fahr cut in. "Beginning next year, on the king's sixteenth birthday, he will take over the throne. But at that time, you have the power to create a royal council of advisers. A council who can overrule the king if they have a majority."

"And let me guess . . . you would be on that council?" Elister said.

"Naturally," Fahr agreed. "As would you and the queen."

"Interesting. This idea has merit." Elister was silent for a moment. Then, "I have an additional request, however, before I could consider this option. I would require the presence on the council of a scientist of my choosing."

"Absolutely not," Fahr said. "These scientists do not belong to our country. They should not be granted power over its citizens."

"We must have a scientist on this council," Elister argued. "You cannot halt progress, Fahr. Times are changing, and we must embrace them."

"Oh, absolutely. And I have begun to appreciate some of the scientists. But none of them can be allowed onto this council. They already exert too much control as it is."

"Then I'm afraid we're at an impasse," Elister said.

"What now?" Lailu whispered.

"Serve the next course?" Greg suggested. They both looked at Slipshod, who nodded once, and they got up and loaded their trays with platters of fish, fresh from the oven and smelling delectable. Lailu was especially proud of the glaze she'd made, with the perfect amount of lebinola spice, if she said so herself.

They carried them out into the dining room. No one was speaking; Elister sat with his usual perfect posture, Fahr and Eirad glaring at him from their side of the table. Albert kept mopping his bald head with a handkerchief, while Krypton had sunk so low in his chair, it was a wonder he hadn't slid onto the floor. And Wren sat so still, she might have been part of the furniture herself. Only Ryon looked like he was casually dining with friends. "Ah, the main course," he said, grinning. "I'm starved."

"I was so hoping we would come to some sort of arrangement." Elister sighed. "It would have been much more convenient. But if not, then I am prepared to change the nature of this meeting. Wren?"

Wren blinked. "Yes?" Her voice came out in a terrified wisp.

"I believe it's time."

"I . . . I can't."

Elister steepled his fingers together in front of his face, studying her. "Interesting. Perhaps not your mother's daughter after all?"

Wren flinched. Without looking at anyone, she pulled a small metal box from her apron pocket and handed it over to Elister.

Elister fiddled with the box, pressing buttons and flicking switches. Then he set it on the table and leaned back in his seat. "You have about twenty minutes to change your minds before it'll be too late. I suggest you reconsider your stance, and quickly."

Twenty minutes? Until what? Lailu looked at Greg and Slipshod, both frozen next to her.

"Oh, good. Is this where we get to the blackmail part of the evening?" Eirad rubbed his hands together. "I do so love a good threat. And it turns out, we have one of our own. An opening threat."

"Oh?" Elister raised one careful brow. "I'm assuming you're about to tell me what happened to my missing spy. I presume she's in your custody?"

"She is," Fahr agreed. "For now, at least."

Lailu caught her breath. "My mom?" she squeaked.

Fahr ignored her, but Eirad nodded. "Sorry, little chef. But all is fair in war and business, and this is a little bit of both. And she was spying on us."

"Actually, she was spying on the king," Elister clarified.

"You would spy on your king?" Master Slipshod drew himself up, but he deflated at a single glance from Elister.

"It is my job as regent of this country to ensure our underage king is not making any foolish . . . alliances, or promises." Elister cut another bite of fish, chewed, and swallowed, like he didn't have a care in the world. Like her mom's fate meant nothing to him. It was the first time Lailu had ever been angry to see someone enjoying her food.

Elister met Lailu's gaze over the table, and it was like he was whispering those words in his office again: *Know which pieces are expendable, which can be sacrificed to bring you closer to your goal.* Lailu went cold all over. Someone who treated people like pawns in a game could not be allowed to run their kingdom. Not any longer.

Still watching her, he said, "It will be an unfortunate sacrifice, but such is the nature of spies. They come and they go."

Everyone looked over at Ryon.

"Why are you looking at me?" he demanded. "Do I look like a spy?"

"Yes," Greg said.

Ryon frowned at him. "I've never liked you, you know that?"

"Mutual," Greg muttered.

"I don't think you quite understand the danger to yourself," Eirad said sharply. "This spy has been working for you for years. She knows many of your secrets."

"She'll never talk." Elister took another bite.

"I tell you, she will sing like a bird," Eirad snapped. "We have ways—"

"Would this be a bad time to admit I let her go?" Ryon spoke up.

Stunned silence. Into it, Wren whispered, "Fifteen minutes."

"You did *what*?" Fahr demanded, finding his voice.

"I told you to stop trusting him," Eirad said. "Repeatedly. But you allowed him to handle these important tasks, and now look: betrayal. Just as I warned would happen."

"Okay, first of all," Ryon said, holding up both hands, "you didn't *allow* me to do anything. You needed my help. And second, this was hardly a betrayal. I didn't do this to purposely sabotage you."

Fahr had gone white-lipped with fury. "I have stood by you all these years."

"Have you really, though?" Ryon asked. "How many 'loyalty tests' have I had to pass? I'm tired of them, and this most recent one pitted my loyalty to you against my loyalty to my friend." He shrugged. "Lailu actually accepts me for who I am and not what I can do for her. So I chose friendship." He winked at Lailu, who had gone pink.

"I still say he's shady," Greg muttered.

"Definitely," Lailu agreed, beaming at Ryon. Her mother was safe. Ryon had rescued her, because he was her friend. And just like that, her feelings for him became as clear as glass noodles.

Ryon was the only person she knew who never saw her as a poor scholarship student, or a rival to beat, or even as a little sister to protect. He saw her as herself. And when she looked at him, she didn't calculate all the ways he could be useful. Instead, their relationship was based on something deeper, an understanding that they were the same, both outsiders constantly trying to prove they belonged. And while he might be a sneaking, skulking spy, he was also Ryon, the boy who made her laugh and irritated her, and who would, when it came down to it, have her back. Just like she'd always have his.

But he was also the boy who would leave when he wanted, and return when he wanted. And even if she thought Ryon was kind of cute—okay, very cute—she had decided long ago that she would never end up like her father, always waiting for someone to return. Ryon had become one of her best friends, but she knew it would never be more than friendship between them.

When she fell in love, it would be with a boy who stayed.

"I *am* sorry, though, brother," Ryon began.

"Don't call me that. You are no longer any brother of mine."

Ryon raised his eyebrows. "Just like that, huh?" He flicked imaginary dust off his shoulders. "Well, I suppose it was inevitable." He said it like it didn't matter, but Lailu remembered his face after the Week of Masks, how devastated he'd been to find out Fahr had anything to do with that. He'd once really looked up to his half brother. For all she knew, Fahr was the only family he had.

"This has been . . . entertaining . . . but it seems you have lost one of your chess pieces. Which puts you at a disadvantage." Elister finished eating his fish and dabbed at his mouth with a napkin. "Will you reconsider my offer?"

"A spot on the council . . . a council where you and your pet scientist would be able to overrule us every time." Fahr shook his head. "I don't think so."

Elister set his napkin gently on the table in front of him. "You know, I've often wondered what your people would do if they were deprived of their leaders."

"Is that a threat?" Fahr asked softly.

"Not at all, merely a question. I have my own theory, of course. I believe—and I'm staking quite a bit on this—that without the two of you, the rest of the elves would take a long time to reorganize. Much like a snake without any fangs, your people would no longer be a threat."

Lailu wasn't sure who moved first, but suddenly Eirad had his knife out, curved blade glinting in the light of the candelabras above them, just as Elister's crescent blades left his hands.

Eirad winced, dropping his knife, blood blossoming from a gash in his shoulder.

Krypton yelped and fell backward out of his chair, while Albert clutched his fork and knife and hunkered down. Lailu wasn't sure what to do; in a hunt, she would be prepared. But these were people, and she wasn't sure which ones were her enemies. All of them? None of them? Uneasily, she put a hand to the knife at her hip.

Fahr stood, chair falling backward, green light flaring around his fingers.

"That, my friend, was a mistake," Elister told Fahr.

"I doubt it." Fahr flicked his fingers, and the green of his magic expanded, then abruptly shot back at him. He cried out and shook his hands, but his magic didn't go away. Instead, tiny tendrils of it attacked him like a nest of ravenous vibbers, driving him back into the wall.

Ryon leaped from his chair and ran over to his half brother's side. As soon as he touched Fahr, the green flickered and then vanished like river fog on a hot summer's day.

In a blur of movement, Eirad was there too, shoving Ryon away. "We don't need your help," he snarled.

Ryon backed up, hands in the air, and left Eirad to check on Fahr, who seemed dazed but unhurt.

"What happened?" Lailu asked Albert.

He pointed at her door with his fork, and she noticed the horseshoe Wren had nailed up there earlier. The clear glass orbs were pulsing with the same green as Fahr's magic. "It's a completed mal-canterarc. Starling was working on it before she . . ." Albert adjusted his grip on his fork. "It was her final project commissioned by the general of Beolann. She must have brought it with her when we escaped."

"And I finished it," Wren said. She sat up straighter, triumphant. "*I* finished it. And it worked!"

"You truly are amazing," Elister told her warmly. "I'm so proud."

Wren's eyes glistened, tears threatening to spill over. She scrubbed her arm across her face, sniffling loudly.

"Is something wrong?" Elister frowned.

"You're proud of me," Wren sobbed. "*Me.*"

"We don't need magic to kill you," Fahr said, rising unsteadily to his feet. "If it comes to that."

Elister stood, his arms at his sides, fingers twitching. "Shall we test this?"

"Um, how about dessert? Anyone?" Lailu asked desperately, looking around for support. Her gaze landed on her front door just as it opened and two people stepped inside: Hannah, her hair twisted back up into buns and clipped in place with her

Ryon-blood-red gems, and a slender teenage boy with shoulder-length hair curling gently around his delicate face. A boy she recognized immediately.

The King of Savoria.

"Ten minutes," Wren said into the sudden silence.

38

PAWNS REVOLTING

"Your Majesty!" Elister bowed hastily. "You really should not be here. It isn't safe."

"Why not?" the king asked. He glanced curiously around the room, at the chairs that had toppled over, at the two elves crouched in the corner, at the scientists doing their best to appear invisible, and at Wren, standing white-lipped and trembling by the window.

Elister strode over to the king. Master Slipshod moved faster, putting himself between them, his hand on the hilt of the chef's knife at his waist.

"Not necessary, Sullivan," King Savon said. "But thank you."

Lord Elister frowned at the chef and then turned to the king, speaking in a soft, urgent voice.

"I . . . have no idea what's going on," Greg whispered.

"Me either," Lailu whispered back. "But only Elister has eaten the food." She looked at the other plates, untouched on the table. "Maybe we can move the rest of it into the kitchen?"

Greg gaped at her.

"What? Our feasts always seem to get destroyed, and we worked so hard on this one."

"This is really not the time to worry about the food."

Lailu scowled. "There is always time to worry about the food."

"Really, I insist, for your own safety you *must* leave," Elister snapped, loud enough that the whole room turned to him.

"Must I?" King Savon asked.

"Stop acting like a child!"

The king stiffened, nostrils flaring.

Ding!

"You'll never believe this," Vahn exclaimed, rushing inside, "but I found another feather, right here on your doorstep, and . . . and . . . Oh. Sorry to interrupt." He noticed the king and went pale. "Your Majesty." He bowed deeply, clutching a hat to his head. When he straightened, the thing in his hand caught the light.

A single long, reddish-gold feather.

Lailu's eyes widened, and Greg clutched at her arm, both of them remembering Slipshod's words: *If you anger a phoenix, it will use a tail feather to mark your territory as its own. And then it will hunt you down.*

"That feather was on my doorstep?" she croaked, her throat dry and tight.

"I'm wondering if it fell out of a pack." Vahn twirled the feather gleefully. "Finally! A spot of good luck."

"No," Lailu said. "No, it's not. You need to get that out of here."

"Oh, naturally. I plan to give it to Paulie, just as soon as I can be taken through the barrier."

"The barrier is down," Elister said.

"Actually, sir, it's not . . . ," Vahn said slowly. "I already checked."

Elister looked over at Eirad.

"We only promised to take it down," Eirad said smugly. "We never said anything about *keeping* it down. We made a few changes to it, a few . . . adjustments."

"Our magic outside of this place still works quite effectively," Fahr added. "The new barrier is shrinking, and quickly. Soon it will completely encase Mystic Cooking."

"If this is true, then how was the king able to come through?" Elister asked.

"I told you, we made a few adjustments," Fahr said. "Anyone can now come into *our* side of the city, but once you are here, you cannot cross back. Not without our help. Without our . . . permission."

"So, this was a trap?" Elister raised his brows, then turned to the king. "Do you see now how you cannot trust the elves?"

"What about your own trap?" King Savon asked. "Your own plans? Why should I trust *you* over them?"

"Whoa," Greg whispered. He glanced sideways at Lailu. "Almost feels like we should be making popcorn, or something."

"This is serious, Greg," Lailu whispered back.

"So is my popcorn. I make it with extra butter, freshly ground sea salt, and just a pinch of pixie paprika."

That actually sounded pretty good, but Lailu refused to let herself be distracted.

"Your Majesty, don't let others cloud your judgment—" Elister began.

"Since when have you ever cared about *my* judgment?" King Savon snapped. "I am just another tool to you. You pretend to care so long as you're able to hold on to power yourself."

Elister flinched as if the king had slapped him. "That is not true. I made a promise to your father that—"

"I saw the documents," the king said, voice harsh. "I know you were planning on remaining in power much longer than you told my mother. And anyone who tried to stop you, like Fahr here, you would remove. Because that's what you do, isn't it? You remove those who stand between you and power, Elister the Bloody."

Elister actually took a step back, his face white.

He had earned that nickname years ago when he'd mercilessly killed all contesters to the throne of Savoria immediately after the old king died, leaving only one possible option: the late king's young son. Afterward, the queen had made him co-regent of Savoria until such time as the king completed his schooling and apprenticeship.

"When were you planning on removing *me?*" the king asked.

"Never. Your Majesty, I . . . I would never—"

"I don't believe you. And it hurts me, Elister." The king put a hand to his heart. "You practically raised me, and . . ." He stopped, frowning. "What is that?"

The walls and floor vibrated, dishes on the table rattling. Something was coming. Something large. "Wren?" Lailu asked.

Wren shook her head. "Still five minutes," she whispered. "That's not mine."

Lailu looked at that feather in Vahn's hand. Outside the noise had grown louder, building into a hum. But it didn't sound like an animal. It sounded like . . . people?

And then her door burst open again.

Slipshod pulled the king back farther into the restaurant, drawing his knife and standing in front of him, while Elister blocked the door.

Outside a whole crowd of people had surrounded Mystic Cooking. Familiar people, wearing their worker's smocks and bowler hats and carrying pitchforks, torches, knives, whatever they could gather, and chanting, "Down with Elister the Bloody!" while others simply chanted over and over, "Murderer! Murderer!" among other cries of "Gilded Island is built on our backs!" and "*Our* sweat turns to *your* gold!" and things Lailu couldn't quite distinguish beneath the anger and desperation. It felt like a whole tide of skilly-wigs washing up on Mystic Cooking's shores, all perfectly harmless on their own, but together like this they could drown everything.

Elister's jaw tightened.

"Didn't count on that, did you?" Fahr said. "That's the problem with someone like you. You're too removed to remember the people."

"The people, who are being herded over in this direction by your barrier?" Elister said dryly.

"Check and mate." Eirad smirked.

Elister drew another set of crescent blades from hidden sheaths in his vest and turned to face the growing crowd.

"Are you honestly going to start cutting up your own people?" Fahr asked.

"Why not? I *am* Elister the Bloody, am I not?" Elister said bitterly. "Time to earn my nickname."

"We'd better get you out of here," Slipshod whispered, pulling the king toward the kitchen. "We don't want them to see you."

"But . . . why?" King Savon looked shocked. "What could they possibly have against me?"

Lailu's eyes narrowed on the king's silk-lined coat, his high-quality shoes, the way he stood there so secure in his position. Everything about him screamed Gilded Island aristocracy. The mob out there would break his fragile bones and eat him alive.

"I can take him through the barrier and back to the palace," Ryon murmured, moving to their sides. He glanced at Hannah. "You never should have brought him here in the first place."

Hannah looked away, her cheeks coloring.

"She didn't *bring* me," the king said, nostrils flaring. "I insisted on coming. I'm here to confront Elister and—"

"And you've done a beautiful job of it," Hannah soothed. "But you're not safe here. And our country needs you."

"Stand down!" Elister ordered the crowd. "I repeat, stand down!"

"You left us to burn," one man yelled, and with a start Lailu recognized him as one of the Wolfpine villagers.

"You ordered us to come to work when the barrier went up, and my son was trapped on Gilded Island. Just because he didn't want to lose his job!" another woman screamed.

And from there a whole flood of anger washed forth.

Lailu spared one last glance and saw Ryon, Slipshod, and Krypton disappearing through her kitchen with the king.

"All of your grievances have a time and a place," Elister said, his own voice carrying over. "But that is not here or now."

"Then when?" the Wolfpine villager demanded, shoving his way into the restaurant.

Elister raised his blades.

Lailu looked at Elister, with his weapons glinting, his jaw set. Her eyes trailed from him to Fahr and Eirad, who had set this whole thing in motion and were doing nothing, *nothing*, to protect the people they'd essentially coerced into coming here. And then she looked at Albert, huddled in the corner, and Wren, staring absently at her remote.

None of them cared about these people. The elves, and the scientists, and the aristocrats of Gilded Island. They each had their own agendas, their own little chess games, and people like Lailu and those who lived near her were all treated as nothing more than pawns to be moved around the board. And Lailu was done with it.

"You leave these people alone." Lailu moved to stand between Elister and the Wolfpine villager.

Elister studied her. "Are you challenging me, Miss Loganberry?"

Lailu drew her knife. "That's Master Loganberry. And yes, I am."

"You don't stand a chance, and you and I both know it. You'll lose this fight."

Lailu swallowed. She remembered how fast Elister had moved when he'd sliced and diced a spy in front of her, and more recently, when he'd killed the Butcher right here in this very restaurant. She knew she was good, one of the best, when it came to hunting mystic beasts. But Elister was right: she didn't stand a chance in a fight against him.

But maybe that didn't matter. Maybe by standing up, by finally choosing a side, she'd already won.

She lifted her chin and shifted her weight. Her knife felt solid in her hand, and the background dropped away, the sounds of Greg calling her name, of Hannah, of the people behind them. It all vanished, and her world became just her, her knife, and Elister.

Elister smiled, one quick flash of teeth, and then he lunged forward. His knives were so fast she blocked them only on instinct, her body moving and reacting faster than her eyes could track the movements. She blocked, spun, dodged, sliced in with her knife, blocked again, and ducked. Already sweat beaded her brow and soaked her shirt. She couldn't catch her breath, her lungs burning like she was drowning, the clang of metal against metal impossibly loud.

Elister looked like he was taking a stroll through a sun-drenched park, like this was the easiest thing in the world for him. He pressed the attack, and all Lailu could do—barely—was block again and again. It felt like hours passed, or maybe years, but really Lailu knew it had been barely a minute.

A sharp slice of pain in her arm, and she cried out and stumbled to one knee.

"Step aside," Elister told her.

"No," Lailu gasped. Her left arm was on fire, blood trickling down her sleeve, but she pushed herself back to her feet.

And she realized that she wasn't standing alone; Greg had moved to her left, his own knife out. It was one of his favorite blades, with a serrated edge, trembling slightly in his grip. And on her right . . . "You got Mr. Smacky?" Lailu panted.

Hannah twirled her frying pan and nodded grimly.

"So this is how it's to be?" Elister sighed. "Very well." But before he could press the attack again, Vahn stepped between them.

"What are you doing?" Elister demanded. "You work *for* me. You can't challenge me."

"I work for Savoria, and I can't let you threaten these people."

"I will strip you of your hero-ship."

Vahn gulped. "I . . . I know. But I still swore an oath to defend the defenseless."

"We're *not* defenseless," Hannah snapped.

"Still." Vahn drew his sword. "This is my battle. You'll have to get through me to—ack!"

Elister slashed directly at Vahn's face, and only a quick parry saved him. Lailu wanted to help, but they were circling each other, moving so fast she was afraid she'd just trip Vahn.

"We couldn't help you, either," Greg whispered, tugging Lailu away. "I wanted to jump in sooner, but I thought I might just get in your way."

"Do you think . . . his curse . . . ?" Hannah's forehead creased in worry, and she hovered on the edge of the fight, Mr. Smacky at the ready. "And what's with the hat?"

"His hair got burned by the phoenix," Lailu explained.

"No!" Hannah gasped.

"I thought you hated him," Greg said, wrapping a large cloth napkin around Lailu's bleeding arm.

"Him, maybe. But his hair was innocent." Hannah sighed. "And beautiful."

"This doesn't look too deep," Greg said, tying off the cloth. "But you'll want to—"

And then people outside were screaming and scattering as a gigantic shadow fell over Lailu's restaurant. Vahn and Elister didn't seem to notice, but everyone else froze and looked up as whatever it was went past, shrieking, the noise like hot air escaping a teakettle. Almost . . . mechanical.

"What is it?" Lailu asked. "Wren? Wren!"

Wren turned away from the window. She'd picked up the box she'd given Elister and was clutching it against her chest like a shield. "It's time," she said, her gaze locking on Lailu. "One . . . two . . . three . . ."

Instinctively Lailu kicked the table over, dishes flying everywhere. "Duck!" She yanked Greg and Hannah behind the table just as something huge smashed through her windows and took off part of her wall.

39

Epic Battle

*L*ailu slowly straightened from her crouch, Greg and Hannah on either side, huddling so close their shoulders touched as they peered through the dust.

Something huge and monstrous stood in the middle of Mystic Cooking, steam pouring from its nostril slits, its eyes the electric blue of the spi-trons. It looked like a mountain dragon, only *wrong*, the same way Starling's automatons had looked like grotesque people. Spikes ran down its back, ending at the tip of a metallic, flattened tail shaped like a small shovel. And when its lips drew back, it displayed teeth made from the jagged edges of steak knives.

Wren walked toward it like she was in a trance.

"Don't!" Lailu cried, standing from her crouch behind the table. Wren had warned her that she couldn't control this thing, whatever it was.

"It won't hurt me," Wren said, putting a hand on its side. "I'm its creator." It towered over her, its long neck extended, body crouched, and still its head scraped against the ceiling, knocking down the candelabra, its feet snapping chairs into splinters as it stomped restlessly in place.

"A drago-tron," Lailu whispered.

"I designed it to kill you," Wren said matter-of-factly. "It's why I gave it these teeth, so you would be ripped apart by your own cooking implements."

"That's . . . lovely," Lailu muttered, suddenly very glad to have a solid table in front of her, and wishing it were five times thicker. "I thought you didn't want to kill me anymore?"

Wren's face twisted. "I . . . I don't know." She looked up at the drago-tron, and it tilted its head, like it was silently communicating with her.

"Lailu," Hannah gasped, grabbing her arm. "Vahn . . ."

Lailu turned. Vahn was still fighting Elister on the other side of the restaurant. Vahn was younger and in better shape, but Elister had years of experience and a ruthlessness that Vahn would never be able to match. Already Vahn was bleeding from a cut down the side of his face and another on his left shoulder. And there was that curse. Miraculously, he hadn't tripped or dropped his sword yet, but how long could that last?

The two of them circled each other, moving so fast it was impossible to see where one ended and the other began, except in brief flashes when they paused, each shifting their weight, weighing the other. Lailu instinctively noted all of the things that could mess Vahn up: a toppled chair, a fallen napkin, a couple of people standing just a little too close. Every single one of them was a tripping hazard, a potential disaster. Even there, in the corner, the glittering phoenix feather. Vahn must have dropped it during their fight.

"Watch it!" Greg shoved Lailu just as the drago-tron's tail slammed into the table in front of them, turning it into splinters.

"Oops," Wren said.

"Oops?" Lailu said.

The drago-tron opened its mouth and roared, and a piece of glass clinging to the window behind it fell and shattered. "I'm trying to send it back out, really," Wren said, "but it's not listening to this." She held up the box.

"Ahh!"

Lailu spun.

Vahn's right arm hung at his side, blood trickling from his fingers. He'd lost his hat somewhere along the way, his charred hair clinging to the back of his neck and head in patches.

Sweat soaked the back of Elister's silk tunic and dampened his gray-streaked hair, but it was obvious he was close to winning this fight. He lunged in, his blade flashing straight for Vahn's unprotected neck.

Vahn stepped back, somehow leaping over the fallen chair behind him and kicking it forward. It slammed into Elister's legs, toppling him, but he turned it into a roll and sprang up to his feet, both crescent blades gripped in his fingertips, prepared to throw—

Whack!

Elister crumpled to the ground. "That's for messing with our restaurant," Hannah said, standing over him with Mr. Smacky.

Vahn crawled forward and checked Elister. "Just unconscious," he announced. "Nice timing," he added. "You are amazing with that thing."

"Now, that is a compliment I'll accept, even from you." She spun Mr. Smacky around in a loop and tucked it under her arm.

"Holy canola oil," Greg breathed.

Lailu blinked. "Hey, that's pretty good."

"Thanks! You can borrow it, if you like."

"I might."

"Notice *I'm* not greedy with *my* expressions."

"Is this really the time for—ack!" Lailu ducked as steam shot out in a geyser from the drago-tron's open gaping mouth. Staying low, she crawled toward the elves. Eirad lounged in the corner, amused by the show, while Fahr still seemed a little dazed next to him.

"You could help!" Lailu snapped at Eirad.

"I was overcome with an urge to be helpful recently, in this very place," Eirad said. "And I swore in that moment not to make that mistake again."

Lailu scowled. "Wren! What's happening over there?"

"I'm still trying," Wren grunted, jabbing at buttons.

"Where is Albert? He could help too," Greg said.

Lailu looked around the room. Albert was gone. She sighed. She shouldn't have been surprised.

"I don't need any—" Wren started.

The drago-tron's tail shot down out of nowhere, the shovel end slamming into the remote and smashing it against the floor.

"Well, that's not good," Wren muttered.

It lifted its front feet and slammed them down, then shuffled back and forth, its eyes flaring, glowing a chilling electric blue as it spun around the room, steam oozing from its nostril slits. It began vibrating, the metal scales clacking against one another. Wren moved back a few steps, fear stamped across her face. Obviously this thing was out of control, and who knew what it would do. Explode? Attack them?

Outside, Lailu could hear people getting louder, crying, screaming. Why weren't they leaving? Why weren't they . . . ? "The barrier," she realized. It must be pushing everyone closer and closer to Mystic Cooking. To this beast *inside* Mystic Cooking. "They're trapped here." She turned on Fahr, pointing at him with her knife. "You keep claiming Elister is forgetting about the people. You claim the elves care about them. You claim you protect your city, so protect it!"

"What?" Fahr blinked, shocked.

"Let them go. If this thing starts going berserk, they're not safe out there."

Fahr regarded her, then turned to Eirad. "The chef is right. Get the city folk away from here."

"But—" Eirad began.

"Do it. They are our people now. We must protect them. I'll take care of this . . . monstrosity."

Eirad frowned, but he did as he was told, slipping outside the restaurant.

Lailu saw Vahn sling an unconscious Elister over his shoulder. "I'll hurry back," he promised. "I'm just taking him to safety." As he ducked outside, the door fell off its hinges, crashing to the ground behind him. Then Lailu, Greg, Hannah, Fahr, and Wren were alone with the drago-tron.

"We took down a dragon once before, and we'll do it again." Hannah spun Mr. Smacky.

Fahr spread his fingers, green fire gathering in the palms of his hands, the air in the restaurant thickening until it became suffocating, like trying to breathe through pudding.

"I'm not sure . . ." Lailu glanced at her broken door lying on the floor of Mystic Cooking, Wren's horseshoe buried beneath it. It must have stopped working; Fahr forced his magic out in a wave that crashed into the drago-tron, glittering against its scales and turning its eyes a vivid forest green. It reared back, its body vibrating.

"Stop!" Wren yelled. "It's like the horseshoe; the more magic you pour into it, the more powerful it gets."

The drago-tron opened its mouth, and green flames poured forth in a river of fire. Fahr barely dodged in time.

Greg pulled his extra knife from the spare sheath in his boot as Lailu drew her own. This drago-tron was made of metal instead of flesh, but Lailu remembered how Wren had studied mystic beasts before, how she'd had a whole hideout full of their skeletons and charts describing their anatomy. She had probably designed this thing to be as close to a real-life mountain dragon as possible using metal, springs, and clockwork gears.

The drago-tron snorted and stomped, and then it charged forward.

Lailu rolled out of the way, trusting Greg and Hannah to both take care of themselves. She came up below another table and used her own momentum to knock that over as the beast shrieked, boiling-hot steam pouring from its open mouth and sizzling in the air above her head. All around her platters of expertly seasoned sea-wyrm crashed to the ground, exactly as predicted. Lailu winced. It was always the food that suffered.

Greg threw a chair at the drago-tron, which Fahr turned into a spinning blade. The drago-tron smacked it down with a metal paw, then spun toward Greg. And that was when Lailu saw it: carefully hidden under a plate of metal was a gap, and in that gap lay a bundle of wires. Just like the nerve bundle at the nape of a real mountain dragon's neck.

Lailu didn't give herself time to think; she lunged forward, leaping up off the edge of the table, and drove her knife right into that gap to slice through the wires.

Sparks shot out like blood, and Lailu dropped and rolled away as the dragon twitched and jerked.

"Wow, you've gotten a lot better at that," Hannah said.

"Thanks." Lailu grinned and waited for the dragon to collapse. And waited.

"Uh . . . I don't know if that worked," Greg said.

"What did you *do?*" Wren demanded. She had to duck under a table as the drago-tron's tail sliced through the air where her head had been a second before. "Don't attack *me!* Argh, all of its safety mechanisms are completely destroyed!"

It flipped over Wren's table with one massive paw and swiped at her, its talons raking against her leather apron. Hannah smacked it in the back with Mr. Smacky, the sound of metal against metal reverberating through the restaurant. "Not helpful," Hannah said, giving her frying pan a look of deepest betrayal.

"What now?" Greg asked Lailu as they all inched back. The drago-tron kept jerking one way, then the other, charging forward and stomping on tables, then twitching, sparks flashing and flaring from in between its metal plates. Fahr had moved back and was muttering to himself, his face illuminated by a soft green glow. Hopefully he was working on something that would stop this thing, but just in case, Lailu knew it was time for her to come up with a plan.

As usual.

"Are there other wires we should cut?" Lailu asked Wren.

"Maybe, if you can get inside its leg joints," Wren said. "But I purposely designed it to make that impossible."

"Great," Lailu muttered. She narrowed her eyes, searching for other weak points and flaws.

"Do you hear . . . yelling?" Greg asked.

"That's the people rioting outside," Hannah said.

"No, I think it's coming from downstairs," Greg said.

"My cellar," Lailu realized. "Did Albert run down there?" She hesitated. Before she could make up her mind, a shriek tore through the night. A very familiar, birdlike shriek.

A fireball flew through the already partially destroyed wall of Mystic Cooking, then materialized into the phoenix, and everything was fire and feathers and roaring, stomping metal.

40

FEATHER OFFERING

$\mathcal{W}$ ren worked her way back to huddle near Lailu, her eyes wide beneath her wild curls.

The drago-tron snorted, stomping its feet like it didn't know what to make of this new foe. It seemed like the more magic it absorbed, the more self-aware it became. But the phoenix didn't care about anyone in the room except Lailu. It found her, those beady eyes narrowing, the cruel beak curving in a smile that was all malice, no humor at all. Flames flickered and spat around it as it lazily flapped its wings.

Lailu sprinted away from her friends, rolling on the ground and coming up with the tail feather.

The phoenix shrieked in fury, gliding toward her . . .

"O God of Cookery, protect me," Lailu prayed, holding out

the feather in both hands. If this didn't work, she was toast. "This feather is yours! I give it to you." Heat scorched her face, and she shrank back, tears streaming from her eyes, sweat sliding down her back. A second passed, and another. Lailu managed to peer through the crackling flame.

The phoenix towered in front of her, eyes sharp on her face. It slowly lowered its wings, but instead of fire blasting from them, Lailu felt nothing but the gentle caress of a warm wind. She got the impression it was still waiting for something more, however.

"Um . . . I'm really sorry about the powder," Lailu tried. She could see her own reflection in the bird's eyes. "And I promise . . . I promise never to hunt a phoenix again."

The tail feather in Lailu's hands flickered like flame and then vanished.

"Lailu!" Hannah screamed as the drago-tron brought its tail crashing down on her. Lailu barely had time to throw her arms up over her head.

Embers fell, burning holes in her sleeves, but she wasn't crushed. She peered through her laced fingers at the phoenix standing over her, shielding her with its wing. Maybe it really *was* a protector of Savoria! "Thank you," Lailu whispered.

"No," Wren gasped. "The drago-tron absorbs magic!"

Flames funneled rapidly away from the phoenix and into the drago-tron, swirling around it. If Fahr's magic had given it the temporary ability to shoot out green fire, what kind of fire capabilities would the phoenix give it?

Lailu sprinted back to her friends, leaping over shattered furniture, while behind her the phoenix shrieked, its scream deafening, and then the silence after even worse.

Lailu risked a quick glance back. Nothing remained of the phoenix but a pile of ashes. "No," she breathed.

"It'll rise again," Greg said grimly, "which is more than I can say for the rest of us."

The drago-tron roared triumphantly, flames flickering all around its body. Some of its metal plates glowed red-hot, the wire casings inside beginning to melt.

Lailu measured the distance to the door and knew they would never make it in time. There was no escape. She and Hannah exchanged a look, and Lailu could tell her oldest friend knew it too. Hannah took Lailu's hand in her free one and closed her eyes.

Something slammed into Lailu, sending her right through the kitchen curtain and smashing her against her stove. She blinked, green light flickering around her and spots dancing in her vision as Greg, Hannah, and Wren all struggled to their feet next to her.

Flame engulfed the drago-tron and poured outward in an expanding, unstoppable ball. Only Fahr remained in the restaurant, his hands up, sweat pouring down his face. The heat was so intense the walls wept, the air filled with smoke, scorching everything. And still Fahr stood there.

"He's trying to contain it," Wren said, her forehead creased. "Why?"

"He promised to protect his city," Lailu whispered. "The elves can't lie."

"But . . . it will kill him." Wren looked like she couldn't believe it. Wren, who believed the elves were soulless creatures incapable of feeling pain.

Green fire danced and flickered around the fireball that had been the drago-tron, the whole thing still growing by the second. Lailu realized Fahr was creating a barrier like the one that had surrounded the city, using that to contain the beast. But it wouldn't last much longer. Already he was being pushed back. He fell heavily to one knee, his hands still up, lips drawn back in a silent snarl.

"We need to run," Greg said. "Now. While he's buying us time."

"Will the fire destroy the drago-tron?" Lailu asked Wren.

"I . . . don't think so. Not the phoenix fire, because it's magic in nature, and the drago-tron feeds *on* magic. It would have to be a real fire, some kind of explosion."

"What's its weak point?" Lailu asked.

"Lailu, we *don't* have time for this," Greg said, trying to pull her toward the door. She shook him off.

"Its heart," Wren whispered. "It has a core at its heart. If that's destroyed . . ."

The trapdoor opened, and Albert hopped out. "Your generator," he gasped. "I've managed to stabilize it, but it won't last. We need to run. Run!" And he sprinted to the back door.

Lailu stared down at that open cellar, then back at the maelstrom of flame that had been her dining room. Her beautiful, well-cared-for dining room . . . damaged beyond repair, destroyed, and . . . and she forced herself not to think about that. Not right now.

Because she had an idea, a stupid, brilliant idea. Something that might take out this drago-tron. She just she wasn't sure *she'd* survive it. But if she didn't do something, then this . . . *thing* . . . could escape. And just outside Mystic Cooking were a ton of vulnerable people.

She made up her mind, then looked at Greg and Hannah and Wren. "Run," she agreed. But she made sure they all went first.

Hannah darted out, then Greg, who glanced back, hesitating just outside the door. He must have seen something on Lailu's face, because he stopped, turning back.

But too late.

Lailu slammed the door and slid their shiny new lock into place, courtesy of the freeloading scientists. Then she realized Wren was still in there. "Butterknives! Wren, you need to get out too."

"I know what you're planning. And . . ." Wren took a deep breath. "I'm going to do it instead. You should run. Survive. And I'll take care of this."

The door buckled as someone outside threw themselves at it. "Lailu!" Greg yelled, his voice muffled slightly. "Lailu, what are you doing?"

"Absolutely not," Lailu said. "This is *my* restaurant."

"And that's *my* drago-tron."

"Lailu! Open the door! Open! The! Door!"

"Together, then," Lailu said reluctantly. Wren nodded.

In her dining room, the roar of the flame grew louder and louder until it was the shriek of a blizzard tearing down the mountain. Fahr shrieked with it, black clouds of smoke billowing outward, pouring into the kitchen. They were almost out of time.

"I'm sorry," Lailu whispered. She wasn't sure who she was apologizing to. Her friends? Her family? Or just to Greg? They'd never had that talk.

She wished she'd been brave enough, now.

Maybe she was apologizing to Mystic Cooking itself, her restaurant, which had absorbed all her hopes, all those dreams, those hours of work and sweat, the aromas of a hundred meals and the plans for hundreds more. And now this would be it. This would be the end.

For both of them.

Fahr screamed one final time, and a wave of heat cascaded from the dining room, roaring into the kitchen. Lailu threw herself down the cellar steps, Wren on her heels. She didn't have time for wishes and regrets. And she wasn't about to let Wren take the heat now either.

This was her restaurant, and if anyone was going to destroy it, it would be her.

41

GENERATOR PROBLEMS

*L*ailu sucked in the chill air of her cellar gratefully. Wren closed the trapdoor, and it felt like she'd just stepped into the shade on a hot summer day. Nails scrabbled at the floor overhead, and something crashed that might have been the stove.

Lailu winced, remembering her opening day, her dad and brothers buying her that stove, all that she had gone through to get this restaurant, to keep it . . .

She couldn't think of her dad or her brothers right now. "Let's get this over with," she said instead.

They both approached the generator, lurking next to the icebox like some kind of metal kraken. Lailu could see the pipe Albert was always worried about vibrating slightly, small puffs of steam drifting from its top while lights flashed on and off around it.

"Neon stabilized this?" Wren studied the generator, seemingly impressed.

"Yeah. With Krypton, and sometimes Zelda and Iggy."

"Zelda and Iggy?" Wren blinked, then recognition dawned. "Oh yes, you mean Zinc and Magnesium. I remember kicking all of them out. Neon just because he was weak, and Magnesium, too. Krypton annoyed me. I actually quite liked Zinc, but she goes where her brother goes, and . . . and I'm babbling, aren't I? I'm just . . . I'm scared."

"Can we set this to explode and then escape?" Lailu asked.

Wren tilted her head, considering. "Yes."

"Really?" Hope unfurled in Lailu's chest. "Okay. So, what should we do?"

Crash! Bam! Scrape-scrape-scrape.

"We should hurry," Wren said firmly. She glanced at the icebox and then at Lailu. "We need to cool down the generator first and then"—she pulled a vial out of her pocket—"we sprinkle this. But just a pinch."

"What's that?"

"Mal-cantation powder. The last of my stash. I thought I'd get to make some more. . . ."

"You will," Lailu said. "When we finish this."

Wren nodded. "When we finish," she whispered. She squeezed her eyes shut, then opened them. "My mother . . . She wasn't the nicest person. But she was the smartest person I've ever known. I wanted to be like her. But I'm not."

"You're really smart," Lailu protested.

"No, that's not what I meant." Wren managed a small, sad smile. "I meant I'm not as ruthless as she was. And I think maybe that's a good thing. Now, open the icebox."

Lailu opened it.

"Can you scrape out some ice from the back?"

Lailu pulled her knife out and leaned forward, sticking her head and shoulders inside.

Wren shoved her from behind.

"Hey!" Lailu sank her knife into the side, catching her balance, but too late; Wren slammed the door shut, and a second later there was a series of pops and bangs and the hissing of steam escaping very quickly. Wren was setting off the generator herself. She'd actually managed to lie to Lailu. Wren, who was never good at hyperbole or sarcasm, had lied to Lailu's face. To save her.

To sacrifice herself.

Lailu had spent her whole life training to be a master chef, and not just any master chef, but the *best* master chef. She had leaped onto the necks of dragons, outrun a charging hydra, and successfully wrestled down a raegnar. Her body knew what to do, and she reacted instantly, kicking the door open, lunging forward, and grabbing Wren by the back of her leather apron.

"Don't—" Wren started, as behind her the generator blew its top, fire bubbling out, smoke billowing in all directions.

Lailu yanked Wren inside the icebox with her, pulled the door shut, and whispered one last prayer to Chushi as the world erupted outside.

Lailu blinked blearily. It was cold, and dark, so dark for a second she thought she might be in a cave. And then it all hit her in a quick flash of memories.

She sat up abruptly.

Smack!

"Ow . . ." Lailu rubbed her sore head.

"Lailu? You're awake?" Wren said eagerly.

"Yes," Lailu grumbled. "We're still in my icebox, aren't we?"

"Yeah," Wren said.

"How long?"

"I don't know. I've been awake for a little while. And it's getting hotter. See, the ice is all slushy now."

Lailu felt the walls, her fingers sinking in slightly. The air felt stuffy too. And while Lailu and Wren both fit inside, it was hardly comfortable. For the first time in her life, Lailu was glad she was so short.

She tried the door, shoving and pushing, but it didn't budge at all. Either the door had been melded shut by the blast, or something heavy lay on the other side, blocking it. She didn't want to think about what that could be. She didn't want to think about her restaurant, or what might be left of it.

"What if no one ever finds us?" Wren's voice sounded so small in the pitch-blackness.

"Someone will find us." *I hope*, Lailu added silently. *O God of Cookery, please help someone find us.*

"It's getting harder to breathe in here," Wren said.

"You sound sleepy."

"I am sleepy," Wren murmured.

"Don't you dare, Wren." Lailu nudged the other girl. "We're not suffocating in here, you hear me? We just survived a phoenix, a mechanical-dragon attack, *and* an explosion; we are *not* being defeated by an icebox!" Lailu used the hilt of her knife to bang at the door again. She wanted to scream and rage until there was no air left.

"Wait!" Wren put a hand on Lailu's arm. "Do you hear something?"

Lailu put her ear to the door. There was the barest of dents from where she'd whacked it repeatedly. These things were good quality. If she survived, she'd have to tell Slipshod it was a good purchase ... And then she heard something scraping, and voices. People calling her name. "Lailu! Lailu!"

"They're just calling for you. No one cares if I die." Wren sniffled.

"I care," Lailu said.

"Why? I tried to kill you, you know."

"Yeah, but you also saved me."

"And you saved me." Wren shifted. "It was easier to hate you before."

"I'm ... sorry?"

"Still, I don't know if we could ever really be friends again."

Lailu thought about everything she and Wren had been through in the past few weeks. "No," she sighed. "Probably not." She went back to slamming her knife hilt into the door, more fiercely than ever.

Crack!

The smallest sliver of golden light trickled in through a tiny little hole, and Lailu wanted to cry.

"You did it," Wren said. "Finally."

Lailu dug the edge of her knife into that crack and wriggled it, for once not caring if she damaged the blade. They were going to make it. They were really going to make it.

"Over there!" Hannah called from outside, and then there was a flurry of activity right over the icebox.

"Back up!" Albert ordered. Blue flame licked through the edges of the hole, and Lailu scrambled back as far as she could, which was only about an inch. A moment later the whole side of the icebox was ripped away.

Lailu blinked at the sudden light. Albert stood framed in it, wearing a pair of oversize goggles and holding some kind of long skinny pipe attached to a box.

"Lailu!" Hannah and Lianna dragged her out, both hugging her and laughing and crying all at the same time.

"I'm okay, I'm okay," Lailu said, wriggling. "You're more suffocating than that thing." She jerked her chin at the icebox, and they let her go. A second later and Greg grabbed her, hugging her harder than Lianna and Hannah combined. It actually wasn't the worst thing ever, she decided. Maybe some hugs were okay.

Finally he let her go. "What the apple peeler were you thinking?" he demanded.

Lailu frowned. "I thought you weren't going to steal that one."

"Actually, it's kind of grown on me." He grinned, and then his grin slid off his face, his expression crumbling, and for a second she thought he was about to cry. "I thought . . ." He turned away, wiping his face on his sleeve. "I thought you were dead."

"I thought I might be dead too," Lailu admitted. "But then I remembered I never got you back for that first chicken hunt. So I decided to survive."

Greg laughed. "I always knew pure spite was your greatest strength."

"She gets it from me," Lianna said proudly, dropping a hand on Lailu's shoulder.

"When did you get back?" Lailu asked her mom.

"Ryon got me." Lianna nodded over her shoulder. "He had me stay somewhere outside the city, so the elves wouldn't know. And by 'stay,' I mean he locked me in."

"He *locked* you *in*?" Lailu demanded.

"Oh yes. Apparently he didn't trust me when I said I'd wait for him to get back." Lianna smirked. "Smart of him. Still . . . I'm sorry I wasn't here. Maybe I could have done something to prevent, well, *that*." She pointed.

Lailu glanced over and got the shock of her life. Where Mystic Cooking had stood there was nothing but a few charred pieces of wood and the cracked foundation. All the grass had burnt to a crisp, and even the well was gone, completely flattened. Lailu almost couldn't believe it, her mind carefully wrapping this information away—*Mystic Cooking is gone*—and cushioning it, letting her wait to process it fully.

That was when she noticed Ryon kneeling at the edge of Mystic

Cooking's foundation, staring down at something that glowed a vivid forest green.

The green of Fahr's magic . . . in the shape of Fahr's body. Lailu had never seen an elf die before. No one she knew had. Was this what happened? Did their magic protect their physical bodies?

"Fahr died," she whispered. "He died saving us."

"I know," Lianna said. "And so does Ryon."

Tears fell from Ryon's unsmiling gray eyes as he leaned over to kiss his brother's head. Fahr had told Ryon he was no brother of his. It broke Lailu's heart when she realized those were the last words he'd said to her friend.

When Ryon straightened, the glow of Fahr's body intensified into several hundred points, like a beautiful elven constellation, and then broke apart, and a swarm of pixies rushed up into the sky and away.

Lailu gaped, then exchanged a look with her mother.

"I had no idea either," her mom said.

"But . . . what does that even mean?" Lailu asked.

"I think it means his magic is returning to the forest. And so is he." Lianna jerked her chin back, and now Lailu noticed the small, gently glowing sapling that had been left behind.

Lailu turned around. It was too painful to see Ryon crouched over that tiny, fragile tree. Instead, she watched Wren accepting a cup of water from Zelda.

Lianna followed her gaze. "She'll be okay," she said. "Everyone except Albert is happy to work with her again, and even he'll come around. Eventually. Plus there's always Elister. He's quite fond of

Wren. Did you know he told me he was thinking of formally adopting her?"

"He did? Probably because of her magic-stopping invention." Lailu remembered Elister saying how proud he was.

"No, he told me this right after Starling died. He just . . . didn't want to rush in. Thought it would be insensitive. I think he's a little lonely, honestly. He appreciates Wren. She's smart, eager to learn, and she always says what she means."

Lailu thought of how Wren had tricked her into going inside the icebox. "Not always," she said. Her numbness was beginning to fade now, and she was forced to face the fact that Mystic Cooking was really, truly gone. What would happen to *her* now? "I guess . . ." Lailu sniffled. "I guess I'll have to go work for a household or something."

"That's just silly," Greg said, taking her hand. "Come work with me. We work well together. Mystic Cooking will be up and running again in no time!"

"We'll see." Lailu pulled her hand free. "I need to . . . see if Ryon is okay." She walked away, her boots crushing what was left of her dreams, grinding it into ash that the wind would carry away until eventually not even that would remain to mark the place where Mystic Cooking had once stood.

A feather floated down to Lailu, a beautiful red-gold feather like an offering of peace. The phoenix was a guardian of Savoria; fire could not destroy its magic, especially the regenerative power in its tail feather. She caught it, running her fingers through its soft, downy edges, but its healing capabilities could not fix the hurt she felt now.

Gently, Lailu placed the feather down on the ashes of Mystic Cooking and watched in amazement as a tiny phoenix flickered into life, like a candle being lit from a match. It sprang from the rubble. Then, shrieking with delight, it circled Lailu three times before flying off into the evening sky.

42

OPENING DAY

ailu watched the dust motes dance in the sunlight. The inn's bed had lumps, and hard patches, and bits of stuffing that stuck out and scratched at her skin, yet she could not drag herself out of it.

Mystic Cooking was gone.

She'd learned her lesson about borrowing money, so that meant she'd have to work for someone else. For years. Years! And then maybe she'd be able to buy a new place.

She felt like a pot with all the stew scraped out, nothing but crusty bits of leftover food and emptiness. And she knew that was silly. She was lucky. *Really* lucky. She'd survived, and so had all the people who mattered most to her. But even that knowledge did nothing to fill the pit inside her where Mystic Cooking used to reside.

Someone turned a key in the door, but Lailu didn't even bother to raise her head. What was the point?

"Honey, you awake?" Her mother came into view, carrying a tray of food with a newspaper tucked firmly under one arm. "Hungry?"

Lailu shook her head. "I might never be hungry again."

"Oh, stop with the dramatics. You'll be okay. You just need to give things a little time." Her mom set the tray down on the bedside table. "Eat a little, would you? No one trusts a chef who's too skinny."

"Am I even a chef anymore?"

Lianna gave her a look.

Lailu sighed and sat up. "I might be a little dramatic," she admitted, and to apologize, she nibbled on a stale piece of toast. "Greg said I could work for him," she remembered.

"Hmm," her mom said neutrally.

"Do you think that would work? I mean, we're friends now. I think. But if he became my boss . . ." Lailu remembered all the worst things about Greg from their time in school together, how he'd teased her mercilessly and charmed the teachers and taken all the credit. Then she thought of the Greg she'd known these past few months, who'd closed his restaurant to help her, who'd hunted with her and cooked with her like it was the most natural thing in the world.

Greg, who held her hand. Who hugged her so hard she thought he'd never let her go. Maybe they weren't friends. Maybe they could be . . . something else. Something more.

But not if he was her boss. It would never work. Her own pride would make it impossible, not to mention Greg's natural insufferability.

"I don't think I'm qualified to answer that question for you,"

Lianna said. "I think you'll have to decide for yourself. But it would probably be a good idea for you to see Greg today and discuss it."

"Today?" Lailu frowned. "I can't today."

"Why not?"

"I have big plans."

"Doing what?" Lianna narrowed her eyes. "Moping in bed?"

"I'm not moping," Lailu muttered. "I'm mourning."

"You've been in mourning for three days! Besides, I hear Greg baked some fresh apple pies."

Lailu shrugged, but actually, that sounded pretty good. Greg always baked apple pies for funerals. And they'd had a funeral for their hydra feast during the Week of Masks, so why not have another for Mystic Cooking?

Mystic Cooking. Dead and burned and gone forever.

Lailu looked down, the room swimming.

"Oh, honey." Her mom put an arm around her shoulders. "Why don't you use this as an opportunity to take a little break? Come home with me, just for a short visit. Your dad and your brothers would be so happy to see you, and you could tell them all about your adventures here in the city."

Lailu sniffed and wiped her eyes on the back of her hand. "That sounds nice, Mom," she whispered. She picked up the glass of water, then put it down again when she noticed the floaters in it. Maybe it *was* time to leave this inn. "Are you ever going to tell them you're a spy?" she asked.

"About that . . ." Lianna shook open the newspaper and passed it to Lailu.

Fall From Grace

After the tragic events that destroyed renowned restaurant Mystic Cooking, Lord Elister has decided to step down from his position as co-regent of Savoria. He offered this official statement on his decision:

"I have served my country and my king to the best of my abilities, but we have decided that the king has come of age where he shall take the reins of this wonderful country himself. I will, of course, remain on as his loyal adviser and the head of his Royal Council."

Also in this council will be the king's mother, Queen Alina, local scientist Albert [no last name provided], and, surprisingly, the new elven leader, Eirad. When approached for comment, Eirad refused to discuss his decision, but merely offered this correction:

"If Elister thinks he's the head of this council, he's about to learn a thing or two. And I look forward to that lesson."

Several people close to the throne have speculated that this decision to step down was not Lord Elister's choice and have mentioned that the king has very little faith in his once closest adviser. Of course, none of these sources wanted to be quoted on this. . . .

(story continued on page 12)

Lailu looked up. "Does this mean your spying days are over?"

Lianna adjusted her colorful shawl. "It means that they are uncertain. I highly doubt that the king will cease using Elister's spying resources, but it still seems like a good time to take a little break and spend time at home."

"Elister was ready to let you die." Lailu scowled.

"It's not personal, honey."

"It is to me."

Lianna smiled. "I know."

"And Eirad decided to take Fahr's spot on the council?" Lailu frowned. She was surprised he'd been willing to go along with that. She didn't want to remember his expression when he'd come back to see Fahr's remains. He'd looked down on that small sapling, and his face had crumpled, as if his insides were more desolate than her restaurant would ever be. As if he were just as destroyed. He'd made a sound deep in his chest, a high, keening sound, his hands curling into fists that he pressed against his forehead. And then he'd straightened, and all of that emotion had slipped behind his eyes and out of sight.

Lailu's heart ached just thinking about it. She'd never seen anything as sad as the way he had taken that hurt and buried it back beneath his mask.

"I'm concerned about it too," Lianna admitted. "I doubt he'll have Savoria's best interests at heart. Or its citizens."

Lailu thought of all the people left stranded when the barrier went up, the ones Elister forgot about. Eirad had listened to Fahr when he'd said to protect them. Maybe he'd continue to respect that. She pictured his cruel smile and cold blue eyes. Or maybe he wouldn't. "I hope the king knows what he's getting himself into, is all," Lailu muttered, glancing back down at the paper. Another headline shouted up at her:

She tossed the paper on the bed, not wanting to read any more. A new restaurant, on today of all days. Obviously someone was glad Mystic Cooking was gone. They were practically building on her corpse.

"Look at that scowl. There's the Lailu I know and love." Lianna smoothed Lailu's pigtails and stood. "Hannah's waiting outside. She brought over a new outfit for you."

"Why?" Lailu asked sulkily.

"So you can look nice when you see Greg this morning."

"I never said I was—"

The door opened and Hannah burst in, a garment bag in her arms.

"I'll leave you two alone," Lianna said. She gave Lailu another quick hug. "See you at Gilded Island." She slipped outside, closing the door behind her.

"You're up!" Hannah dropped her bag and threw her arms around Lailu, then let her go. "Sorry, I know—"

"How I feel about hugs." Lailu attempted a smile. "Between you and my mom, I've gotten my fill today." She thought of Greg again, and her cheeks grew warm.

"You feeling okay? You look a little flushed."

"Mom said you brought over clothing for me?" Lailu asked, not wanting to discuss Greg or her lack of a restaurant.

Hannah grinned. "Are you ready for this?" She opened the garment bag with a flourish.

Lailu just stared at the outfit, sure her eyes were tricking her. It looked exactly like the kind of clothing that she would pick out to wear, although better made.

Hannah laughed. "Not what you were expecting? I've learned my lesson. No fluffy dresses, no pink, no high-heeled shoes . . . but honestly, I'm starting to like this more practical look better myself." She indicated her own trousers and vest. "And I made you these. Blood-free, I might add." She handed Lailu two silver hair nets with tiny dragon clips. The dragons each wore fluffy chef's hats and tiny aprons.

"Those are the cutest things ever." Lailu touched the dragons, then let her hand fall back into her lap, suddenly sad again.

"Here, let me do your hair, and then you'd better get dressed or we'll be late."

"Late for what?"

"Oh, you know. To go see Greg."

Lailu sighed, but let Hannah fix her hair up. "Any word from Ryon?" Lailu asked.

Hannah's fingers froze for a second, then continued efficiently twisting Lailu's black hair into buns. "No. He's taking Fahr's death really hard. I'm just giving him some space. Before the explosion, and the dinner, and all that, he told me . . ." She swallowed. "He told me he didn't want me to spy with him anymore. That he couldn't trust me. You know, after this." She tapped one of Lailu's hair nets.

"Oh, Hannah, I'm sure he didn't mean it."

"No, I'm sure he did. And I understand. I shouldn't have gone behind his back like that. But I didn't trust him. I knew something was going on with him. And anyhow, did you see how pretty those gems were?"

"They were pretty. Gruesome, but pretty."

Hannah smiled. "I was hoping to change his mind by spying on my own. And I did find documents that proved that Elister intended to hold on to power, and with those King Savon was able to get his mother to back him in removing Elister. Pretty useful, right?" Hannah put in the second clip and sat back, admiring her work. "So adorable! Ah, I can't wait to see Greg's reaction."

Lailu refused to be distracted. "Would you keep spying, even without Ryon?"

Hannah hesitated. "Maybe. King Savon asked me, but I haven't answered yet. I'm still hoping Ryon will . . . well . . . But no matter what, I have to admit I've picked up a lot from Ryon." She winked.

Lailu groaned. "Of all the traits you could have gotten from him, why that one?"

"Hmm . . . maybe because I didn't have a lot of good options," Hannah said.

Lailu scowled.

"Kidding! Kidding! Wow, that was an ugly expression." Hannah shuddered exaggeratedly. "Now, get dressed already so we can go!"

The day seemed disgustingly pleasant given everything that had happened. The sky contained only half as many clouds, the autumn air felt a little warmer, and even the people seemed a little too cheerful.

"Hey, Lailu!" they called.

"Hi, Lailu!"

"Hey, look, it's Lailu!"

Lailu turned to Hannah as they walked through the poor district. "What's going on?"

Hannah tugged on a pair of rhinestone gloves. Lailu really hoped they weren't "re-homed." "What can I say? You're kind of a hero in these parts."

"Me?"

"Yes, you." She looped her arm through Lailu's, pulling her along. "Don't dawdle. I told you, we'll be late."

"Late for what?" Lailu demanded again, but Hannah ignored her.

They passed into the marketplace, and Bairn called out to her. "Let me know when you need me to deliver your supplies! On the house!"

"Dad, you don't need to . . . ," Seala started. Lailu was glad to see the guard was okay, although she'd been forced to give up guarding; Eirad had sent her back to this side of the city after she'd promised not to work for Elister again. A much-less-sinister fate than Lailu had expected. It made her wonder if Eirad was really as terrible as he wanted everyone to believe.

"On the house," Bairn insisted. "Just say the word."

Lailu winced and waved at him, but kept moving. If he didn't know about Mystic Cooking, she didn't feel like telling him. Maybe she could get a refund later and use it for her trip home.

The people turned less friendly as Hannah and Lailu crossed over the bridge to Gilded Island. Lailu had expected that, but not all the stares and whispers. While the attention felt as uncomfortable as crumbs down the shirt, they didn't seem to be filled with the usual kinds of malice, just curiosity.

"Hannah . . . why are they staring at me?"

Hannah laughed. "Because they all think you had a hand in Lord Elister's fall from power."

"No, that can't be it."

"Seriously, that's what they think," Hannah said. "But you would already know all this had you read the morning paper."

"I read enough of it," Lailu muttered.

"So, did you see the bit about Vahn?" Hannah asked, her tone oh so casual.

"Um . . . maybe I should have read a little further," Lailu admitted. "What about Vahn?"

Hannah sighed. "Once again, he's the golden boy. He gets to keep his hero title, and the king even has a special secret quest lined up for him. So unfair."

Lailu, remembering how Vahn had risked that title defending the people against Elister, couldn't be sorry. "Paulie must have lifted his curse," she realized.

"That's the most irritating part; she didn't. But then, he didn't need her to."

"What? Why not?"

"Because that selfish jerk somehow managed to be unselfish for the first time in his life, and he broke his own curse."

"Huh," Lailu said. "Maybe he's not completely terrible."

"Doubtful," Hannah said, but she looked less mad than she usually did when discussing Vahn. "He also shaved his head. Nothing but stubble."

"Oh?"

"It doesn't look terrible," Hannah admitted. "I really wanted it to."

Lailu managed a laugh before they turned the corner onto the street that led to LaSilvian's Kitchen, and the laughter went sour in her throat. A line already stretched from the front doors to the end of the block. Greg would probably be getting all of her customers now.

"Lailu, look!" Hannah pointed at Greg's restaurant.

It was huge, large enough to swallow Mystic Cooking in one bite. "Kind of hard to miss, isn't it—" Lailu stopped, her jaw dropping. He'd changed the prominent sign in front. It no longer read LaSilvian's Kitchen, but instead . . .

"Mystic Cooking," Lailu breathed, her breath hitching. Her eyes burned, the sign blurring. "He changed the sign."

"Hey, look. It's Master Loganberry!" someone called. And suddenly all eyes turned to her.

"Hannah, help!" Lailu whispered. "I think I'm stuck."

"Want me to pinch you awake?" Hannah teased.

The front doors opened, and Greg stepped out of the new Mystic Cooking, his fluffy white chef's hat jammed over his unruly curls and an uncertain smile plastered across his face. "Lailu!" He hurried over, his arms out like he wanted to hug her again, but at the last moment he stopped and folded them instead. "I thought . . . But of course you wouldn't . . . But I was worried that you might not come," he blurted. "So, have you decided? Will you work with me?"

With me.

Finally Lailu understood. "As partners?" she asked.

"It has always been as partners," Greg said. "I wouldn't have it any other way."

She looked back up at the sign, at those two familiar words. Mystic Cooking, here. On Gilded Island. She was where she'd always dreamed of being, right in the center of the city, on one of the best streets.

She had done it. So why did her stomach feel like a clenched fist?

"Come on!" Hannah looped her arms through Lailu's and Greg's and practically yanked them to the front doors. "Just wait until you see what's inside," she told Lailu.

They moved past the long line of people, everyone pointing, laughing, and talking excitedly. Lailu even saw someone who looked like a scientist taking their picture.

A roar of excited voices shouted, "Surprise!" Lailu stumbled to a halt, overwhelmed by all the people. People she didn't recognize, all wearing fancy clothing, the latest styles. All lifting elegant wineglasses in her direction or pushing forward to shake her hand.

This was Greg's usual clientele. All of these people. She was getting a taste of his life.

"Master Loganberry," said a voice she recognized. Dante LaSilvian, Greg's snooty uncle, appeared at her side. For once he didn't curl his lip at the sight of her. Instead, he took one of her limp hands in his and bowed over it. "It is an honor to have you join us."

Lailu pulled her hand free and took a small step back. She looked around at the crowd, all those people grinning. None of them actually cared about her. She was famous for the moment only, the flavor of the day, something exciting for them to all gawk at before returning to their normal lives.

Meanwhile the people from her side of the city, the ones who had actually been involved, the ones who came to Mystic Cooking... none of them could afford to come out here. None of them would have a restaurant of their own anymore.

Suddenly it felt like she was back in that icebox, slowly suffocating. She turned and sprinted out of the restaurant.

"Lailu! Lailu, wait!" Greg raced after her, catching up before she'd gone more than a few feet.

Tears streamed down Lailu's face, and she couldn't stop them. "I'm sorry," she sobbed. "I can't. I just . . . I can't."

Greg glanced around, then pulled her into an alley between two buildings, where they'd have a little more privacy. "You can't?" he asked. "Or you won't?"

"Both."

He stared hard at her for a second, and then his shoulders slumped. "It's me, isn't it? I told you I liked you, and now you don't want to work with me, and—"

"It's not that at all. It's . . ." Lailu took a deep breath, her throat catching. "I . . . I like you too, Greg. I never thought I'd say that. But I do." She sniffed and wiped at her eyes, remembering all the times Greg had tormented her in school, but then how he had helped her every time she'd needed him. Hunting with her. Sharing his equipment. Cooking with her. And more than that, how knowing he had her back had made everything else tolerable. So many people in her life came and went as they pleased that having just one person who would never leave her made her feel . . . secure.

Which was why this was so hard to do.

"If you like me, then why—" Greg began.

And Lailu did two things she'd never thought she would do.

She kissed Gregorian LaSilvian.

And she walked away from a once-in-a-lifetime offer: to own a restaurant on Gilded Island.

43

MYSTIC COOKING

One month later...

Are you sure about this?" Hannah asked for the hundredth time. "I mean, this place is probably cursed. Especially if Eirad was willing to just give it to you."

"He didn't just give it to me," Lailu muttered. "I told you, we made a deal."

"Deals with elves. I'd think you, of all people, would know better."

"It'll be fine," Lailu said. "Besides, it doesn't look cursed, not now that Wren helped make it all spiffy and modern."

Hannah shook her head. "I still can't believe that makes you feel better."

Lailu shrugged. She and Wren weren't friends, exactly. But after Lailu turned down the chance to join Greg, she'd spent the rest of the day wandering the city. And she'd decided that she wasn't ready to run back to her village. She was the youngest master chef to graduate from the Academy in more than three hundred years. If she wanted to start another restaurant, she'd start another restaurant. And she'd realized she knew just the place.

When she'd gone to Eirad to negotiate, she found out Slipshod had covered the remainder of her previous debt to the elves, so Eirad told her she could have this building—he'd even magically repair the fire damage—in exchange for her willingness to overlook a certain magical doorway that the elves might, from time to time, take advantage of. Lailu was a little uneasy about that deal, no matter what she told Hannah. Still, this way she didn't actually owe them anything, and Eirad had agreed to move the doorway from its original location to the far side of her wine cellar, where it would be safer.

After that, everything else just clicked into place. Wren had offered to help, and this time it had seemed genuine. According to Wren, this would even the scales between them. Maybe, with a little more time, they could even start over. They'd have time; after Wren finished helping with Mystic Cooking, she began working with Elister on the new science wing of the Academy, but she promised she'd drop by the restaurant occasionally. She also made Elister pay for some of the upgrades to it, since he'd promised to cover the cost of any damage to Mystic Cooking after Wren put her malcanterarc on the door and he'd never paid for their uneaten feast. Even the king had offered money to Lailu, although she'd turned that gift down. Elister owed her, so she could accept his payment. Taking money from the king would mean she'd owe him, even if he never wanted it paid back.

Lailu refused to owe anyone anything again. Not if she could help it. Instead, she'd done whatever work she could on the side—hunts for other chefs, catering dinner parties, errands and rebuilding work for her old neighbors—pouring all the money she earned into her new restaurant. It wasn't perfect yet. But it was pretty close.

There was just one thing that was still bothering Lailu today, like the hint of a wrong spice in an otherwise excellently prepared feast. "Have you, um, gotten any notes lately?" she asked Hannah.

Hannah gave her a sideways look. "What kind of notes?"

"Oh, no specific kind. Just, you know, notes."

"No, Greg hasn't written," Hannah sighed. "Yet. But he'll come around."

"I don't know," Lailu admitted miserably. "I think I messed everything up." She'd avoided Greg ever since she'd turned down his offer—and kissed him!—and now it was too late. She'd ruined everything, and it was all her fault, and just thinking about Greg made her stomach twist and churn and simmer like a pot about to boil over.

"Oh, honey, I'm sure you didn't mess it all up. It will be okay. Really."

But Lailu knew Hannah was wrong. Lailu had written Greg a note a week ago, hoping to somehow make it right, but if he didn't want to respond . . . Well, she couldn't really blame him. She knew how it felt to be abandoned.

Her face burned and she busied herself with the special. It was a big day today, after all. A day to conquer her fears and start fresh all around. Not a day to dwell on the past.

"Mmm. Smells amazing," Hannah said. "I can't believe you never made this before."

"And I never will again," Lailu grumbled. "One time only. An opening-day special." She finished adding the seasoning and then stepped back. "Do you think anyone will show up?"

Hannah smiled. "Lailu, honey, of course people will show up. I'm the only one who thinks this place is cursed, and even I showed up. Now, let's go outside and flip the sign over, yeah?"

"Can you handle it? I need to finish—"

"I really think you should come with me," Hannah said firmly.

Lailu frowned. "Okay. If you insist."

"I do."

Shrugging, Lailu followed her friend out of the kitchen, admiring the new flooring they'd put in, the furniture some of her former neighbors had built for her, the candelabras with all electric lights that Wren had installed. The building itself was much larger than her old space, a three-story establishment instead of two, and closer to the middle of town. But not too close. Nowhere near Gilded Island, and not a far walk from the outskirts where Lailu had lived.

It felt . . . right, to be here, in the place where she and Slipshod had once signed a terrible contract with a shady loan shark. Back then, this place had been the Crow's Nest. After that loan shark died, Starling Volan had taken over this place and turned it into a secret lab. And then she died.

Lailu frowned. Maybe it really was cursed. She stopped at the new shrine her mom had sent back from home and said a quick prayer to Chushi. Then she lit a candle beneath the two pictures she'd had hung on the wall above the shrine. One of them showed a much younger Starling Volan, the scientist who had invented the modern stove and revolutionized the world of cooking, who had saved some of her people from an oppressive country and worked tirelessly on new projects here in Savoria. She wasn't the nicest person, but Lailu could appreciate her work ethic. And maybe this would help put her spirit to rest.

The other picture was one of Fahr. Also not the nicest person, but he'd ruled over the elves for generations, remaining in relative peace with his human neighbors. And he'd saved her life. She wasn't sure why he'd done that, why his last act had been to save her, but unlike her other debt to the elves, this was one she would never be able to repay.

"Hurry up, Lailu!" Hannah called.

"There's no rush," Lailu grumbled, hurrying anyway. "We won't open for another hour. . . ." She stopped in the doorway.

A line of people milled around outside, and when they saw Lailu, they cheered.

"Well? Are you going to let them in, or what?" Hannah asked.

"I . . . They're here to eat?"

"Obviously. Now, if you don't hurry and open, I'm going to start promising appetizers on the house—"

"Welcome to Mystic Cooking!" Lailu said quickly. "Come in!"

"Oh, and I think someone outside wants to talk to you," Hannah added, nudging Lailu forward. "I'll seat everyone."

"Who?" But then Lailu saw him, hanging outside her doors.

Hannah grinned. "Good luck!"

Lailu swallowed, then forced herself to walk one step at a time until she was outside. "Hey, Greg," she whispered, not quite looking at him.

"Hey, Lailu," he whispered back. "I like what you've done with the place. Much less murderous."

"Thanks."

"Also, why are we whispering?"

"I . . . have no idea."

"Me neither."

Lailu did look up then, her eyes meeting Greg's. He was studying her face like maybe he'd find a brand-new recipe buried behind it. And she realized she'd missed him, almost as much as she missed her old Mystic Cooking. "I see you got my note," she said.

"I did. And I see you've stopped avoiding me."

Lailu looked down at her feet. "I'm sorry," she whispered. She risked another glance up. Greg didn't seem angry, but he also wasn't saying anything. "Really sorry," she added.

Greg turned to look at Mystic Cooking, studying the sign that had once been a crow. Next to the letters of Mystic Cooking perched a new bird, this one red-gold, its beak curved in the hint of a wicked smile. "Is that a phoenix?"

"I figured it was poetic," Lailu said.

"Ah, I can see that. Like you're the tail feather that brought Mystic Cooking back to life."

Lailu stiffened. "I am not a tail feather."

"You might be a little bit of a tail feather."

"What does that even mean?" Lailu crossed her arms. "I didn't invite you out here to insult me, you know."

"Then why did you invite me? You ignore me for a month, and then you—" He stopped and sniffed the air, his eyes widening. "No way! Are you really cooking what I think you're cooking?"

"It's . . . sort of an apology," Lailu admitted, twisting her hands together.

He grinned. "I guess I have to accept. I was going to make you work longer for it, but that's a pretty hard apology to top."

Relief rushed through Lailu, and she allowed herself one small smile back before she took a deep breath and blurted, "I also have a business proposal for you." When Greg didn't answer, she made herself say the words: "Do you want to cook with me? Here?" She waited, every muscle tense. This was no LaSilvian's, and she'd turned him down when he'd asked her. There was no way he'd be interested. Would he?

Greg tilted his head. "Maybe."

"Maybe?" Hope filled her chest.

"Would it be as partners?"

Lailu smiled. "I wouldn't have it any other way."

He laughed and took her hand. "Neither would I, my little tail feather." He pulled her inside Mystic Cooking.

"For the last time, I am not—" Words failed Lailu, and she gaped at the scene in front of her.

Every seat was filled with people she recognized. They were her old neighbors, Albert and the small group of scientists who had taken refuge at Mystic Cooking, and all the folks whom Lailu had invited over when the elves put up their barrier. Even some of the villagers of Wolfpine had stuck around. Vahn waved to her from the back, sporting his newly buzzed haircut and sitting beside a somber Ryon. Even Seala and Jonah Gumple, the guards she'd once disliked so much, had come out for her opening day.

All of the people held glasses, and they raised them the moment Lailu stepped inside, saluting her and cheering.

"What is this?" Lailu gawked as Hannah handed her a glass and one for Greg.

"I had wine sent ahead," Greg said. "I know you prefer Debonaire, but I'm hoping this one time you'll make an exception."

Lailu laughed, and it was almost a sob. She couldn't believe this. She'd never had so many people so happy to see her. Her. Not just her cooking. It felt like . . . like belonging.

"And my answer is yes," Greg added.

Lailu turned to him, beaming. "Really?" Her vision blurred, tears trickling down her face, and for once she didn't care if Greg saw her crying.

"As long as I get to say 'what the spatula' whenever I want. Also, we have got to talk about your lebinola issues."

Lailu's tears dried up, and she scowled. "I don't have any lebinola issues."

"Oh, come on, I can smell lebinola spice right now!"

"Well, you'd better get used to it."

He grinned. "I can't wait."

Lailu found herself grinning back. She turned as Master Slipshod stepped forward. "To Master Chef Loganberry," he said, raising his own glass in a toast. "And to Mystic Cooking."

Lailu raised her own glass. So many emotions battled inside of her, but she knew that this was how an opening day was supposed to be.

Epilogue

NEW RESTAURANT RISES FROM THE ASHES

Master Chef Lailu Loganberry has reopened the doors to her highly anticipated restaurant, Mystic Cooking. Loganberry is apparently the youngest master chef to come from Chef Academy in three hundred years. Joining her in this venture is her talented former classmate Master Chef Gregorian Jocelyn LaSilvian, in a business partnership that can only be described as shocking.

"I always suspected they were more than just rivals," said Jonah Gumple, longtime fan of LaSilvian and his cuisine. Gumple admits to "openly weeping" upon hearing the news that LaSilvian's Kitchen would be closing its doors, although he says he has since come around to this new joint venture. "They won me over by serving my very favorite dish for opening day."

Loganberry and LaSilvian prepared an excellent fyrian chicken feast for the first hundred people lucky enough to get in. According to Loganberry, this will be the one and only time this particular beast is served there. According to LaSilvian, however, it will be a regular staple at their restaurant. Is this difference in opinion proof of a troubled working relationship?

"Nope," says a source close to the chefs. "This is just business as usual for them."

(story continued on page 7)

ACKNOWLEDGMENTS

We are incredibly grateful to everyone involved in making Lailu's final adventure in this series possible. First, our amazing agent, Jennifer Azantian, who has been a rock star from the beginning. You took our dream and made it a reality, and we are so happy to be a part of the ALA family. Also a thank-you to the rest of the team, Ben Baxter and Masha Gunic, who were part of Lailu's support crew from the very first book.

To our fantastic editors, Sarah McCabe and Fiona Simpson, who helped us find the best possible version of this story. Working with you on this series has been such a wonderful experience. And to Mara Anastas, Chriscynethia Floyd, Heather Palisi, Katherine Devendorf, Bernadette Flinn, Lauren Hoffman, Christina Pecorale, and the rest of the team at Aladdin who have helped make this story into a book—thank you for all that you do! Also thank you to Angela Li for the stunning cover illustrations. We've loved them all, but this one especially; that phoenix really lights up the sky!

Writing the final book of this series has been bittersweet, and we owe a lot to all the writers who have supported us along the way. There are too many to name, but we need to give a shout-out to our very first writing group, DMQ, and our friend Takeshi Young. You may have failed at that NaNoWriMo all those years ago . . . and at every NaNo since, but those early days really felt like the beginning of all of this. Thank you to our first critique group: Alan Wehrman, Meg Mezeske, Colleen Smith, Miles Zarathustra, and Joan McMillan.

And a special thank-you to some of the other writers who have been our beta readers and our commiserators on this journey, including Moana Whipple, April Stearns, Stephanie Garber, Teresa Yea, Sarah Glenn Marsh, Elizabeth Briggs, Suzi Guina, Katie Nelson, Kaitlin Hundscheid, Jennifer Camiccia, Tara Creel, and Justin Stewart. Also our fellow 2017 MG debuts, who constantly remind us why we love middle grade and the people who write it.

To our family: you were there for us before Lailu's journey had even begun, and we know you'll be there for the next great adventure. Lyn and Bruce Lang, who opened their home to this "cellar dweller" and made writing this book logistically possible; Christy and Paul Buncic, who introduced us to anime when we were kids—this story wouldn't have happened without you; Rosi Reed, who thankfully did not plot revenge after the downfall of the redheaded scientist; Ed Reed, permanent tiger buddy and enthusiastic supporter; Ember Chen, who has been a real instructor on time management; and Rose and Rich Bartkowski, our parents and the ones who first encouraged our creativity and imaginations.

And to our partners, Sean Lang and Nick Chen, who have been our strongest support when we needed it. We couldn't have done this without you.

Finally, our biggest thank-you of all is to our readers. You're the reason we are here. Thank you for joining us on this adventure.